NIGHTFALL

NIGHTFALL

Ellen Connor

BERKLEY SENSATION, NEW YORK

THE BERKLEY PUBLISHING GROUP
Published by the Penguin Group
Penguin Group (USA) Inc.
375 Hudson Street, New York, New York 10014, USA
Penguin Group (Canada), 90 Eglinton Avenue East, Suite 700, Toronto, Ontario M4P 2Y3, Canada
(a division of Pearson Penguin Canada Inc.)
Penguin Books Ltd., 80 Strand, London WC2R 0RL, England
Penguin Group Ireland, 25 St. Stephen's Green, Dublin 2, Ireland (a division of Penguin Books Ltd.)
Penguin Group (Australia), 250 Camberwell Road, Camberwell, Victoria 3124, Australia
(a division of Pearson Australia Group Pty. Ltd.)
Penguin Books India Pvt. Ltd., 11 Community Centre, Panchsheel Park, New Delhi—110 017, India
Penguin Group (NZ), 67 Apollo Drive, Rosedale, Auckland 0632, New Zealand
(a division of Pearson New Zealand Ltd.)
Penguin Books (South Africa) (Pty.) Ltd., 24 Sturdee Avenue, Rosebank, Johannesburg 2196,
South Africa

Penguin Books Ltd., Registered Offices: 80 Strand, London WC2R 0RL, England

This book is an original publication of The Berkley Publishing Group.

This is a work of fiction. Names, characters, places, and incidents either are the product of the author's imagination or are used fictitiously, and any resemblance to actual persons, living or dead, business establishments, events, or locales is entirely coincidental. The publisher does not have any control over and does not assume any responsibility for author or third-party websites or their content.

PRINTING HISTORY
Berkley Sensation trade paperback edition / June 2011

Library of Congress Cataloging-in-Publication Data

Connor, Ellen, 1976–
   Nightfall / Ellen Connor.—Berkley Sensation trade pbk. ed.
      p.   cm.
   ISBN 978-0-425-24169-1
   1. End of the world—Fiction.   2. Supernatural—Fiction.   I. Title.
   PS3603.05475N54   2011
   813'.6—dc22   2011005550

PRINTED IN THE UNITED STATES OF AMERICA

10 9 8 7 6 5 4 3 2 1

For our husbands,
who would love us even at the end of the world

ACKNOWLEDGMENTS

Heartfelt thanks go out to three generous, talented individuals, whose input at various stages proved invaluable: Bree Bridges, Stefanie Gostautas, and Liz Powell. We convey additional thanks to Laura Bradford for sticking by us when this idea and partnership must have seemed crazy. Mad appreciation to Cindy Hwang and Anne Sowards—first for taking a chance—and then making this story bigger (and better) than we'd imagined. The whole Berkley Sensation crew is fantastic, and we thank everyone involved in bringing this book to fruition: from copyedits to art to marketing and sales. You're a great team, and we're so fortunate to have you working with us. Thanks to Fedora Chen for her fabulous proofreading.

As always, we could not succeed without the support of family. With love and respect, we thank Andres, Andrea, and Alek as well as Keven, Juliette, Ilsa, and Dennis and Kathleen Stone. Thanks for your patience and understanding of our idiosyncrasies.

Additional thanks to Larissa Ione, Lauren Dane, Donna J. Herren, Carolyn Jewel, and Megan Hart, plus Joelle Charbonneau-Blanco, Patti Ann Colt, Cathleen DeLong, Deb Gross, and Kelly Schaub. You're all great friends and listeners, who offered much-needed support over the course of this project.

Finally, we thank our readers. We hope *Nightfall* strikes you as fresh, enticing, and different. Let us know what you think at author.ellen.connor @gmail.com and learn about upcoming books at www.EllenConnor.com.

PROLOGUE

Time wends in an infinite circle, bringing all that has been back into the world again. What was, will be once more. Nothing is ever lost to those who remember.

Towers will be built of metal and glass, and these towers will fall. This marks the turning of the tide. This marks the return of magic to the world, and the beginning of a second Dark Age. Fearsome creatures will prowl the earth, and the continents shall be remade in storms eternal. Mountains will crumble. A great wave will rise up and drown a city. Watch for these portents, and you will know you live in the time of prophecy.

Unbelievers will mock you when you seek the signs of coming cataclysm. They will call you mad, but in you rests the promise that all shall not be entirely lost, all of our history unwritten. To you I speak down through the centuries. I, too, have been thought mad for my speaking dreams. But neither mockery nor malice will quell the truth. Therefore, gather your resolve, you faithful. It all rests upon you.

—Translated from the ancient Chinese prophet Xi'an Xi's personal writings

In the mid-twenty-first century, the power grid collapsed. No warning. Religious citizens called it the Rapture or the end times, but there came no blood rain or plague of locusts.

It began in eastern Europe. The land went dark, with total radio and satellite silence. No one knew what had happened; the news simply ceased. But plenty in North America harbored speculations about reactor core meltdowns and weapons of mass destruction.

Next came the easternmost cities of the Western Hemisphere—as if a dark wind swept in from across the Atlantic. Electrical and nuclear substations simply stopped functioning, becoming inert blocks of dead matter. Despite working day and night, technicians could not repair the equipment. Planes fell out of the sky when they tried to land. Cars with computer chips turned into giant paperweights, though older ones went unaffected.

With accustomed sources of power gone and catastrophe imminent, people took to the streets seeking answers. They found violence.

The beginnings of mob rule.

Refining fuel became difficult. The outbreak of the first Fuel War ushered in an era of prophets, all of whom offered stories to explain the madness.

Glass shattered and buildings burned. Economies crumbled, only to be reborn in black market trade. In the city that never sleeps, the government imposed martial law and assigned curfews. The National Guard troops arrived, geared for combat. The populace rebelled, demanding answers. Some blamed terrorist cells as tensions escalated. Hate crimes quadrupled, and the U.S. military killed its own citizens on American soil.

The East Coast lost contact with the rest of the continent. Then states west of the Mississippi seceded, leaving the struggling easterners to their fate. While it could, the New United States pretended nothing was wrong. People went about their business and believed the chaos couldn't touch them.

But the wave followed at an inexorable pace. No one could outrun the change.

This encroaching Dark Age changed the world and the way people lived. Survivors scrounged whatever they could carry and pushed westward, out of the dead zone. Politicians could provide no answers. The military fought on, using old weapons and guarding meaningless borders. Desperate for news and hope, people turned on their radios, seeking the company of other voices in the dark. Dwindling human populations tried to find one another, only to be ambushed by unscrupulous road gangs. Raiders, like the powerful O'Malley organization, and other profit-minded privateers flourished in wider sweeps of territory.

Then the first transformations began—people into monsters—and the world changed again, this time forever.

ONE

"Don't move."

The hot rush of breath against her nape made Jenna juggle her keys and then drop them. Pepper spray dangled from her key ring, received as a gag gift, but at hearing that raw, gravelly voice, she lost all control of higher motor functions. A shiver jumped up her spine.

Something prodded her back. A gun? Jenna didn't even shift.

Her reply came out in a nervous squeak. "Are you mugging me? I don't have much cash on hand."

Liar.

Her dad had always insisted she keep at least five hundred in the house in case of emergencies. He hadn't liked banks, lines of credit, or the government. Sure, he'd successfully predicted a time when skills would become the real commerce and that the entire world monetary system would fail. But trouble had clung to her father like ticks on a hound, so she didn't agree with his philosophies. He'd gone around quoting obscure prophecy and claiming insight into great magical doings to come, and she wanted nothing to do with any of his crazy friends. She'd seen what his life of paranoia and sacrifice had done to her mother.

Hence the move to quiet, dull, out-of-the-way Culver. In an unstable time, this had seemed like the last place trouble could find her.

Of course, she'd heard the talk of trouble on the East Coast—blackouts and riots—but nothing ever seemed real until it knocked on the door. She had been expecting the troubles to push west for some time, just more dramatically than a guy with a gun.

Muggings didn't go down in Culver. This was a place where people clung with blindered determination to a dying way of life. They ignored updates from the New Media Coalition, which controlled all cell phone and Internet access on the new network. They went to their jobs and pretended supply line problems hadn't affected them. If people drank home brew now, instead of Bud Light, nobody mentioned it.

So what the hell?

Maybe this guy was an escaped con from the correctional facility in North Bend. It wasn't unheard of for them to break out and live rough until they emerged in dire need of food and supplies. Her breath puffed out in a smoky devil's sigh. Cold. It was so cold. He'd need winter gear too. If Jenna gave him what he wanted, he might go away. She hoped.

Because of her dad, she nursed a secret soft spot for outlaws and renegades, but that didn't ease the fear in her stomach.

She stayed calm. "I have stuff inside you can use. Soup, an insulated sleeping bag, pretty much everything you need to rough it. You don't have to steal from me. I'll give you the stuff. No strings."

Silence.

Maybe she should be worried about something else. Something worse. Jenna couldn't even make herself shape the words mentally. Things like that never happened in Culver. She should have been safe walking down the driveway to get her mail. Her mind had been on heading into town and joining Deb and Mara at the Louie: liquor, laughter, friends—not defending against an armed assailant.

"Are you Jenna Barclay?" he asked.

Her heart thudded in her ears. She wondered if she ought to lie. Would that make it worse? Fear tasted sharp on her tongue. She wouldn't give a desperate man a reason to hurt her. Sometimes they didn't need a reason, but she'd play it smart. And she'd walk away from this.

"Yes," she managed to say. "I'm Jenna. What do you want?"

Instead of answering that question, he returned to one she'd already posed. "No, this isn't a mugging."

Surely they weren't conversing while he held a gun on her. She felt the barrels through the thick down of her jacket and refused to think about bullets tearing through her flesh, blood-spattered feathers wafting up.

No running, no sudden moves. She'd be all right. She just had to make him think of her as a person. Not an object he could take into the forest and have fun with.

"Then what is it?"

"It's a kidnapping," he said, and stuffed a cloth in her mouth.

He moved too quickly for thought—even faster than the panic that followed his words. Jenna heard a ripping noise before he sealed a strip of duct tape over her mouth. When he slung her over his shoulder, her stomach slammed against his back. The wind was knocked right out of her, and she had the irrational thought that he smelled like the forest—a tangy whisper of pine, cut with fresh air and moss.

Hauling Jenna as if she weighed nothing, he squatted, snatched her keys, and sprinted up the drive toward her garage. He levered her up one-handed and taped her ankles. Her wrists came next, and that was when the fear sunk all the way in.

He wasn't kidding.

Jenna thrashed and fought. If she let him take her away from here, she'd never see home again. She didn't care about the threat of a bullet. A quick death would be better than whatever he had in mind.

Tears seared the corners of her eyes and felt hotter because her skin had chilled in the late autumn air.

But he handled her struggles with impersonal proficiency. She managed to elbow him in the sternum, and he didn't even grunt. Iron man. Unmoved. Maybe begging would work. "Nobody will pay the ransom," she tried to say, but it came out more like, "Mmdy wuh puh," before she gave up.

Oh God. Oh God. Oh God—

Nightmare. It had to be. She'd wake up soon.

Terror flared like a struck match as he popped the trunk of her car. He deposited her inside with curious care. Once he closed the metal top, it would be like a tomb.

No. Please, please, please.

With the setting sun behind him in a nimbus of fire, he looked like a dark god, broad shoulders and features blurred by her tears. But Jenna saw one thing clearly. He wasn't wearing a mask, and that meant he wasn't ever letting her go.

The trunk slammed.

Minutes turned into hours, and hours into eternity. After she died a million times in her mind, in almost as many different ways, the car slowed and stopped. She listened to the engine ticking over.

A key clicked in the lock. Jenna expected her captor to yank her roughly out of the trunk, so she braced. He might not need an excuse to hurt her. To her surprise, he drew her up with the care one would use with a sleeping child. His gentle hands belied the tape across her mouth and her bound limbs.

Wordlessly, he set her on her feet. As her blinking eyes adjusted to the rich twilight, she realized there was no reason he'd fear she might run. In addition to the hobbles on her ankles, they stood in the middle of a deep forest. They might still be in Oregon—she'd lost track of time while he drove—but in a remote region she'd never seen.

A reassuring bulge in her left pocket meant that her cell phone had made it out of the trunk with her. She just needed to bide her time and humor him until she could text someone for help. The New U.S. Rangers could track her phone and find her that way. Though she'd complained about the lack of privacy under the new regime—since the federal government had relocated to Fresno—right now, Jenna appreciated the hell out of their insistence on spying on citizens.

I just have to stay calm, stall him, and make him think I'm buying whatever he's selling.

She stood quietly, awaiting instructions. Crazies liked feeling in control, didn't they? She wouldn't give him any reason to search her—or worse. Giving the man a quick once-over, she reassessed what she'd hoped back in her driveway. He didn't need winter gear. A knit cap stretched over his skull, and he wore dark heavy-gauge jeans and a woodland camouflage jacket that looked military. He slung a *serious* semiautomatic rifle across his back. The gun he'd poked between her shoulder blades must be the nine-millimeter in his hip holster.

Fighting him was completely out of the question. A one-man army. *Oh shit.*

"I'm sorry it had to be like that," he said, his voice rough. "But we needed to get away from the city. You wouldn't believe me without proof."

Believe what? She'd already seen half the world come to a screeching halt.

Jenna stared at him in silence. How was she supposed to answer through the duct tape anyway? Not that there was any point. It was a stretch to call a burg like Culver a city. Not that crazy people needed to make sense. A frisson ran through her as the sun filtered out of the dense foliage entirely, drenching the world in shadow. Nightfall had never looked so sinister.

"Anyway, we should get inside. We can talk in the cabin. It's freezing out here, and I promised your dad I'd keep you safe."

That was pure bullshit. Mitch Barclay had been dead since she was twelve, and even before that, he'd never been particularly interested in her well-being—except when it suited him. He'd faded in and out of her life like a ghost, each time seeming a little less connected to reality. His final visit had been so strange that she hadn't wanted to see him again. He'd come just to stare at her, it seemed, like he could x-ray the inside of her head.

The man knelt and peeled the tape from around her ankles. She wanted to run, but taking off ill prepared in the cold might be stupider than staying put. Besides, her feet had gone completely numb. Blood rushed back in splinters of pain.

Distracting herself, Jenna tried to memorize the dwelling's exterior. Maybe she could put some detail in her text message. They stood in a clearing ringed by heavy trees. The split-log cabin looked like someone's hunting retreat, rustic but not shabby or poorly maintained.

When the man straightened, he was bigger than she'd realized, perhaps as much as a foot taller than her own five foot six. His swarthy skin bespoke some mixed ancestry, and he was built like a Mack truck. Solid muscle. Quite simply, she could hit him with a brick and he wouldn't even notice.

She'd have to outsmart him.

With a gesture, he indicated she should precede him toward the cabin. It wasn't good manners as much as him keeping an eye on her. She stumbled a little, her legs still stiff and tingling. He steadied her with a surprising hand on her back. She flinched and pulled away, but a small part of her was thankful that she hadn't fallen. *Keep it together. Stay calm.*

Jenna crossed the tidy porch, her shoes clunking against the plank wooden floor. Dread churned her nausea when she reached the door. He leaned past her and opened it—again, probably not a courtesy so much as recognizing the limitations of her bound hands. The inside of the cabin matched the exterior: woven rugs, hand-carved furniture with homey sewn cushions, and a big stone fireplace. Avocado appliances decked out an antiquated kitchenette, and a ladder led up to what might be a loft.

"Go in," he said. "I need to take care of some things. Then I'll cut you loose, so you can ask all the questions I see burning in your eyes."

TWO

Mason watched from the doorway as Jenna settled onto the oversized wing-backed chair. Despite an expression stricken with fear, she did so with grace. The massive seat would better suit a lumberjack, all but dwarfing her. She kept her back straight, bound hands in her lap, and those cool green eyes aimed at the barren fireplace.

He wanted to be surprised at finding Mitch's daughter graceful and collected. Prophetic, canny, even capable—that would make sense. Mitch Barclay had definitely been resourceful. But graceful? Never. Yet Mason had felt it when he'd scooped Jenna into the trunk. Through the winter coat and her belated struggles, he'd held a dancer's body. Long limbs and resilient muscles. His own muscles had responded, blood and bone finding a match in her strength.

Strength they'd both need to survive the coming storm.

Turning, Mason locked the door behind him and stalked through the dusk to check the windows. Bolted and blackened. He climbed the metal extension ladder. His pulse kept the moderate rhythm of steady movement, amplified by the urgency of preparation. As he paused atop the roof, he inhaled. The nighttime forest breathed with him, the snap and spice of cold evergreen air.

After making sure the barbed-wire screen and charcoal filter over the chimney were secure, he climbed down and collapsed the ladder. He shoved it into the tiny cellar with the rest of the ammo and supplies, then snapped the padlock.

Next was Jenna's car. He'd taken a chance driving so close to the cabin, valuing speed over stealth. Now he checked the ignition, harboring slight hope that it would flare to life. A turn of the key produced nothing—not even a click. The little hybrid was too new, too wired with computer-based circuitry. They might have used his '78 Bronco, but not for long. The Fuel Wars would hit the west in time, and the Bronco would be harder to hide. Better to make a clean break with old luxuries.

Accepting that the car was a useless relic, he grabbed the emergency gas can from the trunk. At least its fuel would still come in handy. He used his hunting knife to slice a three-foot length of garden hose and shoved it into the tank. Eyes closed, he sucked and sucked on the filthy green rubber, his lungs bursting. Gasoline filled his mouth. He sputtered and spit, then caught the flow of fuel in the can.

When he'd completely drained the car, he popped it into neutral. One hand on the open driver's-side door and the other on the steering wheel, he rocked the foreign compact back and forth. Sweat soaked the T-shirt beneath his camo field jacket. The car edged forward. Momentum took control. Grunting, pushing until his shoulders burned, he steered it into the woods, then dragged netting laced with branches over the gold metallic paint job.

Good. Everything as he'd planned.

Mason looked back toward the cabin. It stood small, squat, and blanketed in darkness. A shiver touched the nape of his neck, quickly followed by the primal call for safety. Get indoors. *Now.*

Minutes later, arms laden with firewood and the rifle across his back, he kicked the cabin's only door with his heavy work boots—and caught Jenna in the midst of a getaway. Her ass hung halfway out a window. His toolbox lay open beneath her dangling feet. A serrated kitchen knife had taken her place on the chair, with strips of dull silver duct tape scattered on the floor.

Crossing the cabin with long strides, Mason flung the split logs toward the fireplace, where they crashed like bowling pins. He stripped off his work gloves and grabbed two handfuls of female. Hips, to be exact. That soft upper-thigh part of the hip where a little extra flesh tempted a man to squeeze. He tightened his fingers. Her surprised yelp sent a rush of blood to his cock.

"Let go of me!" She kicked backward. He yanked her back into the cabin, her head smacking the window frame. "Ow! Shit!"

Every instinct told him to protect this woman, but his nerves were already shot to shit after getting her out of town—and knowing what was to come. He'd *seen* it.

He spun her and pushed her against the stout log wall. "Where would you go?"

"Home!"

Her knee came up between his legs. Mason deflected the desperate attack with his forearm. She twisted and tried to spin free, forcing him to let go of her hips. He settled for her wrists, still red from the duct tape, and pinned her hands above her head.

"My name is Mason," he said, pushing his body flush to hers. That thump of blood increased. Fighting had always done that to him. Violence and sex together. "If you leave now, you'll find yourself walking back to Culver. No water. No flashlight. No vehicle."

Pale green eyes widened. "What'd you do with my car?"

"It's in the woods, and the gas from the tank is in a can."

"*Why?*"

"I'm saving your life. I know you don't see it, but it's the truth." He inhaled through his nose, regaining control of his fight response.

"At least acknowledge that heading back to civilization isn't a good choice. . . because I'm carrying a semiautomatic rifle."

She nodded, a mere tilt of her head.

"I'm letting go of you." He could hurt her, but keeping her safe *and* cooperative would require more than brute force. "I said you could ask questions. Can we do that now?"

A sneer twisted her lips. "You're asking me? I don't have a choice."

Mason closed his eyes briefly. No choice. She wasn't far from the truth.

He glanced down, realizing he dwarfed her just like that massive chair. "Look at me, Jenna. If I wanted to hurt you, I could've done it already. Can you admit that too?"

"That doesn't mean you won't."

Easing the pressure from those slender wrists, Mason lowered their arms and tugged her away from the wall. She stumbled and steadied herself with a palm against his chest. Her nostrils flared, animal-like. Full lips the color of a ripe peach fell open.

He quickly unzipped her down coat and stripped it off. Like a soldier sizing up the enemy, he took in her athletic build, the swell of her breasts beneath a thin T-shirt, and jeans that fit like a glove.

"Now you have no coat either. Sit here," he said, pushing her shoulders until she sat on a bench at the kitchen table. He ran his palms over the thistle of his cropped hair, scrubbing the tension from his scalp, and sat across from her. "Go ahead, if you want. Ask."

"Ask what? I don't even know where to start."

"Ask me if I intend to hurt you."

Her clear eyes turned cloudy. She glanced at the open window. Her shoulder muscles tensed, as if preparing for flight. But she swallowed. The fear faded. She appraised him with a coolness that reminded him of her father—curious but detached, two steps removed from this world. Late in life, Mitch had possessed a shaman's eyes, and he had carried that weight in bowed shoulders. His glimpses of what was to come had nearly broken him.

"Fine," she said, tight and clipped. "Do you plan to hurt me?"

"No."

"Good. Can I go now?"

"No."

"Why not?"

"It's not safe out there."

Eyebrows two shades darker than her blond ponytail pulled into a frown. "Probably because someone disabled my car and took my coat."

"We're safer here."

"From what, kidnapping psychos?"

"No, you already have one of those," he said with a tight grin.

Her lips quirked. She slanted her gaze to the floor.

Mason wasn't used to sitting, no matter her obvious need for something as normal as conversation. It dug under his skin. So he gave up on stillness. After removing the magazine from his rifle and stashing it in his pants pocket, he walked to the toolbox beneath the window.

Jenna gasped. He spun, looking for what had surprised her. But nothing in the cabin had changed. Instead she stared at the sixteen-pound hammer in his hands.

His exhalation sounded more tired than he wanted to admit. "Relax. I'm just going to fix the window. And then dinner." He pulled the window shut, speaking past the two galvanized nails clutched between his teeth. "You're hungry, right?"

"I can't eat nails," she muttered.

She crossed bare arms around her middle, which pushed her breasts front and center. Suddenly Mason had no taste for food, especially not a winter's worth of generic canned goods. Jenna's body, both lush and tight, would be feast enough for any man. He hadn't indulged in sex for months, and she made him all too aware of that fact. An unwelcome distraction.

He pounded the nail with two sharp strikes and replaced the tar paper. "I had tuna in mind," he said at last. "We have lots of tuna."

THREE

So he wasn't the raving brand of crazy. Good to know.

Huddled in her chair, Jenna watched him put together a rudimentary tuna casserole. He hadn't added enough water to the cream of mushroom soup, so it would turn out gluey, but he probably wasn't the kind to take criticism well. Not that it mattered. She wasn't going to stick around long enough to eat.

He'd said she could ask questions. Time to test that.

"Where are we?" Location would shape her escape plans. Too long of a walk would be impossible without survival gear.

Jenna didn't expect him to answer. Honestly, it would be stupid if he meant to keep her.

"North of Culver," he said readily. "Several hours, halfway to the Washington state line."

She tried to bring up a mental map of Oregon, but either her geography was lacking, or she was too shaken to concentrate. "What do you want with me?"

Mason glanced up from the casserole dish. "Me personally? Nothing. I'm just keeping a promise, like I said."

At the second reference to her father, Jenna's heart sank. *Christ, Mitch . . . what've you done?*

Now she knew what flavor of crazy he favored: the same as her dad. Before he'd died, Mitch Barclay kept a basement full of old newspaper clippings—prognostications of some cataclysmic event. When Jenna was nine, he'd joined some group chock-full of crackpots and conspiracy theorists. They'd obsessed over portents and signs, discussed magic theory, and tried to talk to spirits. For obvious reasons, they took the troubles in the east as proof of their convictions. But that was years ago. Since the calamity hadn't yet pushed west, the New U.S. government insisted it had run its course.

Mitch had preached the coming of a bleak age of destructive magic. If he had lived in a city instead of a compound in the woods, he would be the crazy guy on the corner, holding a hand-lettered THE END IS NIGH sign. Even until recently, his followers would turn up at the house from time to time, generally content with a bowl of soup. None had ever stuffed her in a trunk.

"Here," Mason said, digging into a pocket of his jacket. "He left this for you."

Jenna eyed the trifolded paper. A letter from Mitch from beyond the grave. As if she needed more reasons to freak out.

But strangely enough, she needed *something* familiar, even if it was just Mitch being himself. She snatched the letter and retreated to a corner by the fireplace.

Dear Jenna,

If you're reading this, it means I'm gone. I was always sorry I couldn't be around more. I know your mother made excuses for me because that was her way, and I know you were disappointed in the kind of father I turned out to be. It wasn't because I didn't care, I promise you. I just had other work I needed to be doing.

I can imagine your expression. You never held a job for more than six months in your life, *you're probably thinking. And while that's true in certain terms, by other reckonings, I had a calling, one I was faithful to until my dying day.*

These next words will be the most important you'll ever read, my darling girl. There's a Dark Age dawning, and it's more than just the hint of bad things to come. The world as you know it is coming to an end. It's more than bombings, earthquakes, inexplicable weather patterns, and unnatural geological phenomena. Everything passes. Time is a wheel, and the age of technology is spinning away. Soon, magic will return, or a power our primitive ancestors would name so. Past a certain point, names lose their meaning. What will be will be.

I knew I'd never live to see what's foretold come to pass, so I did my best to make sure you'd live. Because you have to. I can't say more because you wouldn't believe me if I did. Some things you simply have to see for yourself.

The wolf shall dwell with the lamb, and the leopard shall lie down with the kid, and the calf and the lion and the fatling together, and a little child shall lead them.

Remember those words. Remember what I taught you, those long-ago summers in the woods. Remember it all, dear girl. There's going to be a heavy weight on your shoulders one day soon, but I know you can bear it. Oh, and one thing more: when the dark man comes for you, don't be afraid. It is as it was meant to be.

Your loving father,
Mitchell P. Barclay

Jenna wiped at her eyes, fighting to keep from crying out of sheer anger. How dare he? After all these years. Forget Mitch. Forget dire portents and doom. She'd heard that same song since she was a toddler. What she really needed was to get the hell out of this cabin and back to town.

"Have you read it?" she asked her captor.

He seemed offended by the possibility. "No, but I have a good guess about what's in it."

Jenna kept her face and voice neutral. "What do you think's going to happen in Culver?"

"You might need to see it for yourself."

"Try me." She worked on making her expression inviting when she really wanted to scream and keep screaming until somebody came to help. But like every other time in her life, she knew that wasn't going to happen. She'd have to save herself.

"I know you have a cell phone in your pocket," he said.

Jenna froze, wondering why he hadn't taken it away. With Mason out sabotaging her car, she had dialed but found no signal. She'd cursed the thickness of the woods and the remote area. Still, she might get a bar somewhere. Then the New U.S. Rangers could go all Big Brother on her ass. Sometimes it was *good* when people could find you.

Her voice quavered—and she hated that weakness—as she asked, "Do you want it?"

He shook his head. "It won't do you any good."

Relief swamped her. Maybe he didn't know the area as well as he thought. If she went up one of those trees, she might get enough altitude for a signal.

"And why is that?" she asked.

Mason put the finishing touches on the casserole and popped it into the wood-burning stove—an incongruous scene because he still wore the camouflage jacket. He'd taken off the knit cap. His dark, skull-cut hair accentuated the hard lines of his face and thick muscles along his neck and shoulders. Not the kind of guy Jenna would imagine in a kitchen. Ever. Between the warmth and the smell of food, the cabin had gained an unsettlingly cozy air. But she didn't want to be snug and toasty here with him; she wanted to go home.

"By now, all cell signals have gone down," he said, his eyes grave and dark like a night unbroken by the moon. "Even here."

Jenna shrugged. "Big deal. They already failed once, remember? And then the new government built new towers."

"That was just a portent, not the real deal." Then he went on as if she hadn't interrupted. "Television stations will fail next. Only old analog radios will play, and most likely, by this time next week, we'll be blanketed in complete radio silence as well . . . because there won't be people to man the controls. You wouldn't believe what it's like out east right now."

That sounded like more of her dad's paranoid apocalypse fantasies, but hearing it from Mason frightened her more than Mitch's most vehement rants. The New Media Coalition chose not to cover events beyond their borders, preaching self-sufficiency and isolationism.

"How do you know what happens there?"

Mason didn't reply. Probably he had nothing true to say.

A shiver rolled through her. They were so secluded out here. Jenna almost believed they could be the last people on earth. Doubtless that was how he wanted her to feel, helpless and dependent on him for her survival. He wouldn't break her with cruelty. Instead he used ominous whispers.

Jenna extrapolated one significant fact from his doom-and-gloom prediction. "So, you don't care if I call my friend and let her know I won't be joining her for drinks?"

The sudden warmth of his smile struck her like a fist in the solar plexus. "Not at all."

Still, she wouldn't let the opportunity go to waste. She dug her cell out of her pocket and dialed. Nothing. Weirder than that, the phone read "network failure" instead of "out of network" or "no signal." Alarm rose up in her throat, threatening to choke her.

Jenna kept an eye on him as she slipped from her chair and moved around the cabin, but no change in location fixed the signal. She shook it, while Mason watched her with an inscrutable look. The display shimmered and went black—even though she'd just charged the thing. She mashed buttons, trying to get the menu back, but the phone became an inert piece of carbon in her palm.

"Digital electronics won't work anymore," he told her. "Already your car won't start. The computer circuitry won't survive this, so it's useless. I'm sorry."

"You must've done something to my phone." Her voice shook.

Mason's brows rose in gentle derision. "While it was in your pocket in the trunk? Or while you were in the cabin alone?"

"Maybe you have some kind of damping device in here."

"Feel free to look around." His amused expression said she was the loony one.

Clenching her hands into fists, she fought the urge to go shrill. She needed to keep a level head. Antagonizing him would only get her hurt.

Jenna took several deep breaths until she could control her tone. "I don't know *how*, but you're doing something."

"I'm baking a tuna casserole." For the first time, he sounded tired. "I don't have anything to do with the rest. I'm just trying to weather it."

"What's causing this?"

At that, he propped his elbows on the counter. "What's the point? The government has filled your head with promises they can't keep."

"Indulge me."

"You don't have to understand why someone stabbed you to die from it. All I know is what I've seen working with Mitch. And judging from what's out there now, the change will be dangerous and chaotic, and it'll cull the hell out of the human populace."

"Oh?" She tried to look encouraging. Maybe he'd elaborate. With a beginning like that, the rest was bound to be entertaining.

"I'm sure Mitch tried to explain in his letter. There's nothing more I can add. I'm not a prophecy guy."

"So you believe that stuff he said . . . about the Dark Age? And that this *change* has broken my cell phone and my car?"

"Not just yours, but technology failure is the least of our worries."

"What are you talking about?"

His eyes darkened, taking on a more somber cast. "Did you watch the news last night, the report about the riot at the penitentiary outside Culver?"

Jenna rubbed her upper arms as the news footage flashed through her mind. She normally didn't watch the news, but she'd wanted to see Stacy make her television debut as the stand-in weather girl. Her friend had been so thrilled to hire on with the New Media Coalition. But before Stacy came on, the lead story had been filled with gruesome images of prisoners beating one another. Then the cameras had gone out and the feed returned to the TV station.

"I saw it," she said, throat tight. "They set riot dogs on them."

"Those weren't riot dogs." He shrugged. "But that's when I knew it was time. I swore to your dad that I'd make sure you survived."

"Why would he care?" she snapped. "He didn't while he was alive. What hold did he have on you anyway, to make you do this?"

"He saved my life."

FOUR

Mason strode to the fireplace. He stacked the wood he'd tossed aside but didn't light it. Only for emergencies. Not comfort. The woodstove would do for now.

"Let's make a deal," he said. "Eat dinner with me, and I'll tell you how I met your father."

"Look, just call him Mitch. I did. He sired me, but that's about it."

"From the way he talked about you, I thought you were close."

That seemed to take her by surprise. She matched his frown, twirling the end of her ponytail around her forefinger. "Now I *know* you're shitting me."

He grinned despite everything. Something about Jenna Barclay tempted him. If—no, *when*—she became aware of her effect on him, he'd lose part of himself. She'd hold his attraction over his head like an anvil.

The ridiculous mental image reminded him of Saturday morning cartoons. He'd been four years old and oblivious to anything beyond the TV screen. But nothing so normal as vegging on a Saturday morning would ever happen again. No more homes and towns, no more modern life. None of it. The last bastion of western resistance was falling.

That meant he needed to keep control.

Besides, at that moment, another of his body's needs had to be satisfied: his stomach growled. He hadn't eaten in two days, not since before that thing tried to devour his leg. He'd chopped off its head. Mason had barely escaped the motel parking lot. While cleaning up, he'd seen the footage of the prison riot and knew their time was done. *Promises to keep.* Which was the reason he'd been hanging around a one-horse town like Culver.

He returned to the kitchen and retrieved the casserole. Like he'd learned in the military, he approached his chores in linear fashion. *One thing at a time until the area is secure.* So food first. Preferably with Jenna. Next, he'd find a way to keep her in the cabin without tying her down.

The noodles sticking out from the tuna goo were overcooked, all brown and crispy from the woodstove's uneven heat. They would have been better off eating the ingredients straight from the can.

He gestured to the dish. "So, are you going to have any of this?"

"I'm not eating with you," she said, shaking her head. "I'm not talking to you. I'm not going to be your friend or your confidante or your shrink. I want to go home."

Mason swallowed his temper and set the table, as if she'd agreed. But he didn't wait for her to get off her ass and join him. Even the charred casserole was enough to turn his stomach ferocious. He ate in silence, needing the fuel.

Even after twenty minutes, she hadn't budged. He knew because he kept his eye on the clock—not that time would mean much anymore. Not like the trains and buses would be running, or folks waiting to punch out after a hard shift. Nothing left but daytime and nighttime. Safe times and times to hide. That was all.

He almost smiled. There was freedom in letting certain aspects of the modern world go.

Then, just when he was beginning to lose hope—not that she would eat, but that she might be too mulish to see sense—Jenna stood. She didn't meet his eyes as she sat before her plate. But she served up the food. And she ate.

"Now talk," she said simply.

And Mason had his answer.

However long it took, he'd have a partner. Mitch had said as much when describing his clever and practical daughter—the daughter who felt none of the same affection in return.

Mason had made his promise with a worst-case scenario in mind. He'd try. And if Jenna Barclay proved too stubborn or stupid to take hold of the lifeline he offered, he'd be discharged from that promise. Now he saw her as the kind of woman who'd grasp any possibility of survival, just like she swallowed those overcooked noodles along with her pride.

"I never knew my folks and grew up in foster care," he said, his throat tight. "A lot of being smacked around but not a lot of supervision. I knocked off my first convenience store when I was fourteen."

Jenna gazed at him steadily. He found no accusation or pity on her face. Just enough curiosity to suggest she was paying attention.

"Not much of a future, starting out that way," she said.

"No future outside of the penal system, no. But Mitch got me out of it. Broke the cycle."

"Never took him for the big-brother type."

Mason shoved away his empty plate. "Me and two buddies held up a liquor store. Hadn't been to school in years. The dude behind the counter opened fire. I caught one in the leg." He resisted the urge to rub his upper thigh, the place that ached whenever he thought of his youth. Stupid kid. "But instead of waiting for the cops, I took off for the woods."

"Where Mitch and his pals used to make camp." Jenna rubbed the back of her neck, like she was tired or sore, and Mason caught sight of her reddened wrists. He felt a twinge of regret. "Don't tell me you fell in with those crazies."

"I did."

She snorted. "Hardly better than a cult."

"They had order and honor at least. Mitch took care of my leg and taught me survival skills. I was young. I'd never known anything like it. His people knew all about old-timey shit, making soap and herbal medicines. It was pretty weird. I thought most of them were crazy. At first."

Jenna sipped from her water glass and looked down at her own empty plate, practically licked clean. She shrugged. "Guess I was hungry after all."

"Seems so."

"How long ago was this?"

"Fifteen years now."

"I was in junior high," she said, her expression souring. "There I was, pulling good grades and captain of the volleyball team while he was trouncing around the woods with some delinquent. I mean, seriously, can you respect a man like that?"

"Yeah. But my perspective was different."

"I'll say."

"He talked about you all the time," Mason said. "How proud he was of you."

"Bullshit."

"No bull. He had an envelope full of letters about you. I guess your mom sent them." He stood and rounded the table, daring to put his hands on her shoulders.

She flinched. "Don't touch me."

But he didn't let go. The tension he found there begged for some release. He began with his thumbs on the back of her neck, hoping to ease the ache she'd unconsciously revealed.

"Look, Jenna, he didn't think he had anything to offer you. I was just somebody the world threw away, and he tried to make use of me. But he didn't want this life for you—until there was no choice."

"Bullshit," she said again, with less conviction.

Did she notice how she'd leaned into his touch? Mason did. That small measure of trust returned him to thoughts of sex. Damn, but he was in a bad way. Being cooped up with her for the foreseeable future wouldn't help.

He leaned over, his lips near her ear. "No bullshit, Jenna. The times he was around you and your mom, what did he do?"

"Drink. And fidget. He always wanted to be out there." She gestured toward the window and trees that lay beyond. "Preparing. Preaching. Whatever. After a while she told him not to come around anymore. I was . . . relieved."

Sliding onto the bench, Mason took her hands. "I never saw him take a drink. Not ever. And he was calm in the woods."

"I remember," she whispered, her eyes unfocused.

"Eventually, he told me to get out of the woods and learn more, the things he couldn't teach me. I got my GED and I joined the military. And no matter how he did by you, he made me a man. He saved my life."

Reality returned to her. He saw it happen, like switching off a light. She yanked her hands back into her lap. "Fine. Say I believe you about Mitch and the stupid promise you made. What does he have to do with you kidnapping me?"

"You're right."

Mason stood and fetched their coats. He held them in the air between their bodies, waiting.

She eyed it with suspicion. "What?"

"You wanted to get out of here, so let's do it."

"So you can kill me in the woods?"

Mason laughed tightly. "Why not here? And why not hours ago?"

"I don't know, but I'm not going out there with you." Her gaze darted to the blacked windows.

"C'mon." Without waiting, he grabbed his nine-millimeter and a Maglite.

Jenna didn't miss his preparations. "I'm not stupid, you know. You're not going to get any trouble out of me."

"Not from you, no."

"You're trying to scare me and it won't work."

"It'd better."

Ten minutes later, with Jenna trailing like a sleepwalker, they stood in a small clearing just north of the cabin. Mason didn't trust her compliance. She was still thinking, doubting his word, and that would get them both killed.

God, he didn't want to get rough with her, but she wasn't getting away from him. She couldn't. Her life depended on him—his will, his cool, his knowledge. But his survival depended on her too.

"C'mere," he said quietly.

She didn't move.

So he went to her instead. Something good and calm opened in his chest when she didn't shy away.

"Listen, Jenna."

"What now? More stories?"

"No, *listen*. Listen to the forest."

The stillness enveloped them, a dark and unnatural stillness that gnawed at bones and wore away at the mind like a drip, drip, drip of water. No moon shone through the quiet leaves. No animals moved among the foliage. Although they stood in the trees, among those countless living plants, breathing each other's poison air, there wasn't a single noise to indicate life.

Jenna stood at his side. He could barely see her in the thick black soup of night, but he heard her frantic breathing.

"Where is everything?" she whispered.

"Mitch took you camping, right? When you were younger?"

"It creeps me out, you knowing stuff like that."

"Did he or didn't he?"

"Yeah, when I was a kid. And you were right. He never hit the bottle out here. For him, being in the woods was normal." She inhaled deeply, unsteadily. "But this . . . *this* isn't normal."

He took her hand, the only solid, real, warm thing in the forest. "Everything I've said is God's honest truth."

She tightened her fingers as a shiver worked down her arm. "There's no God here."

FIVE

From out of the enveloping darkness, Jenna caught the faint baying of distant hounds. Only they didn't sound like any dogs she'd ever heard. Their howls echoed with an unwholesome wetness, as if they keened through blood. Her heart skipped a beat. The cold cut through her jacket like icy knives.

The second-scariest part? Mason was the most harmless thing in the woods.

"We have to get back to the cabin." He tugged her hand. "You're not ready for a fight."

"Will I be?" she murmured, frozen and dazed.

He leveled a steady look on her, his secrets hidden in the near dark. "Yes."

Jenna had no time to think about that. She stumbled as he pulled her back toward the cabin, scattering something white that glittered like crystal. Mason glanced her way, seeming to read her without even trying.

"Rock salt," he said without missing a stride. "It'll put them off our scent."

Jenna hunched into her jacket, feeling naked and undone. The dogs sounded closer now. She smelled them too, a noxious stench that reminded her of graveyards. In her mind's eye, she could almost see hideous skeletal things with flesh barely clinging to bone. But that was crazy. They were just dogs, some strays gone feral.

Shadows flashed in her peripheral vision. She put on more speed, the feeling of life-or-death hitting her hard. The threat was intuitive, on a soul-deep level, and kicked her flight response into high gear. Dry, brittle branches whipped her face as they ran. They felt like bony fingers clawing at her skin. She swallowed a scream.

I want to wake up now. Time to wake up. The only reply to her desperation came in the form of Mason's warm fingers twined with hers.

She remembered her father's warning voice: *If you run, predators will chase you.* Sounds of that pursuit crashed through the trees behind them. She heard some of the creatures breaking off, maybe confused by the salt Mason had strewn across their trail. But the dogs didn't stop.

Animals went for the weakest prey first. Mason was only running—not turning to fight—because she was there. He was trying to protect her, like he said he'd promised Mitch.

Her breath came in shallow gasps as they entered the clearing. Golden slivers of light edged the cabin's blacked-out windows, offering a hot rush of relief. They'd made it. Jenna scrambled up to the front door. Her hands trembled as she tried to work the knob. Terror and the cold made her clumsy.

Two creatures broke from the shadow of the trees. They'd been dogs at some point. Now they were something else entirely. Something . . . *other*. What she'd imagined of their appearance was entirely accurate. *How?*

Only she'd missed the awful way the air shimmered around their gaunt bodies, cloudy like the haze off a sun-scorched pavement. Her blood congealed as they turned their ghoulish muzzles toward her, cloudy eyes gleaming garnet red in the dark. So unreal, so eerie, that ghastly shimmer urged her to look away. But if she did, she'd be their dinner. Although the demon dogs weren't like anything from nature, the law of predator and prey remained.

Mason planted both feet to face them. "Get inside!"

Jenna didn't know what world she'd stepped into, but she felt trapped on the other side of the looking glass. No old rules, if there were any rules at all. She stumbled into the cabin and slammed the door. She leaned against it, her heart pounding and her senses muddled.

A gunshot shattered the silence. Several more shots rang out. How long before he ran out of ammo? Mason was her only link to normalcy, and he was out in the cold, fighting those things—no matter what they were. He'd intended to prove a point, but what the hell would happen to her if he died?

Fear warred with self-preservation. When her breathing stabilized, she crept to the window and peeled back the blacking. With his ammo gone, Mason fought the creatures bare-handed, except for his jumbo Maglite. He was big and strong, but there were two demon dogs. Not good odds.

She didn't like the look of the foul, viscous slobber running from their jaws as they lunged. If they bit him . . . well, she didn't know enough about this crazy new world to predict what might happen. But animal bites were never good.

Jenna cast a desperate look around the cabin. She couldn't leave him alone out there, not when she was the reason they'd ventured out in the first place.

"You're not Mitch's daughter for nothing," she said aloud. "*Do* something."

Her gaze settled on the dead fireplace. A good-sized log sat on top of the woodpile. It would make a killer club. Before she could rethink, Jenna snagged it. She soaked the end in lighter fluid and lit it with embers from the stove. She took a deep breath and flung open the door in time to see Mason stagger to his knees. He had latched both hands on a monster's shoulders, holding it away from his throat with pure brute strength. The second dog was poised to spring. The air around them popped and sizzled, raising the hairs on her forearms as if she'd just caught the scent of an electrical fire.

Jenna launched herself off the porch and clobbered the second beast with a home-run swing. Something snapped and gave with a sickening lurch. Its back legs collapsed.

Mason twisted the other one's head off. Clean. Off.

Jenna's dog still twitched, snarling, trying to crawl. She leaped back, away from the slimy, jagged fangs. Cemetery stench pervaded the clearing. The wavering air around its body stilled as it died.

"I told you to stay inside," Mason bit out. He came to his feet with a subtle unsteadiness, telling her the contest had been closer than he would likely admit.

"You're welcome," she muttered. "What do we do with *them*?"

"Leave them. Don't touch." He scented the air. "We should take cover before more show up."

"Yeah . . . okay." She followed him back into the cabin, overcome with trembling.

Maybe she'd risked her life for nothing. Maybe he could dispatch twelve of those rotting monsters all by himself. Jenna sank down against the wall without stripping out of her coat. It seemed beyond cold in the cabin. Her teeth chattered, so she clenched her jaw.

What the hell *were* those things?

For the first time, she dared to think the worst. What if Mason was right? Maybe the troubles had finally reached the West Coast. What if people and cities and civilization were all toast? No more girls' night at the Louie. No more midnight phone calls when Mara's latest loser left her disappointed. No more libraries, or days at the family-owned financial firm where she'd worked since breast cancer took her mom.

Could it *all* be gone? *Really?*

She wrapped her arms around her legs and rested her face on her knees. *No crying.* Tears never solved anything. She'd learned that lesson at the first father-daughter day at school. When Mitch had been off in the woods somewhere, the other kids ran sack races with their dads. But maybe being Mad Mitch Barclay's daughter would finally pay off in terms of survival, if not inheritance or good memories.

Beyond the ringing in her head, she heard Mason moving around, probably washing the demon dog stink off him. Then she smelled a coppery tang. Blood. They'd hurt him. Worry rushed through her, completely disproportionate to their acquaintance. But she might need him to live through this nightmare. Only natural.

She brought her head up, and her breath caught. He'd taken off his shirt, revealing a scarred back—not the result of a whipping or other abuse. Mason looked more like a gladiator, each wound telling the story of some battle he'd survived. Had she handpicked someone to kick ass and take names on her behalf, she couldn't have done a better job.

Well played, Mitch.

Muscles played beneath his coffee-with-cream skin as he ran a damp rag across his shoulder. Slow and measured movements. She saw iron control in the way he dealt with the aftermath of the attack.

As if feeling her gaze on him, he turned.

Blood spilled down from his chest, but the wound looked like claw marks, not a bite. Jenna didn't know why she feared that possibility, but bad things were transmitted in *regular* saliva, let alone that of unnatural monsters. She wondered if the sickness she'd smelled in the night wind was contagious.

"Aren't you going to yell at me some more?" she asked, pushing to her feet. "Tell me how dumb I was for not listening to you?"

He paused, one hand on a first-aid kit. "I guess you know that already. It's why you're almost green and pretty close to tossing up your tuna casserole."

No censure in his tone. She liked that.

"Things are . . . really messed up out there." She had to smile at her understatement.

"Yeah," he said. "Look, I'm sorry about this. I really am. I didn't mean to scare you, but we didn't have time to talk it out. Towns will be worse than the woods—more people, better hunting. Predators stay where the food is until it's gone, then come looking for stragglers like us."

She couldn't imagine. Having people referred to as food sent cold shivers down to her toes.

He went on with a faint smile, "But I could do worse than to have somebody at my back who'll take on one of those with a flaming block of wood."

"I must have more nerve than sense." Jenna took a step toward him. "Let me help you."

He hesitated, as if considering her motives. She noticed that when he relinquished the med kit, his fingers trembled slightly. So, he wasn't Superman.

Although the gouge was deep and would scar, Jenna knew she couldn't sew up a human being. Mason hissed with the first touch of peroxide, but didn't make another sound. He might as well have been a pillar of scarred brown marble, his gaze fixed over her shoulder. His bare skin felt incredibly warm beneath her fingers, or maybe that was just in contrast to the lingering chill.

"It's been a long time since anybody did anything for me," he said quietly.

"Not even Mitch?"

It bothered her more than she wanted to let on, knowing he'd spent time with her father—time that should have been hers. Maybe if she'd been born a boy, she would have been allowed to join his private army. Mitch had been dead for years, but she couldn't shake her bitterness.

"*Especially* Mitch," he said.

Jenna frowned. "I don't get it."

"He wasn't my dad, and he didn't want to be. He was trying to get me ready for a cataclysm nobody else believed in. He wanted to make me tough enough to stand against what was coming."

In the firelight, she saw in his tired face traces of hardship she'd never known. "Did he succeed?"

His eyes went distant. "I don't know."

SIX

Five days passed like a dream. Mason could never believe the science behind dreams, that even the most elaborate ones lasted mere minutes. Apparently time slowed in the subconscious, but it ground to a goddamn halt in the cabin. Five days of sharing space with Jenna. Five days of silences and meals and a crude little bathroom. Five days of lying awake on the sofa while she slept in the loft.

What would kill them first, the creatures or the boredom?

Mason sat at the kitchen table and threaded a worn piece of cheesecloth through the barrel of his AR-15, cleaning the rifle for the first time—the first time that day.

Tomorrow, if he still breathed, he'd clean the damn thing again.

Jenna, meanwhile, sat in the wing-backed chair, her legs curled beneath her and an open paperback propped on her knees. The moldy little library on the built-in shelves next to the fireplace had found its first and only patron.

He wanted to hate her for seeming so content, but he needed her. At least, Mitch had said he did. Everything else the old man predicted had come true over the course of long years, so he held his patience. And Mason liked not having to fight with her—at least not since she discovered how he'd raided her closet back home, packing for the trek into the woods. No, that hadn't been pretty. But ever since, they'd reached a sort of armistice.

Not bad. Just more waiting. The whole damn winter would be that way.

Until the silence yielded to something he hadn't expected to hear again. Other people.

"What was that?" Jenna pulled her head up from the book. A faraway expression changed her face, green eyes looking inward.

"Stay here," he said, leaving the assault rifle but grabbing his nine-millimeter.

"Where am I going to go?"

But did she listen? No. She followed him to the front door, where the calls and shouts had grown louder, more distinct. He heard the name Robert and the unmistakable crack of an adolescent male voice.

Mason gripped the butt of the gun and kicked off the safety. "Who's there?"

"Help us! Hello? Someone let us in!"

A cacophony followed, each pleading for the same favor. He'd known this might happen, but hadn't expected it to be so gut wrenching. The reality of facing such a choice pressed against his sternum. Throat tight, the tendons of his fingers aching, he flipped the safety back on and returned to his disassembled rifle.

Jenna stayed at the door, staring at him. *Here we go.*

"What are you—" She swiveled between him and the wooden barrier separating them from the evil in the new world and from the people in the old one. "What're you doing?"

"Cleaning my gun."

"What about them?"

"They're on their own," he said, speaking deliberately. "They'll find shelter in the woods. Or not. Either way, they're not our problem."

"I can't believe this." Her blond ponytail swished as she shook her head. "What if Mitch had done this to you? Said, 'Get lost, kid'?"

"He didn't, which is why I owe him."

All of his arguments lined up in a row, nice and neat. He'd practiced them for years. She didn't stand a chance. *Neither do those people.*

"Look." His temper made him sharper than he meant to be. "I'm obligated only to you and myself."

"Yeah, because of some promise you made. Right." She frowned, her bottom lip tucked under a row of straight, white teeth—more the look of a bashful child than a woman in warrior mode.

"We're not opening the door," he said flatly.

"Yes, we are! Those are people. You remember people? There's a kid out there. I can hear him cussing."

"All I hear is a liability."

She stalked to the kitchen and slammed her fist on the table, rattling the rifle parts against each other. "I don't care. I'm here too. I get a say."

Dark circles sat heavily beneath her eyes. Mason figured she was tired, restless, and scared. Emotion clouded her judgment, and he wanted to make renewed use of the duct tape. "This isn't a democracy, Jenna."

"Are you really going to leave them out there?"

"Yep. Now shut up about it. Please."

"Well, it's good you still have your manners," she said, crossing her arms across a faded gray T-shirt. "Please and thank you. Fat lot of good that'll do if there aren't any people left."

"We're not letting them in."

"Forget it." She crossed to the door and retrieved her coat from a hook. "I'll throw in with them instead. You're not making it hard to choose."

"Is this what I get for saving your life?"

"I'm not condemning them on your word. No way."

Mason raked blunt fingernails across his scalp, avoiding her eyes. This *really* wasn't going the way he'd intended. "Jenna, wait—"

She jerked her head. "Did you hear that?"

"What?"

"The . . . those—damn, what do you call them?" Eyes panicked, she gestured. "Those demon dogs. Can't you hear them?"

Outside, the voices sped right past frantic to hysterical. Shouts transformed into terrified shrieks. Fists pounded and feet kicked so that the door danced on its hinges.

Before Mason could stop her, she wrenched open the locks. Bodies tumbled into the cabin. Jenna skittered out of the way and stood motionless in the threshold. After jumping over a few people, Mason joined her. His arm brushing hers, he watched the snarling dogs as they circled the far end of the clearing. The moon glowed softly, not enough to reveal more than the suggestion of movement.

"They're not attacking," she said.

"Planning."

Jenna scanned the darkness, eyes intent. "Planning?"

"Get back."

Mason slammed the door and cursed, resting his head against the wood. No amount of wishing would make any of this go away. So he turned and faced—a quick head count—*five* new burdens. That included one oddly silent little girl. *Great.*

"Thank you," Jenna whispered.

Anger cooked inside his chest like a swallow of boiling water. "Don't thank me, because I don't want the credit or the blame. *You* did this."

The newcomers stared at them. Some had already pushed off the floor, finding chairs. Mason walked back to the kitchen, closer to his weapons. No one was going *Lord of the Flies* on him with his own guns, not when they had bigger enemies to confront.

He stood behind the table and assessed the group. A girl, maybe nine years old, and behind her stood a fair-skinned redhead in her forties. Mother and daughter shared the same wide indigo eyes. Then there was a punk in Goth gear, bristling with attitude, and a middle-aged man who looked like a former athlete gone to seed. He had his arm around a chunky librarian type, who wore horn-rim glasses.

Not promising.

"Roll call," he said harshly. "I don't want your names yet, just some information. Did anyone grow up on a farm?"

"What does it matter?" The Goth boy, about fifteen with black hair, scowled from the wing-backed chair. Jenna's book lay on the floor beside his oversized combat boots.

"Because you might be used to slaughtering animals," Mason said. "You'll need that now. No hesitation. I guess you already know what we're up against." He waited as the words sank in. Mouths dropped opened, but no one contradicted him. "Anybody?"

No one.

"Anyone an avid camper? Former military? Know how to light a fire without matches? Anyone ever fired a gun?" Not a one. "Fucking hell." He jabbed a finger toward where Jenna stood beside the fireplace. "I told you this was a bad idea."

She lifted her brows. "You going to throw them out?"

"Wait," the aging athlete said. "Who put him in charge?"

"It's my house." Mason inhaled and quickly reassembled the AR-15. Thirty seconds of sure, easy rhythm, the stuff of long practice and certainty.

He set his weapon aside and splayed his hands across the table. "Did anyone listen to the radio?"

The kid laughed. "Can't listen to anything. It's all toast."

"Cut the sarcasm," Mason said. "I'm talking about whatever comes on the air. Anybody?"

He had her now. He'd known the truth from Mitch's stories, but watching it spread across Jenna's face was a just reward. She rubbed her hands up and down her forearms. Slowly, finally, she nodded.

The librarian-looking lady was pale and sweaty. She sank down to the floor, holding her ankle. "What does radio have to do with those . . . things? Oh God—all those people."

Mason spared Jenna a glance. Her eyes had gone wide, her face pale.

"We can debate forever," he said, "but you can't deny the threat. The wolves are at the door. The change is here—and whether you believe it or not, it's cataclysmic." He paused to fill his lungs with air, scented by the stink of too many frightened bodies. "The more adaptable and flexible you were in your old life, the better you're going to handle this one."

The new people spoke all at once, too many shrill questions, too much fear. His head felt like it would split in two. He didn't need this. He'd gladly go back to the waiting and boredom.

"You need food and sleep," Mason shouted over the clamor.

He turned from the small, noisy rabble and rubbed his temples. Later, when no one was looking, he'd down a few aspirin. No sense in showing weakness. Strength and order would get them through.

"How did you know I listened to the radio?" Jenna stood at his elbow, her expression a tangle of questions. Her posture and the way she touched his forearm said she might be back on his side.

"Doesn't matter," he said.

"Seriously, did Mitch tell you? Or did you spy on me?"

He placed both hands on her shoulders and gave a little shake. "It was Mitch. I'm not a stalker, for God's sake. Now are you with me or not?"

"Answer me something first. Did *you* listen to the radio?"

"No," he said tightly. "I alphabetized my CDs by artist, then title. DVDs and books too. My time in the military never wore off."

She glanced at where he still gripped her shoulders. "So what does that mean?"

"I'm not very good at . . . at adapting." He held her gaze. Mitch had spotted that weakness almost from the start. Not for the first time, Mason wondered if the promise to protect Jenna had been intended for his survival too. "I soak up the damage, not roll with the punches. Which means I need you as much as you need me."

"Hello? You two? Can we get some help?" The big man knelt beside the woman with horn-rims. "Edna's been bit."

SEVEN

The plump woman trembled where she sprawled on the floor. She wore a gray-flowered dress. Dirty layers of fluffy chiffon had been ripped and snarled, like a Sunday school teacher fallen on hard times. Behind the lenses of her glasses, one of which was fractured, her eyes appeared odd and filmy. She leaned down to rub her calf, then hesitated.

Mason just looked pissed. "Anyone have a medical background?"

"I do," the redhead said. "I was a nurse's aide but I have basic EMT training as well. There just wasn't any work near Penny's school, and I didn't want to uproot her."

His expression said he wasn't interested in her life story. "Check her out. See how bad it is." He turned away, but not before Jenna glimpsed the sick dismay in his eyes.

Whatever happened to a bite victim would be bad.

The aide knelt and said softly, "Let me take a lock, all right? Here, loosen your fingers."

Edna bent her head, studying her injured calf with remarkable dispassion. "It doesn't feel right."

"The skin is broken." The redhead spoke as if she were instructing a class of interns. "Puncture wounds consistent with an animal bite. Are you in much pain?"

"It burns."

Despite herself, Jenna stepped closer. She wanted to see what a bite would mean. The skin circling the wound had darkened, turning ash gray. The holes themselves were an unwholesome purple, as if a bruise had slid inward, eating through muscle. The thought made Jenna shiver.

"Is your tetanus shot current?" the redhead asked.

"That's the least of her worries," Mason muttered.

Jenna leveled a look that said he better not scare the kids. *Damn.* Now they had children to worry about, thanks to her. But she couldn't have left them to die.

A cold feeling crept into her bones. What if she'd sentenced them to a slower death? With so many extra mouths to feed, how long would the canned goods last? And what would happen to Edna? Jenna wondered if she'd done wrong in opening the door, even if it had been the compassionate choice.

No. Think logically. More people mean a higher chance of survival.

The trick would be getting out of the cabin and back to civilization without those demon dogs snacking on them. Surely, there had to be somewhere safe. These woods didn't exactly qualify as "safe." The mother would fight hard for her daughter, the kind of determination that might make a difference. On the other hand, the athlete-gone-to-seed resembled a worshipful puppy at the injured woman's side, and both of them were weak, out of shape. And the kid—he was a wild card.

She crossed to Mason and spoke in whispers. "How bad will this get?"

His silencing look said he couldn't answer in front of the strangers.

"Listen up," he announced, loud enough to draw all their attention. "If you stay here, it's because I let you. That means doing whatever I say, when I say it. No asking why."

"Okay." The redhead's quick agreement made Jenna think she'd do anything to keep her little girl indoors.

Nobody else objected, which showed they had sense. The girl moved quietly to the hearth and curled up on the floor. She had yet to speak a single word. Maybe she was in shock, traumatized in ways that would take months, if not years, to overcome.

Jenna shuddered, trying not to imagine what this little group had seen. If Mason hadn't shoved her in the trunk, she might be a casualty by now.

Everyone relaxed a little once the nurse's aide had bandaged the bite mark. At least they didn't need to look at it. Jenna went into the kitchen and started another casserole—canned chicken this time. To make enough for everyone required extra cans of each ingredient. Mason cut her a sharp look as if he was thinking the same thing. She scowled right back at him.

"I want names now." He settled onto one of the kitchen table benches with the assault rifle across his knees. "And the abridged version of how you wound up at my door."

The man spoke for them. "I am—I *was*—the assistant coach for the Wabaugh JV football program. Bob Suleski." He shifted as if he'd rise to shake hands, but Mason curled his fingers around the rifle's grip. Robert sank back into his chair, then tilted his head. "This is Edna Cartwright, the school guidance counselor."

Edna pushed up her horn-rims and managed a wan smile. "Go Wolverines."

If Jenna had recognized it, the name of the school might have provided her an idea of their location. But she'd never heard of Wabaugh.

"Edna and I, we carpool together," Bob added.

Mason smiled. "How environmentally responsible of you," he said, his voice a dark rasp. "And what about you, kid?"

The Goth flipped ink black hair out of his eyes. "I'm Midnight. I go to Wabaugh. Or I did," he added, sounding uneasy.

He couldn't be more than fifteen, slender in a bony, boyish way. His feet were huge in contrast to the rest of him, his face pale and pretty. Jenna doubted his parents had named him Midnight. He might be Ed or Steve, maybe James, and he needed to get over himself fast.

By his impatient sigh, Mason must have shared her estimation. "Not your handle, kid. Your *name.*"

"Tru." His posture became defensive. "It's my real name, okay? My mom named me after Truman Capote."

"And I'm Angela Sheehan," the redhead added. "My daughter's Penny."

Edna, Bob, Angela, Penny, and Tru. Jenna committed their names to memory. She liked to think it was a nod to the idea they'd all survive long enough for such courtesies to matter.

"I'm Jenna," she said from the kitchenette, scooping the casserole into its dish. "And this is Mason."

No surprise that Mason brushed off her attempt at being civil. "I'll ask again: How'd you get here? How'd you find us?"

Jenna realized the reason for his single-mindedness. *If they found us, so could something else.* Her stomach dropped.

"You probably won't believe me," Angela said, her voice low. "But it was Penny. We fled in Bob's SUV, but it stalled, like the whole electrical system popped at once. As soon as it stopped, she ran for the woods, so I chased her. The rest followed. She led us here, like she knew exactly where you'd be."

Jenna glanced at the girl where she sat on the rug, a white stuffed bear clutched to her chest. Her eyes looked impossibly huge in her pale face, pools of twilight blue framed by flyaway corn-silk hair.

Penny knew something. Jenna saw it in her haunted eyes, but the little girl jammed a thumb in her mouth and turned away.

"She's telling the truth," Bob muttered. "I thought it was crazy, but after some of the things I've seen in the last few days . . ." He trailed off, shrugging. "Everyone else was . . . well—God there was just so much *blood*." He pinched his eyes shut. "None of it makes sense, but 'there are more things in heaven and earth than are dreamt of in your philosophy.'"

Tru rolled his eyes. "Aw, quit the Shakespeare, would ya, Coach?"

From looking at the kid, Jenna suspected he had a cartload of issues. She imagined a row of neat, self-inflicted cuts beneath his long sleeve, and then wondered at her conviction. It wasn't suspicion; it was *knowledge*. She'd felt the same thing out in the woods, imagining how those demon dogs would look.

Okay, what the hell . . . ?

Bob's eyes went dull and distant. "When that *thing* bit Edna, I just kicked it. Kept kicking it."

"Yeah, it kinda didn't look the same when he got through with it," Tru said, grinning.

Jenna took a deep breath. She wanted to pound it out of all of them. What happened? *What happened out there?* But part of her didn't want to know, because that would mean it was true—that the troubles in the east had finally crossed the Mississippi. Nothing would ever be the same.

Old words came to her. *The wolf shall dwell with the lamb, and the leopard shall lie down with the kid, and the calf and the lion and the fatling together, and a little child shall lead them.* She remembered them from what Mitch had written. Right then, she wanted to read the letter over again. Maybe it contained more information she could use. But that would wait until they sorted out this mess.

Jenna leaned against the kitchen counter and looked at the group.

She could imagine Mason as a wolf or a leopard, maybe a lion. But according to that verse, there should be eight of them. And not everyone would survive. She knew that. In Old Testament terms, fatlings and lambs were often sacrificed.

"You were smart, all of you," Mason said, cutting into her thoughts. "I'm amazed you made it all the way out here without gear or training."

Without turning his back on their uninvited guests, he crossed to the hearth and knelt in front of Penny. She regarded him with big unblinking eyes.

"So you're their leader, huh? I should do business with you?" To Jenna's surprise, his tone remained patient and gentle. The girl peered up at him, thumb in her mouth. The idea of her being in charge of *anything* was strangely endearing, but Jenna couldn't imagine following her through a monster-infested wood. "How'd you know we were here?"

No reply. Just that big-eyed stare.

Breaking the fraught silence, Bob asked, "Hey, does that radio still work?"

Mason shrugged. He walked to a nearby coffee table and clicked on the analog radio, then fiddled with the dial. Static hissed through one channel after another. Nothing at all on FM. The eeriness of *nothing* was hard to overcome. Jenna shivered once, then popped the casserole into the stove. Mason switched to AM and scanned slowly, his fierce concentration making her want to touch the twin lines between his brows.

The thought shocked her. No, she didn't want *that*. Jenna shook her head reflexively. She wanted to hear another human voice. That was all. She'd just been cooped up with him for too long.

By the time Mason hit 1500 on AM, she'd almost lost hope.

". . . if anyone hears this, I'm at the nature outpost and research station. Those things are all over the area. Everyone else is dead. I'm broadcasting on all emergency frequencies. I repeat, if anyone hears this . . ." The man sounded weary. "Ah, what the fuck's the point?"

Prescience skittered through Jenna like cold wind on her skin. *There's our number eight.*

EIGHT

Mason enforced rationing after their first meal.

Beside him at the kitchen counter, Jenna put a pan of water on the stove to boil while he opened yet another round of tuna, peas, and condensed soup. She wouldn't meet his eyes and had yet to speak about what was on her mind—not their guests. Something deeper. Her body radiated unease, burrowing beneath his own skin.

Strange, the idea that he could gauge her thoughts. But he trusted his instincts. This new awareness of her was instinctual. When they'd first been in the cabin together, Mason had fought unexpected sexual impulses. Those impulses remained—an uncanny awareness of her as a woman. Now the hair on the backs of his arms stood on end too.

"There won't be enough food for the whole winter."

He looked down into green eyes that seemed to have aged in only a few days. "No."

Jenna inhaled deeply and pushed the air out of her mouth. "I don't regret it."

Her unexpected allure, insufficient resources, and the stink of fearful bodies didn't wear on his nerves like their two biggest problems.

Edna. And Dr. Chris Welsh at the nature station.

Mason had known about the place, of course. He had spent weeks mapping everything in these woods, but he hadn't imagined anybody there would survive the change.

"Hey, radio fans." The stranger's voice crackled out of the little transistor. "Next, we have sports. Those bloody Dogs mopped up again! They're on a hot streak, eh?"

Tru sighed. "This guy is lame. He deserves to be eaten."

"Watch it," Robert said, glancing at Edna.

"What'll you make me do, eh, Bob? Run laps? Or maybe you'd like a little alone time with me in the locker room." Tru stuck two fingers in his mouth and sucked with gusto.

Bob's face darkened to a shade just short of furious. He had a temper under that nice-guy exterior. "Do that any better, *Midnight*, and folks'll think you have experience."

"Only 'cause you forced me, perv."

Mason watched the interplay with a sense of detachment he didn't want to lose. To care about these people would be a wasted effort. They'd be dead before he learned their birthdays.

But dissent in the ranks couldn't be ignored. If they fought each other, they'd be willing to challenge Mason too. For his sake and Jenna's, he couldn't allow that.

"Weather report," Welsh went on. "Couldn't tell you, frankly. Haven't been out of the basement in, well . . . days. Let's say seven. So still late fall. Okay, weatherman Chris says ass cold for the foreseeable future. Here's hoping I see spring."

They'd listened to him like Roosevelt's fireside chats, forty-eight hours on from first hearing his transmission. His voice revealed a lot. First up, he was a native of western Canada. Second, he was alone and losing his grip. Sometimes his words slurred as if he'd been drinking or suffering insomnia. Mason wouldn't blame him for either.

Among the babble he admitted was to preserve his own sanity, Welsh provided clues about his background. He'd studied cougars in the Rockies, and he'd hot-wired the ham radio he used for his broad-casts. That had Mason thinking zoological knowledge and technical know-how. Maybe even cold-weather survival skills to complement his own.

Welsh also had a stockpile of food. About four hours into the show, he'd narrated a list of provisions at the station. They would need every scrap of those supplies to survive the winter.

Edna moaned, the wounded animal in the corner. Her skin had taken on a gray sheen, almost silver with the way she sweated. Not much longer now.

Mason stalked from the tiny kitchen to switch off the radio. Fatigued eyes looked up at him from where they'd scattered around the fireplace.

"Enough," he said. "It's time for the hard news."

The ever-present sneer on Tru's face seemed designed to rankle anyone old enough to vote. "You get off on ordering people around?"

"And you get off on carving up your arms. We all have our ways of coping."

Tru paled. A good guess, but Mason regretted the hasty slam. Shithead or not, he was still just a kid. With the whole world in chaos, the adults in the cabin were all he had left to rebel against.

"I have something to show all of you," he went on, returning to the kitchen.

Jenna watched him with impassive eyes and said nothing as he opened every cabinet—the full extent of their supplies laid bare.

He crossed his arms and leaned against the counter. "I equipped this cabin with provisions enough to sustain two people through the winter."

"Cozy," Tru muttered.

"Two people, kid—not seven."

One by one, the adults and even Tru glanced to where Edna rested half-conscious on the floor. Okay, six people.

"When the snow comes, we'll be trapped here," Mason said. "There won't be any game to hunt because all the animals have fled."

"That's true." Angela glanced to where her daughter lay curled with her teddy bear, always checking to see if her daughter would be scared by harsh facts. But Penny seemed more interested in the world behind her deep blue eyes.

"I noticed it too." Jenna moved next to him, spreading an unfamiliar tingle along his skin.

"So no fresh game," Mason said. "We can't sustain our numbers here."

"We could chew on beefy boy." Tru hooked a thumb at Robert.

Mason ignored him. "I'd hoped the snow would be here by now, because the demon dogs don't do well in the cold. But at this point, it's to our advantage that the weather's held."

Bob stood up and stretched. "How do you know about the dogs?"

"I just do."

"Show him. All of them." Jenna touched between his shoulder blades and sent a shiver down his backbone. "That's how you got these, right?"

An image flashed in his mind. A lamb. And fangs lunging for its neck.

Jenna flinched and yanked her hand away. For long moments, they stared at each other. Pupils dilated, her unblinking scrutiny dug into his bone marrow. Her nostrils flared like a predator catching the scent of its next meal. And Mason wanted to kiss her. Nothing to do with romance or even desire. No, the kiss his body needed was deep and primal, the kind that led straight to sex.

She shook her head, looking as dazed as he felt. "Take off your shirt, Mason."

That wasn't going to help, but he obeyed her quiet command. With one quick jerk of cotton, his T-shirt lay on the ground. He stood facing Jenna and the kitchen, his back to the others. He heard their gasps, distant somehow, as Jenna's gaze moved over his bare chest like a touch. He couldn't move or speak or breathe. She traced every inch of skin, her expression predatory.

If she didn't stop looking at him like that, he was going to make unconventional use of the kitchen counter, no matter who watched. Need and power hammered in his blood.

"What the hell *is* this?" he asked her.

His low, private whisper broke the hold. She looked away, and Mason faced the odd congregation.

"Let's just say I've been fighting these things for some time," he said. "They used to be people. I saw them up and down the East Coast, moving inland by degrees, devouring everything and spreading their evil."

"I heard about that," Angela whispered. "But it just sounded too ridiculous. It would've been on the news, people turning into creatures. The New Media Coalition said—"

"Forget what they told you." Mason retrieved his shirt and pulled it back on. "Eastern Europe went silent first, yeah? It's been years since anyone heard reliable news from across the pond. It's our turn now. The change has been transforming the world for a long time, but it's moved on to producing those monsters. They're unpredictable, and smarter than they look. One advantage we have is that they don't like the snow. But no matter who they used to be, they're our enemies now. Never forget that."

Silence greeted his statement. He could only hope they were strong enough to steel themselves and ditch the lives they'd known before. That hard break was the only way to deal with the new reality.

Jenna broke the tension. "How's Edna doing?"

"I'm awake," the woman answered as Bob knelt to check on her. "If you know about those creatures, then you know what's happening to me."

Aw, shit. She was so damn lucid. Preternaturally so. No incoherence despite a sky-high fever, which meant she was that *other* kind of doomed. This wouldn't be pretty.

He crouched on the hearth of the cold fireplace, a few feet from her pallet below the built-in bookshelves. "You have probably two days. No more than four."

Edna nodded.

"This is ridiculous," Bob said. "She's got a bite, that's all. She'll be fine."

Mason studied her. "What do you think, Edna? What's it feel like to you?"

Her eyes looked cataract-covered, glazed with thick white mucus. A fine trembling claimed her entire body. "My skin itches—not the bite, but all over," she said through chattering teeth. "Worse than the flu."

"I know. I'm sorry."

"And . . ." She shook her head and looked to the ceiling.

"Edna?" Bob put a hand on hers, but Mason noticed how he hesitated before touching her. "What is it?"

"I keep dreaming of spiders."

"And you guys think *I'm* messed up," Tru said bitterly.

Edna didn't seem to hear him. "I *was* a spider. Isn't that strange? I worried about the cold because it was my time to die, but I kept working to make sure the eggs were all right."

A shiver chased across Mason's scalp.

"*Charlotte's Web*," Angela said, hushed.

"Yes, like Charlotte. I *was* Charlotte."

"Edna," Mason said. "You have to listen to me. Soon, your body will try to . . . shift. And it'll most likely fail. It's not a pretty death. But I can end it for you. If you want me to."

Robert's face twisted, horror stricken. "You're kidding, right? This is sick!"

"Is she a danger to the rest of us?" Angela's eyes gained a keen, hard look.

"I don't think so," Mason said wearily.

"So you're thinking of killing her?" Bob scrambled to his feet and stood like a linebacker. "I won't let you. She's a *guidance counselor*, for Christ's sake!"

"Robert, let him talk," Edna said softly. "I can barely even see. What choice do I have?"

"You can choose to die now." Mason stood, his words calm but his posture a silent counter to Robert's threatening stance. "Or you can help us."

"Help us get creeped the fuck out," Tru mumbled. "Mission accomplished."

Her milky gaze found Mason's. "How?"

"We need to get to that nature station, or we'll starve. It's about three miles from here in a secluded patch of woods. I'll need two days of short daylight patrols to figure out the most direct route by foot. And I'll train everyone on the firearms—crash course. Then we'll go."

Edna nodded again. "And me?"

Mason closed his eyes. He could shoot her—and he would, if she asked it of him—but not even he was strong enough to look at her directly now. "You'll stay here. As bait."

NINE

"This is a Thompson .308," Mason said. "You aim it at anything you don't mean to shoot and I'll take your goddamn head off. Got it?"

Tru nodded. The sharp comment he'd been ready to spit out didn't come. He'd never held a weapon before, and that gave him pause. The rifle wasn't like the shooters he played, though it had been a long-ass time since any new games came out. It wasn't exactly a priority for the new regime. But this gun had weight. The wood and metal were smooth beneath his fingers.

The awe didn't last long.

Whenever Mason said it was safe, they practiced. The god of ordnance stalked among them, correcting their stances until Tru's hands cramped. But Mason always acted before an attack. Maybe he could detect the creatures from farther away, sense them somehow. Whatever. He hustled them inside just before the creatures got in range.

The frenzy could last for hours. Angela cradled her girl. Bob sat by Edna pretty much all the time. Tru couldn't sleep when the dogs prowled around the cabin, seeking a way in. He would sit with his knees drawn up, trying not to look at anybody. Mason claimed to have years of experience killing monsters, and now the big dude was trying to get them combat ready before the guidance counselor went all *Alien* on the hardwood floor.

When the dogs gave up, they went back outside. Tru got good at controlling the Thompson. Of everyone but Mason, he was the best shot. Gaming had taught him excellent hand-eye coordination, if nothing else. Funny, the thing his mom had screamed about most might do some good.

No. He wouldn't think about her.

Not everyone would make it, but Tru didn't speak up. He just sank himself in the mindless drills. Fire, reload. Hard to believe, but he was better off now than the dipshits who'd picked on him at Wabaugh. The kids with the shiny cars and the easy cheerleaders—they'd been turned into kibble. Tru had seen them mauled and eaten.

He reloaded and fired and hit the target six times out of seven.

When Mason came by a few minutes later, he narrowed his eyes. "Why aren't you working?"

"I'm as good as I'm gonna be, Pops. You really want me to blow my ammo on that dummy?" He gestured to the target made from pillows and clothing. "We'll need it for the real deal."

"Show me. Head shot, right now."

Adults were assholes. With a faint sigh, Tru raised the Thompson, sighted, and blasted the target. A new hole sprang up slightly off center between its drawn-on eyes. "Do I get a hall pass now, Teach? Better yet, can I go inside? She's never gonna get it." He cocked his head at Angela. "And it's fucking cold."

"Watch your mouth," the blonde snapped.

Tru rolled his eyes. "Or what?"

Her green eyes looked as cold as arctic ice. Jenna was her name. Not like it mattered. Their numbers would be whittled down in this suicide run.

Jenna raised her rifle, a Remington, and landed a slug beside his.

"I'm in no mood," she said, her gaze locked on his. "We have a child here. You want to keep messing with me?"

Tru hunched his shoulders. "Okay, sorry. I'll try not to cuss so much."

The other old folks were too ginger when handling their weapons. They didn't hold them with enough authority, so the kickback threw off their aim. He wanted to tell the big dude to give it up. Some people just didn't have survival instinct.

Then, it was time to go.

"It's three miles over bad ground." Mason looked pretty badass in his knit cap and camos. Eagle, globe, and anchor on the sleeve. Old-style Marines, for sure. "We'll be moving fast, and I'll want you all sharp. Nobody goes off alone—that excludes me. I have to scout to make sure it's safe. When we take off, as far as you're concerned, I am *God* for the day. Any questions?"

Nope. No questions. They'd been over the plan until Tru could recite it in his sleep.

He stopped slouching long enough to present his rifle for inspection. "I'm cocked, locked, and ready to rock."

Mason nodded. "Good work, kid."

"You gonna let me try yours someday?" he asked, eyeing Mason's AR-15. A serious piece of weaponry.

The big dude raised an eyebrow. "Hell, no."

Angela still didn't have the knack with her gun. She held it away from her body as if she expected it to go off in her hands. Mason had given her the smallest caliber he had, a little .22, the kind kids used for shooting squirrels. Overall, it didn't bode well for the mission. The sky hung heavy with threatening snow, a gray day for mission impossible. Trees stood as silent sentinels, barren with the threat of the first heavy winter storm. Tru could taste it in the bite of the air, dampness that wouldn't come as rain. Soon everything would be blanketed white.

Jenna had devised an Indian-style back sling out of an old sheet so that Bob could carry the kid. Tru marched with the others, fully geared. Everyone carried provisions from the cabin. The Thompson felt like an extension of his arm. He wasn't worried. His whole life had been a long shot anyway. Either he'd make it, or he'd die wearing a backpack stuffed with cans of tuna.

Then Edna screamed. The monsters were growling in the distance. Howls filled the chilly air.

They're coming.

And holy fuck he wanted to get away from Edna. *Now.* She jerked like the kids who had gone crazy at school. Mason propped her up against a tree and wrapped her convulsing body in a blanket. He'd filled a number of plastic bags with a compound mix of various household chemicals that would pack a nasty punch. Then he circled her with a stream of gasoline, drawing a line with it back toward the woods.

She flailed harder.

"Get back!" Mason hustled away. "Let's move out. Now!"

Bob looked ready to hurl, his gaze glued to Edna's epileptic freakout. Tru couldn't look away either, but he never lowered his rifle. Her fit made the blanket ripple—at least he thought that was why—until she flung the cover away.

Ange screamed.

"Oh my God," Jenna breathed.

But Tru was speechless.

Edna wasn't a person anymore. She looked *inside out.* And that wasn't even the worst. New limbs protruded from her torso, covered in fine black hair. They all flailed in unison, and her round middle bloated further beneath his horrified gaze. She carried a faint glow like the dogs, corrupted in the same way. Tru wanted to look away, only he couldn't, because her bulging, milky eyes had frozen him in place. He felt like he might piss his pants.

The dogs closed, scenting weakness. She would be their food. Shit, he didn't want to see that.

"I said now, people!" Mason shouted.

This time everyone listened, hightailing it for the woods. Tru fought the urge to look back as the dogs found Edna, their first target. He heard them tearing at her, horrible in a way he'd never dreamed possible. God knew he'd never liked the woman, but nobody deserved to go out like that.

"Jenna, take them," Mason said. "Go now." He lit a match at the edge of the clearing and touched off the stream of gasoline.

The blond woman led the way into the woods, but Tru wasn't sure if she was tough enough for the job. Just before he rounded a bend, an explosion cut the air and pushed a mild heat against his back. Edna screamed in agony, then went silent.

Tru swallowed hard. Now *he* was the one who'd be sick.

"Tru!" Jenna called. "Get your ass in gear, you're falling behind."

"Fine. Coming."

They hustled on for another ten minutes. Tru couldn't force Edna out of his head. *We could all end up like that. Dog food. Or pulled apart from the inside if we get bit.* His thoughts looped on how they'd used Edna. A sick, twisted, practical plan. One only Mason could have come up with. Tru didn't know if he admired or feared him. Maybe a little of both.

"Stop it," the big dude growled eventually. "I know what you're thinking, all of you. But she was out of time and she saved our lives."

The coach only muttered, "You're a son of a bitch," in reply.

He might give Mason shit, but Bob lacked the skills to lead. Tru didn't doubt the big dude would put him down like one of those demon dogs if the coach tried anything.

Mason shrugged. "If you don't like it, find another party. I don't remember inviting you anyway."

Tru stifled a quiet laugh. During the rare moments she wasn't high, his mom had always said he'd end up dead in a ditch. She was sweet that way. But if a crappy home life didn't turn you into a murderous sociopath, it laid great groundwork for surviving the end of the world.

The silence was creepy as hell. Mason made it clear they shouldn't yap all the way, but Tru had forgotten what it was like out here. No animals. No insects. Just the sound of their breathing and their feet rasping over dead wood and fallen leaves. He wanted to cover up that unnatural quiet, pretend it wasn't real.

He walked on, listening to Angela inhale and exhale as if in meditation. Maybe it kept her calm. Calm was good. And for all his bulk, Bob seemed to be doing okay, even as he carried the kid. Good thing they hadn't been stuck with the decrepit math teacher instead.

Despite the cold, sweat formed on his palms. How long had they been walking? Three miles was the target, but he had no way of telling the time or marking miles. Branches slapped his face as they passed through the trees. There was no path. Out here, he felt so exposed. Anything could eat him. *At least I'd make a bony fucking snack.*

And winding up fast food seemed better than the alternative— better than going out in monster form, like Edna.

Mason held up a hand, signaling them to stop just before a clearing. "We're coming up on the worst part of this trek," he said, rechecking his weapon. He sounded tenser than Tru had heard before. Nervous? *No way.* "I'd hoped to avoid it. But with the gear we're carrying, we wouldn't be able to pick our way across rougher terrain."

Raw cemetery stench wafted in on the still air, carrying the scent of open graves and putrid flesh. Angela rubbed her nose. "What is it? What's in there?"

"Tru, up on point with me," Mason snapped. "Jenna, you're rearguard. I want the girl in the middle." At last he turned to the redhead, his grim face fixed with resolve. "It's a pit."

TEN

Mason crept to the left along the edge of the clearing, focusing on steady, even movements.

On a long list of situations he never wanted to be in again, this one ranked at the top. His gut told him to hightail it. This ragtag cluster of walking meat had no hold on him. He could double back in the span of two heartbeats, grab Jenna from the end of the line, and reclaim their cabin. Because he'd seen pits before. Different terrain. Different human fodder. The end result had been bloody.

Mason didn't need any more scars. Or nightmares.

Tru stepped into the clearing, his pale face serious. Mason had worn that expression in his time—scared shitless but doing his best impersonation of a man.

He knew Jenna had latched onto Penny as her personal symbol of all that was good and worth saving, but Mason couldn't relate to that purity. He respected Penny and the strange vibe she gave off, like the hum of an electrical conduit. But over the last few days of training, he'd started to see Tru differently. The kid was hardened, wounded, and too young to bear it with more than bravado. Mason could relate.

So when the first demon dogs showed, he didn't think. He fought.

"Tru! Flank right. Now!"

He mirrored the kid's movement. Together they formed a pincer around the central graveyard hole. Two pair ran out to meet them. Mason didn't look across the pit to see how Tru handled his opponents. If he could survive, his moment to prove it was now.

Mason stood fast and fired. One of the dogs collapsed, its skull a crushed melon of brain and blood. The other showed no sign of comprehending what had happened, no acknowledgment of its partner's sudden demise. It leaped through the pulsing, unnatural air. All flying fangs and claws, it took Mason's second shot in its gut. The slug ejected through its back, taking bits of fur and spinal bones with it. The thing dropped. Mason stepped on its neck and blew off its head, just in case. Only then could he look straight at its face, like a mirage made solid as its shimmer died away.

A series of four shots rang out on the other side of the pit, followed by a string of curses. Tru's voice cracked with every one, but he still lived.

"Jenna!" Mason cut inward from the trees, nearer the graveyard, and motioned for Tru to do the same. The kid was covered in red. "Bring up the others! Now!"

He felt her presence before he saw her. Yet there she was, a hundred feet away and pointing her rifle the way they'd come, backing slowly around the pit. She felt prickly in his mind now, like even the thought of her was pissed off at him. She'd argued against him going off alone, how he went into the woods to scout.

Tough, he thought.

Prick, came her reply, clear in his mind.

What the hell?

But before he could question that, two more dogs burst from the other end of the clearing. The research station lay a half mile beyond, through a narrow corridor filled with snarls and fangs. Mason shouted a warning, then knelt and fired. One fell, but the other kept coming.

The haze around its body acted as optical camouflage, obscuring its fast approach. Mason raised his rifle sideways in both hands, catching the dog between its chin and shoulders. Its trachea smashed against the barrel. Using momentum, Mason lifted his arms and arched back, flipping the growling, frothing dog behind him.

"I got it," Jenna yelled, advancing at a run. "More coming from Tru's position."

Then Mason did the inconceivable. He let her take the kill. Didn't even hesitate. Simply turned his attention to the next batch and smiled tightly at the sound of Jenna's rifle fire.

"Tighten up. Stay on Jenna. Tru, with me on the other side."

Instead of taking the defensive this time, Mason charged. The acidic fury in his chest urged muscles to go faster, cut sharper. Adrenaline stole thought and replaced it with smooth action, a meta trance of movement. Dodge, spin, fire. Hot gunmetal and cordite layered with the copper smell of blood, that tang heavy beneath the pit's sweet rot. He gulped a cool mouthful of air and fired, fighting clear of a nightmare.

Tru met him at the far end of the clearing, having mirrored Mason on the right side of the great circular grave. For once, the kid had no words. He simply panted, his thin chest pumping up and down. Gore slicked his black hair. In his eyes Mason found something he hadn't expected, something that dragged him down from that high of combat: the need for approval.

He gave it with a simple nod.

And just like that, Tru was back to himself. "Shit, you made out like this would be hard."

"Just like an old shooter?" Video games had been out of production for years, but from the quickness of his reflexes, the kid loved those ancient relics of pre-secession years.

"Just."

"Jenna, bring up the rear," Mason ordered. "Left flank."

Robert led, but Jenna kept them in line as they circled the way Mason had come. She moved in steady strides, no bobbing, her rifle always at the ready.

Angela kept her gaze on Penny. "What is this place?" she whispered.

"Not the time," Mason ground out.

He sensed more than saw the next onslaught, as demon dogs bounded toward them.

But he sensed it from Jenna's perspective.

Left!

She turned toward the woods, her back to the pit. A trio burst through the trees, scattering on sight. No straightforward charge for these bastards. Zigzagging, like blurs of fur and skeletal meat, they zeroed in on Jenna and the others.

"Hold," he shouted at Tru, already hurtling toward the threat. "Watch for more."

Jenna took out the center dog, but that wasn't enough. In fact it seemed like a calculated move. Send one up the middle. Draw fire. Leave the flanks vulnerable.

A sound like a champagne cork went off—Ange popping her .22. She took one down at the knees, a lucky shot. Then Bob stepped up and pumped two bullets into its stomach, his hands shaking too badly to aim for anything smaller.

"The head," Mason said, coming up to them. He fired once to finish the task.

"*Mason!*"

At Jenna's shout, he turned to find a creature loping toward the rest, an old-time beast of legend. Over five feet tall, it possessed the fangs and claws of a wolf on a distinctly humanoid form. The monster studied them as it ran, its eyes translucent silver coins. Choosing its victim. A stream of thick, yellow mucus dripped from its yawning jaws. From where he stood some ten feet away, Mason smelled its wet, putrid fur and heard the sandpaper rasp of its breath.

In a blur of motion, the beast sprang. Mason pulled the trigger but only managed to change its course. It leaped for the coach. Whether by instinct or intent, Bob dove into the pit.

The monster wasn't as nimble in its pseudo-human form. Mason caught it around the legs and kept it from leaping after the coach and Penny. After two hard rolls away from the pit, he straddled its smaller, more compact body.

Taloned claws sunk into his thighs, tearing. Mason grunted. The icy shock of pain yielded to a drenching wash of his own blood. But no amount of damage short of death would stop him. Mason forced himself to look at it. Doing so was almost impossible, like forcing two opposing magnets together. Reflex wanted to shift his gaze to the side, to look away. But he managed. Couldn't have been more than a second or two, but he saw emotion in the thing's moonstone eyes. Rage, fear—and understanding. Its body went slack, all fight gone. Pinning its arms with his knees, Mason drew his shotgun and fired. The man-beast exploded.

"Robert, grab hold!" Jenna's voice dragged Mason back.

The pit spanned forty feet across, half as deep, but the edges were shallower. Inside, lying rotten and piled in layers, were the bodies of half-gnawed humans and malformed creatures. Some of them were like that decapitated beast, more humanoid, while others looked like dogs turned inside out. From his time back east, he knew the monsters used these pits as food storage, for lean times when fresher meat couldn't be found.

Lying on her stomach, leaning half over the side, Jenna extended her Remington into the pit. "C'mon, Bob. Grab it!"

Mason slung his weapon across his back and found Angela kneeling on the hard, bloodstained ground. She called Penny's name, low and controlled. This woman was stronger than she looked, or it might be all show for her kid's sake. Either way, he appreciated it.

"Tru, get up here!" he called.

When the kid hustled up, he took in the scene and whispered, "Twisted."

"I need you to watch our backs." Mason scanned the area, but that strange buzzing sense of seeing outside himself had faded. The woods had gone deathly still again, but he didn't trust it. "I need to help Jenna haul them out."

Angela touched his arm. "Penny's down there."

"Focus on the woods," he said to Tru. "If it moves, shoot it and yell for me."

The kid reloaded, his hands steady. "Won't need you, Pops."

Mason approached the pit. Stink he could practically see wafted up. *An unholy place.* But he'd recognized that three years before—in Indiana.

He slid alongside Jenna on his belly. She vibrated next to him, her mind a raging repetition of images and words. He didn't know what to make of those sensations, feeling what she felt, glimpsing things through her eyes, but he took comfort in them. They were in hell, but they weren't alone.

Jenna leaned farther over the edge and urged Bob to try again. His slick fingertips grazed the tip of the barrel, but he couldn't grab hold.

Mason tried. Still no good. "I hope this thing isn't loaded."

"Can't remember how many rounds I used," she muttered.

"Stack bodies, Coach," he called down. "That's the only way we can reach you."

Jenna made a sound in the back of her throat. "Where's Penny?"

His heart stilled, then double-timed its rhythm as he watched Bob, seeing what Jenna recognized. As the coach piled mutated corpses, he did so while wearing an empty sling.

ELEVEN

Mason slapped a hand across Ange's lips before she could panic. "Quiet or they're on us again."

Jenna turned away and shrugged out of her backpack. Mason wouldn't hurt the woman—at least she didn't think so—and they had to focus on finding Penny. From inside the pit, Coach muttered imprecations beneath his breath. Couldn't worry about him either.

Where the hell is the girl?

They must have lost track of her when the final wave came at them. Penny could have slipped free during the fight, nimble as a monkey. He'd been distracted. Understandable.

Jenna circled the perimeter with a cupped hand, calling softly. "Penny, where are you? We need to get out of here. This is a bad place, sweetie."

Tru snorted quietly behind her. "She's not gonna answer. There's something wrong with her brain. Haven't you noticed?"

"Just keep watch," she snapped.

When she came to a tangled thicket, she saw a small gap beneath. Kneeling, she peered into the shadows. A pale triangle of a face peeped back at her. Penny lay on her stomach, protecting the stuffed bear with her tiny body. Jenna didn't know whether that was brave or heartbreaking. The way her chest felt must mean some combination of the two.

"You can come out now. The monsters are gone."

The child didn't answer, but she wriggled out on elbows and knees, careful not to leave the bear behind. Jenna took her hand and led her the fifty yards back to her mother. Angela's blue eyes went wide, shining with tears, and she snatched Penny into her arms.

"Baby, I was so worried. It was clever of you to hide, but please, *please* don't scare me like that again." She stroked the girl's moon-pale hair with shaking fingers.

Now that the immediate threat had passed, Jenna let her gaze sweep in a slow circuit, taking stock of their surroundings. *Christ.*

Th other woman shivered, tightening her arms around her daughter. "This is hell."

The trees hung heavy with sickly moss, tangled so tightly overhead it blocked any chance of sunlight. Underfoot, the ground felt unnaturally soft, slick, and sweet with the smell of rotten things. The pit was filled with bleached bones and liquefying corpses. Good to know they decomposed, becoming part of the topsoil like everything else.

"We need to bail," Tru said. "I have a bad feeling about this."

Mason flashed him a smile. "You and me both, Skywalker. Let's find the fastest way to get the coach out of there."

Jenna moved to the edge of the pit, where Bob had managed to clamber about halfway up. "I'm thinking human chain. Mason, hold my feet?"

"Gotcha," he said, coming up behind her.

His hands curled around her ankles. She didn't hesitate to shimmy down the side of the hole, headfirst. Muck and a foul sort of grease slicked her shirt and oozed between her fingers, but seeing the desperation on Bob's face made it worthwhile. She couldn't imagine the horror of being trapped with all those corpses. A shudder rocked through her.

A flash of orange caught her eye. Those were . . no. Couldn't be. But it was. On one of the dead, she saw part of a number inked onto an orange jumpsuit.

"Mason?" Her voice shook. "Why is this hole full of dead convicts?"

"Is this time to chat?" he said, teeth clenched. "Just do your job. Get him out of there."

Anger churned, but he was right. This wasn't the time.

"Take my hands," she said to Bob.

The coach latched onto her wrists. Mason inched backward while Ange and Tru anchored him. A slow, arduous process. Slime crawled into her shirt as she slid up. Mud and guts slicked Bob's hands. Her arms began to ache, wrists and forearms burning.

"Jesus," Tru said with a grunt. "Fewer burgers and more tofu, Coach."

They hauled him up so far that he could use his legs in the dirt, helping to scramble out. They fell into a filthy pile. Mason rolled to his feet immediately, spinning to sweep the area. Tru followed his example.

"You son of a bitch," Ange bit out as soon as Bob got up. "You lost my daughter! What's wrong with you?"

Coach looked defensive. "I'm telling you, she was there when I jumped."

"Shut it," Mason said. "And pick it up, people. We're stepping triple time the rest of the way."

"Hit it, Pops." Tru fell in, rifle in hand.

Mason took off at a dead run, calling over his shoulder. "I'm scouting the last leg. I'll fire two short bursts if I hit trouble before I get there. Tru, take point. Ange and Bob in the center."

"I'm carrying Penny," the redhead said curtly, holding her daughter close.

"Don't care," Mason called back. "Just don't slow us down. Jenna, rearguard. Move out."

Jenna ran as if there were demons at her heels, which was seriously close to the truth. The backpack weighed like a bag of stones between her shoulders, pulling her, slowing her. With every thudding footfall, she relived that beast's otherworldly growl. In her mind's eye, she saw Mason struggling with it. An ache sprung up, too fierce for tears, as she considered what it must have been like for him all these years, fighting against the damage inflicted by the change. She'd never met anyone so alone.

I'm here. And I'm on your side. You're not a one-man army anymore.

A flicker of warmth touched her, as if Mason had skimmed his palm down her back and settled his comforting touch at the base of her spine. She actually looked over her shoulder to make sure she was still guarding the rear. Nobody. Nothing but dark, still forest.

Damn it.

Images flickered in her brain as they ran. She caught glimpses of what lay around the next corner. A sort of déjà vu, only more helpful. Jenna knew when to duck, when branches would swing back, and when to jog left to avoid ruts in the path. Every moment echoed as if she'd already run the route. How was that possible?

The demon dogs bayed in the distance, their howls wet as if rotten lungs had filled with slime.

"We have incoming," she shouted to Tru. "How much farther? Can you see Mason?"

"He's up ahead, working on the door," the kid called back. "Three hundred yards from us. You'll see the building in ten."

They rounded another bend and sure enough, a two-story white structure stood in the midst of a clearing. During his broadcasts, Dr. Welsh had confirmed it had a basement too.

"Locked," Mason said as she ran to meet him. "Should've figured that, but we don't have any way to call him."

Jenna took a quick survey. Everyone had endured the final sprint except for the coach. He bent over in the field, huffing for air. A hundred yards separated him from the outpost.

"Come on, Bob," Tru shouted. "Get the lead out!"

Finally he straightened, looking nauseated and flushed as he chugged toward them.

"More on the way," she told Mason, watching Bob close the distance. "We need to get inside fast. No telling how many we pissed off."

Mason swore. "Locks aren't my thing."

Angela drew Penny against her, squeezing her eyes shut as if in prayer.

God can't help you now, lady.

"Lemme try," Tru said. "Give me the bobby pin from Penny's hair." His hands were steady as he folded it open, peeled off the plastic tip, and slid it into the lock.

The howling drew closer. Jenna could smell them now, heard them tearing through the trees. She shuddered. *Not like this. We didn't go through all that—and sacrifice Edna—for nothing.*

Edna. Oh God.

The demon dogs burst out of the woods, rapidly gaining on the coach. She cupped her hands over her mouth like a small megaphone. "Bob! *Run!*"

But he couldn't. He had nothing left to give.

The monsters hit him in seconds. One lunge took out his hamstring. He went down, screaming in agony. They tore at him from all sides, devouring his flesh in bloody gulps. Jenna spun, hammering on the door. She needed to cry or throw up or scream. Any of the above.

Mason gave her a little shake. "Remember who you are, Barclay. Get your weapon."

Right. This would be like target practice while the dogs feasted. She leveled her weapon on the nearest one and shot. Mason fired in a fan, hitting as many targets as he could. Two dogs blew up in an explosion of chunky bone and gray matter.

Four spun away from Bob's corpse and charged. Mason dropped one. "How we coming, Tru?"

Jenna braced herself. She was too low on ammo to lay down heavy fire, so she needed to make each slug count. Drawing on what Mitch had taught her, she calmed herself by force of will. Pumped. Sighted. And shot. One smacked right between a dog's eyes. Severing the spinal column or inflicting serious brain damage seemed to work best. Anything else might cripple them, but they just kept coming. Her dog went down, shuddered, and tried to get up again. Hideous red foam frothed out of its mouth and down its neck.

"Shit, I'm out. Cover me." Mason rummaged in his ammo pouch for another magazine.

"Got it!" Tru kicked the heavy door open and hauled Angela and Penny in with him.

"Move, Barclay!"

"I go nowhere without you," she said.

The third bore down on them, all filth and iridescent rot. It lunged at Mason. He hadn't been able to reload and instead fought the thing with his bare hands, holding snapping jaws away from his throat with pure brute force. His arms strained. With a roar, Mason twisted its head backward. An awful pop sounded. He jumped to his feet and reloaded with smooth movements, practiced and calm.

She didn't like the way the last one hung back, watching the fight. It wasn't charging, but Jenna didn't intend to let it escape. She raised her Remington, sighted, and took the shot. But she hadn't factored the wind. Instead of a clean hit, she got it in the neck. Red sprayed all over the fallen leaves.

The thing fell to one side, tremors running through its body. At first she thought it was just death throes, as the nervous system shut down. But it twisted and writhed, the tattered fur squirming as if worms burrowed beneath the skin. By the time the motion stopped, a man lay there instead of an animal. A very dead man.

She took a step toward the corpse. "What the hell—?"

"Oh no you don't." Mason snagged her arm, eyes dark and feral. Not so calm anymore. "Stay put."

"And if I don't?"

For a moment, he stared at her so hard she thought she might catch fire. That look—just that *look*—was more intense than any kiss she'd ever had. Her pulse pounded in her ears, the aftermath of violence. Her adrenaline spiked into something else. She became aware of every inch of her skin, sensitized by a thousand sinful touches.

Then Mason went caveman and tossed her over one shoulder. He ducked past the heavy steel door, taking them to safety. But Jenna didn't feel safe.

"We get inside," he growled. "And then we'll discuss your failure to follow directions."

TWELVE

With aching muscles, Mason hauled Jenna into the hallway and slammed the door behind them. Locked. *Good.*

Coming down from an adrenaline kick left him light-headed. His chest smoldered with a sick combination of fatigue, fear, and heady success. They'd survived. Shit—most of them. It was too much to contemplate, like trying to stare down the sun.

He set Jenna on her feet, then shouldered his weapon. She stumbled back a pace and caught her balance against the wall, branding him with cool green eyes. This woman knew too much, read too many ugly truths inside him. And she made him *want.*

No, that word wasn't nearly strong enough.

"You listen to me, or you die. Is that understood?"

She brushed a strand of hair away from her cheek. "Sounds like a threat, not a warning."

"You're driving me insane."

Good. Kiss me.

The thought smacked into his brain with force enough to hammer through solid concrete.

"No," he said aloud.

One dark eyebrow lifted, taunting him. *Why not? You want to.*

His jaw worked as he tried to find words to protest. They would be lies. He'd wanted her for days, warily circling her in that small cabin. So why hesitate?

Because she scared the shit out of him.

Smiling, she said, "I'm a scary chick."

"How are you doing that? What *is* this?"

At first she mocked him. "Didn't Mitch tell you about it?" But she softened at his obvious fury. "I don't know. But I'm getting it too." Jenna touched his forearm then, her hands pale and smooth where his skin was dark. That simple caress undid him.

Mason grabbed the back of her neck and dragged her mouth to his. Their bodies slammed together. Momentum drove her back against the wall, and he knew he'd regret being so brutal. *Later.*

In that moment, he felt mean. Every instinct said to protect his woman—all other promises and motivations flying free—but he wanted to control her too. No chance of that. He stroked his tongue past her lips and tasted her as he'd needed to for days. The light-headedness intensified until only Jenna remained. Solid. Real. Flushed and pulsing with life.

Yielding to the urge to claim her, he refused to let her run even if she wanted to. But she only responded with a fierce, gathering heat. She strained to get closer, took everything, dove deeper still. He nipped at her tongue. Her coppery taste swirled with the salty tang of the sweat around her mouth.

Madness.

Her body felt good, welcoming and demanding at the same time. She made a little sound in her throat. Arching, she hitched a leg around his hip. Her knee slid across the vicious claw wound on his other thigh.

He let her go, staggering back. "Shit!"

"Christ. Sorry."

"That hurt."

Gingerly, she tested her lip. "Well, you bit me."

He limped the half step to her, looming above but feeling humbled by whatever the hell had sparked between them. After a brief hesitation, he put his palm to her cheek, marveling at the smooth skin. Vital and alive. "You bit me first."

Gazing up, Jenna sucked in a shaky breath. She looked tired and small, but she managed a halfhearted laugh.

"What?" he asked.

"You remember when you were a kid, wanting to be blood sisters, uh, *brothers*, with your best friend? I always chickened out. Seemed too . . . dangerous."

He swallowed hard. Mason had no recollection of any best friends. Ever. Too many moves. Too many new moms and dads and half-assed siblings. But he recognized the danger she was talking about.

"Still does," he whispered.

"Hey, Pops! We found the basement door." Tru barreled around the corner and skidded to a stop, his combat boots as subtle as a locomotive. "Oh, awkward."

"We're coming." Eyes still fixed on Jenna, he said, "This isn't over."

She stepped away and glanced down at her spattered shirt and jeans. "Shit, I look like I moonlight as a butcher."

Mason grinned. "Just the way I like you. Tru, where's Ange?"

"Downstairs."

That turned out to be the entrance to the basement, a solid steel door just shy of a bank safe. Angela was calling, her voice echoing back down the hallway. Mason pushed in front of her with more force than he intended, but the aftereffects of that firefight and his kiss with Jenna made him blunt. She stopped shouting and stepped back.

He tried Morse code on the steel, then just pounding his fists. Nothing worked. "Don't suppose you can pick this one, eh, Tru?"

"Not a chance."

"This is pointless." Mason started to usher them back out. "Maybe there's another—"

A shotgun blast leveled the top third of the door. Mason dove, covering Jenna and Tru, with Ange and Penny sprawled out farther down the hall. His eardrums splintered, all sound ringing and cloudy. Rubble and shards of steel peppered his back. The world tipped. Blackness seeped across his vision like a slow-moving fog.

When he awoke, he lay beneath lights bright enough to scour his eyeballs. A few blinking seconds later and he realized he was stretched on an elevated examination table. Ange sat with Penny on the floor. Jenna stood next to a man sporting John Lennon glasses. He wore khakis, a white button-down shirt smudged with blood—Mason's blood?—and an expression just short of scared shitless.

"How come there's power?" Heads turned when Mason growled the question.

"Hey," Tru said from his perch on the lab counter. "You okay?" The kid looked relieved. Jenna did too.

When she saw him stir, she stepped to his side and ran her hand lightly over his head. "You were starting to worry me."

Mason elbowed up on the table. His back screamed, but he ignored it. "How long've I been out?"

"An hour," she said. "Long enough for Dr. Shotgun to help me patch up the damage."

"Do I need to apologize again?" The light tone didn't fit the man's somber face. He ran shaky hands through his straight, slightly shaggy hair. "I've been down here for . . . well, I don't know how long. The noises—I was sleeping, woke up and . . . panicked. I'm sorry."

"You're Welsh?" Mason asked.

"Yes."

"I might accept your apology if you tell me how you have electricity."

Dr. Welsh stood from his stool by the long lab counter and ambled forward, hands in his pleated pockets. "Hydroelectric power pumped by an underground generator. Pretty nice, huh?"

"This isn't just a basement," Mason said. "It's a bunker."

"That's what I always thought. Glad of it too."

"So you have hot water?" Ange asked.

"Yup."

Jenna cocked an eyebrow. "I should've kissed this guy."

"You still could," Welsh said, his smile affable as he looked Jenna up and down. Mason had the sudden urge to try taking the man's head off. "But I recommend you shower first."

"*He* didn't mind," she said, hooking a thumb toward Mason.

Welsh shook his head. "If survival means kissing somebody who smells like you, I want no part of it."

"Wuss," Tru said.

"Certified. Look, do you have to sit right there? I have research—"

Mason laughed as he pulled upright. His back felt pricked by a thousand hot needles. "You listened to a lot of CDs, didn't you, Welsh?"

"Probably while he was ironing his Dockers," Tru added. "*Très* cool, Harvard."

"No," the doctor said, frowning slightly. "Never had the time. And I went to Cornell."

Tru smirked. "Whatever, Harvard."

Jenna sighed and sliced the air in a dismissive gesture. "Enough. Can somebody hazard a guess about that thing at the pit?"

Tru hopped down from the counter. "The one on two feet? He was messed up. Like, Edna levels of messed up."

"Wait," Welsh said. "What?"

Jenna shrugged. Apparently they'd come so far that a beast-man cross was merely shrug worthy. Take it in stride or go mad. "This monster we saw in the woods," she said. "Out by that pit."

Welsh seemed frustrated as well as perplexed. "What pit? And who's Edna?"

Mason found he enjoyed the doctor's muddle of frustrations. *Only natural. The guy shot me.*

"Dude," Tru said with a sigh. "You are seriously behind."

While Mason sat quietly, the others spent the next twenty minutes telling Dr. Welsh how they'd assembled, heard the ham radio broadcasts, and made the suicide run.

He used the time to assess their unsuspecting host, a guy as tight-wound as they came—all hospital corners and spit shines. A man living by himself for more than a week, isolated and losing his grip, could have let the place go to seed. But every surface in the bunker-style basement lab gleamed, and rows of neat books, clothes, journals, foodstuffs, and medicines lined shelves stacked four high.

Despite his panicky trigger finger and the fist-worthy way he eyed Jenna's rack, Welsh seemed like a thinker, maybe one who could sort out this new natural order. If any such thing still existed.

Mason took another look at those shelves, gratified by the provisions they'd have available for their defense: first aid, books, blankets, matches, hygiene products.

"And then there's the one outside," Jenna finished.

Listening, Welsh paled. But his eyes lit with a curious fire at the news. "A dead one?"

"Yeah," Ange said. "The thing turned into a *man* after it died. Jenna killed it."

"She shoots, she scores." Tru made a crowd-goes-wild noise from where he'd settled on the floor. He was cleaning his rifle. Good soldier.

Welsh seemed oddly focused. "So there's a body outside?"

Mason sat a little straighter. "What of it?"

The scientist seemed like a man who knew how to pick his battles. Apparently this was one he wanted to try, because his posture and expression gained a hard, intense edge. He met Mason's gaze directly, pure confrontation. "Because I'm going to autopsy it."

THIRTEEN

Jenna snagged Chris before he went off on his fool's errand. "Where's the shower?"

"End of the hall," he answered, oblivious to anything but retrieving his specimen.

"Hope you got an ax," Mason said. "Don't even think of bringing that corpse in here whole."

A good policy, chopping off the head. Just in case. As the men set off, Jenna still shivered uneasily. But she'd be damned if she died dirty.

Mason didn't mind.

She didn't glance his way. Couldn't. Just thinking about their kiss curled a wave of heat through her. For a mad moment, with his big body pressed flush against hers, she'd wanted to crawl inside his skin.

Stop it. A quick shake of her head drew the eyes of the former nurse's aide. Ange regarded her with a silent question.

"I'll be quick," Jenna promised. "I'm sure you and Penny would love a bath too."

Her auburn hair a bird's nest of tangles, the other woman nodded. "You have *no* idea."

Jenna snagged a change of clothes from her pack and walked out into the hall. The bunker was decidedly industrial, plain gray tile bounded by cement walls. She followed the corridor down to where, as promised, she found a utility room complete with shower. Chris had said it was meant for rinsing off chemicals after an industrial accident, so it didn't have a curtain or even a proper stall. A nozzle sprouted from the wall, and a six-inch concrete rim framed the drain.

To hell with niceties. While she stripped, she wondered what the cities would be like. Would skyscrapers be full of monsters now? All those dark rooms teeming with fanged and fearsome things? Terrifying to contemplate.

Naked, she hopped in. The water never got all the way hot, but even lukewarm felt better than good. She soaped her whole body twice, arching to expose her sore muscles to the water. Almost as nice as a massage.

Since the shampoo would need to last a long time, she used a tiny dot and nursed it into a high lather. Eventually they'd learn to make their own toiletries. All survivors, assuming there were other pockets out there, would be living in the Dark Ages. Sooner or later.

The cool air raised goose bumps as she toweled off and scrambled into her underwear. She slid on a pair of clean jeans, and with a little sigh, wrapped herself in a blue hooded sweatshirt. No way would she put those shoes back on until she scrubbed off the filth, so she pulled on a pair of thick socks, ready to turn the shower over.

Ange and Penny sat in the hall just outside.

"Wait, you don't have any clean clothes," Jenna said.

"Penny has a change in my bag. I got in the habit of keeping a clean set when she was a baby. I just never stopped."

"Helpful."

Jenna tried a smile, though she couldn't relate. More to the point, she couldn't remember her own mother being so prepared. Clea Barclay didn't believe in planning; she'd preferred laughter and spontaneity. The contrast between Mitch and her mom had been almost painful at times, but their ability to make the best out of bad situations must have brought them together in the first place.

She turned her thoughts to the immediate problem. Ange was a few inches taller and carried a little more weight. "Let me check. I might have something that will fit you."

She went back to the main room and knelt just inside the door, digging through her bag. Yep, gray yoga pants with a ton of give. She usually wore them as pajamas but doubted the other woman would complain. Then she dragged out an old T-shirt.

She returned to Ange, who'd stood up to stretch. Penny peered from around her thigh. God, that poor kid. The Dark Age would probably kill her.

Jenna handed over the clothes. "Do you think we'll make it?"

Through the week, let alone through the winter. That part went unspoken.

The other woman squared her shoulders, like she'd turned a corner in her mind. "We can. We have to. Women are the strong ones, you know? Men go around being all badass, but we're the glue that keeps everything together."

"I'm more like rubber cement," she said with a sigh. "That stuff sticks, but it stretches and stretches until it's going two miles in either direction. And when it snaps, it isn't pretty." She nodded toward the shower. "But enough of that. Get cleaned up before the guys jump line."

Ange nodded her thanks.

Jenna moved off to give them privacy. From two rooms away, she heard the lighter pitch of Tru's voice, responding to something the doctor had said. Maybe they'd managed to drag the dead thing inside.

So what was Mason doing? She should check on his injuries, even if that meant revisiting that damn kiss. He might do it again, for all she knew, but she wasn't unwilling.

But her stomach rumbled, and she needed to check out the cooking facilities before she tried to go all Betty Crocker on everybody. She checked back down the hall, finding a big room with no exits to the left. That appeared to be a lab for various experiments. Nobody inside. Just equipment. She moved on.

Back out in the hall, she explored further and turned into a smaller room filled with lab tables, presumably for examining dead specimens; it was clean, white, and filled with sterile supplies, cabinets, and shelving. She found Tru arguing with their host.

"What do you mean, you can't find it?" Tru asked. "It was in front, like, a hundred yards out."

"Well, it's gone now. Maybe the dogs you described dragged it back with them."

"Or ate it. They're good at that."

Chris rubbed the back of his neck. "There's nothing I can do without a specimen."

"You could always head out there and bag one yourself." Tru held his rifle between them like a peace offering, but his posture said, *Eat me*.

"No, thanks."

"Aw, poor trigger-happy Harvard."

That was enough for Jenna. At least bickering gave them something to do.

Two more rooms lined either side of the hall before she reached a utility area. On the left, she found a dormitory, one big space divided into three individual chambers containing two bunks each. She could tell where Chris had been sleeping because a neat stack of notes waited for him beside one mattress, along with an eyeglass case.

The last room on the right appeared to have been devoted to botanical research and contained a fully hydroponic Omega Garden, lavish with greenery. The air was lush and clean, welcoming in a way that she hadn't experienced since leaving home. She wasn't surprised to find Mason in there, sitting alone.

He still needed a shower, but they'd done the best they could using the lab sink. *So much blood.* Jenna inhaled sharply, controlling her reaction to his injury. If she never felt that sick and helpless again—well, that'd be a good thing.

Mason raised his head. Maybe he'd heard her breathing. His face was hard and remote. Newly etched lines attested to the pain of his wounds.

She hesitated, unsure of herself. "Should I go?"

His voice rasped like velvet over rusty metal. "Stay. Go. Do what you want."

That didn't sound promising, but neither did she want to be by herself, jumping at shadows and noises. Ange was in the shower, and the others still bickered over lack of a corpse. Not much choice. She crossed the floor and sat down four feet away, more than an arm's length.

"It's nice in here," she mumbled, finding herself tongue-tied.

How ridiculously banal.

Heat rose in her cheeks. *Damn it.* Were things going to be weird after that kiss? She didn't want it to be. It shouldn't be. Just a gut reaction, the whole affirmation-of-life thing.

Mason wouldn't look at her. "I thought you'd still be chatting with Dr. Shotgun. You owe him a kiss for putting me on my ass. That's what you've been after, right? Ever since I threw you in the trunk?"

"That's the *last* thing I want."

He skewered her with a cold glare. "Really? I heard you, Jenna. I wasn't out the whole time. I'm remembering pieces."

Frantically, she thought back. What the hell had she said during those crazy moments while they worked on his wounds? Nothing she could even remember, but it seemed to have made an impression on Mason.

"I feel like I know you," he mimicked in a precious falsetto. "We've been listening to you for *days*, Dr. Welsh. We should start your fan club."

Jenna blinked. She'd just thought the conversation silly and ironic. It wasn't like Chris Welsh had any other listeners. She didn't understand the leap from joking—a coping mechanism in the midst of a tense moment—to Mason imagining *this*.

"You think I want to see you hurt?"

"Doesn't matter," he snapped. "Just do me one favor. *Listen* when I talk. I have reasons, and I've been doing this a hell of a lot longer than you." He smiled, showing teeth. "We've just scratched the surface here. And I mean to keep you safe."

"Because you promised Mitch," she said, stung.

Black as obsidian, his gaze met hers. "Got that right."

Good thing she hadn't come to him for comfort. Maybe, somewhere deep down, she'd hoped for a little softness, some solace after surviving another day fraught with long odds. If he'd pulled her close and let her listen to his heartbeat for a little while, she wouldn't have said no. Wouldn't have hesitated. But he looked about as welcoming as the cement wall. His chest, she remembered, was definitely as hard.

So, apparently, was his heart.

She nodded quietly. "Fine. I get it. I'm going to check on Ange and Penny."

FOURTEEN

Mason felt her absence like the end of a rainstorm. One minute his mind was clouded over with the interference she always brought. The next . . . nothing. A door slammed shut. That sound echoed through his brain, setting off a series of small inward explosions. The greenery of the Omega Garden spun him into another, more distant forest.

Morbid curiosity and visceral shock held him transfixed. He hadn't wanted to look at his teammates. Jeff was the youngest, blond and fair. He didn't need to shave more than once a week. Mason came next in relative youth. Thomas, weathered and in his forties, had worked with Mitch the longest. He didn't rattle easily, but now held his rifle with both hands as if to cover their shake. Axel was as good with his guns as he was with a hog, and he could be counted on. If they stayed cool, maybe they'd all walk away.

Mason stared at the corpses. The stench turned his insides to water. He'd noticed a scent like it—close but more tangy and cloying—when his thigh wound had gone putrid, before Mitch took him in. The unforgettable rot of infection.

Forget brimstone. Hell smelled like this.

Then he noticed the profound silence the monsters brought with them. Utter quiet. No living animals. Even the trees seemed to hold themselves unnaturally still. No insects buzzed their death sounds. The eastern states had become a battleground, where nothing sane or good survived.

Mitch leaned in. "Watch yourself, kid. This place ain't right. There's heavy magic here."

The old man looked up at the trees draped in thick moss and crossed himself. That show of deference lodged fear like a piece of shrapnel in Mason's side. Mitch had always been devout in his way but to his own beliefs. Crossing himself made it seem as if he also needed God's personal intervention. Not that Mason believed, but he liked Mitch and the crew. They were family, pretty much the only one he'd ever known. When they told him where they were headed—and why—he'd thought they were crazy.

Now he knew he was too.

Howls wafted from the trees, slow and distant, and gathered strength.

Mitch circled two fingers in the air. "Fan out."

The team moved, backs to the pit and their weapons up. Shotguns. Old bolt-loaders.

A dozen dogs burst through the underbrush and attacked.

"Incoming," Mason shouted. "Jeff, watch your back!"

His brain couldn't take in that much detail. Not so quickly. Blood and teeth, screams and snarls, and the feeling that none of it was solid. Not real. Sure, he'd heard the stories and the news reports, but some things you couldn't believe in your gut until you *saw* them. Until they tried to kill you.

He fired anyway. His rifle kicked against his shoulder as he pulled the trigger again and again.

"Hold your positions!" Mitch shouted.

They might've stood a chance had they fought as a special forces unit, guarding each other. But they lacked the experience. All of them, even Mitch. His training couldn't prepare anyone for this. Not really. With shaking hands, Jeff popped off a few rounds, but fear screwed with his aim. A monster lunged, knocking him down, and tore out his throat in a bloody rush.

After the boy fell, the other two men scattered. Mason never would have believed it of Thomas or Axel, but when faced with death, they ran.

Mitch fired. "Get back here!"

Mason met him behind the pit. They stood back-to-back. In a moment of surreal stillness, he watched the monstrous pack disembowel Thomas. Then a pair broke for Axel, tugging the other man from different sides, working in tandem, dragging him to the ground. Limbs became strips of meat. Waving air currents danced above them as if directly above a campfire. Hypnotic. Almost alive.

Mitch elbowed him hard. "Wake up, kid," he said, face streaked with dirt and sweat. "Aim for the head. Gut shots don't keep 'em down."

The older man knelt, forming two-tier coverage. But no matter how many times they reloaded and fired, the monsters kept coming. Mason's ammo ran out first. He used the butt of his rifle like a club as the last four animals closed in. Mitch swiveled on his knees and fired, blowing one's brains to bits.

But to protect Mason, he turned his back. The beasts didn't miss their chance. They grabbed the older man by his calves and pulled.

"Mitch!"

Mason stomped on the back of one putrid canine neck, then smashed down with the rifle. He kicked and punched, railed and grunted, as the demon dogs continued their frenzy. But when the last beast lay twitching and dying, Mitch was a clawed-up wreck.

Breathless, Mason stumbled over to where his mentor lay fighting for each intake of air. He took Mitch's head in his lap.

"Hey, kid." Mitch coughed up blood, his chest a gaping wound. Bone pushed into the sick shadows. "Damn, I wish I had a cigarette."

"Can't help you," Mason said, bile in his mouth.

"A favor, then."

"Anything."

Mitch's face went pale, the blood a nasty, dark contrast. "Save my Jenna, okay? Whatever it takes."

He'd heard about the little girl before. She had to be, what, twelve now? No way was she ready for this shit. Maybe she'd never need to be. Maybe Mitch was wrong in thinking the grim magic would push west.

Maybe.

"I promise," he said thickly.

"Then get out of here. Go west. Get some book learning, kid. Don't die like me."

Mitch raised his hand to look at where his skin had been shorn back. His entire body trembled. Convulsions overtook him as his systems shut down in quick succession. Release came mercilessly fast, but then he didn't have far to go between those injuries and death. He didn't deserve this.

A noise from the other side of the trees shook Mason out of his grief. He'd die like the others if he didn't get out. But dying wasn't an option. He had a promise to keep. On full alert, he pulled to his feet. Fire burned through his injuries. He didn't know how much fight still pulsed inside, but this last one wasn't taking him down.

He grabbed the enemy with his bare hands.

Where the hell was his gun? *Son of a bitch.*

"Damn, Mason, let go of me!"

Echo. Reverb.

Monsters don't talk. The world shivered and flared black, then came back into focus through white-hot sparks.

He found himself in the garden room. The person he held fought back.

A shimmer of awareness skated along Mason's skin, that same awareness he'd used in the woods to push his mind outside of itself, to see things his eyes couldn't see. Except this time felt more foreign. Farther out. Images stretched and warped like a string of taffy. At the end of it waited a fracturing, volcanic power he couldn't begin to identify.

And with a lion's roar, that bright power pushed back. *Hard*.

Mason yanked back into himself and let go of Tru. Forcing the adrenaline out of his bloodstream, he concentrated on breathing through his nose. When people got jumpy, others got killed. Welsh had nearly proven that. He sure as hell wasn't going to do the same.

"Did you have to grab me?" Tru glowered and shoved dark hair out of his eyes. "I didn't think you swung that way."

"You should know better than to sneak up on me."

Tru looked down at his boots. "Sneaking? In these? Are you high? Maybe Harvard's growing weed in one of these things."

He wore a white button-down shirt that was slightly too big, the sleeves lined with neatly ironed creases. Mason raised an eyebrow. "The doc's wardrobe?"

"Yeah, but don't make a big deal of it, okay?"

"I won't." His pulse settled. "And I'm sorry. What are you doing here anyway?"

Tru's face turned an uncomfortable shade of pink. "Nothing, man. Forget it."

He turned to go, shifting something from behind his back. Mason caught his arm and tugged. For some reason he didn't want to examine too closely, the idea of Tru hiding things from him sat heavy in his gut.

"What do you have?"

"Nothing, damn it." Tru yanked his arm but couldn't break free.

Mason snatched a box from his hands. A first-aid kit. He went still. "You hurt?"

"I said, forget it. I don't need your help."

Shaking his head, Mason released the kid's arm. Tru could run if he wanted. But maybe he'd stay.

He did. Warily.

"I didn't ask if you needed help," Mason said. "I asked if you're hurt, because I'm concerned. If you saw someone with a first-aid kit, you'd wonder the same thing."

Tru opened his mouth as if to protest, then dropped his eyes. "So?"

"So tell me."

He recognized Tru's reaction, when kindness looked like cheddar in a trap. Before he joined the military, he'd felt as suspicious when Mitch wanted to help him for no apparent reason. People just didn't offer something for nothing.

But at least Tru seemed to consider his options. He slumped against the nearest wall and slid to the floor, sitting there with his arms draped over bent knees. Then, his eyes focused on an indistinct middle distance, he unbuttoned one pristine white cuff and rolled the sleeve up to his elbow.

Swallowing, Mason glanced at the first-aid kit he still held. "Can I see?"

Eyes averted, he nodded.

Mason simply walked over and knelt. Maybe the direct approach, something man to man, would save a scrap of the kid's pride.

But the injuries he found weren't the slashing, random, bloody scrapes of the dogs' claws. Instead a dozen evenly spaced, two-inch razor-blade cuts climbed the inside of Tru's forearm like the slats of a ladder, all of them scabbed over. Two or three had crusted with a layer of pale green infection.

Déjà vu washed down Mason's spine. In the cabin, he'd known the kid was a cutter. But how? Stereotypes and worst-case scenarios aside, how had he *known*?

"Normally I can keep them clean." Tru's voice sounded strangled. Every tense angle of his lean body spoke of utter humiliation. "But not lately. And I didn't know what that junk from the pit would do, you know?"

"Yeah. Same on the left one?"

Tru rolled up the other sleeve and presented both arms like a perp waiting for handcuffs. "Pretty sick, huh?"

"We all have our ways of coping. You can do it yourself, or I can help. Your choice."

Studying the med kit in Mason's hands, he nodded—both permission and silent request.

Mason worked in silence, using peroxide to clean the cuts. Although the boy flinched on occasion, he never said a word. No hiss of pain. Pride was an amazing anesthetic. Then Mason applied the antibiotic ointment, wrapped the area in gauze bandages, and busied himself with closing up the first-aid kit as Tru rebuttoned the cuffs, concealing the scene of the crime.

"Where's your blade now?" Mason asked quietly.

"You gonna confiscate it?" The kid had donned his armor again, standing up and glaring. But most of the bite was gone. He looked almost relieved.

Mason shrugged. "Nah. It's your choice."

"Good."

"But would you do something for me?"

Tru stopped but didn't turn away from his chosen flight path, back through the Omega Garden. He simply stood there, shoulders hunched, waiting for the inevitable recrimination or scolding. God, he was young. Mason felt the urge to drop-kick whatever asshole had instilled that cringe in him.

"What?"

"There's only six of us, right? Jenna, me, a mom and her kid, and a jumpy scientist—these are *not* the makings of a first-rate combat unit. We need you, and we need you healthy." He paused, hoping his tacit request would sink in. "Got it?"

Exhaling slowly, Tru lost his whipped-dog posture. He looked Mason in the eye and tossed him a nasty grin. "Got it. But that means you stay away from the ganja."

FIFTEEN

"Men stink," Jenna said.

Angela glanced up from the nature magazine she'd found stashed in a corner of the lab. Jenna lay slumped onto the opposite bunk. Together they used the room as a lounge because Penny lay sleeping next door, curled around her teddy bear. She'd finally dozed off after Ange realized she could use the rest more than food. Jenna hadn't needed to point it out, either, which was a good sign.

The room wasn't much bigger than a prison cell, just cots the naturalists could use to catch a few winks in between bouts of obsessive research. Jenna found it awkward to share such close space with strangers, even after all they'd endured.

"Yeah, they do," Ange said heavily. "Which one are we talking about, by the way? Squirrelly, half grown, or scary?"

Jenna quirked a smile. "Scary, I suppose."

"So what did he do?"

She scowled. "Nothing."

"Doesn't sound like nothing."

"He's infuriating. He growls if I don't do exactly as he says, even if my way saves his ass."

Ange shrugged and set the magazine aside. "Maybe he doesn't like seeing you put yourself at risk, especially for him. He seems like he's used to being self-sufficient."

"You suck at this," Jenna said in disgust. "You're supposed to tell me I'm right, no matter how dumb I sound, and then offer me chocolate."

"Crap. No wonder I don't have any friends. Oh, wait, that's because I'm a single mom with a shitty job. No joke, by the way. I empty bed pans."

"Not anymore," Jenna murmured. "As far as I know, we're all continent. But we have bigger worries now."

She gazed up at the ceiling, weary beyond all bearing. The air seemed different outside since Mason had stolen her from Culver. Each breath snapped with an odd electricity. It tingled in her throat, like the first tickle of a cold or a chemical burn after breathing disinfectant fumes.

"Tell me about it," Ange said. "But there must be other survivors, right? The east wasn't decimated. We still get trucks now and then from the O'Malley corporation." She was obviously thinking aloud. "So if we could find them, maybe things would get better."

"We'll just have to learn the new rules."

"I have no idea what I'm doing here," Ange said softly.

That plaintive tone of voice offered clear insight into her way of thinking. She was scared. Maybe even too scared to continue. And she was silently asking for help, but Jenna had none to give. She could only do what she'd always done in the face of disappointment and difficulty. Keep trudging. Hold back the emotion that clouded thought. Her parents hadn't left her with too many other options— Mitch because of his irresponsible gallivanting, and her mother for always waiting for him to come home.

She stretched on her bunk, deciding that Ange needed a quick change of subject. "If this was a decent girls' night, we'd have liquor. Wait, hold that thought. I'll be back."

Jenna liked the woman well enough, though she was nothing like the friends she'd left behind. The fact that Ange was a mom—and quite a bit older—made for an interesting variety in perspective. Aside from those last few months caring for her mother, Jenna had never needed to put anyone's needs above her own.

But all things considered, she could have done worse for end-of-the-world companions.

She hurried down the hall to rummage through the cabinets in all the rooms. Then she found what she had hoped to find.

"Jackpot," Jenna said as she came back into the room.

Ange raised her magazine in greeting. "Did you know that the Pygmy elephant may have separated from the Asian elephant as long as three hundred thousand years ago?"

"No." She grinned. "Did they try marital counseling first?"

"Cute. What've you got?"

"Party in a cup. Well. More or less." Jenna swirled a fat cello-shaped bottle. Cognac glowed a rich, deep amber as she held it to the light.

"Hennessy. Nice."

At one time, years ago, this bottle ran a hundred and fifty bucks, easy. Well, it *would* have. Now it could very well be priceless. Replacing it might be damn near impossible. Doubtless someone had stashed it for celebratory purposes, intending to drink to a breakthrough after years of research. This wasn't liquor you guzzled to get drunk; it should be sipped from a fine crystal snifter.

Jenna offered a beaker instead. "Feel like having a drink?"

"My ex was a mean drunk, so ordinarily I'd say no. But under the circumstances, I'm not sure it matters. Count me in."

"Yeah, and ordinarily I'd be worried about keeping watch and making sure my head was on straight, but right now, I just don't *care*." Her voice shook with frustration. "I'm so damn tired of all this."

Tired of fighting, tired of Mason being . . . Mason.

"Don't you wish you could have a little-kid-style meltdown?"

"I never did that, even when I was little." Her mother had always been too fragile to take much by way of nonsense. The first and only all-out tantrum Jenna threw in a supermarket had resulted in as many tears from her stricken mother. Shaking out of the past, Jenna filled the two beakers and handed one to Ange. "But right now it almost sounds tempting."

"Too bad you're a grown-up."

Jenna lifted her glass, her lips twisting. "To being a grown-up."

Half an hour later, everything looked rosier. She and Ange had downed the cognac much faster than it was meant to be drunk. Jenna had a serious buzz to prove it. Everyone else she'd ever known might be dead, but that thought didn't depress her as it would have at the start of the day. Ange was her new best friend.

She proved it by listening to the woman talk about Pygmy elephants.

"I mean, there were less than a thousand of them left. You know, before." Ange shook her head. "What's going to happen to them?"

"I have no idea." Jenna's brow wrinkled. "Where the hell is Borneo anyway?"

"How much of this did we have?" Ange asked, her words slurred.

"Um." Jenna peered at the bottle. "Half."

"Crap. We should stop." But she took another sip, still wrinkling her nose as if it was the first. "I wanted to study them, did ya know that? I was going to be Dian Fossey of the elephants. Never got there. Life stinks."

Jenna's laugh felt like a bubble in her throat. "You wanted to be the Elephant Woman?"

Ange shook her head. "I'd imagined myself in the woods, all natural and organic. You know, I'd befriend native tribes and crouch in bushes to watch animals in their natural habitat. Keep a journal. Document everything. Maybe I'd write an article for *National Geographic* to show off my scholastic prowess."

The soft light in their shared quarters tempted Jenna to close her eyes. Everything softened in a peaceful haze. "Can women have prowess?"

"I think so," Ange said with a giggle. "Why let the guys have it all?"

"So why didn't you?"

"I did a few semesters at University of Oregon, but my folks made too much for financial aid. Loans only did so much, so I kept having to take years off to work. Every time I quit, it got harder to go back. The kids in my classes seemed to get younger every year, but it was just me getting older. I got to feeling like there was no point, that I'd be forty before I ever graduated."

"The booze is making you maudlin," Jenna said, although she felt it too.

"I'm due a bit of maudlin."

"And somewhere along the way you got knocked up?"

Ange sighed. She rubbed the back of her head where red hair was knotted in a sloppy ponytail. "Yeah. My ex was a real piece of work."

"You married him?"

"Nah, ex-boyfriend. I'm grateful he doesn't—didn't—know about Penny. He'd have found some way to hurt her, even if it just meant taking her from me." She pushed out a heavy exhale. "What a great life, right?"

"Better than some," Jenna said. "I had a friend who got a great job out of college. Melissa was gorgeous. After a whirlwind courtship and a fairy-tale wedding, she had her dream man. They bought a little storybook cottage and took long vacations in the Bahamas. Then she died of pancreatic cancer."

"No shit." Ange shook her head. "Was there a moral to this story?"

"Even if life *doesn't* suck, you still die?"

"Damn." Ange laughed so hard she snorted. "Is it wrong that I'm having fun with you? I feel like I should be all guilt stricken because I'm not dour enough."

"Mason would probably say so," Jenna muttered. "But his rules shouldn't apply to normal people."

"What's your deal with him anyway? You treat him like a hated ex-husband."

"It's not like that," she said. "Or maybe it is, except without the good times and sex before it all went bad."

"Harsh," Ange said.

Jenna sat up too quickly, as if she could escape from how uncomfortable she became when talking about Mason. "I know it's not fair, but I can't help blaming him that I'm in this situation. I'd be dead by now—I know that—if he hadn't come for me. But sometimes I wonder if that would've been better."

The other woman's eyes were weary beyond bearing. "Would've been easier anyway. I'd never say so in front of Penny, but . . . I'm glad my parents are gone. I can't imagine my mother living through this."

Jenna remembered her fragile mother and shook her head. "Mine either."

"What was she like?"

It had to be the booze. Ordinarily, she wouldn't waste time talking about the past, but Jenna's eyes filled with tears. "Small. Delicate. People said I have her eyes. I always thought she looked breakable, and it was worse after my dad left."

"They didn't get along?"

"He thought he could save the world," she said quietly. "Somehow he saw all this coming, wanted to convert everyone before it was too late. In some ways, I wish he'd devoted himself wholly to doomsday and not bothered with us at all. Then I wouldn't have needed to pick up the pieces after he walked away."

And Christ, that had been hard. Her mother had never been a

strong, independent person. When Mitch had stuck around, she looked to him for support. Once he'd left for good, nine-year-old Jenna stepped up. She recalled her mother crying in the night because she was so lonely, longing for the man who preferred living in the woods to spending his life with the woman who loved him.

His death had actually seemed a kindness. He wasn't ever coming back. That had firmed her mother's resolve. She'd stopped moping and had given Jenna a few good years. But cancer had worn away that happiness. Her spirit consumed, Clea Barclay had wasted away until she was little more than skin and bones and melancholy eyes. At age seventeen, Jenna had sat beside her mom's hospital bed. No dances or dates. Instead she had watched her mother—out of her head on pain meds and crying for Mitch—as she died.

Jenna hadn't been enough for either of them.

She would *never* wind up like her mother. Not ever. A man like Mason wouldn't be satisfied until he'd suborned her will. Mitch had been much the same when he was home. Too used to being in charge—the head prophet and font of all wisdom for the other crazy people—he failed to see when anyone else had thoughts or feelings or dreams.

Once she'd graduated from high school, Jenna hadn't wanted to think about college. So much of her energies had been depleted with her mother's illness that she needed time to recover. Like with Ange, the years had passed and she had grown accustomed to her routine: a five-day workweek and weekends with her friends. But she'd always held back, fearing what would happen if she ever let herself get too close—let alone fall in love.

Deep down lurked that old refrain. *You don't want to end up like Mom.*

"So both your parents are gone too?"

"Yep," Jenna said. "We're both orphans."

They shared a smile over the absurdity of that statement. Then Ange stretched and sighed. "Are you tired? Maybe I'm just old."

"You're not."

"Forty-four feels it."

"Quit with the pity party. I was gonna fix something to eat," Jenna mumbled. "But maybe . . . just breakfast instead. Tomorrow."

Ange toppled sideways and curled on her bunk. They shared non-sense talk that got them giggling like kids at a slumber party. The half-emptied bottle of cognac sat on the floor between them. Slowly, Jenna's eyes drifted shut and she let the velvet dark blanket everything.

For a brief, blissful time, she knew nothing. Not even dreams.

A scream split the tranquility. Pure terror, accompanied by a crash and a thud. Voices blended into panic soup. Jenna couldn't make out individual words. She sat up too quickly and whacked her elbow on the wall.

"Shit! What now?"

SIXTEEN

Mason stood with his nine-millimeter cocked and aimed. That scream still bounced like a pinball around his sleep-fogged head. "Damn it, what the hell is going on?"

"You tell me," Tru said, sprawled on the floor next to his bunk. He swiveled his eyes between the gun Mason held and where it was pointed—at Penny's eggshell white face. "But might I suggest that you stay away from children?"

"Save it."

Mason yanked Penny away from the door and checked the hallway. All clear. He punched a button on the intercom just inside the dorm entryway and buzzed the lab.

"Yeah, what's up?" Welsh sounded wired. Didn't he ever sleep?

"Any break in the perimeter?"

"Um, what?"

"Any monsters get in here?"

The doc laughed, sort of scattered and disbelieving. "You think I'd be answering you with words if they had? More like gurgles or screams or—"

"Straight answers, Harvard," Tru called.

"No, nothing. It's been quiet. What's going on?"

Rather than reply, Mason slid the nine-millimeter onto a high shelf. His head feeling like a nest of hornets, he scrubbed his face with shaky hands, as unpredictable and edgy as he'd ever been.

"What is she doing in our room?"

Tru laughed, his ragged black hair sticking up in odd places. "Just take your head meds and talk to her. Like you did at the cabin, remember?"

Although he didn't feel the least bit capable of comforting a little girl, Mason took a deep breath. At least she wasn't crying. Despite having a handgun leveled between her wide blue eyes, she didn't regard him with any more fear than she did the rest of the blood-crazy world.

He held out his hand.

Barefoot, her back against Mason's bunk, Penny never took her eyes off his. No blinking. No tears. Not even a quiver across her lower lip. His back burned and itched, a million fire ants crawling under his skin, and her otherworldly stare didn't ease his gnawing discomfort.

"Hey," he said, ignoring the rip of pain along his thigh as he squatted to her level. "How'd you get in here, honey? You scared me."

She nodded—more like a twitch, but Mason felt a glimmer of her meaning. He'd tried talking to her at the cabin, feeling a bizarre sort of affinity for how much she must have seen. And a regret that she'd needed to endure it at all. But she'd never once spoken in return.

Small and fragile as a porcelain doll, she touched his shoulder.

He frowned, fingers clumped into fists at his side. No amount of strength or shouting would pull words from her mouth, which made him useless. "Penny, what happened? Where's your mom?"

But that placid, nearly vacant expression never changed, not even at the mention of her mother. No glimmer of recognition or affection. Penny lifted her hand, let it hover a few inches above his shoulder, then lowered it again. Her touch was so delicate that he could hardly feel it, only a gentle press of warmth.

The corners of her pale lips turned down. She shook her head.

Tru snorted. "Man, she is seriously. Messed. Up. Should I go get Ange?"

Penny's blue eyes widened and trained on the kid. With sure steps, she skirted around Mason to stand before Tru. Her frustration, a silent tension that charged the air, ebbed as she touched his shoulder too. Tru's face twisted into a freaked-out grimace, almost comical. But he held still and kept quiet—a miracle by itself.

Penny smiled. Dimples appeared in her apple cheeks and her lips parted to reveal how her child's face didn't yet fit new grown-up teeth. She scrambled onto Tru's lap, curled into a ball, and stuck a pinkie finger in her mouth.

Mason felt sucker punched. Too much he couldn't possibly understand. But he wasn't half as perplexed as Tru looked. The kid didn't know where to put his hands.

"She suits you," Mason said, hiding a smirk.

"C'mon, get her off me."

Seconds later, Ange burst into the room. "Where's Penny?"

"Don't shout." Jenna shaded her eyes as she stepped in. "We heard a scream."

"If you hadn't opened that Hennessy, you wouldn't be hungover," Ange snapped.

"Yeah," Jenna muttered. "Because I forced you to drink and talk pygmies or elephants or whatever for half the night."

"She's over here, lady." Tru still sounded baffled.

Close enough to touch her sleep-warm skin, Mason inhaled the sweet tang of alcohol clinging to Jenna. "You've been drinking?"

"Not enough. Maybe if I'd finished the bottle, I'd still be asleep. What's going on?"

Angela crossed the room in three strides. "Let go of her!"

"I didn't do anything," Tru said. "She came to me."

"Enough!" Mason grabbed Angela around the waist before she could launch herself at Tru. "You, sit down," he said, planting her hard on his bunk. He held on to his exasperation like a leashed pit bull. "And just—everybody shut up." He pointed at Penny, who'd tucked harder against Tru's pencil-thin body. "She screamed. Who knows why, but she did it inside our room. The door must've been unlocked. But I don't remember hearing her enter, not before the scream."

"Me neither," Tru mumbled, dark circles under his eyes.

"Does she sleepwalk?" Mason asked.

"No. I mean, she didn't." The fight drained out of Ange, leaving the skin around her mouth slack and sagging. She looked older, certainly exhausted. "But I don't know now. We haven't had much chance for sleep. Not since . . . you know."

Mason nodded. "Okay, so maybe she took a little walk? Had a nightmare? Is that possible?"

Jenna glanced toward the door. "No four-footed bogeymen?"

"No, I checked with the doc. Nothing."

"But why'd she come in here? *I'm* her mother," Ange said, crestfallen. "She won't talk to me, and now she won't even come to me when she has a bad dream?"

Jenna put a hand on Angela's forearm. "She's probably just—"

"I shouldn't have been drinking. I try to unwind a little and then this happens!"

"Nothing happened," Mason said too loudly. "She's fine. Let's get her back to sleep."

Not that sleep was likely.

Angela wiped her nose and swished tears from her cheeks. Her freckled skin had flushed pink from crying, and her red hair was disheveled. She knelt on the ground in front of Tru. "Penny, honey? Come to Mama. We'll go back to bed, 'kay? You can sleep with me."

She took hold of Penny's upper arms, but the girl flinched and dug deeper into her burrow. Through it all, Tru's face stayed frozen with that same dumbfounded look.

"Penny, c'mon now, baby." Ange gave another tug, but the girl wasn't going anywhere. "Time to come to bed."

Mason pulled her up again, this time with less force. The woman was obviously hurting, with her only child acting in a way they couldn't understand. But just because he understood didn't mean he knew how to fix it. Which made the whole concept of empathy useless. And frustrating.

Jenna rescued him from the crying woman. She looped an arm around Angela and hugged her while sitting on the bunk. Apparently sharing a drink meant they were best friends.

Great, now we're bonding with these people.

"Maybe we should just leave her where she feels comfortable," Jenna said, her tone conciliatory. "She's had such a tough time of it. If she feels safe with Tru . . ."

The kid squeezed his eyes shut. "Oh *God*—"

"Zip it," Mason said to him.

"But she's *mine*," Ange said. "I'm the one who's been there for her, her whole life. I love her. Why won't she—"

Penny moved, removing her finger from her mouth.

"What was that?" Tru asked quietly.

Mason watched as the girl cupped a hand to the kid's ear. Tru listened with impressive gravity.

Ange leaned in. "What did she say? Tru, please."

Mason watched too. The hairs on his forearms twitched and stood, goose bumps peppering him all over. He shivered, knowing it wasn't pain making him jittery. The air hummed with electricity, the push of a storm over the land. Behind his eyes, he caught something new. Another vision.

A triangle of light spread across the horizon and ripped it in two. Colors burst to life, raining ash over the charred landscape. It had something to do with these two, something they needed to do. Not now, certainly. They were just kids.

But someday.

The picture faded, and his body jerked. A migraine drilled his temples as he sunk to the floor. Though his eyes were open, he saw nothing but black.

Only when Jenna touched him did his vision begin to clear. "Mason, you all right?"

"Did you see it too? What was that?"

She stilled, both hands clutching the caps of his shoulders.

She'll push it aside. She won't admit it. Answer me, damn you.

"I don't know," she whispered, eyes wide. "Like the sky was splitting open."

Before the others could question, he asked Tru, "Did she talk to you?"

The kid's expression remained intent and oddly humble. "Yeah."

"What did she say?" Ange demanded.

"Um, it doesn't make any sense." Tru shrugged. "She wants to know if we'll have Christmas now."

Mason frowned. So did Jenna and Angela, trading their confusion like bread recipes.

I've never baked in my life, came Jenna's voice in his head.

That interference was back, her brainwaves scrambling with his. A bad radio signal, two songs overlapping. The room felt like a cell, and he was locked in with the lunatics. Or them with him.

"Penny." Angela knelt wearing her patient-mom face. "It's not Christmas yet, baby. Not yet."

Just that blank stare. It was the oddest thing Mason had ever seen, as if the only voice she could hear belonged to a black-haired, blue-eyed boy with a bad attitude.

"Tru," Jenna said softly. "Talk to her. Please."

The kid swallowed his obvious discomfort. Again. "Hey, Pen." He brushed the hair from her face and offered a smile. Not a sham. Just friendliness. "We got some time left until Christmas, so that means we have to be good, okay?"

She whispered in his ear.

Tru frowned. "You think so? We'll have to check. You and me, huh, Pen? We'll go check."

The intercom buzzed. Angela yelped. Jenna muttered a curse under her breath.

"Hey, where is everyone?" Welsh called. "You should get up here and see this."

"Hold on," Mason answered, looking at the kid. He just knew these two things were related—whatever the scientist wanted them to see and what Penny had whispered. "Tru?"

"She thinks it's Christmas because of the snow. Asked if we can make snowmen."

"Snow?" Mason repeated.

"That's why I rang," Welsh said. "Come and see. It's gorgeous."

SEVENTEEN

Jenna was standing at the window when Tru came up beside her. In another life, they'd be out there making snow angels with the kids, but they couldn't spare the energy for play. And the woods were alive with monsters.

At the next set of panes, Penny watched with her mother. They'd all come upstairs to see the first sign of winter blanketing the earth. Everything was white and still, dark boughs spattered with ice, all spangled with crystal. Jenna could almost forget Bob's hellish death when they'd reached this sanctuary, almost forget what the pristine whiteness hid.

Almost.

Although she wouldn't mind eating some aspirin, she felt better for her indulgence. Nothing besides sex helped her relax more than drinking, and Mason's prickly demeanor meant a casual fling was off the menu. Sleep wouldn't hurt. She had no idea what time it was, but her stomach grumbled.

"She had a bad dream," Tru said.

"That was why she screamed?"

The kid nodded. "She wouldn't tell me how she got into our room, though. I guess maybe Mason and me were just sleeping deeper than we realized."

"It was a hell of a day."

"Sure was."

"You like it?" She gestured at the icy flakes.

"'The snow floats down upon us, mingled with rain,'" Tru murmured. "'It eddies around pale lilac lamps, and falls . . .'"

She glanced at him, her eyebrows raised. "Did you write that?"

"No." His tone said she was an idiot for asking. "Conrad Aiken. *The House of Dust.* No? Jesus, the guy only won a Pulitzer. He had a seriously fucked-up home life too. His dad killed his mom, shot himself, then left him to find the bodies. Eleven years old."

Well, that explained Tru's interest, a macabre at-least-I'm-better-off-than-that kind of therapy. But she wouldn't let herself be baited. She turned back toward the snow. With a huff of disgust, the kid took off to talk to Chris.

Mason came up on her other side. He radiated heat that she detected on a radar that didn't apply to anyone else. She might recognize Ange by her tread or Penny by her odd quietness, but Mason was the only one she could ID based on how her skin prickled to life.

"We made it," he said. "We just have to hunker down until spring. And maybe we'll have a real shot at this."

"How does this help us?"

"Like I said, demon dogs don't like the cold. They should turn their attention to survival, not us."

Maybe that explained his quiet sense of contentment. "So we'll have some time to rest and recover before the battle begins again." She glanced at the bulge of bandages beneath his shirt. "Some of us need it more than others."

"Funny."

An odd surety came over her as she watched his profile for a minute longer. "You're . . . surprised, aren't you? You didn't think we'd last this long."

His voice rumbled in that delicious bass, so distracting that she found it hard to focus on his words. "Honestly? No. Especially not after we picked up the dead weight. I thought taking in these strays would be the death of us both."

"We lost a couple." Maybe he could be casual about it, but she refused.

"There was no saving the woman," he said, his voice hard. "And Bob was too tired."

She managed an ironic smile. "Culling the herd. Isn't that what they call it?"

"Something like that."

Because he looked so weary and worn, she couldn't work up enough indignation to argue. Maybe he believed what he said, all the way to the bone. Sharp words from her would just waste her energy, and nothing would change his mind.

"Is anyone hungry?" Jenna asked the room.

To her surprise, Penny gave her a long look and a very brief nod. It wasn't speech, but it was communication. That had to be a good thing. Ange responded with a smile, stroking her daughter's hair.

"So, Chris, where's what passes for the kitchen in this place?"

"There's the break area." He beckoned her toward the door and led her down the top-floor hallway. Chris had long legs, and she worked to keep up with his efficient strides. He waved a hand at two conference rooms. "We used these for presenting our findings and slideshows from time in the field."

"You had the whole station. Why hunker down in the basement?"

"Didn't like all the windows."

Jenna shuddered. She could imagine all too easily one of those monsters taking a running start and launching itself through the glass.

Chris pushed open the swinging galley-style door and flicked on the light. He nudged up his wire-rimmed specs and leaned against the doorframe, but even that casual pose wasn't casual. More like how he thought grown men acted relaxed. Despite their differences, in some ways he reminded her of Mason—only barely fitting in with real people.

"This is it," he said. "Where I used to zap all my ramen noodles."

Shit. No stove. No oven. Just a useless microwave, a fridge, and a coffeemaker surrounded by vinyl chairs and scarred lounge tables. As far as cooking was concerned, she could have done better in the cabin. She tried not to think about all the fresh bread she could have made.

"Here," Chris said, pointing to the kitchenette's far corner. "I jury-rigged this propane grill so that it vents out through the roof. Just use as little fuel as you can. And it can get hot in here if you let it run too long."

"Nothing fancy, then."

"Afraid not."

"Where are the supplies?"

"Some in here, but the rest is downstairs in the main storage closet." He rubbed the back of his neck. "We stocked up on canned goods every fall, in case we'd get snowed in. Um, do you need any help?"

"No, I'm fine."

"Great," he said, his relief obvious.

She nodded and backtracked to the stairs leading to the bunker—the bunker with the broken door. They seriously needed to do something about that. She wanted more metal between her and those things, a secure fallback position.

Damn, she was starting to think like Mason.

In the storage closet, she found potted meat, cases of canned peas and potatoes, and endless boxes of macaroni and cheese—enough to make a meal.

Making the casserole, however, took some ingenuity. She cooked the pasta on the propane grill, combined it in a big plastic bowl, and dumped in the peas. She flash-grilled the meat until it was slightly brown on the outside, then tossed it in with the pasta.

All she found was plastic tableware and reusable plastic picnic plates, but that would work as well as any. With a sigh, she took in the less-than-inviting picture the meal presented on the round break table.

Well, whatever kept the body together.

"Food's on!" she called. "You guys probably don't want to eat this when it's cold."

"That doesn't smell bad," Tru said as he slunk in.

She flashed him a smile and wasn't surprised when Mason was the last to arrive. "I hope nobody's a vegetarian."

"You'd think I would be," Chris said, seating himself. "But no. I like the way meat tastes."

Ange watched him for an extra heartbeat than was necessary, her expression almost wistful. She shook free and helped Penny into her chair. "Me too. I went through a vegetarian phase, fueled by animal-rights activism, and then I'd get this mondo craving for a cheese-burger." She shook her head. "I'm such a hypocrite."

"It's natural." Chris smiled. "We have canine teeth for a reason."

Ange took up her fork, shaking her head. "Don't mention teeth."

"Here you go," Jenna said, handing the bowl to her right. "Penny needs to eat."

"Thanks." The other woman nodded as she scooped some of the casserole. Penny looked none too convinced of its merits, an expression just short of emotion. It was progress. "You like mac and cheese, right, honey? This is good stuff."

That's a stretch, but it'll suffice.

Tru grabbed his share next and stared at his plate, his expression hard to read. When he caught Jenna studying him, he grinned.

"You're not gonna make me say grace while we're doing this family thing?"

"Nah," she said, carefully casual.

She figured him out then, his shy aggression and confusion. Only at the end of the world did somebody cook for him. And she ached a little over it, even as she puzzled at the insight. These days, she knew too much without understanding why. Hopefully, she'd have a chance to examine her ability to communicate with Mason, and the odd, almost prophetic vision they'd shared.

Mitch would love the hell out of this shit.

Tru's hesitation didn't last long. He dug in. Practically inhaling his food, he was almost done by the time Jenna got the bowl back.

"This is good." Chris sounded surprised. "I like how you made the meat a little crunchy on the outside."

Jenna grinned. "Yeah, I could teach a class on survival cuisine."

Mason ate in silence beneath a thundercloud scowl. She tried to ignore him, but when a man his size brooded, everyone else had to take notice. In a moment of weakness, she'd tried to get closer to him. She'd tried to make a connection that obviously could never be. Mason had no give, no flex. He was all iron, and that had to hurt. She hated that she wanted to check his bandages and draw his head into her lap. She hated that she was dumb enough to want to take care of him, even though he saw her as a promise to be kept—an obligation, not a person in her own right.

Mitch strikes again.

Determined not to feed his ego with her attention, she focused elsewhere. "So, Chris, what do you do for fun around here, other than play with tissue samples?"

"What's wrong with tissue samples?" he asked, grinning.

Tru grunted. "Sick, Harvard."

"Cornell, remember? Not Harvard." He swallowed a forkful of

pasta. "I've been experimenting with what works and what doesn't. Thought a definition would serve us well."

"What did you find out?" Ange asked. She passed her gaze between Chris and Penny. Always back to Penny. This woman would do anything—and Jenna did believe *anything*—for her child.

"Nothing with computer technology. Mason told us that much and it bears out. Cell phones, car electronics, the display panel on that stupid microwave—anything with a chip is toast. My guess is that it's simply too complex to survive radical environmental changes. Simple machines work fine—those that run on electricity or combustible fuels. The change isn't affecting basic rules of chemistry or physics. For now, gears still turn and fire still burns. Hey, that rhymes."

Tru made a wanking motion. "Lame."

"But it all depends on fuel," Jenna said tightly. "Or a power source, like the hydroelectric setup."

"Exactly." Chris pushed his empty plate away. "Now, how about table trivia? Not to be confused with table tennis, of course, although we might have paddles somewhere."

"Paddles? Way pervy, dude," Tru said.

Mason made a sound Jenna took for disgust. He didn't appear to like their host much. No real surprise there.

But Ange didn't let Mason's antipathy discourage her shine. "How do we play?"

"Well, we're stuck together for a long winter, so we may as well get to know each other better, right?" He fiddled with the earpiece of his glasses. "So we go around the table and offer two facts—one true, the other a lie. The person on the left has to guess which is true, and the one with the most right answers wins."

"Wins what?" Tru muttered. "A Bunsen burner?"

"Dessert." He stood and rummaged in the cabinets until he drew forth a chocolate bar. "Someone must've been saving this for ages, so

I can't say how fresh it is. But this seems like a special occasion, what with the snow and all."

Jenna shrugged. "I'll have a go."

"I'm in," Angela said.

Tru leaned back in his seat, looking every inch the insolent teenager. "What about you, Pops?"

Mason raised a brow. "Do I look like somebody who competes for a candy bar?"

"No," Jenna said softly. "You look like a grouchy son of a"—she slanted a pointed look at Penny, who looked slightly less scared than usual—"witch. Shut up and play."

They locked eyes, struggling for . . . something, lost in their fight until it felt like the room had emptied. Pure heat lanced through her. She might have done something embarrassing, if Tru hadn't snared her attention by thumping the legs of his chair.

Mason stood. "Play games if you want."

But the kids split the chocolate. Satisfied he'd gotten the last word with her, even if it went unspoken, he strode away without looking back.

EIGHTEEN

The slow dusk marked the snow with streaks of blue shadow. Grinning at the fierce wind blowing up a third blizzard, Mason took a deep breath. Food would be tight, not to mention mind-numbingly monotonous, but they were snuggled tight as ticks. The demon dog packs would fall back under the icy cold, doing whatever they did when winter came. Hibernate? Starve? It didn't matter. After Mitch died, he hadn't stuck around back east long enough to find out. He'd gone west, as promised, to learn things, become a man, and wait to keep his promise.

Mason imagined that pit covered by snow. The rot still existed, waiting beneath the bleached layer of white. The greater battle for survival still awaited them.

Come spring, he would be ready.

Bring it on.

In the meantime, he had other problems—ones he felt completely incapable of handling. Penny hadn't spoken since the night of the first snowfall three weeks before, and Tru's crisis-time cooperation had disintegrated into bored teenaged whining. The food. The chores.

The lack of anything to do. And the good doctor was a pain in the ass, the way he was always looking at Jenna.

Jenna.

The thought of her snapped his body to full alert. His skin prickled, heart beating a hectic rhythm, and his cock went hard as an iron pipe. Standing there alone, he let need trigger his sexual launch sequence. He remembered those few scant days they'd been trapped together in the cabin, imagining long winter nights of openmouthed kisses and animal sex.

They'd stolen one taste, after Bob was killed. But that was the problem. Every thought, from mundane to erotic, raced back to the threat they faced.

Still, no matter the wall between them, she changed the bandages on his back each morning. They hardly spoke, but she touched him. He held still and lost a piece of himself each time, knowing she needed something. From him. In that strange place at the base of his skull, her interference coalesced into blurry road signs he could never quite read. But mostly he felt her anger.

No matter how fucked up that was, he didn't want to lose it.

He shivered. Turning, he found Jenna in the doorway.

She'd gotten better at hiding behind a passive expression, but he still sensed her restlessness. Her bangs had grown so long as to hang over her eyes. Highlights colored halfway down her hair, but the roots were nearly as brown as her brows. Her cheekbones were sharper, her lips thin.

"Snow's falling again. So as long as we still have heat, we'll be good."

Her footfalls muffled by socks, she crossed the room and stood beside him along the wide bank of windows. "Chris says the hydroelectric is powered off a hot spring. He's come here four winters in a row and it's never frozen."

"Chris."

Green eyes met his. "That *is* his name."

Mason looked up, tracing the line of sealant along the window casing. The spinal bones along the back of his neck felt rusted and sore. "Mine's John."

She inhaled, butterfly quiet. Her surprise was worth that bit of honesty. "John Mason?"

"That's right."

There had to be an easier way of doing this, the talking but not talking. He squelched a flicker of envy when he remembered an old silent movie clip, where a caveman dragged his woman by her hair. He didn't need the hair-pulling part, but a little brute force would feel pretty damn good.

"You never thought this far, did you?"

"Didn't think I needed to," he said. "We should've wintered at the cabin."

"Figured." Jenna turned to lean against the window, arms crossed and facing him. "I saw this show once about soldiers coming home from war. Everything they'd done and seen stayed with them, so they were traumatized. Clueless about what to do with themselves. Most couldn't adapt to civilian life."

Mason didn't want her to stop talking—this was the longest she'd spoken to him in three weeks—but he sure as hell didn't want to talk about useless soldiers. "This isn't some war, Jenna. There won't be a peace treaty."

"I know."

"And extermination takes time. Neither side will go quietly."

Her mouth worked around some words she couldn't say. Or wouldn't. "There are other people out there, right? People like us, hiding?"

He studied the graceful line of her neck. She had a mole on her left collarbone, peeking out from her sweatshirt. The knife edge of his desire sharpened, but a frightening protectiveness pushed forward.

Sometimes she played so tough—and she was. More than he'd given her credit for.

But right then, she looked about as vulnerable as Penny.

"I don't know," he said quietly. "But it doesn't matter. Not really. We just need to survive the initial upheaval of the change. The longer it takes to adapt, the more vulnerable we'll be."

"And this is how things will be? That's . . ." She shook her head, the ends of her ponytail fanning across her shoulder. "That's shitty. God, I hate this. I don't *want* to be a survivor." She laughed bitterly. "Pathetic, huh?"

"I don't think so, no."

"Mitch would've thought so. 'Suck it up, Barclay.'" Her voice broke.

Mason's breath came in agitated gulps, the kind that shredded a man's pride.

He needed this woman.

He'd known for weeks now that she was tangled up in his future— well beyond the promise he'd made. That promise was an excuse, a reminder of how they'd met, and a reason for claiming her when the time came. But she was stronger than maybe even Mitch had known. Or maybe the old bastard had deserted her for precisely that reason, to teach her the lessons she needed now.

While Mason had been dwelling in a dark place—where he was the kind of man who leveled a gun at a little girl and let his friends die—she led the others. Preparing the food. Organizing chores and rations. She kept Ange busy and made sure Tru and Penny had something to do. The day before, she'd given them books to study, learning about the natural world.

In all likelihood, Mitch had known that she could do this. *Be* this.

Without Jenna, they'd be lost. He knew how to fight, and that was all. The military had taught him. Oh, his excuses were sound. They needed vigilance, information, and patrols. But he'd spent more time in the wild, crisscrossing the country with those damn creatures, than with real people. Nothing new there. So he didn't know what to do when he came inside.

Fingers numb, Mason reached out and traced her jaw to her collarbone. She shivered and pushed his hand away. His throat tensed.

Have I ruined this?

"There wasn't any 'this' to ruin," she answered roughly.

He flinched. "Damn it, how are you *doing* that?"

"Me? You do it too. You tell me!"

"I'm not doing a damn thing. My thoughts are mine, *mine*, but you—"

"I get inside." Her hard laugh scraped across his nerves. "That's ironic. Is that all I get, then? Some stray signals every once in a while?"

"You shouldn't be getting that much. Why is this happening?"

"Magic?"

Magic. That sounded like something Mitch would say. *There's no reason for it, son. It just is, like the wind or the rain. It's up to you to make the best use of it that you can.*

She shrugged, but the tension at the corners of her eyes didn't ease. "Hell if I know," she said. "We could ask Chris. He'd try to reason the magic out of it."

"Fuck him." The idea of Jenna getting into Chris's mind, and vice versa, sizzled through him like a lightning bolt. "Do you . . . can you hear anyone else?"

She moved away from the window, mocking with her faint swagger. "Like . . . who?"

"Anyone."

"Would it bother you?" She laid her hand on his chest, the first time she'd touched him in weeks without medicine as an excuse. "I'm right here, John. Don't lie to me."

His fight-or-flight reflex was just about to choke him. The muscles of his thighs burned like live wires. His heart thrashed under his ribs. Sweat itched beneath the bandages on his back. She'd be able to smell it on him. And through it all, his cock hadn't forgotten how close she stood, near enough to grab and bend her body to his.

Sex and violence, yes. But sex and fear?

Show me.

Mason answered her dare. He let his id off the chain and opened his mind. Flashes of that long-ago day, watching the monsters chew through his friends. Pushing deeper, he showed her the shame of standing over Penny with a loaded gun and the lonely fear of outliving his usefulness—a hollowed-out soldier stuck among regular folks. Memories of Jenna, when she'd crossed shivering arms over her chest. He'd wanted to strip her worn cotton T-shirt and warm her pebbled nipples with his tongue.

Jenna gasped. She pushed against his chest and stumbled back, catching her balance against the bank of windows. Green eyes flared wide. Her breath came in the same erratic hiccups as his.

"What the hell was that?"

He tried to speak, then cleared his throat. "You wanted me to show you."

"I—"

"You didn't know what you asked for, huh?" Mason straightened and inhaled. "Well, now you've seen inside, Jenna. Some of it at least."

"That was . . . way more than we did before. How was that possible?"

He smacked his fist into his hand. "If Mitch was right and this is magic, then who the fuck knows what's possible? Those things out there shouldn't exist—beasts so wrong that you can hardly stand to look at them. Monsters that turn into *men*."

"I guess in comparison, what we have doesn't seem as scary." She tapped a rhythm against the glass. "So what now?"

"When you feel brave enough to peel open your brain, then we'll talk."

"When you feel brave enough to talk instead of intimidate, I'll take you up on that."

They watched each other like wary enemies. That fight-or-flight feeling snuffed out, and even his hard-on took a powder. He just felt . . . tired. "Look, can you change my dressings? My back itches and it's driving me nuts."

"Huh. You're actually asking me?"

"Yeah."

"I'll get the supplies."

She crossed his path, the musky, charged-up smell of her like liquor in his blood. Ripping open base fears had dimmed his arousal, but her scent cranked it back to full power. Mason grabbed her arm before she got too far. "Jenna?"

"What?"

"It would bother the hell out of me if you could do that with anyone else." He brought her wrist to his mouth and kissed the place where her pulse fluttered.

Her sharp inhale was like that whoosh when a match touches gasoline. His body jerked. He bared his teeth and gently bit the pad of flesh at the base of her thumb, daring her in return.

A tremor raced down her arm. "I can't," she whispered. "Only with you."

Cool relief washed through him, but reckless violence, coupled with nearly uncontrollable desire, built a storm inside him. Whatever this was, they were in it together.

NINETEEN

If he thought he could get away with that, he was out of his mind. Time and again, he pushed her to the breaking point. Fear and longing tied her up in such a knotty package that Jenna no longer knew what she wanted. His mouth, his teeth. He shouldn't promise what he didn't intend to deliver. Heat lingered in her palms and ricocheted under her skin.

Which gave her an idea.

She pulled back with a murmur about his bandages and reined in her anger as she fetched the supplies. Oh, she wouldn't hurt him. He'd been hurt enough, all scars and pain. But a woman had other means of making a man pay.

The way Mason tracked her return with his eyes gave her hope, though she pretended not to notice. He carried himself like a starving animal. But desperate creatures could take a hand off at the wrist. She just needed to be quick.

As Mason shrugged out of his T-shirt, she stifled the base, needy reaction that always slid through her at the sight of his thick muscles. She peeled tape away from his smooth brown skin, lifting the stained gauze pads with delicacy born of practice. He wouldn't let anyone else do this, not that they were lining up. At first she'd told herself that meant something, but as the weeks passed, she realized she was convenient. Nothing more.

If only he'd give her an inkling that she meant more to him than an obligation. But he never did. So she indulged in a resentment she knew was childish.

"You're healing well," she said quietly.

His back bore fresh new scars, pink-silver and slightly ridged, in addition to the old. Cursorily, she wiped them with peroxide-soaked pads, but they'd healed over a week ago. In time they'd be nothing but raised lumps, signs to mark where the skin had been so violently broken. That evidence of weakness had to gall him, proving he wasn't invincible or immortal. Or maybe that was the problem. He knew he was flesh and blood.

"Glad to hear it," he said. "I need to be in top form before the thaw."

Was that all he ever thought about? It frustrated and saddened her. She ran her fingertips over a purple mark high on his left shoulder. Tension coiled through his muscles at the caress. Mason didn't do softness. That was how she'd bring him to his knees.

She knew better than to ask how he'd received the older scars. He'd only stonewall her, and now she had the half-formed mental images from his past to sort through—answers for when she was focused enough to understand. He hadn't thrust those images into her mind out of trust or openness, but rather as a punishment for prying. She needed to find the real man beneath those defenses. He'd lived in a world of tooth and claw too long, forgetting that certain things should be shared, not taken.

He needed a reminder.

Jenna had felt at a disadvantage with Mason since he shoved her into the trunk of her own car. *He* had all the answers. *He* chose the time and place for their encounters. If he didn't learn to respect her, he would never consider her a necessary equal.

She brushed her hand over the next scar, this one down low on his back. A sharp breath hissed through his teeth. In her mind's eye, she played a slow waltz of sensual images. Skin on skin. Mouths clinging. Legs tangled together. She showed him a candlelit version of his raw sexual fantasy, his head at her breast, her hands curled to hold him there.

With such lovely distractions, the crack in his armor became a fissure. As she touched and soothed, she gleaned little details of each battle, every attack. The scars told her unspeakable stories. But this time she gained the knowledge on her terms.

Mason made a small sound. She circled him, no longer pretending to work. Though he was too strong for coercion, he could be seduced. By venting his temper, he'd also shown her what he wanted. So she added a new act to those dark moments. After the fighting, after the pain, he would find her waiting. They'd take each other endlessly, sometimes hard and fierce, sometimes slow and soft. She'd tend his wounds and then remind him he was alive—why living was so important.

Instinctively Jenna knew it could be like that between them . . . but not unless he learned to give.

Lightning echoed back. His broad back expanded in a quick inhalation. "You're a witch," he rasped. "I have to kiss you."

"Do it."

Strong arms came around her, hard and hot, dragging her against his body. Jenna didn't wait to seal her mouth to his, lips clinging just as she'd shown him. Mason kissed without finesse, all pressure and demand. He ran his hands down her back, cupped her ass, hauled her closer. She licked his lower lip, then the upper. He answered with a hot lash of tongue, followed by a fierce nip. She sensed his primitive need to take and claim.

"God, you smell good." Burying his face in her neck, drinking her in, he grazed his teeth along the tender column of her throat.

Jenna moaned, her hands fisting against the bunched muscles of his back. Tremors ran through them both, rocking them together. His cock blazed against her belly, hard enough to hammer nails. Deliberately she slid back and forth against that hot length.

But she wasn't tall enough for the friction she wanted, and a soft growl tore from him as he lifted her, bracing her against the window. The glass was a cool contrast to his heat. Mason would burn her up, and she didn't care. She wound her legs around his hips, locking her ankles at his back.

His big hands slid up, fingers splayed to the sides of her breasts. Jenna felt more aware of herself as a woman than she ever had. Compared to Mason, she was small but also incredibly powerful. She made him feel like *this*. He brushed his thumbs against her nipples, sending a spark all the way to her toes. She wanted him like she wanted air or water or sunlight.

"Someone could come in," she whispered.

His response came low and guttural. "Let them watch."

Though she'd never had an exhibitionist streak, dark fire streaked through her at the idea of fucking like animals. Her lips curled away from her teeth in a hungry snarl, and she leaned forward, teething his throat as he'd done hers. They strained together, pure sex impeded by clothing.

Just before she lost her mind entirely, Jenna took a deep breath. And another. It was almost impossible to shove the sex-starved wolf back in its box, but she called on civilized instincts. Her legs fell away from his hips, and she gave him a little shove. He fell back half a step, his expression dazed.

She landed on her feet, but it took everything she had to smile. Pure sham. Her knees damn near gave way. Mason wanted her, more than any man *ever* had. *I can't do this to either of us. I should—No.*

She slammed the lid on her doubts. If she couldn't earn his respect any other way, she'd get his attention with her willpower.

I'm not an animal, a slave to my sexual impulses. We deserve more.

"I think you can go without bandages now. The air will do your skin some good."

He regarded her with stark, simmering desire. "What?" he began. "I mean, you're—"

"Leaving. Don't fuck with me again, or you'll be sorry." She paused. "Wait, you already are."

She was too. Not that she'd admit it aloud. Her legs trembled. She wanted him so badly that her head might explode. Her panties were soaked, and merely walking away was an exercise in frustration. As she headed for the door, she half expected him to give chase.

"Jenna." His too-soft voice came from near the window. "We're not done."

She flashed a smile over one shoulder as she reached the hallway. "Well, it's over for now, 'cause your pants are too tight to chase me. Maybe you'll fare better next round."

Before she'd managed twenty steps toward the stairs, she heard the sound of something breaking. Yeah, she shouldn't see Mason for a while, even if he'd had that coming. At the very least, she'd given him something new to brood about. Jenna quickened her step and jogged down toward the bunker at a sprint, where she found Chris and Tru hard at work with sheet metal and a soldering gun.

"Stay back," Chris said. "We're wearing safety gear, okay?"

She nodded and heeded his warning, leaning against a nearby wall. Her body was still so keyed up. And swear to God, if they couldn't discern her current state of arousal, they were both completely dense. Not that she wanted them to notice. *Oh God.* But she was sure they could see it on her face, how hot her cheeks burned—if they glanced up from soldering.

"I like your thinking. But it's only been, what, a month?"

That might be a slight exaggeration. Jenna didn't mark off time like Ange, trying to keep things normal for Penny. What was the point? No matter how much they wished it, shit would never be the same. It seemed smart to figure out the changed world instead of clinging to the lost one.

"Nag, nag, nag," Chris said. "Next thing you'll be complaining about the way I slack on the yard work."

Though Tru rolled his eyes, Jenna glimpsed a genuine flicker of amusement.

"Well," she said—anything to take her mind off her collision with Mason. "How long has it been since you shoveled the walk? And you never take me *anywhere*."

"Now you do sound like my mom," Tru said.

The kid froze, then returned his attention to holding the sheet metal in place for Chris. Or maybe he was remembering. She wondered what he'd meant. Had his mom bitched a lot, or did he see Jenna in a maternal role? She didn't like either possibility. Hell, Ange was the group mom.

Fortunately, Chris wasn't interested in distractions. "Lift up the panel now. Higher. There we go. Hold it steady."

The soldering gun blazed blue and white as he ran it along the seams, melding a patch onto the top. Until that moment, Jenna hadn't realized burning metal had a smell, but it did, somewhere between hot copper and ozone. She sealed her hands over her nose and waited for them to finish.

But waiting meant thinking. Waiting meant feeling the tremors of need that still shook her body. Her heart pounded like mad. It had taken all of her willpower to walk away. Every bit. Even now she wanted to run back up the stairs. *Hey, Mason, sorry for jerking you around. Can we please finish what we started?*

That would be easy. So easy. But she refused to let him keep dictating the terms.

The guys stepped back to admire their handiwork.

"Looks good," she said.

Chris shrugged and pulled off his safety glasses. The elastic band made his hair spike up in the back. "Thanks. I'm not a professional, but I dabble."

"Color me astonished."

In the weeks since their arrival, Jenna had figured him for a man with boundless curiosity about the way things worked. Too bad that world changed faster than he could keep up.

He was handsome in a professorial sort of way, if a little on the thin side. The scientist often forgot to eat, so his cheekbones were sharp. She preferred Mason's skull-cut hair to Chris's shaggy locks, but he had a pair of very soulful hazel eyes. Jenna had noticed them turned on Angela, more than once, which brought to mind a question.

"What are Ange and Penny doing?"

"She's reading to her from an old *National Geographic*." Tru shook his head. "Poor kid. Like she's not already messed up enough."

"Even money the article's about Pygmy elephants," Jenna murmured.

Tru shook his head. "Nah, I think it was monkeys, actually. Pen likes 'em."

"And Chris likes Ange." Jenna grinned, enjoying the chance to tease. "Did *she* ask you to reinforce the door?"

To her astonishment, his ears reddened. He didn't respond—merely wiped his glasses on his shirtsleeve. She hadn't expected such an obvious reaction, not from the closed-off doc, so she offered a little privacy by shifting her attention to the door. With a last sigh, her pulse steadied. If only she could find her balance with Mason so easily. She'd drawn a line, so to speak, but they still had to live together.

"We shouldn't use this if we don't have to, not while it's cooling," Chris said.

He didn't say what was on her mind, that they'd only close it if something managed to get past the front doors. She tried not to wonder if it would hold against a wave of leaping monsters. Jenna imagined the door bending and breaking as snarling bodies barreled inside. She restrained a shudder.

"It's okay." Chris hesitated and then laid a comforting palm on her shoulder.

She guessed that such gestures didn't come naturally to him. But gift horse and all that. He wasn't Mason, and her body knew the difference. But at least he tried.

"Cozy," Mason said from behind.

Nothing had hinted of his approach—not a whisper of fabric, not a slide of soles against the floor. He was quieter than a ghost when he chose to be. Fury darkened his face. He wanted a fight.

But first the lights went out.

TWENTY

Mason's pulse jacked to a flat-out run. "Weapons, now! And flashlights."

"Wait a minute," Welsh said. "It could be a power-supply problem."

The sound of his disembodied voice reminded Mason of the two days they'd listened to him on the radio. He'd liked the man a lot better then. Now the urge to smack his skull into a steel I-beam curled his fingers into fists. "Could be, Harvard. You want to go check it out on your own? I'll let you volunteer."

"Will you two knock it off?" Jenna stood nearby, the lingering scent of her arousal taunting him. "We need to get Ange and Penny."

After a few clumsy sounds and the crash of a chair being knocked over, a light winked on. Welsh held a giant Maglite under his chin, the glare making two white circles of his eyeglasses. "Did you ever do this at Halloween, being a ghoul?"

Jenna grabbed another flashlight. "You're as much of an idiot as Mason. Find Ange and Penny!"

"Yeah, be back in five," Mason said. "Any emergencies, we stay together as a group."

"So they can kill us in one convenient location?" Welsh asked.

Mason opened the weapons locker and retrieved his AR-15. He stalked over to the scientist. "No, so I don't shoot you." He slammed a clip in the rifle, then shrugged. "You know, by mistake."

Welsh grinned. "How's your back, by the way?"

"Healed. You ready to take another shot at me?"

"Only if you keep acting like a goddamn gorilla."

Jenna growled deep in her throat. "Hey, gorillas—both of you. Can we focus, please?"

"Fine with me," Welsh said, all blameless detachment. "I'll go get the others."

Tru grabbed another flashlight from the storage locker and made to follow Mason and Jenna into the hydroelectric tunnels. Mason shook his head. "Sorry, kid. Go with him."

"Why?"

"Did you notice anything wrong when he scurried out?"

Tru hitched his rifle strap on his shoulder. "Nah, what about it?"

Mason pointed to the nearby table where Chris's weapon lay.

"Man, he forgot his shotgun? What a 'tard." He picked up the extra weapon, then shuffled toward the exit. Over his shoulder he called, "Okay, I'll watch out for the women and the idiot. Don't do anything cool without me."

"Just be back here in five." Mason turned to Jenna, feeling as hostile as her expression. He pushed past her and into the maintenance anteroom. "You ready? Or maybe you're not. Hard to tell."

She followed him, her own weapon primed. "Shut it. And lay off Chris."

His jaw tightened by reflex. "Get a light over here?"

"Say please."

Without waiting for a response, she expertly leveled the light where he needed it. Mason's mute anger slid back into his stomach.

All their shit could wait. After wrestling with the lock, he popped the seal. The door swung open with a rusty squeal, revealing six metal steps.

Their breathing echoed as they descended into the tunnel. At the base of the stairs, Mason stooped beneath the rounded, low-hanging ceiling. The hydroelectric pumps manufactured energy for the complex, but none of that heat filtered down below. He registered the chill as if his skin belonged to another man—distant information about goose bumps and a shiver. Every impulse not devoted to protecting the complex was busy trying to ignore the way Jenna scrambled his senses.

He tipped one ear to the far end of the basement. "Hear that? The generator isn't working."

"That's pretty bad news. No heat and no fresh water."

"Wait. Does that sound like running water to you?"

"Can't tell." She held the flashlight in one hand, while the other rubbed up and down her arm. "Should we call Chris?"

He fought to suppress a snarl. "We don't need him."

"Sorry, didn't realize you had a merit badge in engineering."

"Nope," he said. "But we need to assess the threat before sending him down. If it's a malfunction, fine. Harvard can play at being a plumber. I might even help."

She snorted. "I'd like to see that."

"But if it's something else . . . no way."

"What do you mean 'something else'? You said they take the winter off."

Sure, he'd thought that. But there were no experts on the change. No certainties. Maybe that was why he hadn't been able to relax, even with the snowfall. Still too many unknowns.

Jenna's sudden look of panic choked his impulse to share. He didn't need her losing her nerve too. He'd been far too jumpy lately, and pent-up sexual tension didn't help.

"There." He nodded toward where the light from Jenna's flashlight sliced across the disabled generator.

But her panicked expression didn't ease. She stared at him, eyes darkened by the shadows.

Somewhere smack between his ears began to tickle. The poke-prod feel of her mind peering into his was unmistakable. He smiled, feeling dangerous. "What're you looking for in there?"

"Don't lock me out. What is it, John?"

He enjoyed that familiarity too much, but she did a lot of things he liked. He'd almost lost himself in the soft rhythm of her hands sliding over his skin, over his scars. Her thoughts had tangled with his, not asking permission so much as sliding under the door, through the cracks. She'd woven a tempting net of images and offered them to him—comfort and warmth, safety and reprieve.

Then she'd scorched him from the blood on out, leaving him full of icy rage. To see her with Welsh afterward made his anger worse.

"I won't 'lay off Chris' as long as he keeps at you."

"Since when do you get to have any say over what I—"

"Over what you do? I have *every* say."

"Why the hell is that?"

Mason grabbed her upper arm. Why had she turned him into a begging animal, only to drop him? Bottled tension waited for a spark before he blew wide open. Fear of going too far kept his temper in check. Barely.

"Just remember where you'd be if I hadn't put you in the trunk."

"Yeah, thanks." She yanked free of his grip, but she'd probably have bruises. "But you're not my dad or my jailer. So shut up."

His airway constricted around deep, frigid disappointment. He'd been halfway articulate once. In the cabin, he'd spoken to her without this clogged-up feeling in his chest. But she'd played him for a fool, and it hurt more than he was ready to admit. *When had she become more than Mitch's daughter?* He wanted her too much, and it spilled into everything he did.

"Fine," he said. "You and Ange have fun with 'Chris.'"

"I don't want him."

"And I don't care." He tried for a casual shrug. "I won't be your entertainment anymore."

She pinched her eyes shut and shook her head slowly. "You really are thick."

"Save it. Once we get the power back on, you can explain what really happened up there. Make sure to use small words."

Mason left her where she stood holding the flashlight at a crooked angle. Her posture spoke of defeat or fatigue. *Must be the latter.* The fool woman didn't give up on anything.

Forget it.

He'd meant to distract Jenna, but the conversation had turned against him. He always got it wrong with her, lost in translation. And damn if he didn't have a clue how to make it right. So he walked on.

The water pattering against concrete sounded louder here. Mason found the generator and said, "Bring the light? Please."

Jenna trudged across the tunnel and leveled the Maglite at the generator's gray hull. The dripping made the tunnel feel like a cave.

He remembered Katie, a foster mom he'd had when he was in grade school. She and her boyfriend had bought a fixer-upper in a good neighborhood. But Mason learned to stay clear of their raging arguments. Drunk, sober, it didn't matter. He'd resented how they'd continued to work on that damn house even in the middle of a fight, all foul body language and frosty silences.

At that moment, Jenna reminded him of Katie. Before then, he wouldn't have thought it possible to hold a flashlight sarcastically.

"Here, follow this line back to the wall," he said, pointing to a water hose. "Please."

"You can stop now."

"Just using my manners. Thought you wanted things civilized."

She scowled and followed the hose with the light. Where the line met the wall, water slid past a seal and sprinkled onto the floor. "So the water isn't making it through the generator turbine?"

"Seems that way." He leaned nearer and poked the sealing ring. "See here? The ring is cracked."

"So we should—*ah!*"

The flashlight dropped with a hard metal thunk. She sagged, her knees giving out. Mason barely had time to shoulder his weapon before grabbing her beneath the armpits. He sank to the freezing concrete, slowly easing her with him.

"Jenna?"

Their only light source splayed across the floor, pointing back toward the stairs. A shiver shook her from the heels on up. Her body drooped against his, her head lolling at a sick angle. He snagged the light and shone it on her. Though her eyes remained open, she stared up and away—completely vacant.

"*Jenna?*"

The tingle in his brain intensified.

Back in the woods, when approaching the pit, he'd been assailed by a sense of existing outside of himself, a few steps ahead. He hadn't understood it, merely accepted the advantage of an extra sense, like seeing through a tree rather than around it. Now he forced logic aside and used that sense again.

A pack of demon dogs waited outside in the snow. Circling. Watching.

One of the monsters hunched over and shook. Bones realigned beneath fur. Its spine straightened. Its snout receded. Its limbs lengthened and bulked with different muscles. A thick pelt of fur thinned to reveal white skin covered with dark body hair, until a naked beastly man stood where a dog had been. Claws tipped his unusually long fingers, and teeth protruded from an extreme underbite. He directed his four-legged troops to take different paths around the complex, not with words but with growls and gestures, the air throbbing around his every movement.

Mason's mind banged back to the present. A headache arched over his brow and across his skull. The pain was so intense that tears sprang up.

He called to her in a hectic mental shout.

"John," she croaked, still shivering. "They're coming."

TWENTY-ONE

Tru followed Harvard into the dormitory, listening to him whack his shins on every possible obstacle. He wasn't about to hand the dude the shotgun when navigating the dark seemed such a trial. One of them would eat lead before the lights came back on.

In the distance, Ange whispered to Pen, trying to reassure the girl. Ange was nice . . . and pretty, if you liked older chicks. He didn't, but it wasn't like he would need a date anytime soon.

Up ahead, Harvard shone the light back and forth. "It's okay," he called. "I'm sure it's just a technical malfunction, but we should go up where there's some light."

"Mason said to head back downstairs," Tru muttered under his breath.

"You want to drag them down in the dark?"

Not so much.

Without light, Tru became more aware of noises and smells. Signals came at him from all sides. He brushed by Harvard and found Ange and her daughter huddled together on the bed. Pen's hair caught the light as if she stood beneath the moon.

The woman sat up. "I'm glad to see you two. Where are the others?"

"Checking out the maintenance area in the subbasement," Harvard said. "I'll go see what's up once we get you two out of here."

A strange sensation prickled over Tru's skin. He turned in a slow circle but found nothing to explain the general freakiness. Taking a deep breath, he tightened his grip on his rifle. "I'll take point."

He led the other three back to the stairs without a stumble. Darkened hallways were silent as the grave without the hydraulic hum. Weird that the others followed him without question. Maybe some of that do-as-I-say vibe had rubbed off on him from hanging around with Mason.

Nice.

He bounded up the stairs. It was dark up there too, but not pitch black like the bunker. Shadows swirled; he didn't like how exposed he felt. To get to the observation tower, they needed to cut left and head down to the end of the hall. Not far, but too far for comfort.

Why the hell was Harvard rambling about hoses and nozzles? Tru motioned the two adults to silence. Pen had the sense not to yap, or maybe the poor kid had no brains left at all. He felt for her, but everyone had to make the best of a nasty-ass situation. He'd been doing that for a long fucking time.

His chest hurt, but Tru didn't rub a hand across it to ease the tightness. He wasn't the kid who hid in closets anymore. His combat boots made no noise as he rounded the corner, mimicking Mason's light step. A muffled thump froze him in place. Another came—and another. Bodies slammed into reinforced metal.

"That's the front door," Ange whispered.

The monsters wanted in. Tru exhaled, trying to keep the sound steady. *What now, genius? Up where there's nowhere to hide or back down into the dark?* Part of him wanted to whine. This shouldn't be his call. But among this crew, Mason needed a second. That meant he had to use his brain.

"If something gets in, we won't be able to fight without light," he said softly.

"Upstairs, then." Harvard's face was ghostly in the flashlight beam.

Tru nodded and set off down the hall at a dead run, putting distance between him and the violent, rhythmic assault on the front door. The sound was weird, like tribal drums, primitive and lurking just beyond the walls, waiting to devour them all. The rest followed close behind.

"We'll get a good look," he said, starting up the stairs. "Maybe we can see what's out there."

"We know what's out there," Ange answered.

They hit the second floor, everyone breathless. Ange scooped Pen into her arms and cradled her with a tenderness that made Tru angry and sad at the same time. He wanted to smack her. *You aren't helping her, lady. She has to learn to deal. We all do.* But that wasn't any of his damn business. Besides, what would he know? He'd raised himself on Pop-Tarts and video games.

Rifle at the ready and Harvard's shotgun in his other hand, he ran for the windows. A whole wall of glass let in the twilight, and the contrast stung his eyes. Tru leaned forward to check out the scene below. More snow had fallen, lying a foot deep. The trees wore white shirts frosted in icy diamonds, a Robert Frost scene that wound up on a Christmas card.

But the winter wonderland didn't hold his attention. No, it was the freezing, starving-thin pack of demon dogs. In unison, as if they felt his gaze on them, the monsters threw back their heads and let out unearthly howls.

Jenna felt like she was going to puke. Her whole body shook. She'd known flickers before, but nothing so intense. This was the Grand

Canyon of out-of-body experiences, and she'd just fallen into it. As a teenager, she'd once done a tab of acid that left her feeling almost this bad, but the experience wasn't one she had intended to repeat.

Mason was talking, an old-school vinyl record spinning on at half speed. For a terrifying moment, she'd seen herself in front of that man-beast, mere inches away from dying beneath his bloody claws. His eyes were an eerie blue, pale as a mountain sky.

At some point, Mason had gone from supporting to holding her. Listening to his heartbeat in the dark offered some reassurance. Jenna drank it in, bit by bit, until she reached coherence. Eventually she sat up, disoriented to realize that opening her eyes didn't show her anything. Mason was the only true thing she could find.

"Can you hear them?" he asked.

She suppressed a wry smile. Of course he wouldn't ask if she was okay, if she was feeling better. No, it was right back to business. Maybe that was a backhanded compliment, proof of his confidence in her resilience.

She sat quiet, listening, until a terrible howl broke over her on a subharmonic level. Demon dogs keened their hunger in concert, tearing a shudder across her muscles.

"Yeah, I can hear them." She scrubbed her hands together, conscious again of the cold cement floor. "Like a song for the dying."

"If they don't find food and warmth, their pack will dwindle. That's what I was counting on."

That winter will make our job easier, come spring. Yeah, I know.

Jenna found Mason's hand, the one holding the flashlight, and twirled it toward the wall. Water still burbled out of the wall. "But they couldn't do this, could they?"

"The seal is just cracked. We'll see if Chris has another." He studied the play of light, his hand motionless in hers. "To be honest, I don't know what these things are capable of. I do know they learn. They adjust their tactics according to the behavior of their prey."

Crocodiles did that, she remembered, which only added to the primal response of being hunted. Jenna squeezed her eyes shut, beyond weariness. They'd been fighting for so long, and other than the privilege of surviving another day, they had damned little to show for it. Maybe there was something to be said for quality of life over quantity.

"Do you ever think maybe it's not worth it?" she whispered.

Mason laid a hand against her cheek. Amidst so much cold, his heat shocked her. He radiated energy and resolve.

"I don't know how to give up," he said. "If I did, I would have already, long before I met you. I'm not a man who's ever gonna lay down, Jenna." He paused, and his teeth flashed white in the near dark. "Except maybe for you."

In anybody else, she would have taken it as simple flirtation. But there was nothing simple about Mason. His words offered a glimpse into the labyrinth of his soul. Promise and trust tangled in those words, hints of a softness that didn't equate to surrender.

Jenna gripped his hand in return and smiled. "I guess I'm not the kind who goes down easy either."

"And ain't it a shame," he muttered.

A shimmer of raw lust washed over her. He leaned in, touching his forehead to hers—more intimate than an hour in anybody else's arms. Almost immediately he pulled back, but her mind flashed back to the way he'd kissed her. Her heart went wild.

"For the love of God, don't look at me like that when we have work to do."

"Like what?" The question came out husky, not teasing as she'd intended.

"Like you want to do me here on the floor."

Damn, he wasn't wrong. In trying to teach Mason a lesson, she'd done a number on herself too. Her flesh felt too big for her skin, as if she had a million more nerves in every square inch. He was some kind of drug; the more she had, the more she wanted. Jenna gave herself a little shake, but it took a solid minute to focus on business.

"Is this fixable?" She redirected the light between the leaking hoses. "I mean, we have to get the power back on."

"I'm sure the genius can do something with it. Should be safe to send his ass down to tinker."

"We should let the others know." She shook her head as she looked at the tangle of machinery. Useful, but she'd never figure it out, even after a week with the manual.

Mason helped her up, taking her weight. That was when she heard the digging.

TWENTY-TWO

"What do you mean, you can hear them?"

"I mean just that," she said. "I can hear them digging."

Mason watched her prowl along the east-facing wall. "Jenna, you can't. That concrete is structural. For a place this size, it's probably a foot thick."

"But lately, I hear and see things that I'm not supposed to all the time."

He raked blunt nails along the backs of his forearms, when he really wanted to scratch inside his mind—that nasty tickle he couldn't explain. "Point."

She kept moving, tracing where the flashlight carved a wedge of brightness along the wall. "Help me! Look for anywhere they could get in."

The light she held shone up between their bodies, leaving shadows where her eyes had been. She smelled different to him now. Perfume, detergent, and the smoky tang of the city—all gone. Until that moment, he hadn't noticed how completely the old world had worn away. With Jenna's arms shaking beneath his hands, he knew he'd recognize her scent anywhere.

And he could smell her fear.

"Show me," he whispered.

Gently, he touched his forehead to hers as she opened her mind. He didn't think he'd ever get used to that tapping sensation in his brain. Shuddering, he clung tighter to Jenna's slender arms.

Damn. Damn. Damn.

"You're fighting it," she said. "Don't fight me, Mason."

"I think you like it."

She laughed softly. "Sometimes. Now shut up."

Heat bloomed in the gray matter between his ears. He could almost smell the sulfur. Then came the freefall terror of stepping off the tightrope, only no net awaited him as he plummeted beyond his senses. Out of time. Outside of his own body. Accustomed to using his muscles to make his way in the world, he felt stripped and panicky. Physical strength meant nothing where she asked him to go.

East. Look east.

Swimming through his own thoughts, halfway between basement and sky, Mason saw them. Two dozen hunched demon dogs. Four times as many paws tipped with razor claws.

They dug along the eastern wall.

Shit.

Told you.

You did.

I'm scared.

Need my gun.

Behind the mindless, digging bodies, cold steam pipes poked up from the snow. They were right over the generator array. But why? Did they know it was on the fritz, or were they like any dog, eager to dig, dig, dig?

More over there.

Mason followed Jenna's thoughts and found another pack. Bigger and not as thin, the six monsters paced. Shock troops. And behind them stood the beast-man he'd seen in Jenna's vision.

Her fear tugged him back like a parachute. He fell into his body with a force so violent that he swallowed to keep his stomach down. Jenna clung to his chest, both of them breathless and sticky with bitter sweat.

"Why'd you stop?"

"I don't like it," she muttered.

"Damn, that's weird."

Jenna smiled unexpectedly, given the circumstances. "Magic."

Dear God. She's Mitch's daughter after all. Using what she has, because she must. The old man would be proud.

He nodded. "Let's go." Taking the stairs two at a time, he hiked the rifle strap up his shoulder. "Tru? Welsh? Where are you?"

"You told them to come down here in the dark. Chance of that?"

"Zero."

More stairs. But his heart didn't race and his breathing had calmed. Every flex of muscle felt right and reassuring after the head games they'd played in the basement. He didn't fear fighting. His body. His skills. He trusted both. And after weeks of slowly going insane inside their own little Alamo—waiting, watching, and wanting Jenna—he craved the release of violence.

A clammy cold crept over his skin. Not sweat. Just pure dread. Panic waited there. Though he wanted to fight, he'd willingly rust from the inside out, if it meant keeping the others from harm.

He couldn't think about that, not and keep them all safe. So when Jenna tried to take his hand, he pulled away and clenched aching fingers around the rifle strap. When she tried to find him, that maddening tickle of her mind brushing his, he clamped down hard. No hand to hold. No thoughts to share. He had work to do. If she wanted more, she was after the wrong guy.

But her hurt stabbed like an ice pick between his shoulder blades.

They emerged into the piercing silver light of the observation room, where the others stood frozen along the bank of windows.

"Damn," Welsh whispered. "I've never seen them this close. Do they always . . . gleam like that? The air around them?"

Tru nodded. "Yeah, like you can't look right at them. Freaks me the fuck out."

"Language," Jenna said automatically.

Mason continued his search of the observation deck and found Ange and Penny huddled together on a nearby chair. It was a wonder the little girl had any hair left, the way Ange stroked her head. But Penny didn't look scared. She looked . . . absent. So far gone they couldn't find her.

Welsh looked thoughtful. "It's peripheral. Almost like camouflage. But I've never seen anything like it. There's a refraction of light, but—"

"There's no light," Ange finished.

Tru shook loose of whatever thoughts kept him immobile. "Hey, you guys gotta come see this."

Jenna pushed past Mason, her back stiff. "We heard them howling."

"Man." Welsh let out a low whistle. "That was something."

He slung his AR-15 behind his back and joined the kid at the windows. The pack had slunk into the loose grouping of trees along the perimeter. They'd also left the snow dotted with countless paw prints.

"Our very own Rorschach test," he muttered.

Tru laughed. "I see the Space Needle."

"Where?" Welsh asked.

"Over there, along the base of those trees."

"I don't see—"

"Idiot," Mason said curtly.

With the good sense to look embarrassed, Welsh apologized. "So what'd you find?"

At his back, he felt Jenna's coldness melt while she spoke in quiet whispers to Ange and Penny. She dumped it in his lap with a mental mutter: *Hey, you want to be in charge. Have at it, asshole.*

"A cracked seal on the hose connected to the generator," he said. "Water all over the floor. You wouldn't happen to have another, would you?"

"Should, yeah."

"Look," Tru said, pointing.

From across the snow, those six alpha monsters circled a thinner member of the pack. With hardly any meat left on its protruding bones, the skinny one burrowed his muzzle in the snow, crouching low. The others pounced in unison—ripping, biting, devouring. Two minutes later, a ravaged smudge of bloody snow spread out where the cowering creature had been. The shock troops walked away licking their reddened jowls.

Tru backed away from the window. At first Mason thought it was because of what he'd seen, but then he noticed where Tru had moved: into Ange and Penny's line of sight. The kid was turning into a man, looking to protect those who needed it. Mason tucked away that sense of pride.

"That's how they're surviving," he said quietly.

Knowing they'd been people once dug at his brain. He hadn't given it more than a token thought in years—too busy fighting them to consider the possibilities. *Make the wrong move in the Dark Age and you could end up like that. Any of us could.* Sobering thought.

The scientist merely stared at the grim scene, nonplussed and studying. Mason could almost respect the man when he fired up his brain. Almost. But then Welsh frowned. "Wait, what about the backups? They should've fired up right away—no interruption of power."

"What backups?" Mason asked.

"Two more generators. They're smaller, in an anteroom that abuts the underground spring. The original builders used them as their main power source, but when this place was renovated, they were relegated to backups. They don't produce as much juice. Something about the pressure in the pipes."

Mason stared at the bloody snow, muscles seizing beneath his skin. "The hot spring, can it be accessed from outside?"

"It connects to a water source," Welsh said. "Natural underground tunnels. But I've never been down to the spring myself."

"The anteroom—what's it made out of?"

"Wood. Like I said, it was the original structure."

"And the door connecting to the basement?"

Beside him, Tru inhaled sharply.

Welsh paled. "Um . . . metal? I think."

"Tru, stay with those two. Jenna, the flashlight. Let's go."

Vaguely, Mason heard Ange asking what was going on, but Welsh was right at their heels.

"We know they're digging," Mason said, as much to himself as to the others.

"Digging? We didn't see any—"

"Trust us," Jenna snapped. They burst onto the ground floor and tore across the lab. "We saw it. We just didn't know why."

"Then, could they be looking for a way in?" Welsh asked.

Mason shouldered through the basement door and flipped the safety off his nine-millimeter. "Everybody's upstairs, right?"

"Yeah." Jenna aimed the flashlight. The beam wiggled. "Anything moves, shoot it."

A chill ran down Mason's spine. "If they found a way into the hot spring, I wouldn't put it past them to take out those generators."

"Seriously?" Welsh sounded astonished.

Mason crept down the stairs and tracked his eyes from side to side. "Normal dogs chew things. They mark territory. And these monsters know a lot more than you think. I can't be sure what they remember from before the change, but I know they learn. Now where's this anteroom?"

"End of the hall, past the main generator, and then around the corner to the right."

They passed the generator in silence. Water still sprinkled on the concrete like a recreational fountain in summer. But no kids here. No laughter or sunshine or heat. Just a tension in Mason's gut that constricted into a tighter and tighter knot.

They arrived at the anteroom door, which meant Mason could breathe again. "Good. It's metal."

Welsh leaned against the wall, his face shiny with sweat despite the dank cold in the tunnel. "That's something, right?"

"Shut up," Mason snapped. "Listen."

They didn't need that head voodoo anymore. The sound of faint and rhythmic scratching—like old-timey musicians scraping spoons along a washboard—vibrated through the metal door. Mason touched it. He pushed. The metal gave beneath his fingers.

He stepped away and raised his rifle. "It's not reinforced. Barely better than sheet metal for an outhouse. Jenna, get back."

She complied without protest, readying her weapon.

"What're our options?" Welsh asked.

Mason bristled. "Do you have to talk?"

"Just think about it. Say they're on the other side. You can't shoot them. That'd be like . . ." He cleared his throat. "That'd be like when I shot you."

"Dumb? Jumpy?"

"Yeah. And even if you get the vanguard, the others have an open door."

"He's right." Jenna tucked the hair behind her ear, her profile in shadow. "How would they get in? No one's dug through yet."

"They won't be able to, not all the way," Welsh said. "There's a good layer of granite shale between us and the surface. But there's no telling where the tunnel comes out. Maybe miles away. Some might take a backdoor route in, but that's the only option."

"Not all of them—not yet. So we have time." Mason put his gun away. "What've we got to reinforce this door?"

Jenna flicked the flashlight to the generator. "First, the seal. I want our damn lights back on."

He shook his head. "Protection's more important. Nobody ever died of the dark."

That unearthly group howl sliced the air again, grating against Mason's nerves as a primitive warning—a caveman's awareness of being hunted. Jenna flinched and shivered by his side. But she didn't reach for him that time, not even with her thoughts.

TWENTY-THREE

Chris's lean, scholarly face was unnaturally pale in the ring of light Jenna shone on him. The glasses hid his eyes, leaving his thoughts unreadable. He was still considering the problem of shoring up the door. "I don't know. Let me think."

"Thirty seconds."

Mason's blunt impatience rekindled her anger. Why didn't she learn? Every time she thought she had a handle on how his mind worked—and that they were making progress—he slapped her down.

Chris snapped his fingers and pointed back the way they'd come.

He and Mason carried the empty storage cabinet into the subbasement. At first Jenna couldn't visualize what they meant to do. Blocking the doorway didn't seem like it would work—the monsters would just tip the thing over with brute strength—but the men opened the doors and began to affix them to the walls. Noisy work. But the beasts already knew they were inside, meaty and magically delicious.

Pointedly, she held the light for Chris and ignored Mason. Maybe it was petty. But if he wanted nothing from her, he'd get an assload of it.

Chris drilled more bolts into the concrete, securing the portal.

Another layer of metal would take the monsters longer to push through, if at all. And they couldn't very well chew through it. "That's as good as it gets," he said.

Jenna touched his arm. "Lights next, please. Do you want help finding the part?"

"Sure. It should be upstairs in the maintenance closet. I could use another pair of eyes and a steady hand on the light."

Mason made a sound as they left, but she didn't turn. She left him in the dark, listening to the monsters.

Upstairs she noticed the cold. The heat had been off for a while, a hint of things to come if they didn't fix it fast. Jenna exhaled, testing, and her breath puffed out in visible fog. She touched the butt end of the Maglite, the metal downright chilly.

"We have to get the power back on or we're going to freeze." Her words were an experiment, just as her exhalation had been.

Chris hesitated, as if taking her measure in turn. "Yeah," he said at last. "The clock is ticking. We have a few flammable items that might extend the deadline, but without power, there's not much in the way of ventilation."

"Eventually we'd suffocate."

"If we didn't die in our sleep, we'd smoke ourselves out. Then those things would have us for brunch."

Jenna squared her shoulders. "Then let's go get that seal."

The sooner they did, the sooner things could get back to normal. Such as it was. Boring meals, tension, wondering if each day would be your last. Typical Armageddon stuff.

They made their way down the hall. Chris opened the closet door and Jenna swung the light to make sure nothing lurked in the shadows. Couldn't be too careful. She went in first, and then Chris found a battery-powered lamp. He switched it on and nodded at the blue-white shine.

"Not much juice left," he said. "But enough to help look."

Jenna dug through jumbled stacks of boxes, hoping she'd know what she was looking for if she found it. *Why the hell did anyone save this stuff?* Old holiday decorations. Lightbulbs for ancient fixtures. A busted tire pump.

Chris mumbled to himself, then tossed a box aside in obvious frustration.

"What is it?" she asked.

"I wouldn't organize a closet like this, but I wasn't in charge of maintenance. I mean, who could find anything in here?"

"Glad it wasn't just me."

"So." He cleared his throat. "How'd you two meet? You seem like an odd couple."

Jenna glanced at him, surprised by the personal question. In the four weeks since their arrival, she'd learned that Harvard, as Tru called him, didn't do personal. If he couldn't study it, classify it, or dissect it, he wasn't interested.

"We're *not* a couple. He stuffed me in the trunk of my own car and drove me out to the woods." She sighed. "Good times."

Chris offered a wry laugh. "I actually miss my dissertation days when my adviser was all over my ass to document, document, document. But when I was out in the field studying the big cats, I got caught up in watching them. I'd track them for days, not writing down a thing." He rubbed beneath his Lennon glasses and smiled. "Weird what we miss, isn't it?"

Feeling a certain affinity with him, she ventured further into personal territory. "So what's the story with you and Ange?"

"Nothing. She just likes animals and—"

"You think she's purty."

He almost sounded like Mason when he muttered, "Just find the damn seal."

Mild annoyance carried her through two more crates. The lamp guttered; soon they'd be down to her Maglite. Jenna worked faster.

She almost shrieked with excitement when her fingers closed over hard rubber. "Here!"

In his haste Chris tripped over a box, and she caught him by the shoulders. It might have been a moment with anyone else, but he was too focused on what she held. He examined it under the flickering camping lantern, then swore—a word that sounded wrong coming from him.

"It's too small. We need a six-inch seal. Where'd you find it?" She pointed to a box and watched as he raked through it in frantic motions. Eventually he straightened. "Jenna . . . I'm sorry."

"What're you saying?"

"We're fucked." Mason slid through the doorway. How long had he been standing there? "That's what you mean, right? The power's not coming back on."

"Not unless you can pull a six-inch seal out of your ass." Chris's expression held a surprising amount of anger. Maybe even disdain.

"I wouldn't mind seeing that," Jenna said.

She knew how Mason would feel if she took Chris's side, even if he gave no outward sign. Maybe he looked a little too long at the scientist before letting his gaze slide to her, but otherwise he was iron.

His voice held no anger. Hell, no emotion at all. "It's time we went upstairs. We have some decisions to make."

Upstairs, Tru stood guard. He looked too young to hold his rifle with such expertise, but if Jenna said anything, he'd take it as an affront to his manhood. More machismo. No wonder her eyes went to Ange, where she huddled with Penny beneath a blanket. Jenna felt better equipped to understand her own gender, even if her maternal instincts were practically nil.

Any other child would be crying, but Penny looked at the world with altered eyes. Poor Ange. A kid lacking in any regard might not survive.

Mason pulled up a chair and sat. "Here's the situation. One of the generators is down, and it's not coming back up unless we get our hands on a spare part."

"Which means no power, no heat," Tru said.

"But you can repair it, right, Chris?" Angela looked to him as if he were the Professor from *Gilligan's Island* and could make a radio out of snow, spit, and sticks.

The poor guy seemed to hate disappointing her. "If we had a spare seal."

"Which we don't," Tru guessed. "Well, I'm not sitting in the dark until I freeze to death."

"Hey, I'm not keen on becoming a corpsicle either," Jenna said.

Chris held up his hands. "Hold up, both of you."

Ange's blue gaze bounced from face to face. "What can we do?"

"They'll get in." Mason's matter-of-fact tone silenced everyone, far more chilling than if he'd been loud. "They're persistent. Frankly, I don't know how they've survived this long after the snow. Maybe they've had plenty to eat until now."

People, Jenna thought. *Plenty of other people.* She pinched her eyes shut, but she couldn't help but remember the smorgasbord the dogs had stashed in that pit. If their stores had dwindled, they would seek fresh meat. The warmth of a shelter might be nothing more than a bonus.

"But if we don't act," Mason said, "we'll freeze to death. Or they'll get in. Those are the facts."

Chris folded his arms, surprisingly calm. "What are you thinking?"

"A supply run." Mason fixed his gaze on Jenna. "Two of us head for the nearest town, about forty miles northwest of here. Two or three days, round-trip, depending on weather, monsters, and terrain. We pick up the spare parts and anything else we can use—as much as we can carry. The rest of you stay put and keep the demon dogs out."

Tru shook his head. "Like hell. I'm not babysitting these assholes. You're *not* leaving me behind."

Mason took the kid to the other side of the room. With their heads bent close together, facing away, Jenna couldn't make out what they said. Tru's body language was all protest, but then he glanced at the others. Anger yielded to resignation.

Jenna could relate. She was numb. That was the only applicable word. She should be terrified at the idea of going outside, but maybe the cold had spiked clear through her brain. Despair and acceptance warred for dominance, with neither emotion particularly strong.

"I don't like it," Chris said. "It's damn risky."

Mason focused a narrow stare on him. "You'd rather we all die because you're a pussy?"

Ange glared. "He is not. He's smart and he's being logical. I'm not setting foot out there, and I'm not leaving Penny. Really, can't we make do in here? The pioneers did."

"Ange," Jenna said quietly. "They lived in cabins insulated with moss and mud. They were equipped to use fire for heat and cooking, had adequate ventilation. They planned for lives without power."

Tru slumped against the wall. "We never should've come here."

So began an hour-long argument. They took sides and spat insults. Eventually Jenna tuned out the angry male voices. She curled up with Ange and let the invective wash over her. If she was going out at first light—and she felt pretty resigned to that possibility—then she needed sleep.

They had to try. And by dawn, shivering with cold, everyone else admitted as much.

"I want Tru at the front entrance," Mason was saying. "We'll make a straight line out the door, so I need cover fire."

Tru hoisted his rifle. "I'll take care of it."

Mason toed the front door, radiating nervous tension. "Soon as we're clear, lock up and stand guard. Sleep at your post if you have to, but don't get jumpy."

"Me? Trigger-happy?" The kid snorted. "I'm not Harvard over there."

"Don't joke about this shit."

Jenna watched Tru sober up, impressed as always.

"You won't have any relief until we get back," Mason continued. "On the third day, I need someone here at the front door to unlock the padlocks."

Though nobody thought these monsters could pick a lock, they didn't want to take chances.

Down the hall, Chris's expression drew taut, but he didn't volunteer to pick up his shotgun. "And if you don't make it?"

Mason caught Jenna's eye. "Then you'll have some shitty decisions to make."

She turned her back on all of them. She couldn't think about leaving Tru and Chris with the decision to kill Penny and Ange, because the alternative was just too disgusting. Neither did she say good-bye, in the end, because she needed to pretend she was coming back.

With Mason in the lead, she stepped out into icy hell.

TWENTY-FOUR

Mason's boots crunched over the snow. The steady pattern of freeze and thaw had formed bands of ice, topped with the newest layer of fresh powder. Running would be slippery. If they made it across the clearing, he'd consider it a goddamn miracle.

Jenna stood at his side and readied her rifle. A smile curved her lips. He'd have thought she was brain-damaged if he didn't know any better. "Is it always suicide runs with you?"

"Seems that way. Stay out of my line of fire, understand?"

"Yeah."

Mason checked his rifle, the smooth metal barrel already chilly. "If I fall, you keep going. And vice versa. That seal is the objective."

"Not each other," she said tartly. "Got it."

Her disappointment and sarcasm drilled into his mind, but he pushed it all aside. Useless. Frustrating. And at that moment, dangerous. The dogs at the other side of the compound might still be digging, but he couldn't hear them. They might break off from their task at the first sign of fresh meat. That meant they needed to be wary.

"You're pissed," he said, his eyes roving over the absolutely still clearing. "I know that, but right now I don't care."

"When do you ever?"

Mason grabbed her by the scruff of the neck, bringing their faces close. But he never took his eyes off the open stretch of hell between them and the forest—not that the woods would be much better. "Regardless of how you feel, if you shut me out right now, we'll die. I don't know how we do it, but keep your mind open. I can see my own back when you do."

She shrugged away, eyes narrowed. "You don't want to see what's in my head right now. But this is bigger than you and me."

He turned to the kid standing in the doorway to provide cover fire. "Tru, ready?"

"I was born ready." His tone said he knew it was a cliché.

Jenna primed her weapon. "Let's do this."

Mason set off at a steady rhythm, adrenaline rushing through his veins. He didn't run, but it wasn't an afternoon stroll either. Jenna's footfalls struck the icy snow at a quicker tempo. He forced himself to inhale through his nose. His lungs would be better served by warmer air from the nasal cavities, and the discipline of those unnaturally controlled breaths kept him focused.

"Anything?" she panted, just back and to the left.

"No. Keep moving."

"Not gonna stop to admire the trees."

His backpack bounced with every stride, empty except for ammo. The return trip would be harder, more encumbrance. To think otherwise, that they wouldn't make it back—unacceptable. He centered his focus on the line of trees a hundred yards off.

"Ow. Damn ice."

Mason felt it too. With every step, the hard snow broke around his ankles and scraped like it didn't want to let go. Wind howled in his ears. And this was only the beginning.

"Mason!" Tru's voice cut across the clearing. "Incoming! Heads up!"

"Keep moving," he barked at Jenna. "He has our backs."

Two shots rang out from the outpost door. Running now, Mason seemed able to view the clearing from above. Jenna hung with him, tapping and burning inside his brain. The shock troops had circled, their fangs bared and crusted with rot. Strange dancing currents of frigid air danced around their withered bodies.

He heard them. Panting like he was. Running like he was. It was too soon to stand and fight, or they'd never get away. Tru would buy them time. Draw their wrath.

Damn, Mason hated using the boy like that.

Two more blasts. Echoes ricocheted off the dense wall of trees.

John?

Run, Jenna. Almost there.

Shouts from Tru overlaid in quick-fire panic, followed by the slam of the front door.

He's safe. Thank God.

"We're on our own," he said, breathless.

No amount of discipline could keep his lungs pumping at a steady pace. The adrenaline response was too strong. Each intake felt uneven, burning his throat. He glued his eyes to the trees ahead. If he could get them there, he'd have solid wood at his back—one less side to guard— or he could clamber up and fire from the canopy. So close.

Don't look.

But Jenna did. He felt the sharp jolt of her fear. Three monsters remained, the nearest twenty yards and gaining.

Closing his mind, he hooked his thumb around the trigger. He skidded to a stop, spun, and knelt in one fluid movement. Jenna charged past. Momentum alone would carry her into the trees. With the AR-15 at his shoulder, he squeezed off two quick rounds. His aim was shitty, slugs flying wide in the wind. The beasts gained ground, with the quickest so close he could see its dilated pupils.

Instead of diving away, he held firm. Focus. He took slow aim, sighting away from dead center to where he could better judge their true forms. Then it was just target practice.

The foremost monster slid bloody and still across the icy ground.

The trailing two came up fast. They split in two directions, claws digging against the slip of ice as they cut the distance in half. No bones showed on these two. Their muscles were lean and wiry, jaundiced eyes unflinching. From behind, Jenna's rifle kicked to life. Snow sprayed at the feet of the one on the right, then again.

Mason took her cue and aimed for the one flanking left. His shot shattered its hind leg. The dog yelped and slid full tilt across the slick ground, trailing blood behind it. Another pull of the trigger and it collapsed, skull split in half.

To the right, Jenna's dog lay in a red puddle, the air around it normal and still.

Mason laid his forehead on his bent knee. The muscles of his thighs ached where, weeks earlier, that man-beast's claws had taken hold. Recovery time and little activity meant he was more winded than he preferred.

And they'd only crossed a clearing. Wabaugh was forty miles away. Then forty miles back. With how many monsters in between?

The rest of the pack would come soon, no matter how weak. So they'd leave these six corpses . . .

Five.

He counted again. His heart iced over.

"Mason!"

Gray fur pounced out of the trees, straight for him. He caught an armful of greasy fur and stringy muscles. Bared fangs sliced within inches of his face. Fetid breath stinking of death and old meat hit his nostrils. The air felt different, like fighting through mud. His limbs turned leaden, unresponsive. Only by force of will did he wedge his forearm just under the dog's chin, pushing hard against its windpipe. With his other hand he fought to keep razor claws from flaying his arms.

But the dog had momentum from that leap, and the snow undermined Mason's balance. He fell back, his head cracking against the ice. Stars spun before his eyes. Harsh panting narrowed his senses to pinpricks.

"I can't get a clear shot," Jenna shouted.

"He bites me, you kill us both!"

The others wouldn't make it if he died. He saw it. Felt it. Experiment over. Little group of humans gone—either dog food or freezer burned.

Absolute rage flipped a switch in his head. He powered his legs beneath the beast's soft middle and kicked. The snarling thing flew back, landing awkwardly on its side. Mason scrambled up and drew his nine-millimeter. Jenna's shot and his own hit the dog in two different places—shoulder and rump—sending its body twirling. Another to the head ended its life.

The clearing echoed with the last sounds of gunfire. Dazed, breathless, Mason realized he missed the sound of birds. He used to count on them raising a fuss after discharging his weapon, but now only silence remained.

Until the howling started.

Throughout the woods, like music in surround sound, the howls rose from the roots of the trees to the gray metal clouds. A primal shiver raced down his back, itching his newly healed wounds. The howls gathered and strengthened, but the whining, hair-raising harmonics held no aggression. It was a mourning song. Six warriors sprawled on the field of battle, and these soulless beasts sang.

He'd known they used to be human, but this felt different than abstract knowledge. He didn't like identifying with them. Not in the least.

At the other side of the clearing, a ragged pack of scrawny dogs crept from the trees. Their zombie expressions never altered, just slack-jawed and absent. These were not warriors. They were starving and they wouldn't last much longer. Mason doused a little flicker of hope.

"Mason?" Jenna asked tightly.

"Yeah," he said, straightening. "No more fight in this lot."

The knees of his jeans were wet, and blood seeped from a couple of shallow wounds. His head throbbed. But every inch of skin remained free from bite marks. Good enough.

He strode toward Jenna. Her face was pale except where exercise and cold had turned her cheeks into bright red beacons. Green eyes glazed with the unseeing focus of combat. Left to right, over the snow, she watched the clearing—as animal as the rest of them.

Something about her posture and the set of her expression made his heart double pump. A woman ready for anything. She'd had his back, and she was smart enough to cover her own. His pulse spiked in a way it hadn't before, not when running or doing battle. He swallowed, his mouth dry as ash.

"There were seven?" she asked.

Mason pointed back toward the research station. "Tru only bagged two."

Jenna raised a hand to her brow. Her eyes slid from one corpse to the next, counting. "So one circled to meet us here?"

"I think so. Told you they're learning."

But then she was Jenna again. The disturbing distance he'd noted in her expression faded. She lowered her weapon and cocked a fist on her hip. "You didn't tell me you were going to stop."

"Nope."

"If you had, I could've planned for it. But you don't trust me. Why is that?"

"You don't need to plan. You just need to follow my lead." He adjusted the backpack and shouldered his rifle. "Let's move."

They set off at a fast clip, putting space between themselves and the rest of the starving pack.

A few minutes later, she muttered, "God, you can be such a prick."

"I have one whenever you're ready for it."

"Bite me."

"That can be arranged too."

The woods closed around them like a curtain. Exit stage right. Underbrush laid low by autumn lurked beneath the patchy snow, snagging their feet. The canopy must've kept some precipitation from reaching the ground, because body lengths of dirt stretched dark between the trees. They might make good time if the weather stayed clear.

At least they were moving again. Their strides matched after every third step: his longer, hers quicker. Doubtless she thought he did it to be a dick. In truth, Mason set a hard pace because he knew she could keep up. He didn't tell her so because he needed the distance her anger provided. If he let himself get too close, his attention would be split. Their survival hinged on his focus.

She eased her gaze over the woods. "You think it's safe to shoulder this? My hands are freezing."

Mason shook his head. "Just stay sharp."

"Oh, sure. Hadn't thought of that."

He crunched to a stop. "What's with the attitude?"

"We lived, right? Go team."

They *had* been a team. He'd known she was at his back the whole time, reveling in a sense of partnership he'd rejected for years. And she always wanted more. She craved a real connection, but he couldn't permit the vulnerability. Already, she'd drawn too close for comfort, and he remembered exactly what it felt like to watch his team die.

He needed to prove he was in charge. Maybe it was the aftermath of surviving that violent run, coupled with the edgy knowledge that their journey stretched out like a wasteland. Or maybe the silent warning of her expression—and the need to defy it. Or hell, maybe it just *was*. An alpha struggle.

Mason reached out. The distance between them seemed too far. Blood stained his thumbnail, but that didn't stop him from wanting to touch her. Neither did the blaze of her eyes. Just before his skin met hers, she stepped away. He heard her whisper in his head but couldn't understand its origins.

I will not *wind up like my mother.*

He was left with his hand in midair, palm freezing in the wind. Just like that, he fell into the pain of her previous rejection, consumed with need for her . . . and left wanting.

"I see," he said, jaw locked. "Suit yourself, sweetheart. We have a long trip ahead."

TWENTY-FIVE

Mason turned his back as if it didn't matter what she'd wanted to say. And when had it ever? Always his timetable, his agenda.

It had been like that with her mom and dad too. Whenever Mitch had shown up, he expected his wife to drop everything, cook whatever he wanted, and spend a few days in the bedroom. Then he left her crying. Never had it mattered what she needed. It was always about his damn prophecies. In the end, they'd both died alone because Mitch hadn't been able to commit to a woman the way he could to his religion. Though Jenna had been young, she'd registered the damage.

Not me. That's never going to be me.

She glared at Mason's back. He was a damn machine. Accomplishing his objective was the only priority, no matter what the cost— to himself or to those around him. But Mitch had been that way too. His priorities hadn't included his own flesh and blood. Jenna loathed wanting someone who seemed so much like her old man, making her feel weak and helpless.

"Pick up the pace," he called over his shoulder.

Violence spiked through her, riding the tail end of the fight. No more. She refused to put up with his shit for another minute. With a low growl, she launched herself at his back. Rage gave her strength. She hit him with her full weight, slamming her rifle butt into his shoulder. He stumbled into a tree, though not as hard as she'd have liked.

Mason got his footing quickly and spun. "What the hell is your problem?"

"You." Jenna gave his chest a shove. "You're my problem."

His dark eyes narrowed. "Keep pushing me. See what happens."

"Yeah, 'cause you're such a badass."

"And you're a cock-teasing bitch."

She lashed out with her fist and clipped him hard in the mouth. In reflex, he shoved her away. Jenna staggered, knowing that if he'd punched her, she wouldn't be on her feet. Or conscious. His restraint softened her anger a little. He didn't give it back, even when she hurt him. But that awareness wasn't enough to check her frustration.

Blood trickled down his upper lip where she'd split it against his teeth. His tongue darted out to test the damage, and her fury coiled up with something else. She wanted to kiss him and savor the coppery taste—almost as much as she wanted to smash his head against the ground. She inhaled his scent.

Pupils dilated, a muscle ticked along his jaw. They stared at one another, nothing but snow and icy trees as witness. Jenna worked to calm her labored breathing.

Mason pounced. Their bodies met through layers of clothing, grappling. His hands were hard on her upper arms, then he slammed her head against his chest in a parody of an embrace. Her knee came up, but he twisted away.

Infuriated, Jenna tried again to hurt him. She lashed out with elbows and knees. He contained her with an ease that made her want to howl. Her boots slid in the snow, and he shoved her down. She tried to roll, but he dropped on top of her too fast. Pinned her. In retaliation, she stuffed snow down his back.

Mason settled between her thighs, forcing her still. With a few movements, he demonstrated his dominance and her complete vulnerability. He felt like a force of nature. Wrestling her to the ground had given him an erection, or maybe he just liked violence. He rocked against her.

I own you.

Impressions battered her in kaleidoscopic succession, flashes of rage and jealousy. He'd minded her attention to Chris more than he let on—wanted to beat the man's head against the door instead of helping him fix it. She glimpsed him lurking in the dark, watching them in the maintenance closet, felt his muscles tense when Chris cupped her shoulders. Then it all swirled away in a red haze, lust and anger and pain twined so tightly that none could gain sway.

Mason pressed down along her body, his lips against her ear. Warm breath gusted over her skin. "Not so mouthy now, are you?"

His thrusts evoked a soul-deep response that made her work her hips in answer.

Jenna growled. She tried to sink her teeth into his throat, but he forced her head still. Defeated in that, she dug her nails into the tender flesh at the nape of his neck. He responded with a fierce push. The feelings surging through her were so raw that she didn't know if she wanted to fuck him or kill him. Maybe she'd try both and see how it all worked out.

Thrashing, she lashed out with her leg. He took the opening to shift against her, avoiding her kick. It drove her wild that such a primitive display turned her on. Yet she couldn't deny the impulses clamoring in her head. She wished he didn't feel so good, hot and heavy and built to fill her up.

Their layers of clothing seemed heavy and confining. Her skin ready to combust, she wanted to strip down despite the cold. Teeth bared, she worked her hands beneath his jacket and scored his sides. He pushed harder.

"Don't fight me," he snarled. "You'll lose. Do you understand me? I *will* hurt you."

She turned her head to the side. "You already have. So many times I've lost count. Every time I reach out, you shove me away. I don't know where I stand or what you want from me."

"You're one to talk. What you did in the tower . . . and then Welsh—fuck it. This isn't the time. We're leaving a trail a mile wide here."

"When will it *ever* be the time? You'll leave it until we're mauled to death." She shook her head in weariness and defeat, letting it drop onto the snow. "Get off me. I'll be good."

But he didn't immediately comply. His heated weight contrasted with the chill at her back. Jenna shifted, her breath skipping at his expression. His harsh face held a raw hunger that he couldn't suppress. He ground his hips against her slowly, rhythmically, and she softened, stopped trying to shove him off. Her legs curled around his.

The wolves could catch up to them any minute. If they didn't return with the seal, they'd leave the others to their deaths. Struggling in the snow against one another was worse than foolhardy, and it was her fault. She knew that now, accepting responsibility for it. Part of her didn't care about the cold or the snow or the danger. She whimpered deep in her throat.

"Mason?"

"John." The word sounded torn from him. "I . . . like it when you call me John."

Then he bent his head, kissing her in a way that curled her toes inside her boots. She tasted his bloody lip and the richness of his mouth. His tongue slid against hers, hungry and desperate. From there his hot mouth trailed down her throat. He nipped and claimed. She loved the gentle-fierce bite that made her want to—

A distant howl split the quiet.

Jenna pushed at him and he gave way, letting her scramble to her feet and pick up her weapon. Her anger filtered away, leaving her beaten and tired. They needed to move. As he'd said, they had a lot of ground to cover before dark.

She set off walking, head down, without waiting to see if he would follow. Violence spent, her whole body felt overripe and tender from longing too often denied. She was afraid to look at him, unwilling to see his triumph. So easily he'd tamed her to his will. Again.

He'd set out to prove his dominance, and she'd folded. *Just like my mother.*

His graveled bass voice came from behind, raw with emotion. "I can't let you lead me around by the dick. Do you get that? I'm in charge of keeping us alive. I can't hold your hand when I need to take care of business."

"And you think holding my hand would weaken you?" Her boots crunched over unpacked snow, frosted with ice.

"What?"

Pure puzzlement. He couldn't fake it that well.

Typical man. He didn't even know when he hurt her. What scared her most—he might not even care. Jenna just wished her body didn't remember the pleasure of his weight, the way his touch made her skin sing. If things continued in this fashion, he'd be able to control her with sex. One orgasm and she'd be amenable to whatever he wanted.

"If I reach out, it's because I need you," she said quietly. "And it hurts when you give nothing back. I can only take so much of that. I . . . can't do this alone. I need someone willing to partner me all the way, give me strength when I'm failing."

"You've been messing with *me*. Look, if I don't pick up on your cues, I don't mean anything by it. I'm not used to . . . I mean, I just need my head on straight. There's too much at stake."

Nearly an apology. She let out a shaky sigh. That was more than Mitch had ever said to her mom. It showed he was sorry for not offering what she needed. And maybe she could concede their situations were not the same. They were different than her parents.

She felt compelled to respond in kind. "I'm sorry I hit you."

"I've had worse."

She'd hurt him and he'd retaliated. Nothing was healed between them. Misery permeated her every pore, layered with unspent sexual energy. Why couldn't she want Chris? He was cute. That would be easy, nice—and certainly none of these complications.

Hell of a way to start a hike.

"I'm sure you have," she said softly. "But that doesn't make it right. I shouldn't have taken stuff out on you. The truth is I've been scared so long that if I'm not mad about something, then I'd be cowering in the closet back at the station. I wouldn't have the courage for this mission if I wasn't nursing a grudge. But it's not your fault. I just wish you *respected* me as much as I do you."

There. She'd left herself wide open. He could take his best shot now, make a crack about how she was dumb as a stump and needed to do what she was told. But Mason said nothing. His dark eyes were steady and serious when he acknowledged her words with a nod.

He slid past her, taking point again. Her jacket was cold and wet, but she would never complain. After all, she'd started it.

For the longest time, she simply watched his back. It was humbling that he still trusted her there, after everything. He wore the black knit cap, covering his skull-cut hair. That was Mason, all precision and organization. If she'd just stayed in her box and stopped bothering him with emotional bullshit, they'd have had sex by now. But she didn't want sex from him—well, not *only* sex. And she didn't want a protector either. That was the problem.

She wanted to be as essential to him as he was becoming to her.

But if the situation was truly a matter of life or death, she needed to accept things as they were.

Jenna sighed and forged on. She listened for the sounds of pursuit and howls carried on the wind, but it was eerily still. Her rifle weighed heavier with each passing minute.

More ominously, she still hadn't seen any signs of life. Camping in winter was always a quiet exercise, with animals in hibernation or flying south. But the silence made her nervous. It was too complete. When she looked over her shoulder and saw their footprints in the snow, she shivered. So very alone.

"Should we be using pine needles to wipe those away or something?"

He shrugged. "They'll likely use scent to track us. Woodcraft would just slow us down."

The clouds loomed heavy and gray, eventually opening up. A feathery snow began to fall. She gazed through the dark trees as they hiked, seeking snatches of sky.

They'd been walking about four hours when Mason found a dead tree and dusted off the snow. Jenna sat down, exhausted and grateful. She didn't know how she'd finish the rest of the journey, but maybe she could run on stubbornness. He offered jerky and a drink of water.

"You burn up more fuel trying to stay warm. Eat."

Something made her brave, or maybe it was simply that she had nothing left to lose. "Does this mean you care?"

His absurdly fulsome lashes, dusted with ice, fluttered against hard-hewn cheeks. The silence drew out and she looked away. Jenna ate her jerky without any hope of a reply.

"Yeah," he said at last. "I do care."

Her heart thumped in her ears. He stared at the ground between his feet, making waffle patterns in the snow with his boots. His hands rested on either side of him, braced against the log. Without thinking, she lifted his right hand and pressed it to her cheek, completing the touch he'd offered earlier.

"As more than Mitch's daughter? More than a promise to be kept?"

He exhaled as if it hurt him. "Yeah. I don't have the words, Jenna, but . . . damn, wanting you is a knife in my gut."

It was enough—more than she'd expected, in fact. But she lacked the courage to ask for more. This would get her through the cold. Part of her said she was a sucker for gobbling up the scraps from his table, but she couldn't help it. He mattered so much.

Mason pulled her to her feet. "Break's over."

TWENTY-SIX

Jenna could have taken sandpaper to his skull and done less damage. Mason felt that scoured, inside and out. From the first touch, he'd felt the sizzling, dangerous blend of sex and violence. She'd almost blown his self-control completely. Choke her. Fuck her. Both sounded pretty damn good.

How had he come to this?

Stomping through the woods, his legs growing heavier, he pushed the nausea back in his gut. Tree limbs swung back and forward in the strengthening wind and snow, adding to his dizziness. She'd forced him to admit the most appalling truth—not physical weakness but about what he felt. Excruciating things.

Things that proved he was still human. That realization shouldn't have come as a relief, but it did.

He pulled a compass from the breast pocket of his field jacket and checked their progress. "Another two hours, if I had to guess."

Jenna trudged to a stop beside him and nodded. The skin rimming her eyes drew tight, and her lips angled downward in a near grimace.

He read her. Not her mind, but her body. Fatigue. Resignation.

"You okay?"

She fixed jewel green eyes on him. "Sure. No choice, right?"

Mason huffed a hard breath and ground his molars, but he didn't voice his frustration. He'd only just figured out that sarcasm meant she was hurting.

Give me strength when I'm failing, she'd said.

She seemed to want a friend more than a guardian, which made no sense to him. What use was a friend who couldn't protect her?

But what could it hurt? By all rights they should be dead already, and they might be before the sun set. If they didn't make it to shelter before nightfall, if they couldn't find the spare seal, if the monsters attacked again—too many possibilities. He'd been trying to ward them off, every one. By himself.

Yet she only wanted his damn hand to hold.

"Right," he said roughly.

She bowed her head, loose hair angling across her cheekbones. Her shoulders slumped. She would keep going, just as she always had—for survival's sake and for him.

"Jenna?" Gently, still terrified she'd refuse him, he curved his hand along the base of her skull. She didn't pull away. That gave him strength. "We *do* have to keep going. But I asked if you're okay be-cause . . . I want to know."

He pulled the backpack off her shoulders. A quiet sigh slipped from her lips.

"C'mon. Two minutes won't kill us." He tried to keep his tone light but failed.

"News to me."

"Me too."

A quirk of a smile. Not much, but he latched onto that encourage-ment. Still wary, he cupped her upper arms and eased her against his chest. Kneading, he massaged her neck and shoulders as a means of working out his own frustrations. Her body melted beneath his hands. She moaned, more a vibration against his sternum than a sound.

She'd relaxed, but he knew it was a conscious decision to lean her head against his chest. He accepted it like a gift. Her hair tickled his nose, washing the scent of her across his ragged, needy senses. *Yes, please.* Something other than death and defensiveness and fear-soaked adrenaline.

God, is this what she meant?

Yes. He knew it deep in his bones. Maybe it was time they both had something better to fight for.

"Tell me. No tricks. No games." Mason turned her and tipped her face up to his. Wide green eyes gazed back. Her chin trembled. He'd never seen anyone so capable look so young, so lost. "I'm asking. Are you okay?"

"*No.*"

She let him have it then, the full brunt of her fear. Weeks of mental images. Sleepless nights and days made of terrified hours. Mason almost collapsed under the weight of that pure, surging emotion, but he stood firm. He caught her in his arms and held tight. No passion now. No hostility. They simply clung to each other in an embrace that ripped open his heart.

He didn't know what to do with her tears, so he wrapped his arms even tighter around her trembling body, opening himself. Maybe he could be the comfort she needed. And holding her, absorbing her, the vise around his chest eased. Just a little.

"No, I'm not okay," she said, her words muffled in his coat. "And this . . . this just *sucks.*"

Mason chuckled. "Yeah, it does."

"It's not fair—but I can't say that, right, 'cause at least I'm not dead."

"You can say it." He glanced around the still, ethereal forest. "I won't tell."

"And I hate that it won't ever be over. You can't even tell me with a straight face that it'll be all right. Maybe not now, but someday."

"I can't tell you that, not without lying. Do you want me to?"

"About that?" She laughed shakily. "Yeah, sometimes I do."

Mason kissed her temple. "I'll bear that in mind. Anything else, while we're having confession?"

"Sometimes I hate you for saving me."

He pulled off the black cap and rubbed his head. Cool wind whipped over his skin, a quick punch to the senses—like her words. "I, uh, shit. I don't know what to say."

"You don't need a rebuttal. These are feelings, and there is no answer for them, really. They just are." She smoothed the button flap of his coat as snowflakes frosted her hair. "Your turn."

"My turn what?"

"Are you okay?"

He scraped a thumbnail against his lower lip. "No." Her narrowed gaze prompted him to go on. "My back hurts like a son of a bitch. I'm out of shape—and I'm *never* out of shape. I hate that Penny and Tru have to grow up in this world, and they're the lucky ones because they might forget what it was like before."

"You never said."

"Why would I? I got us into this. I'm the one with the training. So I'm on point all the goddamn time. Would you rather me send you into the woods for a patrol? Ange? Tru? No, so I go. And I—"

He ducked his head. His voice wasn't supposed to crack. What the hell had she done to him? But the grinding pressure eased another notch. He could take a deep, shuddering breath without the crushing pain of responsibility that never let him rest.

"And I hate when you goad me with Welsh." He'd never begged for anything in his life, but he felt himself silently pleading with her. "*Hate* it."

Jenna's hand feathered over his brow, down along his cheek. "I won't do it again. I promise."

A shiver climbed his spine. He didn't hear a thing, but something deeper than his five senses said they needed to move. Quickly.

"Damn it." He grabbed Jenna's gear and shoved it at her. "See? Talking about feelings marks us for puppy chow. You don't want that, do you, Barclay?"

She shouldered the pack and offered a mock salute. "No, sir. Pressing on, sir."

Mason grabbed her hand and tugged. They hit their stride together. His lungs and heart and muscles pumped hard, even as he fell into that deep place where he prepared for battle.

"Hey," she said. "You're crushing my hand."

He looked down. He hadn't let go of her. "Yeah, you'd complain about that now."

The ground sped beneath their feet. Making their stand in the woods wouldn't be as effective as somewhere fortified. A town. A single building would be better. They could hunker down again, like back in the cabin.

A surge of guilt closed his throat. He swallowed. But he had to say it. "You know, we don't need to go back."

Jenna stumbled. "You mean leave them to die?"

"We'd survive. We'd keep going at least."

"What, like perpetuate the species?"

"If that's what you want to call it."

"You assume I'd stay if you cut and run. Let alone anything close to . . . perpetuating."

"You wouldn't?"

"You know I wouldn't," she said tightly, her breath puffing. "Not after all the time we've spent with them." She yanked their intertwined fingers up. "I don't know what this is, but it's not enough for me to let my friends die."

Mine too.

"What was that, John?" Her sugary voice shot up his backbone.

"I said, they're my friends too."

She shook her head, half laughing. "You have a sick way of show-ing it."

"Well, when Tru comes to me to clean his cuts, I don't like to brag up those moments." He shouldn't get off on surprising her, but some-times it was just too sweet to resist.

"You," she started. "You help him?"

"Try to." He didn't like to talk about Tru, or think about him. It was like staring into a mirror, a sad history he couldn't let happen again.

"And you'd leave him, never go back?"

He pulled the compass from his pocket again and made a slight adjustment to their trajectory. The sun sat low on the horizon. Soon darkness would slow their progress, maybe hinder it entirely. The snow would continue to fall. And the beasts hunted at night.

But if he'd navigated correctly, they would be coming up on Wabaugh any minute. Irrationally, he imagined they should be able to see lights soon. Welcoming lights.

Not a chance.

"It was just an idea," he said, taking her hand again. "One that never even occurred to you."

"Does that make me a weakling, then? No survival-of-the-fittest award this year."

"Nah, you already proved that when you opened the cabin door in the first place."

"You still hold that against me?" Her voice hardened.

He stopped. She reeled back toward him, their hands still linked. He let go of her, but not for the reason she probably thought.

"No." Mason bracketed her face between his palms. "I *admire* you for it. All of it. The way you fought me for them. How you've kept them sane and halfway normal. And how going back isn't even a choice for you. You just will."

"You too."

A heavy sigh ripped out of his body. He was exhausted in every possible way. "You don't believe that."

She dropped her eyes. He ought to be fine with her doubt, but it cut deep.

"I've needed you all along, and now you know why," he said. "I know how to fight, but that's not the same as building. That's what *you* do. Don't give up on me."

Please.

The forest snarled around them.

She jumped. "Did you . . . ?"

"Shh." No matter how fast his gaze moved through the trees, he never banished the shadows. Always something hiding, waiting. Watching. The hair on his nape prickled.

Jenna?

Yeah?

Run.

TWENTY-SEVEN

Jenna ran as if her life depended on it. From the growls closing in on them, it did.

Tree branches lashed her face as Mason tugged her along. Earlier, they'd stuck to what seemed like a rough path, one that a hunter might follow. Now he pulled her straight through the underbrush, due west. His urgency caught fire in her veins.

Low on energy, nightfall threatening—they couldn't stand and fight. Sheer numbers would overwhelm them. In the distance the beasts howled again. She could almost make out the message: *Come! We found prey.*

Determined to keep up, Jenna lengthened her strides. Footfalls thundered over dead wood that had collected during recent storms. She stumbled, caught herself on her hands, and scrambled onward. Mason paused long enough to reach out, towing her along. He was breathing just as hard, some combination of exhaustion, fear, and cold.

Shock exploded through her when they broke from the trees and fell down a slope. Mason steered himself into a half slide, but Jenna went headlong, careening in the snow. He jerked her upright, gave her a quick once-over. He didn't waste breath on talk, and she understood why. They hadn't lost the pack; the beasts were gaining on them.

Jenna glimpsed buildings in the distance. Twilight and lengthening shadows made it difficult to gauge how far. She gathered a last burst of vigor and propelled into motion, ignoring aches and pains and parts that had long ago gone numb.

They ran a hundred yards before she noticed the ground felt different with each thud of her feet. Beneath the snow lay a road. Pavement, where cars drove—or at least where they used to. Nothing had been plowed this season.

The howling gained a strident note. *Hurry, they're getting away.*

"Damn right we are," she muttered.

"Jenna?" He glanced over as they sprinted full out for the buildings.

"Don't worry about me."

There were no signs of life. No smoke from chimneys. No lights brightening this endless winter night. They dashed past a blue sign, half obscured by frost:—LCOME TO WABAUGH, WHERE IT ALWAYS FEELS LIKE HOME.

Yeah, if home were a ghost town, and you liked being hunted.

Just past that marker sat a derelict car, covered in a foot of snow. By the raw, sick feeling in her stomach, she knew she didn't want to wipe the window clear.

The first house they came to was a simple white colonial. Jenna slowed. "Maybe we should duck in here? It might be smart to take shelter and find the store in the morning."

Mason paused and swiped his palm across the window. Jenna kept an eye on the road. The howls grew fainter, as if the monsters preferred not to roam too far out of their own territory. *Good.*

"Not this house," Mason said.

If she hadn't been so attuned to his voice, she would have missed the faint tremor.

Jenna spun, wanting to see for herself. This was her chance to find out firsthand what their world had become. Sure, Mason had told her. And she'd heard it from Ange and the others. There had been intermittent reports about the east, and Mitch had been prognosticating doomsday for as long as she could remember. But she'd only seen the demon dogs and . . . Edna. But maybe more proof could help her understand the way the magic worked.

Mason tried to shield her face against his shoulder, but she struggled free, raising up on tiptoe to peer through the pane. Her whole body lurched in revulsion so powerful it couldn't rightly be called a gag reflex. The monster on the living-room floor had a wolf's muzzle, but human eyes stretched open in agony. Its body had twisted into bestial lines, powerful haunches ending in sneaker-covered feet. This thing wouldn't have been able to run on four legs or walk on two. Hideous . . . and unspeakably wrong.

"Ah Jesus," she whispered. "Kind of like Edna."

Mason nodded. "Failed change. Their bodies must not have been strong enough. They die of shock. If someone gets bit but isn't eaten . . . It's like they're tainted by the dark magic." He shrugged. "I don't have all the answers. But there seems to be an epicenter, where the exposure began. Some say as far away as the Ukraine."

She laughed bitterly. "Like a toxic leak? Magic ground zero."

"I'm guessing. But it was unbelievably fucked up in Connecticut. Less so on the Plains."

"You really came all that way, just to save me." Incredulity melted into a feeling brighter and stronger, like Sarah Connor must have felt when she learned Kyle went back in time for her.

"I really did. And I'm fucking glad, not just because I promised Mitch. He taught me so much. You know he used to give lectures? My favorite was when he went on about blood magic. Said it was the strongest kind, that it could be used to cure or curse. Just depended on the hand of the wielder."

"He said a lot of things," she muttered.

Mason jerked his head toward the monstrous corpse on the other side of the window. "Anyway, I suspect we'll see more like that poor bastard before we get out of here. So we should move on."

God help her, but he was right. They passed more frozen corpses in the snow as they walked, all locked in that twisted rictus. Some looked like they'd been trying to turn into big cats, bears, insects. A few were even more alien, unfinished reptilian forms. Their faces had locked in indescribable agony. She wondered why they'd left their dead in the street. Had people evacuated?

Or maybe nobody got out. Maybe there was nobody left to bury the dead.

Mason might have been right. No one had been prepared for a disaster that the government refused to acknowledge. The lawmakers and the military had believed that if they ignored the problem in the east, the chaos wouldn't touch them. Citizens west of the Mississippi had simply gone about their business, unmolested.

Wabaugh, then, presented the hideous results of isolationism as viable policy.

"Do you think there's anyone left?" she asked softly.

Mason shrugged. "Don't know. But I'm not going door-to-door, looking for survivors, if that's what you had in mind."

"No," she said quietly. "I know too much about surviving in this world now to want to take on more dependents."

Their steps flagged as they trudged through town. Under any other circumstances, the walk might have been peaceful, almost idyllic, with unspoiled snow falling lightly on the old-fashioned brick buildings. Wabaugh was the kind of place where people decorated the pine trees in their front yards, strung lights for each other, and sang carols over steaming mugs of cider. Not this year. And never again.

Thankfully, it wasn't a large town. They slogged through the downtown to a brand-new shopping complex on the northern outskirts, anchored by a big-box home improvement store. The cracked orange and white sign beckoned her onward. Smaller shops had once done business at either side: a hair salon, a drugstore, a Chinese takeout place, a shoe store, and a dry cleaners. Across the parking lot, snowy cars hunched like oversized gravestones.

"We made it," she breathed.

Mason squeezed her hand, wearing a funny little smile. "So we did. Let's get inside and warm up."

Though she'd swear she had no reserves left after the shock and horror of the last hour, Jenna broke into a run. This time Mason was hard put to keep up with her. Double doors that read ENTRANCE promised safe haven and untold luxuries. She gave the doors an experimental push. They opened, which meant the place had been unlocked the whole time. That didn't bode well for what they'd find inside.

Tension coiled through her. "You ready?"

"Yeah." He flipped off his rifle's safety. "We'll secure the place first."

Creeping through the store in a state of extreme readiness, they found a few more bodies. Some of the employees seemed to have chewed each other up in a mad fit. They'd started decomposing, but freezing temps kept the stench at bay. Mason grimly piled them onto tarps, rolled them up with twine, and pushed them out the back. Then they went around locking all the doors.

"Let's find that seal," he said at last.

"Now?" She hated the complaint in her voice, but she was so tired.

"If it's not here, we have to try elsewhere. There's another town a few miles north." He paused and looked back at her. "I need to know we've accomplished our mission, okay?"

Jenna nodded, realizing his motivations made sense to her at last. They were finally on the same wavelength. This was just how he worked.

The place was dark and gloomy, giving Jenna a serious case of the creeps. When they found the aisle filled with plumbing supplies, Mason ransacked the seals and tubes. He found three types that looked possible, then compared them to the broken one he'd stowed in his pack.

"Good," he said, finding the match. The tension across his shoulders eased. "Now for us."

Jenna refused to let him out of her sight, so she followed while he collected supplies. She'd never been in a store when it was totally dark and deserted. Grills and garbage cans were equally ominous.

Trying to be helpful, she grabbed a cart. He filled it with batteries, flashlights, cushions, an area rug, and other oddments. She added the ubiquitous candy bars, bags of chips, and salted peanuts from near the checkout aisle. Then she hauled a few sodas from the lifeless refrigerator case. The ambient temperature was such that they held a chill, even without a working fridge.

By the time Mason led her to the garden section, she feared she might fall down. Her teeth chattered from cold and shock. He unzipped the screen of a fabric and mesh gazebo, making them a shelter. After shaking out the area rug, he stripped the pads off several lounge patio chairs to make a mattress. He scattered the bed with cushions, then fit batteries in the lanterns and arranged them in a circle inside. The light helped dispel some of the shadows.

"I wish we could bed down in the employee locker rooms, but then the choice would be security versus freezing to death. There wouldn't be enough ventilation for a fire. As it is, we're going to need to be careful."

"Or else it's beddie-bye for good, huh?"

"That's right," he said quietly. "I'm going to go get a grill. And some charcoal."

"Okay." Her voice sounded small.

He hesitated and then added, "Come with me?"

Thank you.

After collecting the supplies, he got the fire going within a few minutes. The coals burned a merry orange. Mason stationed the grill by the zipper and his guns by the bed.

It was the best they could do. To Jenna, it seemed downright luxurious.

She fell onto the makeshift mattress fully dressed, aching in every muscle, and she couldn't seem to get warm. Mason lay down beside her and pulled a rug over the top of them, soft side down. Jenna chafed her hands together, unable to relax. Though her body was exhausted, her mind couldn't stop its panicky fits and starts.

He found her in the half-light, brushed his fingers against hers. "God, you're freezing. You know what would help?"

"What?"

"Body heat."

"Lame."

"It's true," he said, half grinning. "Take your clothes off."

Her whole body came to life at his words. Eagerly, Jenna stripped out of her jacket and shirt. Her boots came off next, then her socks. Mason helped her with her jeans and threw everything outside their little nest.

Arousal hit her in waves. "You too. You need to warm up too."

It was unexpectedly erotic, stripping him by touch in the dimly lit enclosure. She slid her palms over his bare chest, sharing heat. But she didn't stop there. Slowly, teasingly, she worked his boxers down until her fingers brushed the tight curve of his ass. After all that fight and fear, this was easy.

A shudder rolled through him. "*Jenna.*"

She walked her fingertips downward. "Yeah?"

"Don't. I'm on the edge here."

Desire trickled through her like honey, eclipsing everything else. The world could go to hell for all she cared. Right then they were safe, and a chance like this might never come again.

"Remember that cock you were teasing me about earlier? I want it." In case that wasn't clear enough, she cupped his hard length and stroked.

"Fuck," he snarled, forcing her head back.

"Yeah. Finally."

He rolled onto her and tore down her panties in one motion. His hands were clumsy, shaking with desire. Jenna bucked. She opened up her mind and flooded him with raw need. *No foreplay. Just do it.*

His whole body jerked. He came up on his elbows, his pelvis pressing against hers. She tilted her hips and he slammed inside. No tenderness. No finesse. His cock filled her, stretched her, and then there was no stopping him, no pacing, just the rough, endless push–pull of his body grinding deeper. Shaking, Mason curled his hands into fists at either side of her head. She worked against him in fierce undulations. His throat clenched, strangling on primal sounds. In the half-light, his eyes gleamed feral.

No words now. Their bodies spoke for them, all liquid sighs and hot pounding thrusts. A groan tore from him. He grabbed her hips, lifting her up to meet his hard, fierce strokes. With a low growl, he pulled her thighs farther apart, pushed them upward. She'd have bruises in the morning, and she didn't care.

Lightning spiraled through her and flared across every nerve. He plunged in. Her nails raked his back as she arched and came.

Mason's movements became shallow and quick. He bowed beneath her hands, surging into her again and again. The heat of his jerking orgasm amplified the aftershocks sparkling through her belly.

Panting, he rolled his hips, circling them with the last shimmers of pleasure.

Visibly shaken, he collapsed on her. Within seconds he seemed to think better of that and tried to roll away. She tightened her hold and pulled him close.

"No," she whispered. "Stay."

TWENTY-EIGHT

The walkie-talkie on Mason's hip crackled to life. He'd left its mate on his pillow, right where Jenna would find it.

"John?"

He held down the receiver. "I'm here."

"Where's here?" She sounded groggy and a little disappointed not to have him next to her.

"The electrical aisle." He leaned the list closer to the Coleman lantern he'd set on a shelf, but the light didn't help him understand the doc's chicken scratch any better. "Welsh gave me a list of supplies we might need. So I'm shopping."

"Couldn't sleep?"

Leaning his forehead against the shelf, he shut his eyes. Damn, she knew him.

He could see her there in the little nest he'd made, his primitive gift. She was naked. Her hair lay in tangles. A bruise tinted the skin along her collarbone—from the loving or the fighting? Maybe both. Turning onto her stomach, she stretched long, lean legs beneath that ugly rug. He was struck with the idea of licking the indent behind her knee, before traveling up to nibble the perfect ass he'd dreamed about.

The vision hit him with such power that he could taste her on his tongue, his mouth watering.

You can if you want.

"Quit it," he said, half smiling. "You'll make my walkie-talkies seem obsolete."

"We should grab more for the others. And batteries."

"On it. We should also hit that drugstore across the way before we head back. That kind of stuff will be irreplaceable soon. But the return trip will be a bitch."

"We'll manage."

They spoke more about practicalities, but her invitation hovered in his mind. That she wanted him again set off tiny explosions in his bloodstream.

"I found a turkey-frying thing and filled it with water," he said. The pipes had burst, so he'd chipped away at a block of ice in the store's restroom sink. "It's heating on the grill for you, if you want to wash up."

"You clean already?"

"Yeah."

"Good."

His handset went dead.

Mason exhaled slowly and grabbed the fuses they needed. Two stops later, his cart holding a hodgepodge of goods, he used a pencil nub to cross the last item off the list. He only hoped Welsh had remembered everything vital. They wouldn't make a return trip anytime soon.

Exhausted yet wired, needing a moment to breathe before returning to Jenna, he slid to the concrete floor next to a photo display of fresh, fluffy carpeting in a large living room replete with sunshine. The high-res scene looked like Disneyland. It hadn't been that long since the change, but he couldn't imagine people aspiring to such a dream anymore, all bright windows and gleaming countertops.

Carpeting. Blinds. Exotic hardwoods. Who'd need them anymore? Folks out there lucky enough to be alive would be content with a dry cave.

Forearms draped across his knees, he let his body go quiet and his eyes sag to half-mast. His mind drifted and found Jenna. He always did, across a path of magic and mystery that didn't hold up to logical scrutiny. But who needed logic when he could see her like this? She was standing naked in front of the grill, framed by the entry to the enclosed gazebo. The russet embers cast her skin in a warm glow. She picked up one of the expensive chamois curtains he'd cut into strips for washing, then slid the material against her neck, reveling in the softness. He felt more than saw her shiver.

His cock went rigid. Tight muscles bunched and ached. But he didn't move. Watching her this way—voyeuristic, almost a daydream—seemed safer. He'd been so brutal. They both had, the most vicious way a couple could fuck. A huge part of him didn't trust that he'd be any different if they tried again. Taking still came easier than asking, even after all they'd shared.

But that was just an excuse. He was being a coward. He needed something more from her, the bit of the tenderness she'd offered with her mind—there in the tower. She'd touched him, eased him, shown him how it could be. Just before dropping him cold.

He swallowed hard. No, he didn't trust himself or Jenna. Not fully. So he watched from afar.

She wet the cloth and rubbed hand soap from an industrial-sized refill jug until it lathered. She scrubbed it over her arms and shoulders, beneath her arms, then started down her chest. Collarbone. Breasts. Flat, smooth stomach. Her nipples puckered in the cold. Mason moaned. She bent at the waist and worked from the feet up. Her breasts swayed gently as she worked, and he wanted to cup them, massage them. Instead he rubbed a hand along his cock where it strained against the fly of his jeans.

The walkie-talkie crackled. "You're an idiot."

Eyes still closed, he picked up the handset. "I like watching you."

"Do it in person."

Need and instinct overpowered whatever pride he had left. He made a beeline back to the garden section. Upon reaching the gazebo, everything was as he'd pictured, except now her hair was dripping wet and clean. She shoved a hank of it out of her eyes, then wrapped a length of chamois around her head like a turban. Arms raised, her naked breasts stretched high. Dizziness swept the strength from Mason's muscles, leaving him weak and trembling.

Too much.

We're just getting started.

He closed the distance between them. His feet, if they were still attached to his body, had gone numb. Jenna dipped the cloth in the water and wrung it out, then shot him a look he couldn't understand. But it scorched him.

"I missed a spot." She held out the fabric, water dripping quietly onto the floor.

Mason took it, not surprised to see his hand shaking. His naked chest brushed hers. Their fingers intertwined at their sides, bodies flirting. He inhaled sharply. Jenna simply . . . purred.

"Where?"

She nudged his hand toward the heat between her legs. "Here."

Air sizzled in his lungs. But he was determined to take back a scrap of the control she'd stolen. If she wanted his touch, she'd get it. And more.

Mason knelt. Tight curls hid her softness, but he explored. She tipped her head back, moaning as he used the cloth to clean and stroke. Jenna's fingers latched onto his shoulders. She dug her nails into his skin, sending dark fissures of pleasure deeper, deeper still. He kissed her upper thigh where bruises dotted her flesh, then spread his fingers across each one, finding them a perfect match.

He'd marked her.

"Nothing I didn't want you to do," she whispered.

"Witch."

She made some noise of agreement in her throat, one that turned breathy when he replaced the cloth with his mouth.

Her groan tore a hole in his control, but Mason forced calm, even breaths. He wrapped one arm around her backside, kneading her ass. With the other, he eased two fingers inside her slick pussy. She clenched around him. The clean scent of her sank into his brain. Her taste washed over his tongue as he darted it between her folds, slipping over her clit with a sure, quickening rhythm.

"John," she gasped.

The climax built beneath her skin, rising with the shivers of reaction even while she held completely still. He could have stayed there all night, suckling and nipping, but he pulled away. She moaned. Eyes dusky with passion tipped down toward him.

He didn't break eye contact as he leaned nearer and pressed his mouth against the soft skin of her upper thigh. Baring his teeth, he bit gently. Her breasts rose around a quick inhale. Her mouth opened. And her flesh gave way beneath the pressure he slowly increased. Biting. Testing them both.

When at last she squirmed in his arms, he released her. He kissed the crescent of teeth marks. "Mine," he whispered against her skin.

She shuddered. "Yes."

Mason caught her in his arms and swept her back into the gazebo. After laying her on their makeshift bed, he shucked his pants and resumed his place between her legs. This time he didn't stop. He licked and tasted until her breath came in ragged bursts. Her hands fisted at the back of his head, holding him there. He pushed his fingers inside as the orgasm tightened her muscles.

Her satisfaction dripped into his mind like warm molasses, easing the fierce ache of his own body. He kissed the skin just below her bellybutton and waited for her to come back to him.

She did with a laugh and a deep sigh. "Jesus."

Moments later, she ran a tentative hand along his lower ribs before trailing down to his naked hip. "I'd like to return the favor, John. Tell me what you want."

"A BJ would be nice, but I'm not picky."

She leaned closer. Her breasts brushed against his upper arm. "You're holding out on me. Why?"

His mind flashed to the moment she'd cut him deepest, drawing him in before slapping him down. Jenna followed him there, and understanding shimmered between them.

"I . . . I—" He cleared his throat. "I can't do that again."

"I left you wanting."

"Yes."

"And that hurt."

"God, yes."

"You're hurting. I get it now, John. You're trying. Really trying. I know that."

She was killing him by inches. He sensed what she needed—even now, asking him to reveal his own desires—but he couldn't form the words.

"I felt your teeth on my skin and I trusted you," she said. "Trust me now."

Jenna waited, her fingers feathering against his straining, twitching cock. So he let go. He let the truth fill his thoughts first. Then he voiced them.

"I want you to touch me. Kiss me." He cupped her face. "You showed me that, remember? How it could be."

She nodded, eyes luminous. Kneeling, she tugged him around until he sat cross-legged, his back bowed. She moved behind him and smoothed her hands over his skin, over each painful ridge of scar tissue that marred his back. Nothing remained but Jenna.

Warm lips and damp hair followed in the wake of her hands. She eased those old wounds with gentle kisses, again and again, until the pain was a memory—a dark, twisted memory that she wouldn't ever let return. He read her vow in the aching caresses.

Shuddering, he called to her. Maybe with words. Maybe with his body or his mind. But she came to him, made of fluid grace. She settled onto his lap, enveloping him with a fire that burned and cleansed and set him free. Where before Mason had hammered inside her, frantic, she now set the pace, easing up and over. So slowly. He caught her nipple in his mouth and sucked, all languid tenderness. Her moan flayed his defenses and stripped him to the bone.

She arched, crying out. Even then, finding release again, she dragged out each sensation, grinding her pelvis, pulling his head to her breast.

Mason wrapped his arms around her and held on with the fervency of a dying man—just one more breath, one more moment. One more thrust. But he couldn't hold back. He surrendered to her. He bucked beneath a fierce, hot orgasm.

"Jenna," he groaned. And when he licked his lips, he tasted the salt of his own tears.

TWENTY-NINE

It seemed wrong to be so happy.

God only knew what was happening back at the station, but Jenna couldn't make herself worry. Not now. Time belonged to her and Mason. This day, ostensibly devoted to resting up for the long hike back, couldn't be touched by outside forces.

After they'd made love—and there was no other term for it—he held her. Jenna lay back in his arms, head tucked beneath his chin. She never would have believed him capable of such tenderness, but his hands sifted through her hair with idle delicacy. His heart thumped in a steady, reassuring rhythm, keeping time with hers.

She smiled, shifting to glance at his face softened by the sepia gloom. Even with the ring of flashlights, it wasn't bright in the closed-off gazebo. The sun was up, but they were too far from the windows. Just as well. She didn't want anything to do with the horrors outside.

"I love your voice," she murmured, dreamy. Drifting.

He stirred against her. "That so?"

"Even when you're telling me what to do, it's sexy. Gravelly. I could come just listening to you."

"Huh."

"Plan on putting that to the test?"

Mason touched his mouth to her ear and growled, "I might."

A shiver worked through her. "Had a lot of practice talking dirty, have you?"

But her question gave her a fierce, unwelcome twinge. For the first time, she understood how he must have felt when she paid attention to Chris. The idea of Mason touching anyone else made her want to curl her hands into claws and do some damage.

Mine.

He'd voiced it, but she felt it too.

"No," he said simply.

Jenna tried not to display visible pleasure. Listing a roster of past lovers was useless. Most must be dead by now. He laughed softly, as if he'd glimpsed her feeling. In comfort or reassurance, he stroked the curve of her waist. She felt her own skin when he touched her, strange as that sounded.

Satiny. God, she's soft. Can do this anytime I want—

Her breath hitched. His unspoken wonder did crazy things to her insides.

She'd never spent so much time naked. They hadn't brought spare clothing, instead saving room in their backpacks for extra supplies, so she'd washed their things in the bathroom sink while Mason rigged a laundry line between the aisles. Until those dried, they had only rugs, curtains, and bare skin. Not that she was complaining.

Tilting to the side without leaving his arms, she snagged a candy bar. She unwrapped it and offered him a square of chocolate. A little shimmer of pleasure overtook her at the feel of his mouth on her fingertips. In that moment, humbled and happy, she knew she'd do anything for him. Anything.

Mason broke off a piece. Her eyes slid half closed as he placed it on her tongue. She nibbled his finger along with the chocolate. His arms tightened, but she felt like drawing out the moments before he'd enter her again.

"So tell me, John Mason, what did you want to be when you grew up?" It was a silly question, but she wanted to know—wanted to know *him*.

"A fireman."

So he'd always wanted to be a hero.

Not a hero, came his silent response. *Just valued.*

"So how come you didn't make it happen?" She knew his determination, and she couldn't imagine him giving up on anything he truly set his mind to.

"I grew up."

His tone made her wary, and she didn't want to ruin the moment by poking around in painful places. Today was about pleasure, not past trauma or future threats. Just them. Together.

"Yeah." Jenna brushed a kiss against the curve of his elbow, where he held her. "People have a tendency to do that."

He laughed softly, a real honest-to-God laugh. She closed her eyes and shivered with delight.

"What about you?"

"Normal," she said. "I just wanted to be . . . normal."

"I can never give you that."

Wrapping her arms around him, she held on tight. "You give me something better."

By the way he tensed against her, she guessed he didn't believe her—that he thought she was being kind. So she opened to him and showed him the truth of it. However sad these stolen moments might seem, she'd never known such pure, unfettered joy.

"Jenna," he whispered, and rubbed his rough jaw against her cheek.

In sweet silence, they fed each other the rest of the chocolate bar.

Not an ideal diet, but they could survive on chips and candy and stale peanuts until they got back to the station. Jenna thought maybe she could survive on him.

They talked of little things until late in the day, and then she nestled into him, drifting toward sleep. In the early hours of dawn, she awoke with her bottom tucked against his pelvis. She didn't know if he was fully awake—or just his cock—so she gave a little wriggle.

"Mmm." His big, calloused hand cradled her hip. "Morning."

"It's not quite light yet," she said, arching to him.

He slipped his other arm beneath her, and his palm came up to smooth her breast. Fingertips dusted across her nipples, drawing them from sleepy soft to tight and eager. "Any ideas how we should pass the time before we pack up?"

"I have a few."

Jenna rolled in his arms. This would be her gift to him—pleasure he didn't ask for, and no worry that she'd withhold it. Not again. Not for either of them. He was more relaxed than she'd ever seen, his hard face set in gentle lines. Although she slipped on top of him, she didn't want him to get the wrong idea. Instead she settled on his belly. He had to feel her heat against his skin as she kissed him, softly, tenderly, playing with his lips. That heat drew her, teased her, as she traced his mouth with her tongue.

His hands framed her head, trying to deepen the kiss, but she pulled back. Puzzlement flashed into his eyes, followed by fear. His whole body locked.

"This is for you," she whispered. "Not stopping. Just changing course."

He eased with a quiet sigh. Jenna nuzzled a path to his jaw, then farther down, using her teeth to nibble the column of his throat.

Touch, taste, breathe. She shaped his chest with her fingertips and nuzzled from shoulder to pectoral. She sealed an openmouthed kiss against his nipple, which perked beneath her tongue. He made a soft sound and sank his fingers into her hair, not controlling. Just caressing. She rubbed her mouth over his ribs.

Good.

More.

Their thoughts mingled, a give-and-take of rising desire. His longing swelled through her, guiding her motions, and she licked each line on his abdomen, tracing the muscle groups with her tongue. A shudder rolled across his body with the power of distant thunder. He knew where she was going, and he wanted it.

Jenna didn't make him ask, not for anything. She settled between his thighs and curled her hand around his erection, steadying it for her mouth. Realizing this was the first time she'd held his cock, she spent a moment admiring his hard, powerful size. Breath coming in rasps, Mason watched with lambent eyes. He lifted his hips in a helpless little movement.

God, she loved having such a dominant man laid out for her pleasure, rapt and utterly focused on her. She dipped her head, touched her tongue to the tip.

"Jesus, Jenna." The hands in her hair tangled, demanding more.

But he didn't need to push. Artistry dissolved in a wave of hunger. She wanted him. More of him. *More.* His cock slid smoothly between her lips. She licked, swirling her tongue in a wide, delicious pattern. At first he seemed afraid to move, as if she might stop.

He tasted luscious, felt even better—smooth skin over iron flesh. Jenna rocked faster, both hands on his hips. He found his rhythm after a few jerky lunges, working her mouth in tandem to his fierce breathing. With wild but reverent hands, he kneaded her nape and shoulders, sending sharp pleasure shocks down her spine. Her hips moved in cadence with his, feeling those phantom thrusts.

Mason arched, his body going rigid. She thought he might tear away, but he held her there, letting her take each hot burst into her mouth. Jenna gentled, knowing where to lick, where to press and heighten his sensation as he came down.

He heaved a shuddering breath. "Everything is better with you. *Everything*."

She licked her lips and tried not to seem too smug. "Took you long enough to figure that out."

With a little snarl, he dragged her up his body and positioned her pelvis over his face. With single-minded concentration, he worked with fingers and lips and teeth until she sobbed his name.

Dawn stole toward them, marking the end of their interlude. She didn't want to go, but duty called. Neither spoke as they gathered their supplies, including as many red employee aprons as they could stuff into their packs and wear beneath their coats. The fabric would come in handy.

Jenna's backpack was damn heavy. It would be rough going in the snow. She straightened her shoulders, getting her mind ready for the challenge.

"I hate to leave here," she said as they stood at the door.

"I know what you mean." Mason smiled and brushed a kiss against her mouth. She tasted a delicious echo of herself and wanted to drag him back to their cozy nest. She'd never get enough of him.

"Fond memories of a home improvement store. Who knew?"

"Come on, sweetheart." This time the endearment rolled over her like a sunny day, all sweet warmth. "Sooner home, sooner we get—" He broke off and dropped his eyes.

Home. Oh God. Yes.

But for Jenna, it was a person, not a place. It was Mason. If he took her to a yurt in the Arctic Circle, then *that* would be home.

They spared a last glance for the abandoned store and then un-locked the doors. Stepping out into the cold kicked her like a boot in the face. Snow crunched and wind sliced in sharp bursts. After ransacking the drugstore across the parking lot, adding to the burdens on their backs, Mason plotted their course back. He watched for trouble, always, though nothing but frozen bodies lined the street. They made good time on the iced-over road and soon returned to the woods.

Mason set a brisk pace, but Jenna had no trouble keeping up. Energy coursed through her. She felt reborn, like a butterfly that had slipped free of its chrysalis. Forty miles was nothing. Hell, maybe she'd run. That might be chocolate-for-breakfast talking, but she felt almost cheerful about the walk. At least she'd be with him.

John.

"I can feel you thinking about me."

"Is that bad?"

His voice rumbled low. "No. It's . . . good."

They walked on. The sky had dawned a bright blue overhead, no snow threatening. Not even the winter-bleak trees seemed morbid today. Ice hung like crystal ornaments from their long, graceful limbs, sending a symphony of shards tinkling to earth anytime the wind asked for a dance. If joy were a color that could show upon the skin, she would glow with it. Jenna watched his back and remembered what it was like to run her mouth against his skin, giving solace where there had only been scars.

Deep in daydreams, she didn't hear anything until the beast leaped from the underbrush and sank its teeth into her thigh.

THIRTY

Rage gave Mason more strength than he'd ever known. He landed astride the monster and grabbed its muzzle, yanking up and back. But its teeth clamped fast, jaw locked. Jenna screamed. Her hands pushed at the scrawny, mangy chest.

"Close your eyes!"

She obeyed, wrapping her forearms around her face and twisting away. Mason pinned the demon dog with his knees, then slid his hand back until he found its eye sockets. Two wet squishes gave way beneath his fingers. The creature howled. As soon as its teeth cleared Jenna's flesh, he hauled it off her body and flipped it into the snow. Four bony legs kicked toward the sky. Then Mason blew its brains out with his nine-millimeter.

The shot echoed, faded, until only their breathing remained. He wiped his hands on his jeans and tugged on Jenna's arm. *Get up.* No stopping. Not now. More would come.

"I can't."

"Sweetheart, c'mon." He wouldn't look at her leg. If he didn't look, he wouldn't see the bite.

"John, I mean it. I can't . . . *Stop* it!"

She pulled back until he dropped beside her on the snowy ground. There before his eyes was the torn and bleeding flesh of her upper thigh. Puncture wounds. The mark of death. Nausea ripped a hole in his gut. He choked it down.

They said nothing aloud, but their emotions collided in the center of his brain. She wept; he raged. Pain split his skull, a combination of grief and the anguish Jenna projected. They'd been so close for days, entirely open to each other. Now all her agony and fear became his, defining him, branding him. He pressed his palms on either side of his head and squeezed.

To save his own sanity, he closed his mind.

When he opened his eyes, he could finally sort sound from thought. She wept silently. Tears streaked her face, and hair stuck to her cheeks. Blood stained her right leg from knee to hip, her jeans ripped to strips of cloth.

"Jenna," he said firmly. "Move it. Now."

He stood and yanked the pack off her shoulders. After loosening the straps as slack as possible, he piled it on top of his own. The bulk settled heavily across his back. Next he hoisted Jenna upright and helped her balance on her good leg.

"Keep weight off it. Here, hold under the pack, around my waist. We have to go."

She tried to protest, the words kicking against his brain. And he refused to hear it—literally shut her out. He felt her fury, like an old reflex, but the howl of more demon dogs, somewhere close, coming, spurred a survival instinct she couldn't deny. They trudged through the forest at a half-loping walk, far faster than she could've managed on her own.

Mason kept her upright. He dragged her. And when she cried out, her strength sapped, he hauled her into his arms and carried her.

"Can't," she whispered, her lips against his neck. "Hurt yourself."

"Shut it, Barclay."

His chest was a volcano with its top blown open—burning lungs, thrashing heart, and the sick knowledge that he'd let this happen. She'd woven into him with thoughts of sunshine and home and their walk together. She'd made him look forward to spending the wrong-headed, isolated, godforsaken winter in her arms. They would have been together at least.

But now . . .

"Quit it, Mason."

"I'll think what I want."

She slipped into his head then, a cat burglar with skills he couldn't repulse—not when every thought was devoted to her. Not when his body continued the mindless walk.

You didn't do this.

Should have seen it.

Couldn't.

Should—

She growled at him and kicked, upsetting his grip. His balance gone, they sank to the ground.

"Damn it, Jenna!"

He expected a fight, but she wouldn't look at him. Instead, efficiently, she tore off the bottom half of her ripped pant leg and wound it around her thigh in a makeshift field bandage. He saw Mitch in her movements, although her fingers shook uncontrollably. All he could do was watch.

"You didn't do this," she said again, aloud this time.

"Can we not talk about it?" He shrugged out from the packs but kept the AR-15 slung across his lap. "I don't want your absolution."

"You don't have any choice."

Mason sprang to his feet and slammed his fist into the nearest tree trunk. Bark sliced his skin into rough, raw pieces. He hit it again, again, until she cried his name.

"John! Stop it, please!"

He turned and slumped against the tree. Blood dripped from his knuckles onto the snow at his feet. "I can't—" He swallowed hard. "I can't lose you."

Her skin shone pale in the eerie forest daylight, draped with irregular shadows from the evergreens and bare branches. "You're going to."

"Jenna."

"You know that better than anyone. You've seen it."

"No, not this time." Pushing away from the tree, he paced the little clearing where they'd fallen, his senses open to every sound even as his mind raced, fighting and thinking. "We'll get you back. Maybe Welsh can do something. And Ange was a nurse, right? They'll fix you right up. You'll be . . ."

As good as new.

But he couldn't say it. Even now, he couldn't lie.

"I'm not going back," she whispered.

"Don't be stupid."

She shook her head, settling back on her elbows. "Best-case scenario, I wind up like Edna or those people in town, some half-animal thing. But what if I end up like one of those monsters, huh? I'm not going back because I will not—*will not*—risk the others. I won't risk you."

Mason knelt before her. "Do you know who those beasts were? Convicts and murderers."

"How do you know?"

"I've been fighting them for a long time." He slumped cross-legged on the ground, trying to forget how she'd caressed and kissed him, how she'd made silent vows to take away the pain forever. "Remember at the pit, all those orange jumpsuits? That's where all the monsters came from. They got bit during the prison riots and turned into those demon dogs, mindless and vicious."

"What about Edna? She wasn't a bad person."

"No, which is why she died." He grimaced. "The worst of the worst . . . they make it."

"That's not fair! I mean, shit—none of this is fair. But *really*? Good people turn inside out and die while the scum of the earth get to walk around on all fours? What kind of magic is that?"

"Mitch said evil adapts faster because it cares only about self-preservation. At all costs." He bit the inside of his cheek until it bled. "He also said one day, good people would survive too. They'd learn to channel the magic. Jenna, I have to believe that time is now. He said you'd make it because you have to. I believed him. I promised him. And I'm *not* leaving you."

"You'd take that choice from me?"

"If I have to."

Sweat gathered on her brow. Her lips were chalk white. She tapped the foot of her injured leg, as if keeping time with unheard music— jerky movements made of pain. "No. I won't risk it. We've worked too hard to keep everyone alive. I won't put them in danger. Whatever this is"—she waved a hand over her bite, where blood seeped through the dressing—"it's too unpredictable."

She was giving up. On herself. On him. Her resignation infected the bond between them. Just as he'd shut her out, struggling for a piece of sanity, she was pushing him away. When the wall came down, it sounded like prison doors slamming shut.

"Jenna, don't."

"This is my choice."

The journey alone stretched before him like a nightmare. He'd plod through a quicksand of leaves and snow. He'd hand bundles of spare parts and supplies to Welsh and Ange. Then he'd walk back to the woods. His despair layered with a strong, clear sense of inevitability as he imagined the dog pack tugging his body to the ground, shredding him until nothing but bits of cloth and bone remained.

"Don't you dare," she growled. "Stand up, soldier. People need you. If not Chris and Ange, then Tru and Penny. You think they can last the winter without you?"

"You'd take that choice from me?" He felt no victory though, in quoting her own words back to her. Just a certainty that they'd both hit a brick wall at the end of a long road.

"Fine. I'm coming with you."

Mason jerked his eyes up. Without thought, he laid his palm against her forehead, which was fever-hot already. "You are?"

"'Course," she muttered. "You son of a bitch. You're gonna make an injured woman walk five more miles, just so she can make sure you do the right thing."

"And what's that?"

"Keep going. I have your back, remember?" Jenna touched his cheek. Her eyes shimmered with unshed tears.

He pulled her close, a sob catching in his throat. She hung on tight. Mason buried his face in her hair. Kissed her throat. Heart in pieces, he clutched and stroked and tried to pull her into him, keeping her there. Safe. Like he hadn't been able to do. Her tears fell again, wetting his face. Cold wind burned across salty smudges.

No matter how hard Jenna tried to keep it from him, he heard her fear. *I don't want to die. I don't want to leave you, John.*

Lungs burning, he pulled back just enough to find her mouth with his. Her tongue pushed inside, a pale imitation of the fire she'd burned him with at dawn. Time blurred. Had it only been that morning? He'd felt her writhe beneath him, every cry building with breathy intensity until she flew apart. And just the day before, he'd licked chocolate from the hollow between her breasts. A soft wave of desire and safety had tempted him to think it was all right to *feel*.

But this kiss blazed more with grief than passion, a more poignant good-bye than any words.

"C'mon, soldier," she whispered, her eyes bloodshot. "Let's do this thing. I . . . I don't want to get any weaker."

"How bad does it hurt?"

She laughed shakily. "Pretty damn bad. But it's getting stiff. I need to keep moving."

Mason stood and looped the packs across his back, then helped Jenna to stand. "What are you going to do?"

"I know what you're thinking, but I won't let you. I'll get you to that clearing, and I'll make sure you get inside and safe. But I'm done, John. Swear it." She faced him, digging the fingers of both hands into the skin at his nape. "Promise me you'll keep the others safe."

"And that means leaving you out there in the clearing to die." The words flowed freely now. Panic-driven. "That means shutting the door behind me with you still outside."

"Yes."

"*I can't.*"

"Unlike Mitch, I never asked you to promise anything, but I'm asking now. Please." Her chin quavered. "Don't let me hurt the people I care about."

Mason gathered up the strewn packs, slid his arm around her back and found their rhythm again, that loping, dragging rhythm. He was a machine once more. Maybe if he worked hard enough, kept his eyes focused and his feet moving, he could make that true.

But first he'd have to cut out his heart.

"John?"

"Yeah, Jenna. I promise."

THIRTY-ONE

If Jenna had been a pagan, she might think this was retribution inflicted by jealous gods. Mason's misplaced guilt throbbed at her like a sore tooth, compounding the pain of her wounded thigh, but neither of them could have done a thing to prevent it.

This wasn't a punishment for their pleasure. It simply *was*, like rain or thunder. They'd been lucky to move through the woods unmolested before now. That beast hadn't been hunting in a pack. Instead it had lain in the undergrowth, weak and near starving. She'd been prey. Desperation and survival instinct had driven it forward, just as she and Mason kept trudging forward in the face of long odds. Nothing sinister, just bad luck.

But that didn't make it easier to bear.

If she didn't know it would keep Mason from completing their mission, she'd have eaten a slug already. That wasn't an option anymore.

Jenna made herself keep moving, one foot after another. That was what soldiers did.

She'd been press-ganged into Mason's army, and she wasn't sorry. Not about anything. Saving the others had been the right thing to do.

Making the supply run had been too. Sometimes you could make all the right choices and still wind up boned.

They'd gotten the seal, at least; the others would be okay. Her death would mean something. That was more than most people got, especially these days.

The tears had frozen on her cheeks but not in her heart. Deep inside lay a small child who wanted to shake a fist at heaven and scream. Instead she kept quiet. She knew she had to be strong for Mason.

He had a brittle kind of strength, iron hard, not tensile. Bend him beneath a certain stress and he'd break. Jenna didn't want to take that to her grave. He had to make it. That wasn't altruism; on some level, it was vanity. She wanted a little piece of immortality, that someone would remember her after she was gone.

Children. Yesterday, lying in his arms, she'd indulged in the fantasy of solemn little boys who gazed at her with his dark eyes. She wasn't selfless enough to wish that he'd find someone else and be happy, if other survivors remained. But damn, she wanted him to live.

Misery balled up in her chest, weighting her steps. His sorrow and rage lapped at her resolve like waves on the shore, taking more each time the emotions receded. She lost track of how long they'd walked, and she lacked the skill to gauge the time by the sun overhead.

"You need to lead," she said. "Scout the path. I'll be right behind you."

At least as far as the door.

In the desert of Mason's eyes, she glimpsed a hint of his intentions. Once he'd given Chris the packs, he intended to go with her, away from the others. He'd leave Tru, Ange, and Penny in Chris's care. While the scientist was a good man, he wasn't hard enough. Without Mason, they wouldn't make it.

She couldn't let that happen.

"What you promised, John . . . it wasn't enough."

"What wasn't?" The life had already seeped from his voice, a dead man walking.

I can't go on. Can't lose her. Little worms of grief wriggled out of him and into her, burrowing until she couldn't tell where his pain stopped and hers started.

"You promised not to let me hurt them, but you didn't say you'd stay and look out for them."

Mason shook his head. "You can't ask that of me."

Tears boiled up. The cold froze them in her eyes and matted her lashes with ice. "Yes, I can. Do you trust Chris to hold it together? Who's going to teach Tru what he needs to know? You said once that Mitch saved your life, that he looked at you and saw the man you could be? Where would you be now without him?"

"Dead. And I wish to God I were."

"It was worth it," she said to his rigid back.

"What?"

"Yesterday, with you—it was worth dying for." Pushing deeper, past the fear, she found a core of contentment and offered it to him as proof.

"Jenna, *don't.*"

"Why not?"

He whirled on her then. One of his hands was damn near destroyed, but he didn't seem to notice. "Mitch *died* because of me. Because I wasn't fast enough. I didn't do enough."

"It was a hunting accident." Old memories realigned as she sensed the truth of what he said. A closed-casket funeral. Twelve years old, and she hadn't understood.

"Only if you call having your face chewed off an 'accident.'"

Cold seeped in through her chest, numbing her. It was too much to take in on top of everything else. She wet her frigid lips with her tongue. They dried in the wind, then cracked and bled. But she knew Mason. He was tough and capable, not careless.

Pure bad luck. Just like this.

"It wasn't your fault."

"You have no idea. One by one I watched my whole team die, even Mitch, and there . . . was only me. Just me, Jenna. I went west, like Mitch told me. I tried to build a life, but mostly I was. . . waiting. For you." His jaw flexed. "If I can't save you, I can't save anyone, and the rest of them can go to hell."

There was no reaching him, and that broke her heart. Their friends needed him, but he didn't want to hear it. So she fell quiet as he took the lead, conscious of the blood seeping past her makeshift bandage. Out here, Jenna might as well run around in circles yelling because the scent announced her as dinner. More monsters would come. Soon.

She'd pushed him too far, asked too much of him. He trudged headlong now, no longer scouting the easiest path. She did her best to keep up, but each stride shot agony through her thigh. From up ahead came a thud and a grunt, like the sound of him falling.

"John, where are you?"

She came to the lip of a shallow ravine and heard him swearing at the bottom, out of sight. He'd gone down the hard way. In the distance burbled running water—maybe the river that fed the generators.

"Can you hear me?" she called.

The cussing faded. Jenna heard him reply, his voice distant and to the west. She followed the path, biting back a moan. Her thigh burned. Mason had left churned up snow in his wake, but she couldn't make it down the same way.

Breathe. This isn't the end. You can find him.

If nothing else, to say good-bye. For one more kiss, she'd die happy.

Remembered pleasure sparkled through her. Howling arose in the east, and she struggled through the underbrush, looking for another way down. But she might be alone in this endless winter, surrounded by dead trees and unnatural monsters. *Maybe he decided to make the parting quick.*

No. John would never leave her.

Focus. Find him.

Calming her mind, Jenna tried to open herself to his thoughts, but he'd begun blocking her access just after the bite. Repudiating their connection must have made this easier for him to bear—and who was she to begrudge him that? But that silence made him harder to locate.

Jenna . . .

Desperate fear. Flashes of warmth. Need.

After discovering a shallower path of descent, she tried climbing down. The wound tore wide from the stress, and the bandage wasn't helping anymore. Blood froze and stiffened the denim. She struggled down to level ground and pushed through the tangle of branches, but he was nowhere to be seen. Panic pierced her. They needed to make it back to the station. She wouldn't be the reason four people—including two *children*—froze to death.

Snarls seemed to come from all sides.

"John!" she shouted, no longer caring what else might hear her calls.

She'd never find her way back without him, so she might as well sit down. He had all the supplies, even her rifle. He'd taken the weight to make it easier for her. How the hell could he fight?

A gunshot rang out. Then another. Then the sounds of a struggle and a human cry.

John! No!

He'd live for her, no matter what the cost. Even if that meant her soul. Wrath and purpose fused into something new, harder than steel, more fluid than mercury. This new feeling transcended pain.

Jenna rose—or at least part of her did. It felt like dying. For an eternal, minuscule moment, she stared down at her body from a great distance. Wracked with convulsive shudders, she shook and trembled on the ground. *Was* she dying?

No. She watched as her flesh began to roil and realign. She saw, but did not feel, as bones snapped and refitted into new lines. And then she slammed back, twisted through an unseen wall. Tremors rolled over her. On the other side lay a plain of pure pain. It washed her senses in fire, and her mind snapped in two. The thinking part fell down a deep, dark hole and lay weeping at the bottom.

The other part of her raised its head and sniffed the wind. She lay on her side, trembling and winded. But she was warm. A white paw lifted, tested the snow. *Cold.* She investigated a fallen tree limb and squatted on it.

On the wind came the scent of decay. She growled. Walking things shouldn't smell like that. A need arose, deeper than hunger. *Kill.*

More loud noises. She followed her nose.

The woods offered many trails. She sniffed. *Dead squirrel. Fresh blood. Human stench.*

Fear.

There was something she had to do. Her right hind leg hurt, but it didn't slow her down. She felt strong and sure. Liquid grace rolled through her as she took leap after leap, following the human scent-trail. Her muscles bunched as she bounded through the trees, wind streaming through her fur. *Hunt.* Her stomach growled. *Find meat.*

No. Protect.

Trees offered no obstacle; she wove through them with speed and expertise. On the wind, she recognized the man's scent. He was important. She couldn't remember being touched by human hands, but she wanted his. He would rub between her ears and run strong palms down her belly. He would admire her bright fur and praise her skill. Warmth surged through her quick muscles.

Save. Yes.

She found him ringed by a pack of wrong-dogs. They wore their blood on matted fur and reeked of dead things.

The human made noise. He needed to keep still. They would see him as the greater threat. But they needed to know this bitch owned these woods. She let out a growl to warn the wrong ones they had crossed into her territory.

They paused in their attack and swiveled slimy muzzles in her direction. One of them let out an uncertain whine. Despite their stink, she would let them go if they ran. She would not leave. *Guard.* She raised her hackles and bared her teeth, showing gums. *Stay, and you become prey.*

But they were too hungry. The wrong-dogs offered submission, yellow eyes sliding away with little whimpers, but they returned to their cornered food.

No. Mine.

When the first one lunged for the human, she curled herself low and sprang.

THIRTY-TWO

Mason rolled, the sky trading places with the ground, until he found his rifle. He wrapped his hands around the butt and came upright in a crouch, the barrel leveled. He pegged one demon dog between the eyes. Its brain casing exploded into the wind. He fired again, imploding the sternum of another.

Then he did something he never thought he'd do in the midst of an attack: he lowered his weapon.

His chest aching from cold, quick breaths, he stared at the animals brawling in the snow. The monstrous ones he knew well enough. Three more of them. A fourth lay dead to one side of the scuffle, its esophagus bared to the waning daylight. Hellishly unclean, they stank of humid, rotting meat. Blood and leaves tangled in their fur. These were dirty souls, the remnants of a violent world that no longer existed, one that had become even more deadly.

And they were fighting a wolf.

A she-wolf, he thought, by her lean, compact frame and slender muscles. Her fur bright white with silver tips glistening along her back, the wolf flashed sharper, gleaming teeth at her opponents.

Fresh blood painted her muzzle. She sank those fangs into the nape of the nearest monster, then shook her head until a mouthful of fur and skin tore loose. Her victim yelped and whined, cowering. She readjusted the angle of her neck and pressed a killing bite.

This was no mindless beast, but an honest-to-God animal. A *thinking* animal.

Spinning, she caught the full brunt of a leaping assault. She pitched backward and rolled, jumping free. He could see strategy forming in her bright green eyes as she watched the two remaining dogs with a dark intensity. Her shoulders and haunches relaxed, going limber and loose, as if the demon dogs were nothing more than a nuisance.

He stood. The wolf never looked away, but her posture shifted. She eased around with her back to Mason. The two monsters circled until the wolf growled and held her ground.

What the hell?

He'd never seen a wild animal turn its back to a human being, but she stood deliberately between him and the monsters. Mason took the opportunity to raise the barrel of his rifle and aim. He slid his body until more weight rested on the ball of his right foot. The wolf leaned back into a fierce, powerful coil of muscle and sinew. She sprang left. Mason fired, taking the one on the right with a single shot to the skull.

By the time the smoke cleared and the whimpers ceased, the wolf stood with a dead beast clamped between her jaws. She dropped it, sat back, and lifted her muzzle to the clouds. Her fierce howl split the calm forest air—not the mournful sound the starving pack made, nor the eerie, warning howl of those monsters on the hunt.

No, this was triumph.

Mason slid to the ground. He wound up resting beside the two heavy backpacks he'd shed when the dogs surrounded him.

The wolf turned her green gaze to him. Her chest heaved as she panted. Long canine jaws open, she looked pleased with herself, almost smiling. And why not? Blood covered her from jaw to forelegs, the blood of a hard-fought victory.

"Thanks," he muttered.

She tipped her head, then strode to his side without any apparent fear. Mason frowned, hypnotized by her gaze. Only then did he recognize a silvery aura shimmering around her body. Not so obvious as with the monstrous beasts. His heart eased its frantic pace.

Tentatively, expecting her to flee at any moment, he reached out and rubbed the silken fur behind her pricked ears. But she didn't run; she leaned into his touch. Her trusting, pleased response made him think of a woman's body asking for more.

Jenna.

He leaped to his feet. The wolf scuttled backward. Rifle in hand, Mason jogged back, looking for a path to climb. Where the hell was she? After finding a gap in the steep treelined slope and pushing through, he used roots and brute power to pull himself up. But level with the rest of the wood, he only saw trees. Limitless trunks and branches and shadows.

No sign of his injured lover.

"Jenna!" Fuck the dogs and the forest. He needed her back with him. They didn't have much time. Darkness awaited . . . and good-bye. "Sweetheart, where are you?"

No reply. No birdsong. Not even the wind. His heart struck a frantic rhythm against his breastbone. He held his breath, listening, but that only made the blood beat harder in his ears.

Giving up on his five senses, Mason used the only thing he had left. He closed his eyes and pictured her face—not the way he'd last seen her, grieving and wracked with pain. No, he remembered how the tense bow of her lips went slack as the last tremors of her orgasm faded, leaving her face soft and glowing pink. He reached out across time and physical distance, along the connection they shared.

And she was standing right behind him.

Mason whirled. And found the wolf, sitting, watching him. Her fur shimmered as if she were lit from within.

"Go. Get out of here!"

She didn't move, only blinked. After a big, gaping yawn, she settled onto the ground. One paw crossed over the other, a pillow for her bloodied chin.

Mason shook his head, trying to get rid of the buzzing sensation. Something had snapped. He'd stepped into a very wrong place—more wrong, even, than the hell of the last few weeks. That hell had rules, at least. Kill or be killed. This didn't make any sense at all.

But one logical possibility clawed at him. What if there had been another pack? What if she'd let them have her, resigned to her fate? He'd been carrying everything, even her rifle—trying to make the journey easier. Now . . .

"Jenna!" The bass harmonics of his bellow rattled underneath the forest canopy. His throat ached, but he shouted again.

The wolf whined. Head perked up, she tilted an ear into the chilly winter air. Listening. Then she stood and walked to him again. With the cold black skin of her damp nose, she nuzzled his injured hand, then started to lick at his wounds. Purposefully. Cleaning. His fingers twitched at the tickle of her slick tongue. He reached around with the other hand and rubbed her glossy pelt, scratching down to the skin. The wolf made a companionable sound in her throat, then tenderly butted her forehead against his leg.

Mason knelt and took her big, sleek muzzle between his hands. Green eyes gazed back.

His heart turned in his chest.

"Oh, no. No. No." He jumped up and back. Spinning, looking for any other answer, he fought a tide of dizzying black. "Jenna! Come *on*, Barclay. Where the hell are you?"

Seeming restless, the wolf sat and wrapped around herself. She licked at her right hind leg, cleaning just as she'd washed him. Transfixed, his breath pushing in and out, Mason knelt beside her. He gently pushed her muzzle, still expecting her to nip or run away. But she stayed. She let him touch her leg.

Beneath the fur, puncture marks marred her hide. She'd been bitten. Like Jenna.

The wolf nuzzled against the side of his neck. Mason opened his mind and found Jenna there, beside him, a primal part of her soul within the body of an animal.

A cry tore from his chest. He pushed the wolf away and ran. Tears threatened on the edges of his eyes as he found the packs. After loading a new clip in his AR-15, he strapped the heavy overstuffed burdens onto his back. Black grief layered over everything, but he shoved it into a dark corner of his mind.

A half hour later, he found a path he could navigate with the weight he carried. Mason emerged near the four-foot entrance to a tunnel, where water from a stream disappeared beneath the ground. Judging his position, he guessed this was where the monsters crawled into the earth, strolling right up to the back door of the station's basement.

But he lacked the time to investigate, and he couldn't get trapped underground while burdened, tired, and alone, especially not carrying the supplies. Instead he'd go overland, back across the clearing as they'd planned. More than ready to see this journey ended, he pumped his legs like pistons. No feeling. No stopping. Every thicket of underbrush gave way to momentum. Tree branches, snow, freezing cold— none of it mattered anymore. He didn't even try for stealth.

Bring it on, fuckers.

The clearing loomed ahead of him, but he kept his eyes on the station door. He discharged one shot in the air, whether to catch someone's attention in the tower or to incite the pack, he couldn't decide.

But he wouldn't go out like Bob. Instead he'd fire until snapping jaws ended this nightmare.

Monsters prowled in from the edges. Mason kept moving. Ice broke beneath his feet, while fresh powder crinkled along the surface. The setting sun glazed the snow with cold yellow light.

The front door opened. Welsh poked his head out. Then came Tru, rifle drawn, just like the last moment Mason had seen him. Except now he walked. No haste. No Jenna.

With perfect detachment, he admired Tru's stance. The kid leveled the rifle with easy readiness. In his head, Jenna asked, *Who's going to teach him what he needs to know to survive?*

He flinched. Then he picked up the pace.

The boy shaded his eyes, squinted, and signaled a warning. Mason turned to look. The wolf. She followed at a respectable distance, her shining coat catching the last rays of sunlight.

"Hold fire," he shouted to Tru.

The wolf closed the distance with a few uneven strides. Her wounded back leg must hurt like hell. But the beasts wanted dinner. They wouldn't let the best chance for meat in weeks stroll back into the station. There were fewer monsters by half, but they were all fatter. More cannibalism to stave off death. Mitch's idea—*Evil is adaptable, survival at all costs*—reared its head again. Mason wondered how many prisoners had taken refuge in these woods.

The wolf brushed her tail against him. She growled at the incipient threat, then settled into a coiled stance. Ready for battle. Mason kept the packs on his shoulders. His certainty shifted. *Fuck it.* Not one of those bastards would get a single taste of him today. They'd devoured enough.

"Tru? Cut left! I'll take right. I want a clear path down the middle."

"Got it!"

One after another, their rifles furrowed through the charging beasts. After a few shots to discourage the nearest attackers, Mason took a deep breath and sprinted for the door. Every ounce of energy and grief and grit poured into his limbs. He pumped his fists. Brittle air stung his raw lungs. The wolf matched his stride. That almost-smile shaped her muzzle.

Twenty yards from the station, one of the monsters broke Tru's line and pounced on the wolf. Mason kept running. He slid past Tru, just inside the door, and tossed the packs onto the concrete floor. He turned back to the clearing.

Tru raised his rifle. "What do I do?"

"No change. Just keep them off my back." He snatched the nine-millimeter from his holster and strode unencumbered into the snow.

The kid laid down cover fire, cool and brave, like he had been born for the changed world. And the wolf? She was unbelievably gallant, fighting with heart and skill. But the injury to her back leg slowed her movements. She wouldn't make it, not without him. No matter what she was—no ordinary wolf, he sure as hell knew that much—he needed to return the favor. A life for a life.

One beast sank its fangs into her other leg. She spun and fell, sliding on her side. Her paws scratched the slick snow but found no purchase. Snarling, blackened teeth bared, the dog lunged. Mason fired three shots in close succession. A cold smile crossed his face as the dead, perforated monster hit the ground with a crack.

The rest of the clearing quieted. Tru's silent rifle meant the fight was over. For now. Mason turned to check on the wolf, but she was gone.

Instead Jenna lay sprawled naked on the icy ground.

THIRTY-THREE

Tru had seen a lot of shit in his life, but this . . . this—

His brain couldn't wrap around it. He knew what he'd seen, but . . . flesh didn't reshape itself, at least not without killing the victim. Fangs couldn't just disappear.

But they had. And it looked like it hurt. No wonder Jenna had passed out.

Staring wouldn't change anything; it just made him look like an asshole. Tru sprang to help Mason, who carried Jenna in his arms. Seeing her naked made him feel weird, as if he'd been lurking around outside the shower—which he never did. Still, those were the first tits he'd ever seen in person, so he couldn't help but look.

Thank God Mason didn't notice. He'd have kicked Tru's ass for sure.

After the big guy passed into the station, Tru slammed the door and padlocked it with numb hands. Inside, it was unbelievably cold. Layering every scrap of clothing still hadn't been enough. More than once, he'd wished he had somebody to curl up with. Chris and Ange had snuggled together for at least one of the long, frigid nights. He didn't begrudge anyone a little happiness, but neither could he squash a flicker of envy.

Mason nudged one of the packs toward Harvard. "Got the seals. Go fix it. She's freezing."

The scientist grabbed the packs and headed to the subbasement without a word.

"Where's Ange?" came Mason's next growl.

"Here," she said. "I'll get the first-aid kit."

"Upstairs. Warmer." Mason seemed incapable of speaking in complete sentences, like something had snapped in his brain. He turned and speared Tru with a look. "You. Blanket."

Any other time, he'd mouth off a little, but Tru could see it was not the time to test the big dude. He sprinted up the stairs. Even the milder early evening sun burned his eyes after so much time in the dark. He met Mason in the stairwell and handed over the blanket. The expression on Mason's face as he wrapped Jenna turned Tru's insides watery. Together, they climbed upstairs to the lounge, since heat was supposed to rise, though there hadn't been any for days.

Ange arrived with a flashlight and medical supplies. Mason didn't put Jenna down, just held her in his lap. Tru had seen a mother behave that way once. Her kid had run out into the road to chase a ball and got mashed by a car. She'd knelt on the pavement, rocking the body until the EMTs tore her away. Tru saw that damage written on Mason's face, and he didn't know what to do with it.

Jenna looked scary pale.

Tru put down the rifle. So much for impressing Mason with how well he'd done. God, when would he stop being such a tool?

It would be hard to patch Jenna up in the dark, he thought, and the light through the windows was failing. As if in answer, the fluorescents kicked on. Heat would soon follow.

He rubbed cold hands together. "Go Team Harvard."

"Where's she injured?" Ange asked.

"Thigh." Yep, Mason had gone downright monosyllabic.

The closest thing they had to a nurse peeled the blanket away from Jenna's skin. She sucked in a breath. "Mason . . . that's a bite."

Jaw set, his teeth showed in what couldn't be called a smile. "Yeah."

Ange looked like she'd swallowed a razor blade, but she went about cleaning the wound with sure hands. Then she met his gaze, looking impossibly sad. "You know—"

"*No.*"

She ducked her eyes. "Let me find something for her to wear. When Chris gets back, you can tell us what happened."

"Yeah, man," Tru said. "What'd you do to her?"

He'd meant it as a joke. But Mason turned blasted eyes on him, pulling him into one of those postmodernist paintings where every road led to hell. "I failed her."

Tru stepped away, knocking the backs of his legs against a table. He sat down, feeling young and stupid.

Harvard came upstairs to hover. Ange brought both clean clothes and Penny, who hadn't ever gotten upset about the dark—didn't get upset about much of anything, from what Tru could tell. He wondered if they thought what he did, that her mind wasn't ever coming home.

Mason grabbed the clothes, seeming unable to trust anyone else to touch Jenna. It was like watching a man struggle to dress a sack of rice. Tru turned his face away.

Finally he laid her flat on the couch. Ange draped the blanket over her. "You want to tell us what happened?"

Mason shook his head. "You first."

"I've been guarding the basement door," Tru said. "It's been balls cold. And we've had a couple of near misses. I thought they'd break the hinges a few times, but it held when I leaned on it."

The big dude spun toward Harvard. "You had a kid down there in the dark for three days? What kind of asshole are you?"

"I'm not a kid," Tru gritted out.

But nobody was listening to him because the scientist launched himself at Mason and popped him in the nose.

Chris pressed his aching fist into his palm. His whole forearm trembled, and his knuckles felt like lit coals. He hadn't even rocked the bigger man's head back. But at least Mason grabbed his nose and cussed. Not bad for his first punch since the third grade. No, seventh.

"What the fuck was that for?" Mason demanded.

"I know you've been in the woods awhile, but could you use your indoor voice? You'll scare the kid."

"I said, I'm *not* a kid."

"No, you're an asshole," he snapped. "That better?"

Tru grinned.

"I meant her." Chris hooked a thumb to the corner where Penny sat. "And for the record, we've been trapped here for three days. Don't think you can stomp back in and expect us to jump. Now, facts. Please."

Mason offered a restrained snarl. "Hit me again and I'll take your head off."

"Can we please stop this shit?" Chris rubbed fingers through his hair until it ratted up with tangles. "I'm tired. We're all really, really tired. Grunting and making threats won't help Jenna."

He'd been around animals long enough to know when one was wounded. Jenna's bite was obvious, but Mason positively bristled with pain.

Chris softened his voice. "For the record, asshole here volunteered for the basement."

"And I was armed," Tru muttered.

Mason slumped onto a metal frame chair next to Jenna. Maybe the punch had done some good. After weeks of failed attempts, Chris had finally managed to speak Mason's language.

"She was bitten in the woods on our way back. The fever started up almost right away, but she wanted to keep going, to get me back here with the gear."

As Mason talked, Ange bandaged his thrashed knuckles. Chris liked that about her. More often than anyone else, no matter how she might feel, she kept the outpost running. Only about her daughter did she ever lose her calm.

"We got separated, and I was cornered by a small pack." Mason's eyes went distant. "This . . . *wolf* . . . showed up. She helped me fight them off."

When Tru spoke, his tone matched the somber situation. "I saw it happen. She was a wolf . . . and then she was Jenna."

"A skinwalker?" Ange asked.

Chris glanced at her in surprise. "What does that mean?"

"People like Edna, but who survived," she said. "I didn't believe it. Before everything went to hell, I heard rumors that things were getting better back east. There have been stories from people pushing west . . ."

"About this . . . condition of Jenna's?" Mason asked, his gaze intent.

Ange ducked her head. "I don't know any more than I already said."

He could tell she hated to disappoint Mason with her lack of knowledge. The big man sighed and ran a hand across his face.

Rather than resort to his fist again, Chris took charge with what remained of logic. "Let's think this through. What do we know?" He pointed out the windows, blackened now that the sun was gone. Not that the sun ever left. Not really. But people shouldn't change into wolves, so science wasn't a big help right then. "Those monsters out there. What do we we know about them?"

"They were bad people," Mason said, his voice flat. "Convicts and criminals."

Tru snapped his fingers. "Oh, yeah. The jumpsuits. Remember, at the pit?"

"What else do we know?" Chris asked.

Mason cleared his throat. When Ange let go of him, he flexed against the dressing—and Chris felt a good deal of relief that she wasn't touching him anymore. He blinked. That night spent holding her in the dark must have affected him more strongly than he believed.

"In town, some people were half person, half . . . other animal," Mason said. "All dead."

Chris pulled out a chair and sat. His feet wouldn't stop tapping the tile. "Other animals?"

"Cats, pigs. One looked insectoid, others reptilian." Mason looked toward Jenna with miserable eyes. "They tried to change. Didn't make it."

"I'm assuming these are regular folk, not criminals." Chris couldn't sit still. He started pacing. His brain misfired. Too many variables. No controls. "She didn't shift right away, did she?"

"No," Mason said. "Hours later."

"Under what conditions?"

The tension across Mason's shoulders made him look like an animal about to spring. But his voice didn't give off that warning vibe anymore. "Stressed, I guess. We'd been separated. She must've been looking for me."

"So maybe trauma catalyzes a successful shift," Chris said, uneasy about making assertions without proof. "Pain has a remarkable effect on enzymes. It crystallizes in the brain and . . ." He glanced around, seeing he'd lost his audience. "Not important. Point is—"

"Point is, Jenna could die." Mason's dark eyes narrowed. "You can't tell me otherwise."

Chris found Ange's pale face, peppered with freckles, and tried to smile at the way she looked at him, all quiet and proud. But the smile wouldn't come. "No, I can't."

Mason stood, looking oddly humble. "What *can* you do?"

Well, that's a surprise. He'd never heard so much as a genial request from Mason, let alone one that suggested confidence in Chris's abilities. "I can draw some blood. From Jenna, from a corpse, from all of us. See what I can learn under the microscope. There just has to be a scientific explanation for all of this. I just can't get behind, well, *magic*."

Mason snorted, like he thought Chris was stupid for clinging to the idea that the world made sense.

"What do you need?" Ange asked.

"A dog corpse." He held up his hands at the start of Mason's protest. "Headless is fine."

"Appreciate it." Oddly enough, the man's posture and roughened voice almost held the vibe of an apology. The world had become a darker place if landing a punch was what ensured a little civility.

"You better hurry," Tru said, "before they drag the dead ones off. Like last time."

Chris studied Jenna, where her blanket barely moved. "And what are you going to do with her?"

Mason's hand trembled when he touched her forehead. "I made her a promise. She didn't want to come back here if she could do any of you—us—harm. So I'll keep watch."

As always, Angela's anxiety for Penny showed in her widened eyes. "You mean . . . she could hurt us?"

"No," Mason answered. "I won't let her. But I won't let her die alone either."

THIRTY-FOUR

After gearing up for the cold, a fire ax in his hands, Mason trudged into the snowy night. Although it was only about eight in the evening, the absolute darkness of winter made the hour seem much later. Tru positioned himself in the doorway with his rifle, and Welsh lit the snow with a Maglite in each hand.

"Hurry," Tru said. "I won't be able to see them until they're right on us."

"The doc wants blood and guts. That's what he gets."

No problem. Thirty seconds, in and out.

And Mason felt the distinct urge to eviscerate something in the worst way. He found the misshapen beast he'd pegged three times with his nine-millimeter and chopped off the thing's head. Then he hacked up a good, meaty section of its middle. He shouldered the ax and gathered the grim samples. The cold had already stiffened the corpse.

He shoved the hunk of meat at Welsh. "Have fun."

With the door secured, he retrieved Jenna from upstairs and settled her on his bunk in the dorm. Unconscious, she was much heavier.

Dead weight.

He fisted his injured hand and felt the skin split beneath the bandages. No such thing as dead weight, not with Jenna. She would never be too heavy. Never a burden.

Kneeling at the bedside, he laid a hand over the dressing that covered the broken skin of her thigh. His mind drifted to the wound Edna had suffered and the way it ate at flesh and bone and hope. She'd died screaming, her body twisted from the inside out as it tried to birth some secret thing. Mitch had said that when the magic hit, people would try to turn into their totem animals—that everyone housed an animal soul. That affinity showed in their final forms.

Right then, Mason didn't give a fuck.

He'd done everything Mitch asked. He'd performed the rituals on the cabin for their protection, even the ones he'd thought pointless. But maybe that was all that had saved Jenna and himself from ending up like those poor bastards in Wabaugh.

Mason turned gritty eyes to where a bruise had formed on the inside of Jenna's elbow. Welsh had drawn a sample of her blood like she was a damn lab rat, but she hadn't flinched. Now her slack face was pale and still. Her chest barely moved. She seemed so far away that he doubted she'd whimper if he squeezed the fevered bite beneath his hand. At the moment, her wound was the most vital part of her.

He closed the blanket around her like a cocoon and swept loose tendrils of hair from her face. No fever now. Just cold. Holding out little hope, he leaned in and brushed a kiss against her mouth. His own Snow White—only Jenna didn't stir. Her lips didn't respond. He opened his thoughts, sending a desperate SOS. But even on that unseen highway where their minds once met, he traveled alone.

Mason slumped onto the floor, unable to look at her anymore. God, he ached.

Half-formed questions bumped inside his head, images of a silver-tipped wolf. The way she'd leaned into his touch had provided a fleeting sense of peace that soothed him to the bone. But he wouldn't let them coalesce. Jenna was Jenna. Everything else was a nightmare, and more to the point, it was completely useless if she didn't wake up.

The other possibility, that she could try to hurt one of them, held more immediacy. He wouldn't break his promise. So Mason checked his nine-millimeter and slid in a new clip. The thought of treating Jenna like a contagion and a threat made him ill, but the alternative was so much worse.

A quiet knock at the door brought his head upright. He'd expected Angela, but Tru stood in the doorway. "Hey."

Mason nodded in greeting.

"It's like Christmas with all that stuff you brought back. Well, if you dig presents from a home improvement store. Ange liked the batteries."

The kid slid onto the opposite bunk. As always, his posture reminded Mason of himself—tense and thriving on that tension. But that was a younger version of himself. All Mason felt now was fatigue and gut-deep dread.

"Why?"

"Because of Penny," Tru said. "Ange is always looking for her and she hates the dark."

"Not you though, huh?"

"Whatever. Lights are on now." He shrugged. "I guess I'll stay in the basement."

"Why?"

"I just thought . . ." Tru glanced at Jenna. "You'll stay with her. Take care of her."

Mason stood and shook the numbness out of his legs. "Jenna doesn't change things. We all have our jobs. If you want to stand guard in the basement, that's your choice. But you have backup now."

Funny how a few words could change a person's entire bearing.

Mason had seen it with Jenna, how his words made her happy, gave her a measure of comfort that brawn never did. He just hadn't expected it to have the same effect on anyone else.

But when Tru took to his feet, his uncharacteristic hesitancy was gone. "Yeah, backup's good."

"And I didn't mean it when I said you were a kid, okay?" Mason pinned him with a serious look. "I appreciate what you did here."

Tru beamed, briefly, then donned his don't-give-a-rat's-ass expression. "No problem." Again, his eyes darted to where Jenna rested. "So what now?"

"A lock. I need a lock."

An hour later, he'd soldered a chain across the outside of the dorm door. He'd be able to relieve Tru on point, patrol the perimeter, power through another meal, take a piss—all without wondering if she was stalking through the station looking for fresh meat. He slid the chain in place and thumped the door hard with his forehead.

She'd turned into a goddamn wolf.

Nope. Don't go there.

So back it went, shoved into a corner.

He set off for the showers. Lukewarm water beat against his bare back, peppering his skin the way Jenna had—except her kisses hadn't been the random patter of water. She'd touched him deliberately. She'd found every place that hurt and eased it, until his defenses diffused like steam.

A scream built inside him, gathering from the core abdominal muscles just below his bellybutton, scorching his organs, pushing up through his body until nothing could hold it back. Fear and grief and a hollow, broken need bellowed free, reverberating off the tile walls. Finally, his lungs empty, he dropped to his knees on the shower floor.

Water poured over his head. He scratched his wet scalp. Days of stubble itched like steel wool. Tiredly, he got his knife and wished he could use it on himself—a solution more permanent than scraping the hair off his head. Mason lathered and shaved, needing to impose that minimum of order. His grip on reality was seeping out of his pores. He felt it leaving.

With a last burst of energy, he twisted the shower knob. The water stopped. He shivered. The knee he'd split open on the ice was bleeding again. He watched a thinned rivulet of his blood trickle toward the drain. He didn't know how he was still moving, but he managed. Every movement went sluggish and numb as he toweled off. With a T-shirt and jeans on, he climbed back up to the dorms and unchained Jenna's door.

No change. She wasn't awake, smiling a greeting at him, but neither was she feverish, transformed, feral, dead—too many horrific possibilities. No, at that moment, resting looked pretty good.

So he did.

He slid the nine-millimeter just under the bunk, within arm's reach, and slipped in beside her. His body dwarfed hers and made a joke of the narrow mattress, but he needed to hold her. He snuggled the blanket around them and nuzzled his face in her hair. Catching a hint of musk and snow, he told himself he didn't care. She was Jenna. *His* Jenna. And he would hold her until morning.

Four days passed in a nightmarish haze. Every morning, Mason awoke more exhausted than the night before. The others tiptoed around him, but he held his frustration in check. He knew better now. They didn't need his anger on top of their own worries. So he chained the door shut and trudged out to get food, answering their silent questions with a curt, "No change."

He fed Jenna and rubbed her throat to make her swallow. He cleaned her when her body processed that food. And he wouldn't stop trying, no matter how hopeless it seemed.

Welsh looked as beat up as Mason felt. Where once he'd been clean shaven and neatly pressed, now the doc wore the same clothes

for days, well on his way to a ratty goatee. The specs were all that remained of the scientist they'd first met.

"It just doesn't make any sense," he mumbled as Mason walked by
the lab on the fifth night. Welsh scribbled onto a notepad beside his
microscope.

Mason hoped the guy spent sleepless nights working because he
cared for Jenna—not as a potential lover, but as a human being. Yet
he knew Welsh didn't work that way. Jenna was a riddle to solve.

Fine. Solve it.

He was tired of the radio silence in his head, tired of sorting each
sliver of memory to see if he'd missed something. And damn, he was
tired of stretching out next to the woman he loved without any hope
that she'd open her eyes.

Mason dropped his spoon. It fell to the floor with a clatter, sounding far away. There'd be a splatter of oatmeal on the floor, but he didn't
care.

Love. Goddamn it.

Tru snapped his fingers. "Hey, Mason. You in there, dude?"

I love her.

"Yeah," he said, throat tight.

"Harvard wants to know if you can come see him."

When he arrived in the lab, Mason found Welsh and Ange talking
quietly. Tru trailed him to the doorway and stood watching the pro-
ceedings. And where he went, Penny wouldn't be far behind. Yeah,
there she was in the hallway outside, eyes locked on Tru.

Welsh glanced up with a tired expression. "Glad you're here.
You'll want to check this out."

"What am I looking at?" Mason asking, squinting into the microscope.

"Cells." Welsh nodded to the pile of meat laid out on a nearby slab.
Pins stuck out of various organs and tissues.

"What is this? Ash? Charcoal?"

"Not quite." The scientist peeled off his Lennon glasses and rubbed his eyes. Then he indicated the slab of monster meat. "It's *that*. Looks like tissue, hell, it smells like rotting tissue. But that's how it looks under magnification. Like cinders. Not animal at all."

He tried to hide his irritation. Slides and cells didn't mean Jenna was awake or that Welsh had found a cure. "And?"

"It's not possible, all right? There has to be cellular structure. This . . ." He exhaled like a man admitting defeat. "I can't explain it. It's not science. It's . . . other."

Ange asked, "What does this tell us about Jenna?"

"I wish I knew." Welsh gestured to another set of slides. "This is her sample."

He stood away from the microscope, letting Tru and Ange take turns examining the unnatural evidence. Mason wondered if Welsh would admit the existence of magic now. Denial seemed impossible in the changed world, but maybe the guy was determined not to see what was right in front of him. God knew, the folks in Fresno had done the same thing, until it was too late.

Once they finished, Mason switched slides and peered down at Jenna's blood, swirled on the glass. What he saw astonished him. "This is like her fur."

"What do you mean?" Welsh asked.

"When she was a wolf, her fur . . . glowed. Just a little."

"Yeah," Tru said. "Like she was under a spotlight. Her cells look that way too."

Welsh nodded. "Whatever that means, it's a fundamental difference between her and the beasts."

Mason couldn't breathe. He looked to Welsh for confirmation of his hopes. "You mean, she won't turn into one of them?"

The scientist lifted his shoulders in a who-knows gesture. "I hope not, but I can't be sure. This is beyond anything I've seen before."

"Is she dangerous?" Ange asked.

The back of Mason's neck prickled. "Not when she's unconscious and locked up."

"You don't get to take that chance. Not with my daughter's life."

He tensed his injured hand into a fist. "I wonder what kind of life your kid would have right now if Jenna hadn't opened the cabin door for you."

"Hey, let's not borrow trouble. She has to survive before we worry about whether she's a threat." Welsh seemed to realize what he'd said. "Sorry, man."

Mason nodded, though his gut felt like it held live coals. He fixed a dark, cold stare on Angela. "If it comes to it, we'll take a walk in the woods. Just her and me."

She blanched. "I didn't mean . . . oh God."

Welsh put an awkward arm around her.

So that's how it is. And the leopard shall lie down with the kid.

This wasn't the time for Mitch's prophecies, but the words burned in Mason's head.

"Mama?" Penny stood in the doorway. The pale fabric Ange had fashioned into a nightgown seemed to glow against her porcelain skin. Her filthy bear dangled from slim, graceful little fingers.

It was the first word anyone had heard her speak since the change.

Her face alight with wonder, Ange reached for her daughter. Tears streamed from her eyes even as she smiled. "What is it, baby?"

The girl smiled in return. "Mama, the wolf's awake."

THIRTY-FIVE

Shapes loomed in the dark.

She had never been here before. It smelled strange, and a big thing stood between her and freedom. *No wind.* Faint smell of death. Her blood. Human stink—more than one. It was too warm. Her tongue lolled as she sniffed something familiar. *Good.*

But she heard movement. *Threat?* If they had put her in this place away from trees and freedom, they were her enemies. She curled her lips back and raised her hackles. An angry growl escaped her as the thing moved. Light trailed in.

Backing as far as she could, until her rump met something hard, she stood with her ears forward, threatening. The new thing was human. He stepped in, and she snarled to let him know of her presence. He edged closer. His familiar shape gave her pause.

He kept coming. She coiled her muscles, ready to spring if he did not take her warning. His body folded as he knelt, and in the motion, she breathed his scent. *Hunt-mate.* They had taken prey together, bonded in blood. She remembered this human. He had good hands. She remembered them on her muzzle. The fear trickled away.

Whining softly, she let her fur fall soft against her neck. She edged closer. Sounds spilled from the human. They made no sense to her, but she tried to communicate. She bent forward in a half bow and lashed her tail, letting him know she wouldn't mind playing. He didn't seem to understand, still moving with the slowness of a crippled wolf.

Happy but out of patience, she pounced and nipped gently at his arm, then pranced away. She turned to see if he would try to catch her. Instead he stared at his arm, frozen in place. She huffed out a little breath.

No play?

Maybe he didn't want to. Maybe he was tired.

Chastened by her inability to read him, she slunk forward with her belly low on the ground. He didn't move, but he continued to make those soft mumbling noises. He didn't smell scared. He smelled . . . good. Not like food, but something else she wanted.

When she got close enough for him to touch, she rolled onto her back in a pose of extreme submission. She shouldn't have tried to make him play. Only cubs annoyed pack mates like that. She should have known better.

Slowly, he reached out and rubbed her tummy. *Good.* She wriggled side to side on her back, letting him pet her. Something thunked beside him, and then he put his other hand on her. She didn't try to get away when he lifted her. Instead she sat down and gazed into his eyes.

Water streaked down his face. She licked. *Salty.*

The human made a sound she recognized, a whine of pain. *Hurt?* She licked again, looking for a wound, and he wrapped his front legs around her like he wanted to wrestle, but she didn't think that was right. Then one of his noises reverberated through her.

Jenna.

The word cut through her like a crow's squawk. She cocked her head. He said it again.

I'm Jenna.

Fire followed. She spilled onto her side, whirling, as the world slipped away. She went to that place of pain for the briefest time and spiraled back. Agony impaled her, as if all her bones had shattered at once.

When her vision cleared, Jenna lay in Mason's arms. He stroked her naked stomach as if she were an animal. Worse, he looked as if he had single-handedly fought the armies of darkness.

Days and sensations came back to her in ragged flickers. The bite. The fight. She'd dreamed of hunting as a wolf. *How the hell am I alive?*

She tried to speak, failed, and wet her lips with her tongue. "Taking advantage of me? Must've been a helluva party."

His raw laughter rumbled through her. "Jesus, Jenna. How much do you remember?"

"I'm not sure. I think . . ." She met his dark gaze as the last clouds lifted. "I did, didn't I?"

Mason gave a somber nod. "You shifted."

His tone coiled through her and left a spiral of worry in its wake. "Does that mean I'm a monster now? Or I will be soon?"

"I don't know. You didn't hurt me. You nipped my arm, but it didn't hurt."

"Oh my God. Oh shit. Did I—"

"No." His jaw slashed to the side. "You didn't draw blood."

Tears pushed behind her eyes. She struggled to get free, but he wouldn't let go. He didn't caress her either. On a bone-deep level, she knew if he let her pull away, everything between them would end.

I could hurt you.

You didn't.

They still had this anyway. Jenna took a deep breath and focused on bringing up impenetrable barriers. He shouldn't be tainted by her damage, shouldn't have her disease in his head. When she shifted on his lap, her fingers brushed cold metal on the floor. Blindly, she gripped the object and brought it up. His gun.

Perfect for breaking up with a girl who's gone to the dogs.

Her breath huffed out, an impossible ache in her chest. He'd meant to put her down, if necessary. That should have made her feel better; instead she wanted to scream. No matter how tough he thought he was, he wouldn't have been able to live with that. And fuck the others for letting him carry that weight.

"This is yours," she said, offering the weapon. "You should keep it with you."

In case she went rabid, started seeing them as food.

"That's not going to happen."

"What about the others? You think they'll be willing to take a chance on me?"

He snarled. "They'll do what I say."

"Or you'll exile them? That's not fair, John. If it comes down to it, I'll go. I can survive in the woods." She tried a smile but it hurt her sore, dry lips. "I might even be happy there."

"Can we not talk about this?"

"Fair enough." But how could she go on, pretending things were normal? "I need to take a shower anyway. I smell like wet dog."

When she pulled to her feet, her body felt surprisingly fit. Her thigh carried her weight with only a twinge of sharp pain with that first step. Despite the cold, Jenna didn't dress. She'd lost all sense of modesty, it seemed, because she saw no point in covering up when she would just get naked in a minute anyway. After she gathered up her things, she padded down the hall toward the shower. At this point, what did it matter if someone saw her bare ass?

She hadn't expected him to, but John followed. *Watching over me, or making sure I don't go after anyone?*

He couldn't answer, of course, because she wouldn't let him in.

She felt more conscious of her body, more aware of what it could do, and that meant keeping him at a distance. Her muscles felt sleeker, stronger. The bite on her thigh had healed over. Scents rose up and offered themselves like gifts. Herbs in the garden, a hint of dead flesh. Ange was cooking something upstairs. Jenna found it a little easier to see without light too. Every angle had sharpened.

She navigated the maintenance closet, not noticing that she did so in darkness until John flipped the switch. She turned, stepped into the water, and bent to retrieve the shampoo from a basket of toiletries on the floor. John stood transfixed, watching the water on her skin.

That was balm to her uncertainty. If nothing else, he still liked the way she looked.

She played to it, arching her body as she washed her hair. Her breasts came up. She rubbed her hands through her hair to rinse, and then she knelt to look for the soap, offering him a different view. Jenna lathered slowly. Her fingertips brushed her nipples and the slope of her belly. She remembered the way he had watched her wash. He had touched her there . . . and there. She still felt the weight of his gaze as she let the water run clear. John stood like a man turned to stone.

"You're the best thing I've ever seen," he said quietly.

A savage instinct swelled inside her. She wanted to leap out of the water, onto him, just push him to the ground and take him, all teeth and nails. The strength of the desire made her shudder, but she covered it in the pretense of the water growing cold.

Jenna turned off the tap. Instead of looking for cloth, she gave herself a vigorous shake. *Jesus, what did I do?* Too much to hope he hadn't seen it.

She dressed quickly. Making sure not to touch John, she slid by and went in search of the others—in search of food, light, and companionship. Below that need waited fear. She was none too sure how they would react, if they'd shun her.

Still, huddling in bed wouldn't help. And she was hungry. She smelled the food, willing to eat just about anything.

Except people. Definitely not people.

Edgy and restless, she sprinted down the hall, up the stairs, and down the next hall. John cursed behind her. He still hadn't caught up by the time she reached the second floor.

At first, the others didn't take notice. Chris and Ange were setting the table, all secret smiles. Their hands brushed more than once. But more than the visual cues, Jenna could smell the shift in their chemistry. Slightly musky. The scent of attraction. Bickering over some piece of cutlery, Tru and Penny sat waiting.

Jenna cleared her throat and they turned in unison. Everyone froze, staring. Then Chris took a half step forward, as if to protect the kids. Her smile, born of pleasure from the run, died a painful death.

"I'm sorry," she muttered. Of course they didn't want her around. She must look an awful lot like the enemy right now. "I didn't think. If you don't mind making a plate, I can take it downstairs."

She spun into the hallway and leaned her aching head against the cool wall. But then two things happened more or less at once: John came toward her, and a small hand slipped into hers and tugged.

She glanced down. Penny's eyes were indigo blue, framed in gilded lashes. Ange had borne an exceptionally lovely child, and right then she was smiling.

Penny never smiled.

"Come eat." Tug. "Dinner."

Over Penny's head, Jenna stared at John with soul-deep confusion. But those little fingers twined through hers. Warm. Welcoming. Inexplicably, tears prickled at Jenna's eyes, but it wasn't sadness.

"You heard the kid," he said. "Let's eat."

THIRTY-SIX

During dinner, Chris watched Ange to see if her wariness returned. But no. Jenna's ability to lure Penny to speak seemed to ease that tension. The girl had found her appetite, munching on saltines and wordlessly offering them to her teddy bear. Ange passed the hour wearing a bright smile that did intriguing things to his heart rate.

"You seem distracted," Mason said, his eyes narrowed. "Something you want to share?"

Chris spread his hands flat on the tabletop. *Never used to be a nail-biter.* But the proof was in his ragged, reddened cuticles. "I think we need to talk about this. About Jenna."

She flinched. "What about me?"

"No need to get defensive," he said quietly. "I'm not here to judge. I just want to figure out what we're dealing with." Years of training made what he was about to do very difficult. Chris wasn't a man who just . . . guessed. "But remember, I wouldn't be able to prove anything, not outright. I don't have a control group. I couldn't write a paper—"

"Talk," Mason said bluntly.

Chris grabbed a legal pad from a nearby cabinet. "Okay, so what happens when a population is exposed to a new virus or bacteria?

No, wait, smaller than that. What are the possibilities when an individual is exposed?"

Tru snorted. "You get sick."

"No, faster. What's the easiest option?"

"Death." Ange glanced nervously at Penny.

Chris offered her an encouraging smile. "That's right. The body doesn't have the resources to cope. Think about the Aztecs when the conquistadores landed. Wiped out. That's the first one." He drew a stick figure man on the yellow paper and then a line down to the word *death*. He drew another line and consulted his unlikely students. "What's another option?"

"Resistance," Mason said.

"Good." He penciled in the word *fever* at the bottom of the second line. "The body develops a fever. The white blood cells go crazy and create—if they're lucky—new antibodies. Fever breaks. And then recovery."

Ange paled. "Edna had a fever."

While the others nodded, Chris licked his lips. He shouldn't be so eager about this, but the rush of putting the pieces together had him breathing fast.

"Her body tried to fight back," he said. "So maybe we were mistaken in assuming that the fever was part of an inevitable progression toward death. We're assuming now that people like Edna were trying to change. What if they died because their bodies got it wrong? Maybe death came when their bodies turned inside out, trying to heal." He paused and looked at Jenna. "But you got it right."

"So shifting saved my life?" Jenna's eyes moved from Chris to Mason and back again with sharp, quick movements. She was certainly not the same woman. Fascinating. And freaky. "And all those people we saw in town—half cat, half pig—they died from the cure?"

Chris nodded. "That's my guess."

"Then why'd I live?"

"Well—here's where it's different, right? You shifted, and the fever you developed in the woods never came back. You went into a coma instead, like your body was realigning on the inside. As for the timing . . ." He sketched two more lines down from *fever*, one ending with *shift* and the other with *death*. "Jenna, do you think you could shift at will? Right now, if you had to?"

Ange looked panicked—not fearful exactly, but like Chris had just thrown up on an expensive rug during a dinner party. Almost embarrassed that he'd do such a thing.

But Jenna only grinned, a little wild around the edges. "I don't know."

"Can you try and describe it?" Chris asked.

She frowned, as if looking into herself. "You know in the old days, you'd be in the grocery store and someone would cut in front of you in line? You'd let it pass because it's not worth it to lose your temper." She shrugged. "It's like I'm holding my temper."

Chris nodded, feeding off that rush of discovery. "What triggered it the first time?"

Jenna darted another look at Mason, but this one was so thick with emotion that Chris averted his eyes. "I was worried about John," she whispered.

"So extreme emotion—trauma, like I thought," Chris said. "Do you think you would've been able to do the same thing twelve hours later? Two days later?"

"No," she said firmly. "I was already pretty tired. My leg hurt."

"Then your friend Edna, five days in—maybe she hadn't received that jolt of trauma." Chris shook his head. "On the other hand, maybe it's exposure. The catalyst could be in the air right now, in tiny particles, and more concentrated in the dog bites. We've had weeks of exposure to it. Maybe that potential finally came to fruition. But whatever the combination—Jenna, your timing was *really* good."

"Why didn't you mention all of this when she was unconscious?" Mason asked.

"Why would I?" He glanced down at his lame drawing. "I told you, I can only guess. I didn't want to get your hopes up. We had no way of knowing if she'd awaken or how she'd behave."

"She behaves just fine," Jenna said sourly.

Tru perked up. "Wait, so all of us could be shifters? That'd be awesome."

Mason grunted. "Don't be an idiot."

"Hate to throw a wet blanket on the idea," Chris said. "But you'd have to stick your leg out there, get bit, then hope you managed to shift. Not to mention surviving the coma afterward. Oh, and I'd have to be one hundred percent right about all of this. Long odds, kid."

"Especially that part about you being right," Tru said, grinning. "But wouldn't that kick ass?"

"It might not require a bite," Jenna said. "You're talking about everything like it's science. But it's time to face facts. This is *magic*, and we don't know all the rules."

Chris hated that word. Hated it.

Ange had been sitting there, pale but attentive. Had to give her credit for sticking it out. "But what about the monsters? Why are they different?"

"Don't know." Chris drew one more line off of *fever*. He wrote *monster*. "Brain chemistry? Maybe the way the change affects people already prone to violence."

"What did Mitch say?" Jenna asked Mason. "That evil is faster at adapting to magic?"

"Magic," Chris said woodenly. Back to that again. Ignoring it wouldn't make it go away.

"That's right." Mason's gaze held a challenge. "Unless you have an explanation for those blackened cells."

Tru grinned. "Or shapeshifting."

"Forget it," Mason said roughly, standing. "It doesn't matter. None of this bullshit explains the other weird changes in the world, does it?"

Just like that, Chris's enthusiasm drained away. Even if he figured out every aspect of their situation on a scientific level—which seemed less likely with each revelation—they wouldn't be any better off. His inquiries, no matter their accuracy, didn't guarantee they'd get through winter or survive against the monsters come spring.

Intellectual masturbation.

His shoulders slumped, and a headache flared at his temples. Their group would be better off if he put away his microscopes and found the guts to pick up a rifle.

"Thanks for dinner," Tru muttered before heading back downstairs. He acted like something terrible would happen should he leave his post for more than fifteen minutes. Hell, maybe he was right.

Jenna and Mason excused themselves as soon as their plates were empty.

Chris watched Ange washing up, his mind elsewhere. Penny stayed to help, which was new. She dried the dishes carefully, looking for approval each time she finished one. Dishes done, Ange leaned down and kissed the girl's cheek. Penny's arms went around her neck in a tight hug.

Chris knew he ought to take some comfort in this scene. It should make him feel better that he was part of this family, at least peripherally. Hell, he could have ended up alone and insane. But their obvious closeness did nothing to improve his mood.

"Is it okay if Maisie and I go downstairs and play with Finn?"

Maisie was her bear, but who was Finn? Chris had no idea.

"You mean Tru?" Ange asked.

"Nope." Penny laughed softly. "I mean Finn. He's waiting for me."

An imaginary friend, he guessed. That was as normal as the kid got.

Ange kissed the top of Penny's head. "Just don't go wandering around the subbasement."

"I won't."

Once they were alone, she turned to Chris. "You all right?"

"Why wouldn't I be?"

She sighed and tucked a strand of red hair behind one ear. "Because Mason took you off at the knees."

He shrugged, although his shoulders had stiffened. "I'm used to it."

"That doesn't make it right. We need to know all we can. The rules have changed."

Chris studied her, wondering what she really thought of him. "Do you believe what Mason said? About magic?"

"I think I have to. It's that or go crazy." She touched his arm. "I just wish we could do something useful with it, like cook. Right now, we can only react to changing circumstances, which have become *impossible* to understand. If it's a force, then we should be able to shape it. But we don't know enough."

"My undergrad courses didn't include any hermetic theory. Sorry." Chris knew he sounded bitter.

"Chris?"

"I'm obsolete," he muttered. "Nothing I do helps. Everything I spent years learning is worthless."

Ange shook her head. "Look, Tru may not follow you around like you're some big hero because you can fix a generator, but where would we be without you? Sitting in the dark, freezing to death—that's where." She exhaled softly. "You matter, Chris."

"Do I?" In his tone, he heard himself asking a question.

This probably wasn't the time, and it might end up . . . complicated. He'd never been good at making relationships work, even during the best of times. He shouldn't push for more. But something about the desperation they faced every day made him look at Angela and keep looking.

After crossing the space between them, she put her arms around his waist and gave a gentle squeeze. "You do," she said firmly, her cheek against his chest.

Chris felt as unbending as a hunk of iron, but feminine warmth eased his tension. Her body shaped to his, and he rested his chin on her hair. They stood not speaking, just being, until he murmured his thanks against her temple.

"No problem. Want to watch the snow with me? It's really coming down." She paused, studying him as if she felt as unsure as he did. "Unless you have work to do. You don't have to."

"Well, I do need to . . ." He touched her lightly on the cheek. "You know what? It'll keep."

"Do you mind if we check on Penny first?"

"No. I was going to suggest it."

They went down to the dorms, hand in hand, and peeked through the doorway. Penny sat on her bunk, cradling Masie the bear and humming softly. "Finn, you have a nice voice. I like the funny way you say words. What should we do today?"

Chris smiled. This was . . . well, almost normal. He led the girl's mom away before Penny realized they had been watching.

Maybe it didn't matter if science no longer provided all the answers. He could adapt. Mason would keep an eye on Jenna, so they wouldn't be mauled in the night. Penny had returned to the land of the living, and Ange wanted to spend time with him. Maybe the changed world wasn't as dark as he'd feared.

here. We'll keep walkie-talkies with us to gauge progress and keep in contact. Got it?"

Though it was more or less what Jenna had envisioned, the idea spoken aloud sounded even more kamikaze than it had in her thoughts.

Chris was already shaking his head, not in disagreement but with an expression of disbelief. "Why the tunnels?"

"We won't be safe," John said. "Not if our power source is also a wide-open back door. A collapse will keep them out."

"You'll have to find a place to close it all up while keeping the water flowing." Chris hooked a thumb back to the generator. "Otherwise we'll lose power again."

"Noted," John said. "I know the place, down by the ravine. What do we have for explosives?"

Chris ran through a list of chemicals and quantities, but John kept shaking his head. Finally, the other man threw up his hands. "This isn't a munitions factory, Mason. You can't expect me to keep—oh, wait." A satisfied, masculine smile cut across his face. "Cans of machine lubricant. Two cases of them."

John grinned too, like they were two boys planning firecracker pranks. Typical. The first thing they shared was a genuine interest in blowing shit up.

"Good," John said. "That with the gasoline should do well. We *do* have gas, right?"

"Diesel, sure," Chris said with a nod.

Tru seemed to want to get in on the party. "How does it work?"

"We wrap each can of oil in a gasoline-soaked rag," John said. "Then we pop the can with a slug. Boom."

If it was possible, Ange grew even paler. "That's nuts. You'll blow yourselves up."

Well, yeah, Jenna thought. It wasn't like they had a computer to calculate placement of the explosives. They could be crushed by rubble, eaten, suffocated—an endless variety of ways to die. But it didn't seem so bad if she had John fighting beside her.

Tru put it best. "You got a better idea?"

"No." Ange held tight to Penny. "I'll get supplies."

"Lay in lots of food and water," Jenna added. "Everything you'll need to wait out a siege."

And it would come to that: three against a bestial army. Incalculable odds. In her heart, Jenna knew they needed to say their good-byes beforehand. Leave nothing unsaid.

She lightly caught Ange's arm. "I know you're scared of me. . . and I'm sorry. But I want you to know . . . you've become like a sister to me." She paused, feeling the other woman's tension drain away. "And I love your girl too. I'll do my damnedest to make it safe for her."

She fought off guilt over the thoughts she'd had earlier, regarding her single-minded devotion to John's survival. Conflicting instincts fought within her—human versus animal—and left her sick with self-loathing.

Maybe we aren't meant to survive this. Maybe Mitch was wrong.

Jenna. Her mate filled her head with warmth. *Mitch wasn't wrong. Trust that.*

Ange let out a quiet sob and wrapped an arm around her neck, squeezing until Jenna saw spots. "I'm sorry," she said. "You're still my friend. Please . . . be careful."

"It's out of my hands now," Jenna choked out.

Penny raised up with a dreamy smile and kissed Jenna on the cheek. She'd thought the kid was asleep, but there she was, listening the whole time. She wondered what else Penny had overheard. Did she know what it all meant? She didn't seem scared. Thank God. The girl didn't deserve to spend her last hours in terror.

Jenna turned to Chris as Ange slipped away. "You're the answer man. Maybe that doesn't seem like much right now, but you're here for a reason."

As she finished, Jenna realized she meant it. They all contributed complementary aspects, everything interlocking and working toward the survival of the whole. The old paradigms would fall away, giving birth to something new. Change didn't have to be fatal, not if the organism was healthy and strong.

Chris nodded. "Thanks."

She couldn't read him like she did John, so she didn't know how to take the strange look on his face as he turned to go.

Tru held up his hands. "Don't even try to get emotional with me, woman."

Jenna grinned. "Okay. You know what I'd say anyway."

"Whatever." His pale eyes flicked away and blinked a few times.

"So," John said, "I need one volunteer for the bombs. The other watches the door."

THIRTY-NINE

Mason slung the satchel of two dozen wrapped cans of machine lubricant over his shoulder and readied his rifle. The ax lay heavy between his shoulder blades, as did the bag of spare magazines and flares. Safety goggles pinched against the skin of his forehead. Beside him, Tru held his own weapon as if he'd been born with it. Admiration and a profound sense of sadness kept Mason from meeting the young man's eyes.

Where she waited in the doorway, Jenna looked tense and wary. She'd stood there for an hour with her finger on the trigger, cool green eyes examining every shadow just beyond the safety of the basement. "You boys ready?"

"Sure," Mason said. "We got company yet?"

"Not that I've heard. And I can hear them a long way off now."

"Good. I'll go through first." He leveled his AR-15 and stepped in front of Jenna in the doorway. "I won't be able to move as fast as either of you, not with all this gear. Just think of me as a tank. Got it?" They both nodded. "And if you shoot me, it won't be just a bullet wound. I'll go boom."

Tru shrugged. "As long as Harvard stays put, you're good."

The day when they'd arrived at the station seemed years gone. The cabin, the pre-change world—they'd faded like black-and-white photographs. Only the moment mattered. Mason caught Jenna's eye and looked at her for one long, searing breath.

She nodded, acknowledging all he hadn't said. "Let's get this done."

He edged through the doorway, swinging the barrel of his rifle left and right. A quick check of the two generators there in the original wooden anteroom confirmed that the hoses had been gnawed into strips. He hoped that if they lived through this, Chris would be able to use the new spare parts to get the backups in working order again.

Too far ahead, he heard Jenna say. *Stay with us.*

Mason inhaled. She was right. He hadn't been so scattered in a long time, if ever—perhaps because the stakes were so high. Yet that distraction would get them all killed.

He pulled out a flare, struck it against the heel of his boot, and threw it out of the anteroom, where it landed with a quiet clatter. Leading with the rifle, he pushed into the tunnel. On the all-clear, Jenna and Tru followed and flanked him.

Illuminated by the harsh orange glow of the flare, the long, low-hanging underground cavern waited to their left. The hot spring stream ran along a sunken gulley at their feet, half obscured by stalagmites and rock formations. Water dripped from the tight, arched walls, sporadic but as constant as the flare's even hiss. Shadows stretched in warped arrays along the rock outcroppings.

"Where are they?" Tru whispered.

Mason frowned, easing deeper into the tunnel. They edged farther away from the subbasement entrance. After Mason popped the third flare, there was enough natural light to see. Grim and solemn, he felt more like he was attending a funeral than standing on the verge of the most important battle of his life. No more bloodlust. No more fear. Just a resignation that left him light-headed.

Jenna raised a hand. "Listen."

In a burst of claws scratching against rock, monsters barreled toward them. The scraping echoed. Hectic shadows flickered down the far walls. Mason raised his rifle and fired. Sound slammed in his ears, the bursts like cannon fire in the confined space. Demon dogs yelped and fell. Tru cussed the things, but Mason didn't look at him, just kept his eyes on the targets. He trusted his partners enough to ease into the rhythm of combat. Sight. Fire. Pump another round.

"Reload in shifts," he shouted. "Tru, you first."

He and Jenna closed up as Tru fell back two steps. The three of them traded places over the next minute. Then they pushed forward. Each slavering assault fell beneath their defensive fire. No wasted ammo. No hesitation either. Mason glimpsed the exit, where dawn light filtered through.

"Hold up," he said as the beasts regrouped. "We have to get to where the tunnel meets the ravine. We'll be better able to control the outcome—seal the tunnel without damming the water source."

Jenna's breath came fast but controlled. "There'll be more."

He tipped his head toward the station. "Tru, I want you here. No arguments. Be ready to end any that get through on your side."

"What do you mean on my side?" the kid asked.

Mason flicked his eyes to the four-foot-tall exit. "We'll head out and make our stand. Seal the entrance."

After reloading, Jenna pumped her rifle. "What about the water supply?"

"We take a chance. If they get inside, we're all done." He shrugged out from the satchel of explosives. "With these, we make the choice. Tru, keep the walkie on and be ready to let us in."

Appearing unsure for the first time, the kid nodded slowly. He met Mason's eyes. "Good luck, man."

"You too." Mason watched him back up a few steps before turning to Jenna. "Now you. Out. Through the tunnel. Clear the way so I can set the charges."

"Shit, no." Jenna lifted her rifle as if she'd rather use it on him than obey. "I'm not leaving you. That's the deal, John."

"What, so we can both die here, trying to do this? That doesn't make any sense." He opened the satchel and placed the canisters along various rock ledges, wedging some of them in ceiling cracks. "You're a hell of a lot faster than I am. Get clear and circle back to the front door."

Her mouth twisted. "Why? Why would I do that?"

"Worst-case scenario, and this fails, you'll have no power. No heat. And the tunnel might not be sealed completely. Dogs'll get in or you'll freeze to death. Maybe both. You're all they have, Jenna. Any chance—*any* chance of surviving—will evaporate if we both die."

"I'm not—"

"Enough!" Patience gone, he backed her against the slick, curving wall. "I'm your mate? All that matters?" Her shoulders tensed beneath his hands. "I feel it in you, sweetheart. You'd leave them all. Get me clear, get us both safe. After what you said to me in the woods—you'd do it, wouldn't you?"

"Yes!"

"And if you had to do it again, would you open the door to a scared bunch of strangers?"

"I—"

"Shut up. I see it in your eyes and it makes me sick." He grabbed her chin and leaned in close, anger and deathly fear making his hands shake. "Would you have Chris use my gun? I wonder who he'll do first, Penny or Ange."

Her nostrils flared on a sharp inhale. "That's not fair."

"It's the truth. You said you loved her little girl, but you'd put Ange through that? I don't believe it. Not of you." He smacked the wall with his palm, glad he could still make her flinch, glad his anger still counted for something with this new version of Jenna. "Because if I'm so goddamn important, why'd you let me send Tru away? Why not ask him to set off the explosives?"

"Stop it, John." Sharp fingernails cut into his forearms. "The only way any of this makes sense is if you're still here. With me."

He grabbed the back of her head and pulled her in for a fast, hard, desperate kiss.

"I've changed too, you know," he said. "*You* did this to me. Two months ago—fuck them. Just you and me, right?" He ran a thumb along her swollen bottom lip. His own smile felt numb. "But we need them too. The whole world's gone to shit and we *need* them. You know that."

"Our pack," she whispered.

Mason tucked a strand of hair behind her ear. Worries that had consumed him for weeks cleared out in a quick rush. He could no more protect her now than he could save himself. He simply had to trust that she'd make it, and that he could carry on if she didn't. Their obligations had grown larger than two people. And if she lost sight of that, she wouldn't be his Jenna.

"I thought I'd lost you," he whispered harshly. "But I kept going—for them. You made me promise, remember? I'm not going to let you give up on what's right either, not now. I love you too much to see you abandon that part of yourself."

She bared her teeth, but tears shone in her eyes. "You tell me you love me, then say I could lose you. That's *cruel*."

"Everything's gonna be fine. You'll see."

"You never sugar-coated it for me before."

"That's the truth—the truth I need to hear." After one last kiss, he hauled her away from the wall and gave her a little shove. "Now get out. Don't let me down, Barclay."

For a moment, he didn't think she'd go. She stood as fiercely angry as he'd ever seen. He could see the wolf shimmering within her, the animal snarl and raised hackles. A glow kindled about her lean, trembling body. For a frightening minute, he thought she was about to shift.

Then she closed her eyes and mastered the urge. Jenna planted a kiss on the side of his neck, just below his left earlobe. He touched that place as she bolted out of the cave, her weapon leveled.

Gunfire echoed outside, along with the howls of the dying. Mason turned back to the satchel of explosives, trusting that she'd protect his back while he set the remaining charges. With everything in place, he crawled out into the faint, pale light of dawn. No beasts. No sounds. No sign of Jenna. Now he hoped that the damn canisters would work.

"Be ready, Tru," he shouted back into the tunnel.

He pulled the rifle to his shoulder. At that range, through the scope, every target was huge. He chose the center canister, then picked the next six pockets he'd hit. One time through, like a dress rehearsal, he aimed at each one in turn. His muscles would remember, even if he couldn't see.

Once the tunnel mouth collapsed, well . . . all bets were off.

Mason exhaled. And pulled the trigger.

FORTY

Jenna slid down the hill, keening her fear to the sky. Not for herself. For John. He'd worn the expression of a man who thought it might come down to personal sacrifice. She needed a live lover, not a dead hero. Firing a few warning shots, she took off running, still screaming. She didn't stop until she got the attention of the monsters around the tunnel entrance. Then she paused only to shoot one. She'd upgraded her marksmanship from fair to pretty damn good.

A fierce and mournful howl arose from the rest. Two tore into the fresh corpse with slavering fangs, while the rest decided fresh meat looked more promising. The hunt was on.

Jenna ran.

"Draw them away. Easy for him to say."

What sounded simple enough in theory proved scary as hell in practice. She scrambled up the side of the ravine and ran toward the distant trees. The snow made her footing tricky, hiding threats that would be obvious during any other season. A root tripped her and she landed hard. Half of her spare ammo went bouncing away. No chance to recover it.

Buy time for John.

He needed to set off the explosives without the beasts snapping at his concentration. Any mistake would prove disastrous. The entrance needed to be sealed, no question. If humans weren't to go the way of the woolly mammoth, she would run like she never had before.

Dogs snarled and snapped behind her. Jenna didn't think about what would happen if the pack caught up to her. As she hit level ground, she spun and shot, dropping another one on blood-spattered snow. Red over white. The stark colors stayed with her as she burst into motion again. They raced a bit closer every time she tripped or paused to get a sense of direction. The death of their comrades didn't faze them at all.

But every monster she downed thinned their ranks. Jenna used the trees, weaving with an expertise born of familiarity. She'd weathered a number of bad situations in these woods. This wouldn't be the last.

In the distance, an explosion rose up like a phoenix. He'd done it. Praying John was safe, she just had to survive this game of hide-and-seek.

Jenna pressed into the low boughs of a pine tree, despite the prickle of the needles. The sap wasn't running, but the smell was pungent enough to queer her trail. Any delay to let her catch her breath. If she found a tree that could bear her weight, she might shimmy up and go all tower sniper. No, bad idea. She'd be trapped when the ammo ran out, and she couldn't count on rescue.

Her mind raced as she darted to the other side of the tree. The monsters moved nearby, snuffling and growling to each other. She couldn't fire on one without bringing the lot down on her. Did she have enough bullets for them all? She'd lost track.

Glancing around, she took stock of her surroundings. She couldn't be more than a mile from the station, but that distance would be tough to cover. A target-rich environment, John might call it. She hoped he was all right. Everything would be worth it as long as he survived.

Jenna took a deep breath to steady herself, the exhalation wreathing her head like smoke.

Surely she had most of them after her. Good news, at least. She pushed through the winter-dry thicket. A beast waited on the other side. It launched at her. She brought her rifle up, sighting and firing in the same motion. Ammo slammed through its chest and splattered guts. The monster twitched and lay still, a few scant feet away. She pegged it in the head just to be sure.

A howl rose up nearby, both mourning and an exchange of information. The rest would find her now. Her heart thudded like a drum. She didn't like fighting by herself. Her back felt cold and vulnerable; she'd gotten used to somebody watching it.

Jenna ran. She didn't have time to scout. Just keep moving. She would head toward the station if she knew exactly where it was. The trees made everything look the same. Her footprints and her scent left a trail behind her, but she couldn't worry about that. She was cold, and the leaden morning sky threatened more snow. Black branches lashed her as she fled, tearing at her jacket, her hair her skin.

Two demon dogs slammed out of the trees behind her. She heard them and smelled them, the raw odor of fetid meat and steel-sharp hunger. She spun. They flanked her—clever move. She couldn't swing her rifle fast enough to catch both. Jenna blasted the one on the right. It yelped and fell dead as its partner lunged from the left. Teeth sank into her upper arm, dragging her down. If she hit the ground, her guts would be a feast.

Not today. Not me. I'm not food.

The bite burned like hell, as if acid seeped from its fangs. She tossed the rifle to her left hand and clubbed the beast in the skull with all her strength. No fear now, just rage. The blow stunned it long enough for Jenna to fire. More blood on the snow. She didn't think she could do that again. Her right arm felt weak. Something had torn beneath the skin.

The rifle slid from her fingers. *Too heavy. Slowing me down.*

More howling in the distance. They'd find her soon. She needed help. She needed John.

No, keep it together. She thrust aside her panic and worked quickly, tearing a strip from her shirt and wrapping it around her arm—not a tourniquet, but it would slow the bleeding. She scanned the sky before choosing a direction, but moving fast was no longer an option. She was so tired.

"You need to shift," she said aloud.

But it didn't happen, no matter how much she wanted it. Nothing. She couldn't think herself into being a wolf, not like she'd hoped.

Jenna ramped back up to a run. She thought she was headed home. Going headlong, she tripped over a rock half hidden in the snow and smashed face-first into a fallen tree. Her cheek burned where the bark abraded the skin. Pain shot into her brain. She might have broken her nose. More blood flowing. Jesus, with two wounds, she was a wet dream of a scent trail now.

The howls closed in.

A primitive part of her shuddered. She wasn't a wolf. She was a hunted human. Prey. Walking meat. Her muscles locked with cold and terror. It was all she could do to slink inside a log, hollowed out from long seasons. She huddled and tried to stop the bleeding. They'd find her soon, and Jenna didn't have her rifle—not that she could do anything with her injured right arm. The log was just a place to die.

A growl sounded in her throat.

Her wolf had gone to sleep when she forced it down back at the cave. It had relented, at least until its survival became uncertain. Primal strength surged through her bones, carrying fire in its wake. Her body blazed with agony as the change began. This time she rode it out. She didn't shoot upward, watching from above, not feeling. No, she stayed with it and breathed it. Nothing had ever hurt so badly, liquid agony roiling in her veins. She flashed through that strange no-place again, a place hewn of pain. When she twisted through to the other side, she wore sister-wolf's skin.

But more of Jenna rode along this time. She remembered who she was. On the other side of a dream, she lived as a human female with a man named John. She was hurt and she needed to go home. But first, the wolf had some hunting to do.

She bounded from the log, unimpeded by a sore paw or a wounded muzzle. One sniff put her on their scent. The wrong-dogs stank, and she would hunt them all. She threw back her head and howled, warning that they'd trespassed again.

My woods.

Two stood in the clearing, just past the trees. Her ears flickered. She leaped toward them, rushing headlong through the snow. Her muscles bunched. She sprang and tore at one's throat, the motion smooth and satisfying. She spat. Their meat was rancid, and their blood tasted foul. Then she swiped at the other with a paw, a warning it didn't heed. She threw all her weight forward and savaged his shoulder. It fell, crippled, and she landed a killing bite.

More came, and she fought. Teeth and claws, she tore their flesh and snarled. She was a wolf; they were only rotten mongrels. They died one at a time, but she paid the price. One tore into her wounded foreleg. Another bit her in the side. She took a claw in the chest. Their numbers would eventually overwhelm her. She ached.

More howls sounded in the distance.

Home. She needed to go home. If she died, there would be no more hunts. The wolf turned and sniffed. She found the faint scent of humans, a smell that beckoned her as strongly as raw meat. Her mouth watered. *This way.*

FORTY-ONE

Tru kept an eye on the front door and an ear on the walkie-talkie. He hated waiting.

He'd been in the tunnel when the big boom hit. The entire place shook, and for a minute he'd thought the whole thing might cave in. But none of the dogs snaked through, so he'd hightailed it to the front door. More waiting. He passed the time counting cracks in the wall plaster and wiping bloody grime off his hands.

Dumb fuckin' things. They should know better than to mess with us.

He didn't like remembering they'd once been human. Better to focus on what they'd become. The walkie-talkie crackled to life in his hands, making him jump.

"Everything okay?" Harvard asked.

"Yep. How you guys holding up?"

"Penny's asleep. Ange and I are coping. Did Mason close the tunnel? We heard the blast."

"It looked good on my side." Tru frowned, his head throbbing. "Now they just need to get home."

But that was the hard part. He signed off after promising to keep Harvard posted.

Jenna and Mason had been out there a long time. He told himself not to worry. They knew what they were doing. But if they died, it left his survival in Harvard's hands. Tru didn't like those odds.

His instructions had been to sit tight, ready to lay down cover fire in case things got hot and heavy when they returned. He was a better shot than anything else, but not so good in the woods. He wasn't quiet like Mason. Or Jenna in her wolf form. So it would be stupid to go looking for them, and he wasn't stupid.

He'd sit tight.

A faint scream roused him. Definitely a woman's scream. He'd expected contact on the walkie-talkie first, but he knew the sound of Jenna in trouble. Knowing what Mason would do in his place, Tru unfastened the locks and flung the door open without a second thought. A chill wind swept down the hall, raising goose bumps even through his jacket.

He took in the situation in a glance. Jenna sprawled naked, just past the trees. Blood stained the snow. Having taken a number of wounds, she didn't look like she had the strength to crawl a foot, let alone back to the station.

He squeezed his eyes shut. Dumb to go out there. *Dumb as hell.*

He grabbed his rifle and ran. The dark trees lined up behind her appeared beyond imposing, an unearthly honor guard to ward over her last moments. The sky arced behind her like a gray tomb, and the world revealed only grave hues, all contrast and no color.

Dipshit. He'd read *Lord of the Rings* once too often.

Monsters launched from the shadows. He fired again and again, forming a protective perimeter of hot lead. He wasn't shooting to kill so much as to deter. What he wouldn't give for a full-auto AK right now. If this were a game, he could switch weapons at will, a full arsenal on his back without any weight.

But life wasn't a game.

Tru got lucky and a few dropped, but there were too many to

handle alone—not while protecting Jenna. This had to be the last of the pack. Desperate now. They wouldn't stop coming.

He reached her, then stripped off his jacket and slumped it over her shoulders. The cold air was a relief against his sweaty back.

"Can you walk?" he asked.

She tried to push up, but her right arm folded beneath her. *Jesus.*

"The bites aren't too deep," she said, her voice a raw protest.

Of course, he thought. She'd been protected by a thick layer of winter fur. But exhaustion and shock made her clumsy.

"Get up. C'mon. We're dog food out here."

"Go, Tru." Her head didn't move from where it drooped toward the bloodied snow. "Don't be a hero."

He shot another one and grinned. "Didn't you hear? Superman got old, and I'm up for the job."

"You idiot. Just give me the rifle and run for it. I can cover you."

"Mason would kill me."

For the first time, hope flashed into her eyes. "Is he inside? Waiting?"

Too messed up after all that fighting. She'd have known better if she thought it through. Why would Tru come out after her with Mason around to do the job? So yeah, it was the wrong assumption, but he couldn't tell her the truth. He let her believe.

"On your feet. Up we go."

Tru tugged, ignoring her cry of pain as he shoved her arms into his jacket. It was a fair run back to the station, but otherwise, they were sitting ducks. And Jenna would freeze to death. She fell before they'd gone more than a few steps. Damn. She was going to get him killed. Where the hell was Mason? Jenna was *his* woman.

With Jenna wobbling and faltering, he fired again and then grabbed the walkie-talkie. "Mason, we fucking need you, man."

Silence.

Anger lashed through him, lending strength. Tru spun and flung her over his shoulder. He lacked the bulk for a fireman's carry, so his run turned into a drunken stagger. Then he heard the crunch of the dogs bounding through the snow. They were gaining. The door might as well be ten miles away.

Fuck it. He had to fight. Tru set Jenna down and raised his weapon. What happened next shook him to his core.

Penny appeared on the snow before him. No shoes. No coat. She wore sweat pants and a little pink T-shirt. A glow kindled around her. He had no idea what she was doing out there, or how she'd popped out of thin air. *Magic. Holy shit.*

Beasts crouched all around her, coiling to spring. Tru fired over her head, nailing one in the neck. Blood sprayed everywhere. But the others kept coming. No way he could win this. No way.

Grimly, he fired on. He'd protect these two with his dying breath, even if it killed him.

And it probably would.

"Penny!" Ange screamed.

The girl was just . . . gone. One minute she'd been with them. The next, poof.

There was trouble outside, and Chris just knew Penny had launched into the thick of it. The fierce instinct that pushed up from his gut shocked him speechless. Before his adrenaline failed, he hurried to the main floor. Ange raced hot on his heels. His blood pumped hard, quick enough to make him sick. But he'd just outrun it—outrun the nausea, move faster than the fear.

From the supply room he grabbed the spare shotgun. Gun-shy? Yeah, he was. But he also wanted to see morning. He stuffed the shotgun with all the shells it would hold and hauled on his parka. Then he handed the nine-millimeter to Ange, who held it with more surety than he'd ever seen. And why not? Outside, her child was in danger. Nothing mattered to her more than that.

He flung open the door to a sharp blast of icy wind. His glasses fogged over. He rubbed at them with quick swipes. Jenna sprawled unconscious at Tru's feet. She must have gone wolf at some point because she wore only Tru's jacket. Her legs were nearly as white as the snow, except where vicious wounds gaped red and ugly. Tru stood over her, looking determined but as young as his years, facing down the snarling, starving pack. Penny. . . glowed.

Doesn't matter why. No time to think.

"Over here, you sons of bitches!" Ange called.

They both hurtled onto the battlefield, weapons ready. The woman beside him fired as she ran, trying desperately to draw the attack from her only child. Her aim was off. Never a good shot, the movement and the distance prevented her from doing more than picking holes in the snow. One monster crouched and leaped, taking the girl to the ground. Tru spattered its brains. The light around Penny dimmed as she fell. Chris couldn't see how badly she was hurt.

Goddamn this shotgun. He wasn't in range. His weapon had plenty of stopping power, but little accuracy at such a distance. Firing now would just waste his ammo.

Other dogs slunk closer, trying to get at Jenna. Tru couldn't be everywhere at once, and the monsters grew bolder. They thought they'd won. Chris let out a fierce yell. He and Ange ran on, together. Closer now. Almost close enough.

A deep calm eased the tension from his muscles. He had seen it in big cats, the mountain lions he'd devoted his life to. They limbered and relaxed just before leaping, as if their bodies knew the prey was already dead. The wind wasn't so fierce now. His hands didn't shake.

The beasts leaped. Toward Jenna. Tru. And the fallen child.

"*Penny!*" Ange screamed.

She killed one, wild with motherly rage, as if she no longer feared the gun in her hand. Good for her. They could do this. The demon dogs might have once been people, but they'd lost too much. They couldn't succeed against rational beings, no matter the magic in the world. Bravery mattered. So did solidarity.

He pumped the shotgun. "Tru, down!"

The boy hit the ground, protecting Jenna and Penny with his whole body. If the monsters got them, it would be because they chewed all the way through Tru's back. *Heart of a lion, this kid.*

Chris fired and blew one wide open. Not too many left now. He fired again. With every pull of the trigger, monsters dropped dead. He liked that power. A lot.

Step. Fire. Reload.

Only four left. Turning as a pack away from Tru, where he huddled over fallen friends, they correctly judged Ange and Chris to be the real threats. You just don't fuck with a woman's child. She'll rip your face off with her bare hands. The beasts snarled a message that Jenna would probably understand. Chris didn't care what they had to say. Not even a little.

Raw fury surged through to his soles. *You're not taking anything else from me.*

Weeks of pent-up anger and frustration found release as he plugged round after round into what remained of his old life. The monsters swarmed. For the first time he saw them up close, the unnatural *other* of them. Their awful aura made his skin itch and his brain misfire, tapping into deeply primitive places.

Magic. Awful and unholy.

His scalp tingled with the surety of it. Magic existed. There was no other way to explain this or force it to make sense. *Adapt or die.* That old rule still held true. He'd be damned if his evolutionary progress halted today. Nobody would perish because he couldn't accept reality. The scientist could kill. And he did.

His shotgun sparked until the snow bled red.

Only two left.

Chris reloaded as a beast charged at Ange. With shaking hands, she raised her nine and pulled the trigger. Click. Empty.

"New mag!" he shouted.

But by the terrible resignation in her blue eyes, she knew she didn't have time. Her gun hand dropped to her side. The monster took her down before Chris could raise his shotgun. With ravening fangs, the dog ripped out her throat. Ange's blood sprayed all over the trampled, icy ground.

Five seconds later, Chris blew its head off. He wheeled on the other. Boom. Hole through the torso. Just like he felt.

Five seconds too late.

Later, he might review those five seconds. Relive them in his head, over and over. But he needed to get Jenna and the children inside. Tru wobbled to his feet, his shirt front frosted with snow. His lips were tinged blue. Tears frosted his lashes.

"I couldn't carry her," he said, his young face tight with failure.

Yeah, Chris knew exactly how he felt. *Ange should've made it. I should've been faster.*

No. Not the time for self-recrimination. He didn't know if more monsters prowled the area. He would make use of the temporary quiet to get everyone the hell back inside. Otherwise, Ange had died for nothing. She'd come back as a ghost to kill him in his sleep if he didn't see to Penny.

"You did great. Take Penny. I'll get Jenna." Chris knelt before the woman's frigid body. She wasn't shivering. Not good. He lifted her from the snow. "And if you ever call me 'Harvard' again, I'll throw you out a goddamn window."

Tru shot the nearest dog in the gut, unable to look at Ange's body. It was the one that had killed her. "Whatever, man. I owe you."

Snow and ice and Jenna's limp weight took running off the menu, but Chris kept his eyes on the door. Not far now. Twenty meters—nothing at all. Just a winter stroll. He kept moving, gulps of frozen air burning his throat.

He kicked the door wide and backed in, keeping Jenna's head from smacking against metal. He laid her on the floor and turned to help Tru secure the door.

"I'll get more ammo," the kid said. "We gotta go back out for Mason."

"We stay."

"Who put you in charge?"

Chris grabbed Tru and slammed him into the wall. "I *am* in charge. You want to try me?"

"You're a fucking coward," Tru gritted out, still struggling.

"I just saved your life. You keep it up and I won't bother again." He glanced down to Jenna. "Assuming she doesn't bleed out on the floor, she'll wake up and want to know where Mason is. Either way, it won't be pretty. In fact, she'll probably be downright vicious, even without going wolf. And I haven't even seen what shape Penny's in. I'm going to need your help." When Tru's struggles slowed, logic penetrating his skull, Chris eased up. "We have injured to deal with."

Tru puffed out an angry breath, but he nodded. "I'll take Penny to the dorm. Her arm's bleeding. I can't tell how bad it is." He paused. "I wish Ange was here."

Those words lodged in Chris's heart like a steel blade. "But we have to make do."

Downstairs, he gathered all the first-aid supplies they'd brought back from Wabaugh. He tended Penny first, perhaps as a gesture to her fallen mother. But Jenna also healed faster. She would probably recover before the child, even if her wounds were worse.

Penny had suffered a deep claw mark on her upper arm, likely where the beast gouged as it took her to the ground. Why hadn't it torn out her throat, like the other had done to Ange? *As if the light around her protected her somehow.* Chris lost himself in the mindless work of cleaning and stitching the wound, trying not to remember how ragged and helpless Ange had looked right before she died.

Tru proved a capable assistant as he handed over bandages and antiseptic without a single smart remark. He caught the kid watching Penny with a puzzled look.

"How do you think she got there?" he asked finally.

Chris shook his head. "Magic? Don't look at me that way. I have no clue. Just . . . one minute she was with us, and the next? Gone."

"Yeah." Tru's wondering tone said he wasn't giving up on the topic. "She disappeared in the woods, went missing for a few minutes when the danger got too close. And she scared the crap out of Mason and me by popping up in our room when the door was shut and all."

"Maybe. Probably?" Chris only knew uncertainty. He bowed his head down and kept working, although grief pulled at him like a determined undertow.

Not now. Later. More to do.

FORTY-TWO

Mason shook his head. The clanging in his ears wouldn't ease up. His chest felt heavy and molten. Ice slivers melted on his face. The wind stole his body heat and scattered it into the forest. He looked up, then ripped off the ruined goggles. What remained of the tunnel's entrance lay smoldering beneath a pewter-colored cloud of smoke and soil.

He struggled to his feet and looked down. His coat had been sheared open. Blood formed a spatter pattern on his T-shirt. With unsteady fingers, he touched his chest and found dozens of tiny flecks of shrapnel embedded in his skin.

Great. Now my front matches my back.

Dazed, he found the remains of his ammo bag. One of the explosions must have taken out what he had left, but he didn't remember any of it. He'd fired. Things exploded. Repeat. Until he'd wound up playing kissy face with the frozen turf.

Feeling numb despite his injuries—one benefit to falling into the snow—Mason found his AR-15 and checked the magazine. Empty. A second scan of the area confirmed that his ammo had gone up in the big boom. Although he didn't hear any dogs nearby, his sense of vulnerability sharpened the cold against his exposed skin.

Clutching his field jacket with one hand, he stumbled to the tunnel entrance and double-checked his handiwork. Rock formed a heavy, deep wall. He toed a couple of places, expecting the bulk to give way—maybe a hollow pocket behind a sturdy-looking facade. But nothing moved.

Back door. Locked.

At last.

He turned and caught sight of the ax. Not the most elegant means of defense, but he wasn't about to complain. Pain lanced through his chest when he bent over to retrieve it. Every muscle whined. He felt exhausted and very, very old.

Blinking away the spots, he focused on putting one foot in front of the other. Get back to the station. Get patched up. Find Jenna.

He opened his mind, searching for her. Nothing. Panic skated through his guts. Trying again, breathing to find some level of calm, he reached out. Not even her wolf side howled back at him. He hiked the flat metal ax blade against one shoulder and set off toward the ravine exit. Although worry for Jenna threatened to cloud his senses, he bound and gagged every worst-case scenario.

Just make it back. That's all you have to do. You promised her it would be fine.

With his mind unguarded and searching, he pulled in odd images and sensations—that sick, sliding out-of-body feel. It swelled and darkened until his senses receded, like he'd turned down the volume on the physical world. He fingered the ax haft. The crunch of his boots sounded far away. The back of his neck itched.

He turned.

A single monster stared at him from between two black barren trunks. It tipped its grim, greasy head to the side, jowls tinted with bloodstains. A scraggy pelt hung in limp patches across its back and haunches. Claws like a bear's poked out from its foot pads and dug into the icy snow. A waft of dead carrion stink crept over the chill air.

But Mason didn't move. He could have tried the ax. He could have wrestled the thing until its damn rotted head tore off. But he waited.

Slowly, with the building energy of a thunderhead, the beast's body realigned. Mason had once dislocated his shoulder in a bar fight, and he'd never forget the sound of popping his humerus back into its socket. The dog snapped and wriggled in its own skin with those same popping sounds, bones changing places and shape. He lengthened and grew, his haunches straightening into human legs.

Briefly, Mason thought of Jenna. He'd yet to see her transform, and part of him was damn thankful. But whereas Jenna's silver-tipped wolf eased back into her supple human form, this monstrous creature transformed into a living nightmare. Still deformed. Still rotten. Just a little bit more human.

He was the humanoid thing Mason had seen with Jenna in the basement—the one in charge of this winter horror show. Naked, a layer of thick body hair covered his pale skin. His underbite made lower canine teeth protrude. Bushy eyebrows topped a pronounced brow.

A guttural grumble. A whine. Then a look of frustration that appeared almost human in that wrong, deformed face.

Mason lifted the ax from his shoulder.

The clicking grunts in the monstrous throat came nearer to language. "Hungry," he slurred.

The reality of what he was seeing turned Mason's stomach. He felt pity. After years of fighting these beasts, he felt actual pity. This thing used to be human, just like those putrid dogs. They were caught in a fiendish hell, as much as Mason and the others. The rules of living on Earth had changed, perhaps forever.

"Cold," the grotesque thing spit out.

"I know," Mason found himself saying. He needed to just lop the monster's head off and be done with it—put him out of his misery.

But the remainder of humanity, in the thing, in himself, wouldn't let him. "You need to call off your curs. There's only death here."

"Hungry."

"Sorry. Not gonna happen." Mason gave the ax a few practice twirls.

That aggression angered the beast-man. His back hunched into a distinctly canine pose. He lifted those bear-claw hands and snarled, his human side pulled under by pure animal rage. Mason held up the ax and slashed the air with it. The monster flinched, hustling back a few feet.

"Remember this?" Mason shouted. "Remember home-improvement projects and logging—human things. Remember cars and computers and books? Human things. Remember?" He poked the blade into the space between them, but the beast didn't retreat again.

A bunched tangle of bushes shivered to his right. Mason turned in time to catch a leaping demon dog as it sprang into attack. He chopped it cleanly through the neck. This was the one thing he knew how to do well. Fight. It didn't matter how many lurked in these woods. He'd go down swinging. The beast landed on its back and didn't try to get up. The bony, bloody chest simply heaved.

But Mason was done trying to understand these creatures. He was tired, cold, injured, and pissed off. He sank the ax into the dog's stomach, his hands jerking against the impact of blade on bone. No satisfaction in ending their lives anymore. Simply the knowledge that his species would not endure if theirs thrived. Grim. Unavoidable.

More beasts came, their attacks sluggish and uncoordinated. Their leader, the feral man, slunk back between the naked trees, his face twisted with what looked like disappointment and fear. Mason took each predator as it lunged and fought, each one of them clumsy like toys running low on batteries.

Edging backward, swinging the ax to ward off what remained of their attack, Mason made steady, slow progress. He could see the top of the station from between the last of the trees.

A monster sped from the undergrowth and knocked him behind the knees. The brunt of its slight weight seemed aimed at unbalancing him, not taking him down directly. Feeling sluggish, his chest burning like skin under a tattoo needle, Mason spun. Another repeated the hard knock against the back of his knees. He stumbled. The ax flew from his hands.

When he looked up, he swore. He called himself every foul name he could think of. A ring of the last monsters closed in like a noose. The ax lay useless ten feet away. And Mason's own blood froze on the snow.

The beast-man kicked between a pair of his lackeys and entered the circle. He cracked the knuckles of each hand, then squatted and opened his arms. A direct challenge. Mason could almost imagine that long-ago bar fight, with the hairy, naked, fetid man in front of him standing in for just another sloppy drunk. The curs were his cronies, waiting to finish the job.

So this is it? He'd do barehand, one-on-one combat with a half-animal thing, with the best option being that if he lived long enough, he'd get to ward off another eight beasts.

Mason pushed to his feet and shrugged out of his ruined camo jacket. The air stripped his body heat. Blood chilled across his pectorals. But he'd do this thing.

In the back of his mind, he heard Jenna. She was waking. She was upset and frantic, but thoughts of her filled him with warmth. Whatever had happened to her between the tunnel and the station, she was safe now. The others would patch her up. Instead of saying good-bye to her, he closed the door that linked their souls. He didn't want her to see this, to feel it. And he didn't want her to come out after him.

Something of their love would live on if she did.

But in the quiet of his head, he whispered. *Good-bye, my love.*

"Cold," the thing said again.

Then it threw back his head and howled. The rest chimed in with a collected wail that raised the hair on Mason's arms.

"Yeah, well, I'm cold too, you fucker. Let's go."

The beast-man snapped. He lunged forward, the weight of his body shifting to the right. Mason ducked left and added a shove. The monster fell, sliding against the snow. He grunted and cried out. When the circle of drooling monsters moved to take Mason down, he rose up on all fours and snarled as if to say, *My fight.*

Mason strode forward and kicked. The man grunted and curled into a ball.

"Those are your kidneys." Mason kicked again. "That's your sternum." And again. "And that's your mandible. You remember that? Huh? Language. Anatomy. Maybe you never knew it, but once you had the ability to learn it."

The man spat blood onto the snow. A tooth followed. He growled, "Hungry."

The single-mindedness of his opponent had the power to make Mason shiver. They wouldn't ever stop. They wouldn't relent, because they didn't think about the odds or the fear. Even if half-men monstrosities like this guy managed to come up with a few strategies, they wouldn't ever aspire for more than food and shelter and spreading their corruption.

No shit, a Dark Age. Mitch, I wish you were here.

"That's the difference," Mason said, as much to himself as to his opponent. He felt the dogs growing restless, their frantic energy held in check as if they wore leashes. Only their leader's command held them at bay. "But you won't win this thing—even if I die here."

He dropped the weight of his knee against the man's chest, which collapsed in a sick crack. Unnatural claws scraped at his forearms, but Mason pushed past the weakening defenses. He looped his numb hands around its neck, trusting what he saw rather than what he felt. A quick twist and the life snapped out.

Mason looked to the sky and breathed in. Then the mob hit him from the front, behind, everywhere at once, and his mouth tasted of blood.

FORTY-THREE

Her wounds weren't as bad as they'd seemed, just a dozen slices coupled with exhaustion and cold. Chris had patched up the damage, with quick dressings wrapped up tight. Some soup and hot tea went a long way to making her feel better. She'd thanked Chris and Tru until her voice all but gave out. Now Jenna was dressed and back on her feet. Only residual weakness and a few sharp twinges marked her ordeal.

Except it wasn't over—and it wouldn't be until he came home.

Funny that she could feel this way about the man who'd stuffed her in the trunk of her own car, one who came bearing stories of Armageddon. She paced upstairs, watching the snow. Dead trees, dead white. Apart from the rays of dying sunlight, it was a black-and-white world.

He cut me off.

Fear owned her. A dark part wondered if it was because he hadn't wanted her to experience his death. She didn't know what that would do to her, feeling her mate's life end. Nothing good. Jenna touched her brow to the window, watching the sun go down. Soon there wouldn't be anything out there to see.

She heard someone coming down the hall. Turning, she fixed her features into a semblance of welcome. Tru slid in first, followed by Chris and Penny. It no longer surprised her to see Chris holding the little girl, who gazed at Jenna with sad blue eyes. They all wanted news. Amazing, actually, that they'd managed to hold off this long.

They'd told her about Ange. But Jenna hadn't wept. Not yet. Maybe the tears would come in time.

"He did it," Tru said then. "Nothing will come up through the tunnels. And the water's still flowing up from that underground spring. We're good."

Chris nodded tightly. "He's right. The generators are still going strong. Jenna, you sure you're strong enough to be walking around?"

"People don't get better in beds. They get better by testing their limits." She couldn't believe she'd just quoted Mitch. One day, she'd write down all his truisms. *The Dark Age According to Barclay*. He'd been a huge proponent of walking off injuries, and when that failed, rubbing dirt on them. "I'm not using up our stores, not if I don't have to. And I *can't* rest."

"Understandable." Chris put his hand on her shoulder and her muscles coiled. She leashed the impulse to snap at him. It wasn't smart to handle a wounded wolf whose mate had gone missing. Jenna didn't know what he'd seen in her face, but he took a slow step back.

"Hey, Chris," Tru said. "Maybe you and Penny should go . . . uh, do some stuff."

Huh, I think that's the first time I ever heard the kid call him anything but Harvard.

Jenna didn't apologize as Chris left with Penny. Between John's absence and Ange's death, everything was wrong. A glance out the window showed her that the sun had gone—along with most of her hope. The sky shone like a bruise, twilight fading to mourning purple.

Tru sat on a table, knees splayed. "He'll be okay. Right?" The slight pause before the kid tagged on the question didn't fool Jenna. He needed a positive answer more than the truth.

"If anybody can fight through and make it back, he can. I did what I could to draw them off." She didn't mention the alpha or the cold, or how injuries weakened a body. Likely he knew that as well as she did.

Jenna curled her hands into fists, wanting so badly to run out and look for him. A silent scream built in her throat. Thankfully, for all his general acuity, Tru trusted her. He could feel better for a little while at least.

He smiled. "Yeah, you had an assload of them on you."

"Thanks again. I owe you big-time." She wasn't exaggerating to make him feel better. "I hope I didn't bleed on you too much."

Tru shrugged. "It's weirder to find you in the snow naked."

With a wince, Jenna conceded the point. "So, what do you think? Do I need to keep a cache by the front door, maybe hide some clothes in the woods?"

"It'll be easier, come spring."

Those words loosened a stone in her chest. Tru believed they were going to make it. He thought there would be a spring, and a summer, and another fall—time enough for them to perfect the new rituals and skills that would permit their survival. He believed they would build, like Mason had said was her gift. Jenna considered that possibility. They needed a proper place to live, something designed for a simpler time, with ventilation and different cooking facilities . . .

Just for a second, she let herself believe too.

Tears filled her eyes, but she blinked them back and found a smile. "I hope so. Would it be okay if I hugged you?"

He hunched his shoulders. "I'm not much for that stuff. But if it would make *you* feel better . . ."

"It would."

Looking uneasy, the kid stepped forward, and Jenna wrapped her arms around him. He felt more fragile than he was, all bones and bad attitude. But beneath that beat an incredibly strong heart. She couldn't believe he'd charged out into that mob, all by himself, to save her ass. He hadn't broken. Hadn't run, even when it would make sense in a man twice his age.

John was right. We are pack.

He patted her on the back as if he didn't know what to do with his hands. "You good?"

She nodded. "Look, I'm going to get some blankets and camp out up here. From this side, you can see the front door."

"Watching for him," Tru said.

"Yeah. You want to sit with me?"

"I don't need to hang out in the basement anymore. So I could."

Please do. I don't want to keep this vigil alone.

Maybe he saw some of that in her expression, the need coursing through her. He gave a terse nod. "You stay here. I'll get the supplies."

Jenna turned back to the windows and willed John to break from the trees, to come stumbling across the white expanse of churned snow. He didn't.

Tru kept watch with her until late in the evening. They didn't talk. He fell asleep sometime after midnight, though he might be embarrassed as hell about reaching his limit. In the early morning, Chris came to the doorway and stood there for a minute.

Jenna turned lazily, her head feeling muddy and clouded. "Need something?"

"You should go to bed."

"Would you? If it were someone you loved?"

Chris looked at his hands. "You want some tea?"

It was the kind of offer Ange would have made. By his awful expression, he knew it. Jenna's heart twisted. But she didn't go to him.

"Sure." It would help keep her awake. By way of privation, her hard-core sugar and caffeine addiction had been kicked, so even a little bit wired her up these days.

"Feels good just to do something," Chris said as he brought the drink.

Failure weighed on him even to her distracted eyes. Maybe he felt like he should have done more. Saved the day, somehow, with no losses. That wasn't logical, but something had changed him. Whether it was the fight or the loss, Jenna couldn't know. Chris's fire had gone out, no longer questing after answers in the same way. He wasn't the same man they'd heard talking into a radio without any hope he'd be heard.

She didn't speak any of her thoughts. No sense in it when he had enough to contend with. Jenna lifted the mug for a long drink.

Instinct made her turn. Pain and exhaustion vanished, as if a door had been opened in her heart.

John.

She thrust the cup at Chris and sprinted for the windows. There he was, shambling toward the station. He fell twice while she watched, afraid desperation made her delusional. But no. He got up with a dogged determination that could belong to nobody else, not even a figment of her imagination.

"Tru! Up now! You're not done yet, soldier."

"Wha—?"

"We have one more to bring home."

He snapped to with a speed that saddened her even as she blessed it. Matching Jenna's movements, Tru shrugged into his jacket and laid hands on his rifle. "He's back?"

"Chris," Jenna said on her way out. "Bring the blankets. We're going to get him."

"Right behind you."

Jenna sped downstairs at a dead run with Tru hot on her heels.

"My arm's still a little weak," she told Tru. Though she healed much faster than before, she didn't recover overnight. But most of her wounds already looked four days old. "So I need you on his left."

Tru nodded. "Got it."

He unfastened the locks with a speed born of practice. Jenna burst out of the station, stumbling over the tossed and refrozen snow. It hadn't been obvious from upstairs, but John had lost his pack. No weapons, no ammo. Not even the ax. Hell, half of his clothes were gone. He was covered in blood from head to toe, as if he had been rolling in guts. The foul grime had frozen to his skin, leaving her to guess at how badly he was hurt.

His eyes were fogged, unfocused. When Jenna and Tru ran up, he settled into a fighting stance, despite his struggle to stay standing. Finding him didn't relieve her mind. She fought its frantic surge. They couldn't afford to fight him just to get him safe.

"Stand down," she ordered.

A shudder rolled through him, as if he recognized the authoritative tone. He let them take hold, one on either side. They dragged him back to the station. His weight tugged against Jenna's shoulders. Tru grunted, his breath coming in sharp puffs. Inside, while the kid did up the locks, Chris wrapped John in blankets and helped transport him downstairs.

The next few hours crawled past in an endless nightmare. Jenna's hands shook too much to be of any help to Chris while he cleaned and stitched. One gash showed the pale glint of bone. Jesus. So much raw flesh. So much damage. Too much, even for a man like John.

He needs a real doctor. He needs a blood transfusion.

But she kept her mouth shut, afraid of giving voice to the truth. With Chris's lab experience, nobody could do better—not in their world anyway. Jenna sponged off the blood and helped get him warm, covering bare parts with blankets when they'd finished bandaging. She wanted to lie down with him, but she'd only get in the way.

Eventually, Chris booted her out in the nicest possible way. Jenna only paced. Tru dogged her steps, looking almost as worried. She wasn't setting a good example for the poor kid, but her reason for living lay motionless beyond her reach. Her mate.

Love of my life.

She'd never even told him. Talk about unfinished business. He had to live, if only to hear her say it.

Another hour passed. On her hundredth circuit, she slammed into Tru, who'd fallen out of step. Pain flashed through her sore arm. She snarled.

"Put your fangs away, Jenna," he snapped. "Like you're going to bite *me*. Please."

Whatever she might have said was interrupted by Penny. The little girl wandered out of the dormitory and into the hall. "Breakfast?"

Jenna wouldn't leave her vigil for hell or heaven itself. She looked to Tru. "Can you take this?"

"I'll fix you something, kid," he said. "Come on."

Shortly thereafter, Chris came out of the lab—their impromptu surgery. His arms were red to the elbows, and he wore a heavy frown. Hazel eyes were dark and tired behind the wire-rimmed specs. "I did all I could."

She didn't need to hear the rest. Wounds like Mason had taken required a hell of a lot more equipment and expertise than they could muster. An ache swelled up in her chest.

"And, Jenna," he said. "He's been bitten. Repeatedly. If he doesn't change soon—"

He'll end up like Edna. Like the half-shifted monsters we saw in Wabaugh.

"I'll help you take him to a bunk." She kept her expression blank. Wouldn't think about it. Wouldn't hear it. John had to be fine. "We'll need Tru too. He's heavy."

Once they settled the patient in the dorm they'd shared—God, had it only been the night before?—she said, "Go eat breakfast with Penny. Both of you. I'll take care of him from here."

Role reversal.

The days passed in an agony of fear. She'd never really considered how John must have felt during those days after she was bitten. But she thought about it now, a slow, crawling insanity of waiting and watching every rise of his chest. She contended with his wounds, changing bandages and looking for the abnormal reaction Edna had suffered. Jenna locked herself in with him, along with his trusty nine-millimeter.

She wouldn't open the door to anyone but Tru, and even then, she didn't let him in. She just took the food or drink or whatever medicine they offered and locked up again. Locked herself in with the truth. The man she loved would die a monster.

When John's fever spiked, she went down on her knees—not prayer exactly, but a complete abasement of self. There was nothing she wouldn't sacrifice to have him back. Not pride, not reason, not even . . . sanity, she thought. It wasn't melodrama; she didn't know if she could function without him. His death presented a looming chasm that would swallow her too, even if she tried to fight.

Jenna bathed him. She fed him broth and weak tea. Most of it trickled out of his slack mouth, and the scant medicine they had on hand wasn't enough to fight the fevers ransacking his body. When taking into account the grievous wounds and the unknown effects of the bites, it seemed hopeless. One by one, his systems began shutting down.

She wanted to howl but didn't have the throat for it. Instead she wept. Her tears spattered onto his chest and trickled down to pool in his navel. But he was already leaving her. Jenna rested her brow on his belly. When she had no tears left, her dry eyes just burning salt in their sockets, she raised her head and gazed down at him.

His breathing was shallow now. The first couple of days, he'd raved and thrashed. Now he just lay there. Waiting. Like her.

So she talked.

"I never told you . . . but I love you. Even in the beginning, I wasn't all that scared of you. I think I knew you wouldn't hurt me, even then." She leaned down and framed his face in her hands. "But this, John . . . if you do this, if you walk through that door without me, it'll hurt worse than anything else ever could. Don't do this. Don't break my heart."

It was stupid. Jenna *knew* it was stupid. You couldn't beg someone to get well. But she did until she had no voice left at all. She implored, she threatened, she coerced, and she lost track of what she said. Then she lay down with him and covered them both. Maybe she'd just lie with him until she died too. The doors were locked. It wouldn't hurt any of the others. She pressed her forehead to his.

"John, please. Please don't go."

In the depths of her despair, she heard a small voice. *The most powerful magic there is.*

It wasn't Mitch. Just a memory of what Mason had said in Wabaugh. But as she sat up slowly, a chill rolled over her. *I have absolutely nothing to lose.*

She found Mason's knife, the one he used to scrape the hair off his head. She'd never told him, but she liked watching him do that. With such complete lack of personal vanity, he became fierce and sexy. Before she could rethink the decision, she cut open her palm. Blood welled up, ruby bright. *Does it look . . . different?* Almost like someone had slipped ground diamonds into her veins.

She could change forms. That was magic. Therefore, she believed. With every fiber, she did. Jenna sealed her palm over the worst of Mason's wounds. She remembered reading some novel where a character said, *There are no magic words, only the will behind them.*

"My blood is yours," she whispered. "My strength, yours. Yours, my mate."

For long moments, nothing happened, and she felt *incredibly* stupid. But her faith never flagged. The invisible cord between them went taut, quivering. Heat rushed up her spine, along her shoulder, down, down through her arm and into her palm. If she squinted, Jenna could see the faint glow where her hand pressed against his skin.

Holy shit. It was working. It *had* to be.

She painted him liberally with her blood, touching each of his wounds. When the cut coagulated, she sliced herself again. The drain dragged on for what seemed like hours, until her vision went vague and sparky. Her head felt thick, and the room blurred around distant edges.

Yet she didn't stop until his breathing eased. Jenna had no idea how long she bled for him, but she didn't break the link. She wouldn't, even if it killed her. More heat poured out of her. The faint silver light around her palms bloomed brighter.

The room flashed away in a burst of white; she had nothing more to give. The darkness closed around her.

When she woke in a panic, hours later, his arms were looped around her shoulders. Skin sweaty but cool, his wounds were scabbed over—a gift from her accelerated metabolism. Tears welled in her eyes.

Fucking blood magic, Mitch. We're square now, old man.

"What's this about finding a replacement?" John asked in a rusty voice. "Something about how you're not mourning me if I'm bastard enough to die?"

FORTY-FOUR

Mason didn't speak again. He couldn't, not when Jenna lay beside him, sobbing as if he'd died. He inhaled, testing, but his chest burned. He didn't even want to think about the rest of him. His legs were uncharted territory filled with shadowy horrors he wasn't strong enough to confront. Not yet. Jenna's mental exhaustion pushed and pushed, layering with his, until he couldn't figure out how they both still breathed. No gas left in their tanks.

But his eyes were open, and Jenna was warm and soft against his side.

Gingerly, with every joint blistering in pain, he laid a graceless hand against the back of her head. His wrist was bound in bandages, as were a couple of fingers. She stilled and lifted her face, tears wetting the dark bags beneath her eyes.

He shifted on the bunk, his right shoulder bound tightly. "How long?"

"Five days."

"But I was bit."

She nodded. "I know. Repeatedly."

"So . . ." He closed his eyes, feeling outside of himself. "I didn't . . . shift?"

"No. You had a fever the whole time."

"So how come I'm still alive?"

"Blood magic." She pushed up enough to show him the self-inflicted stigmata on her palms. "Mitch was right. And if I hadn't tried, if I hadn't believed in him, you would have died."

He exhaled slowly, shaking his head in wonder. "Cure or curse. Damn. Do you have any idea how it works?"

"Maybe because we're mated. It tapped into that bond. I'm not sure I could do it with anyone else."

"You better not," he growled softly.

"Do you think this means—?"

"I'm like you?" Mason shrugged. "We won't know until I hit that catalyst Chris was talking about. That perfect storm of pain and emotional impact, or whatever the hell he said."

"Would you mind?"

"I'll be honest," he said, staring upward. "I wouldn't love it. But it's better than the alternative. And I get to be with you. I'll cross that bridge if I come to it."

Jenna studied him critically for a moment and then settled against his side, ardent but careful. "You're a wreck. Your woman should take better care of you."

Eyes closed, Mason indulged in the feel of her hip beneath his hand. "I'll take it under advisement. So tell me . . . did we win out there?"

"Yeah." She stroked a rare bit of skin on his chest that wasn't injured or bandaged. "Chris and Tru checked the tunnel from the inside. You collapsed it completely."

"We still have power?"

"Yup. And Tru said this morning that they haven't seen a single beast in days."

"They gave up," he said, his brain pulling in details from the past. "Outside. You remember that beast-man? The alpha?"

"Yeah."

"I killed him. After that, all his buddies didn't fight as hard. With eight of them—I shouldn't have survived, especially with no weapon. They lost focus. Two of them just walked away and fell over."

"They needed their pack leader to function."

"I think so. He seemed to be in command, as much as those things can be." He paused, his eyes flicking to the nine-millimeter waiting ominously on the opposite bunk. "But you haven't been out of this room to see for yourself."

Jenna stopped the idle stroking. A choked sound escaped her as she buried her face in the crook of his neck. Mason pulled her tighter, closer. Holding Jenna kept the darkness at bay. Things were different now, as if everything had changed while he lay sleeping. No walls. Nothing hidden. Her very blood coursed in his veins, as if he could feel her heart beating through the rhythm of his own. It was unspeakably beautiful, a connection unlike anything he'd ever known or imagined.

Bonded. Mates.

"Of course I didn't leave." She sniffed. "When you didn't follow me home, Chris kept the front door padlocked, or else I'd have been out there trying to find you."

Home. What a weird way to describe the station. After fighting the few monsters that had any drive left, he'd taken every step with *home* as his goal. Home, where Jenna was. He couldn't remember how he'd made it, only that stopping equaled death. Plus, he had promised her everything would be all right. Despite the impossible odds, the punk-ass kid who once robbed convenience stores had turned into a man of honor, worthy to be with such a woman.

"I'll have to thank him for that," he said quietly.

"Don't. You'll piss me off all over again. I've never felt more . . ."

Her hoarse voice seized up. "I . . . God, I was help ess. First waiting for you to come back, then waiting for Chris to patch up what was left of you, and then more damn waiting in here."

Mason started to laugh, a crazy sound that did nothing to ease the ache in his chest. But he kept laughing—then coughing and shuddering.

"What's so funny?"

"You."

"What, it's funny that I love you so much my heart feels broken with it?" She half sat up and pushed a fist between her breasts. "Because that's what it was like. I was *mourning* you, waiting for you to turn into a damn monster or to keel over dead. So you tell me what's so fucking funny."

He grinned. "You missed me."

"Asshole."

"And I think you just said you loved me."

"Not the first time," she said, her cheeks coloring.

"First I've heard."

She looked annoyed for a moment, but then her stubbornness dissolved. "I've told you about a hundred times over the last few days."

"What, is there some quota you've topped out?"

Tears slipped down her cheeks. "I love you."

Mason lifted his arm. He thumbed away the tears, but more dampened her skin. "So we traded vigils, huh? It's a shitty thing to have to do."

"You could say that, yeah." A tentative smile wobbled across her lips. "Can we not do it again, please?"

He stretched his legs, pointed his toes. "Sure. I'm keen on hibernating for a while."

Jenna stared at him. She smiled fully, with open affection shining from her eyes. Not the lust they'd shared before, and something more than the possessive hunger she'd shown after her first shift. No, this was his woman. The woman who loved him. His mate. He'd fight for her. Kill for her. Die for her. But more importantly, he'd build with her.

"I know I've changed. I mean, I'm still me. But there's something else in me now, too. Other urges and instincts. It's hard to put into words. But . . . I'm trying, you know?"

"I know," he said. "And you're not going to do it by yourself. I promise you that."

"More promises? For you they're like orders from on high."

"I keep my word."

"Yes." She leaned over and kissed him softly on the lips. "Yes, you do. And if it turns out down the line that you've got a wild animal inside you, I'll help you deal with that too."

She smelled of sweat and tasted of salty tears. *More*, his body said. But it would be some time before he could make love to her. Holding her, though—that he could do. It would be nice to cradle her in his arms and drift off to sleep. Let his body recover until spring.

But not just yet. There's one last thing I have to do.

"I want to see outside," he said.

"Why?"

"I want to see that we did it. To rest, I gotta be sure they're gone. That we have a chance."

"No way. I kept you from death, but it took damn near everything I had." She extended a hand to show him how it shook. "You're not ready to be walking around. And Chris won't let you either. He padlocked us in, remember? For our own damn protection."

"A pair of dumb animals." He grinned, then pushed into a seated position. Dizziness stole his balance. Pain made him shiver. "But I *need* to see," he said, breathing heavily. "Understand?"

She scrambled off the bed and looked ready to bar his way. Then she stopped. Their minds touched, saying hello again. He felt the wolf lingering inside her, behaving—not leashed but calm.

Gathering his strength, he opened himself and showed her what he feared. He feared relaxing when more work remained. He feared trusting that it was done—not over, because it would *never* be over. But with the station truly secure, they could hold each other through the remainder of the winter and prepare for spring. For the next chapter in a post-change world.

Jenna knelt, her hands enveloped by his. "Just to see?"

"Yes."

"Then we can rest."

"And eat. I'm starving."

"Okay." She hooked her shoulder under his arm and helped him stand. "Two minutes, and then back to bed."

He laughed with a crazy sense of contentment. "Sounds good. But damn, we need a bigger bed."

Twenty minutes passed trying to get John dressed, then even longer for him to summon reserves enough to stay on his feet. Jenna's head was spinning too. She needed a pound of steak and a week of uninterrupted sleep. Still, she didn't protest. For a little while at least, she'd let him have whatever the hell he wanted. She was just too grateful that he was alive.

Then she got on the walkie and rang Tru. Three words. "Let us out."

Jenna kissed John with a leashed desire that left them both trembling.

The sound of unfastening locks drew their attention. Just Tru. He didn't have his rifle, and his pale eyes flicked over how John hung on her good shoulder. "Glad you're up and around."

"Good to see you too . . . kid." Mason grinned as he added the tag that was guaranteed to rile Tru, but the affection in his voice was real.

"I'm not a kid, old man. But maybe now she'll stop crying so the rest of us can sleep."

Jenna arched her brows. The walls were solid cement, and the doors were metal. "You *heard* me?"

"Sure." He shrugged. "You need some help?"

"Yeah," she said. "I'm not sure I can handle him by myself. I'm weak as a cub."

Tru studied her hands. "You got blood all over you, too. Did you get stabby?"

"Kind of," she answered, smiling.

Maybe she'd explain later. She might even tell Tru about their psychic link. He seemed to dig that kind of stuff. Of them all, he'd do well in the changed world. There would be all kinds of adventures, crazy things to see, magic to learn.

"I'm not going upstairs." John leaned on the wall, giving Tru a chance to get on his other side.

"You're not?" Jenna asked.

"Nope. Outside. I want to smell the air. Then I'll go back to bed. Promise."

She exchanged a look with Tru, who shrugged. Together they struggled to the ground floor and down the hall. Jenna didn't understand his drive to go out, except maybe he was feeling buried alive down there. The wolf in her could relate. She wanted a long run without the threat of being eaten, just the sweet crunch of snow beneath her paws, the wind in her fur, and maybe a rabbit in her jaws. Her stomach growled.

"I hear you," John said. "Just give me a minute, okay?"

The kid unlocked the front door and shoved it wide. The wind howled into the hall, but it carried a fresh smell. Jenna didn't know if that had anything to do with the contagion, or the dissipation of the pack prowling their woods, but the early morning air felt fine on her skin, fresh and brisk and true.

The bloody snow had been covered with a pristine top layer, sparkling in the wan sunlight as if frosted with crushed crystal. The sky burned as blue as the waters of the Caribbean. Jenna had visited the islands once, years ago, and this cloudless sky brought the memory of warmth and sunshine back to her, despite the frosty cold.

John stepped outside and gazed toward the woods, where the trees still stood dark and abandoned. Nothing stirred in their depths. Jenna lifted her head, sniffing, but she couldn't find anything unwholesome on the breeze. And echoing from far away came the trilling call of the winter wren, a sign of life returning. She glanced at John, reading in his unchanged expression that he couldn't hear their song. If latent abilities as a skinwalker lurked inside him, he hadn't yet found the spark to bring those accelerated senses to life. Her wolf ears still held the advantage.

"How is it?" Tru asked.

"Quiet," John answered.

Tru cocked his head, eyes widening. "You sure about that?"

There was definitely something different about the boy.

A vee of geese soared overhead, arguing vociferously—the first natural thing she'd seen in so many months. In wonder, Jenna watched them fly until their bodies receded into tiny black dots. The changed world would have real animals again. Wherever they'd hidden for the worst of it, they were back.

"Spring will come," Tru whispered.

Jenna let out the long breath she'd been holding. They weren't locked into eternal winter. The seasons hadn't been toppled by the new world order. She could take comfort in that. Certain things were immutable, like spring after winter.

"Like how much I love you," John murmured against her temple. "We're gonna make it."

The man didn't make empty promises.

They edged back inside. Jenna smiled when Tru locked up. He helped support John as they walked back down the hall, but her mate didn't lean on them as heavily. Walk it off. Sure. But maybe Mitch had gotten it right with all those truisms.

Thanks, Mitch. Dad.

For the first time, she was grateful. Maybe she *would* write *The Dark Age According to Barclay*, if she ever found enough paper. All her life she'd just wanted to be normal with a dad who came home to his family. She'd never have that, but she didn't want it anymore. She was just happy to be alive. So much had been lost; so much more would be. But not then.

They settled John in the lounge. He didn't care to leave the light and she didn't blame him. Then she went to look for food. Chris met her in the hall, both excited and perplexed. The look sat on him like a jaunty hat. Instead of commenting on John's recovery, he poked a slide at her.

"He's got them too," he said. "The weird glowing cells, like the ones we found in you."

"What does that mean?"

"Don't know." Chris paused, then offered an explanation he would have once considered unthinkable. Impossible. "Magic?"

Jenna lifted her brows. "You think so?"

"May as well be. Arthur C. Clarke said, 'Any sufficiently advanced technology is indistinguishable from magic.'" He shrugged. "I'm not going to argue. Not after what I've seen. But I *am* going to test everyone, see what changes have occurred since you were bitten. Who knows. Maybe we all glow."

"You're a dork," she said. "I need to get some food."

In the kitchenette she put together a tray. Penny handed her a plastic fork. She still didn't speak much, but Jenna no longer believed that shyness was because of trauma. This quiet seemed more like grief. She knew then that she would raise the girl to the best of her ability, hoping Ange would have wanted Jenna to step in. They were family now. Sometimes they would fight. But when it came down to it, they loved each other.

"You're okay now," the girl said. "We all are. Finn said so."

Jenna smiled. "Well, if Finn says so."

"I used to read these nature books," the girl said softly. "With my mom, about pack animals. They protect their own. We're like that, right?"

That was the longest speech Jenna had ever heard from the child. It gave her hope that one day Penny would recover. She'd led that ragged group away from Wabaugh and its inexplicable violence. And she had found that little cabin in the woods.

"We are," she promised.

I did that to protect the young. My territory. My mate. My home. I'll take care of it from here, little one.

She felt John searching for her, restless now that she was out of sight. But she also felt the tug of their new bond, too new to sustain much distance. Not that she wanted to be apart from him ever again.

Sweetheart?

Coming.

She knelt before Penny. Though she would never say so out loud, she thought the girl needed to spend more time with people, less time in her head. "I need to get back to John. Maybe you should look for Tru or Chris?"

The girl thought about it. "Tru. He's nice."

Once she left Penny in Tru's company, Jenna went to the lounge, balancing the tray across her arm. First they ate. Then she repeated what Chris had said.

"I guess that means we're adapting," she said. "Learning to use the magic."

John kissed her, and she tucked her head against his shoulder. "If it's true, then we have a chance. Evil may be faster, but we're still here."

They had more than a chance. They had hope. They had love. And it was enough.

EPILOGUE

Mason stacked the last of the split logs on the woodpile. He wiped his forehead with the back of his forearm and leaned against the side of the two-room cabin he'd built into a natural wall formation. The snug little structure was secured by rock on two sides, protected by a granite overhang and a bedrock floor—but with an escape tunnel out the back. Just the way he liked it. The site had taken him four months to find, there in the western foothills of the Rockies. Now he could breathe and rest, proud of what he'd accomplished.

What he and Jenna had accomplished together.

After tipping his canteen to dribble cool water down the back of his neck, he took a long, deep drink. The sun was bright and strong, slipping lower toward the west, but soon the winter snows would return. They had much to do before then.

He put his ax away in the underground tool and ammunition shed, then went to look for Jenna where she worked to harvest the potatoes. The Omega Gardens from the station weren't much good without electricity, and they'd weaned themselves from such luxuries.

Instead, up and around the cabin, along terraces that were accessible only by ladder, their garden was thriving, full of vegetables and berries that would sustain them through the winter.

"Need some help?" he asked.

Jenna pushed her mud-encrusted boot down on the head of the shovel and yanked the handle back. A thatch of new potatoes erupted out of the fertile ground. She grinned.

"That bushel is full," she said, kneeling to pull the potatoes from their earthen home. "You can take it down to the cellar for me."

Mason nodded, but he didn't touch the basket. The sun played over Jenna's hair, the color lightened through time outdoors, not peroxide. Her skin glowed a healthy tan, slicked with a light sheen of sweat. Her compact body was lithe and toned. After nearly two years, he knew her body—knew her feel and her taste—but he never tired of watching her move. She still had that dancer's grace he'd admired so long ago, but her spirit animal laced every movement with savage vigilance.

She hadn't shifted for almost six months, but the wolf was a part of her now. Part of him too. The first time feral skinwalkers had threatened their kids—Penny and Tru—he hadn't resisted that power.

Two wolves now, mated for life. Defending their home.

He recognized that shared spirit in the way she watched the horizon, the way she eased across the ground with a nimble, preternatural calm, the way she cocked her head to listen when a sound might be more than just the wind through the pines.

And he loved her. All of her. Still, and forever. He hadn't thought he could feel like this about a woman, as if she were the whole world wrapped in skin and bone. The mate bond had only grown stronger. Tru was disgusted at the way they communicated in a look and finished each other's sentences.

The kids were inside doing schoolwork, something else that disgusted the boy. He wouldn't be around much longer, especially now that Welsh had set the example of setting out on his own. That assumption saddened Mason. But Tru was nearly a young man. He preferred solitary treks through the woods to being around people, even the ones who loved him. That he supplied most of the meat they salted and dried for winter had become a welcome luxury. Mason much preferred staying close, building their refuge—and stealing private hours with Jenna.

God, you're beautiful.

Jenna paused and met his gaze from across the garden. A welcoming heat blazed from her green eyes. She stood and stretched— intentionally provocative, he thought, with her breasts pushed against her homemade shirt. She crossed through the wilted potato plants and the tangled gourd vines until mere inches separated their bodies. The sparkle of moisture along her upper lip made his mouth go dry.

"We'll never get all these chores done if you keep staring at me," she said, smiling.

He touched her chin. "You like it when I stare at you."

"I do. But we won't be ready for winter if we keep taking these breaks."

"All work and no play . . ."

Jenna captured his hand, pressing his palm flat against her cheek. "Now who would've thought I'd ever hear such a thing from you?"

Mason grinned. It was true. He'd finally let his guard down because he knew he could rely on her to take up the slack. "Tru and Penny won't be done with lessons for another hour at least. We could find a sunny spot in the woods."

She glanced down at her work-worn clothes. "I'm a mess."

"Don't care."

Mason swept her into his arms, pressing his nose to the place where her hair met her nape. He breathed in deeply. The heat and essence of his woman eased into his body. She was his air and his water and his sunshine. The old, hard urge to protect her was still as swift and vital, but so was the need to indulge in what she'd taught him. He could give himself to her without sacrificing an ounce of vigilance, knowing she had his back. They'd survived the worst that the world could throw at two people, and they thrived because they had each other.

When holding her was no longer enough, Mason found her mouth and kissed her deeply. Her hands roamed across his shoulders, down his back, and slipped inside the waistband of his trousers. Her calloused fingers dug into the flesh at the top of his buttocks, dragging his pelvis to hers. A feral growl hummed in her throat.

"And to think you used to have such a lovely work ethic," she said.

"I still do. All my chores for the day are finished."

Jenna indulged him with one more kiss that left him hard and gasping. She wiggled free of his embrace and tossed him a saucy look as she returned to the potato patch. Holding the shovel in his direction, she said, "Then you can help me with mine."

A gust of cool, cool wind sheered down from the north. It feathered against Mason's face and the V of skin at the collar of his shirt. *Winter is coming*, the wind said. No matter how much he wanted to indulge in Jenna, in their bodies coming together with a heat that never dimmed, he knew she was right. The sooner they finished the harvest, the sooner they could enjoy the spoils. All their hard work would ensure cozy, restful, loving months together, bundled against the raging elements. Their world had become much harder and unpredictable, but there were benefits to a simple life, like not sharing his woman with a thousand modern distractions.

He took the shovel and gazed down at her. Her beauty stole his breath, melting him from the inside out. Not for the first time he wondered if Mitch had known. Perhaps during one of his endless ceremonies, staring into the fire, breathing herbal smoke, he'd foreseen this outcome—and had done all he could to nudge things along.

"I love you, Jenna," he said softly.

Surprise no longer lit her expression when he said it. Only happiness. Being able to tell her how he felt without fear made the words all the sweeter to say—and to hear in return, "I love you too, John."

For so long, he'd only been Mason, the soldier. Now he was John. And in her arms, he was so much more.

No matter what else happened, no matter how the world changed—and he knew there'd be fierce upheaval in the years to come—he had everything he wanted or needed. Maybe the Dark Age had dawned, but there was beauty in the darkness too.

Ange kissed the top of Penny's head. "Just don't go wandering around the subbasement."

"I won't."

Once they were alone, she turned to Chris. "You all right?"

"Why wouldn't I be?"

She sighed and tucked a strand of red hair behind one ear. "Because Mason took you off at the knees."

He shrugged, although his shoulders had stiffened. "I'm used to it."

"That doesn't make it right. We need to know all we can. The rules have changed."

Chris studied her, wondering what she really thought of him. "Do you believe what Mason said? About magic?"

"I think I have to. It's that or go crazy." She touched his arm. "I just wish we could do something useful with it, like cook. Right now, we can only react to changing circumstances, which have become *impossible* to understand. If it's a force, then we should be able to shape it. But we don't know enough."

"My undergrad courses didn't include any hermetic theory. Sorry." Chris knew he sounded bitter.

"Chris?"

"I'm obsolete," he muttered. "Nothing I do helps. Everything I spent years learning is worthless."

Ange shook her head. "Look, Tru may not follow you around like you're some big hero because you can fix a generator, but where would we be without you? Sitting in the dark, freezing to death— that's where." She exhaled softly. "You matter, Chris."

"Do I?" In his tone, he heard himself asking a question.

This probably wasn't the time, and it might end up . . . complicated. He'd never been good at making relationships work, even during the best of times. He shouldn't push for more. But something about the desperation they faced every day made him look at Angela and keep looking.

After crossing the space between them, she put her arms around his waist and gave a gentle squeeze. "You do," she said firmly, her cheek against his chest.

Chris felt as unbending as a hunk of iron, but feminine warmth eased his tension. Her body shaped to his, and he rested his chin on her hair. They stood not speaking, just being, until he murmured his thanks against her temple.

"No problem. Want to watch the snow with me? It's really coming down." She paused, studying him as if she felt as unsure as he did. "Unless you have work to do. You don't have to."

"Well, I do need to . . ." He touched her lightly on the cheek. "You know what? It'll keep."

"Do you mind if we check on Penny first?"

"No. I was going to suggest it."

They went down to the dorms, hand in hand, and peeked through the doorway. Penny sat on her bunk, cradling Masie the bear and humming softly. "Finn, you have a nice voice. I like the funny way you say words. What should we do today?"

Chris smiled. This was . . . well, almost normal. He led the girl's mom away before Penny realized they had been watching.

Maybe it didn't matter if science no longer provided all the answers. He could adapt. Mason would keep an eye on Jenna, so they wouldn't be mauled in the night. Penny had returned to the land of the living, and Ange wanted to spend time with him. Maybe the changed world wasn't as dark as he'd feared.

THIRTY-SEVEN

While Jenna sat on the bunk Tru had once used, Mason stripped off his shirt. He felt her eyes on him, assessing his every move the way he'd watched her in the shower. Blatant feminine interest, coupled with memories of her slick, soapy skin, left him aching in places only Jenna could ease. She had a wolf locked up inside her, but he'd become the real animal—restless, caged, wary.

He stood facing the closed door to the dorm room, his head bowed. The bright fluorescent bulbs overhead would show her with unforgiving clarity. No warm lamplight, like there in the gazebo. He no longer thought she'd deny him, but the ground had shifted. They couldn't will the earthquake to stop.

"Dark magic," he said, the words a low rumble. "A Dark Age."

He turned. Jenna's eyes flicked to his bare chest, down his abdomen, and down again to his fly. Her nostrils flared slightly. Green irises darkened. "Good and evil. They might be burning midwives as witches, out there somewhere."

She reached out with her mind and smoothed warm sensations along the base of his neck. His nipples pebbled and his abs tensed. Minds open, looking through her eyes, he could see just how much she enjoyed the view of his naked torso. For the first time, he realized how beautiful she found him, and that moved him in a way that left him raw.

"Then there's this." A smile tipped up the corners of her lips. "Pretty fucking magical."

"You gonna tell Chris?"

"Nah. He'd only try to science it away and then get bummed when he failed. He's having a hard enough time with the monsters, and they're pretty straightforward." She huffed out a little laugh. "Ange better not fall in love with him, or he'll quantify it into the ground."

Mason's chest seized at the mention of that word. He'd loved her. Probably still did. But he didn't know if he had the guts to run with it all the way. What would they face in years to come? Only more potential for loss. He couldn't stop it and he couldn't lock her up. She made him vulnerable. Those days when he thought she would die— that it couldn't spin any other way—had been the worst of his life. The urge to shut her out represented his need for self-preservation, even as she tempted him to share even more.

"How would you explain it?" he asked, sitting on the opposite bed.

Jenna uncrossed her legs and leaned forward, elbows propped on open knees. The pose was more confident than she'd ever used, and the challenge of her boiled in his blood. Rock hard just from being in the same room, he wanted to test her. Tame her.

"You're my mate," she said, her eyes heavy-lidded and intense. "When we couldn't manage with five senses, we found another way to communicate."

His cock throbbed. "Your mate."

"Yes. Do you want me in here with you, or are you just worried about what I might do?"

"I'm not worried."

She stiffened. "That's not an answer."

"What do you want me to say? I've been caring for you for days. And now you're back." *But not the same.* He licked his lips. "Are we just supposed to pick up where we left off?"

"Yes."

"I can't."

"Why not?" The sparkle in her eyes might be a dare. Or hurt. "Because I've changed?"

Sleek and silver, crouched and mistrustful, she'd returned to him. Changed—shit, yes. Irrevocably. But at that moment, she was still Jenna. He wanted her and he feared the vulnerability. Yet by her tight, guarded expression, she expected him to be . . . what? Afraid? Repulsed?

"You're you," he said roughly.

"Yeah. And you're John Mason. You're not a wolf, but you're still a man."

Standing, her movements lithe and certain, she stripped off her sweatshirt and then the cotton T-shirt beneath. No bra. Just sudden, bare flesh. Mason groaned. If she stepped forward, her hard, dark pink nipples would be level with his mouth.

She did.

Rigid and hot, Mason banded her slim waist with his hands. He gave a rough squeeze, mad for the taste of her. "I want you. Still. But damn, Jenna, don't leave me again."

"I can't promise that."

Now he understood her need to hear an encouraging word. He needed the lie right then. *It'll be all right, John. I'll never leave you.* But she told the truth.

"When did you get so strong?" he whispered.

"Somewhere between being thrown in the trunk of my car . . . and right now. You showed me how." Her green eyes were bright and turbulent. "John?"

"Yeah?"

She braced herself with both hands on his shoulders. "Take my pants off."

Mason swallowed hard. They held still, watching each other. Her quirking smile teased, wagering that desire would overcome any remaining doubts. He was inclined to let her win that bet. After the hell of worrying for days, he needed her. Everything else could wait.

He leaned nearer and licked the underside of one breast, his tongue sliding up to the tip of her tight nipple. Her pelvic bones stood out sharply where once she'd been fleshier, rounder, reminding him of how many days he'd force-fed her canned chicken broth while tending her bite wound. Waiting.

He hooked his thumbs under the waistband. One quick tug revealed brown curls. His mouth went dry. "Did you give up on underwear?"

She arched her brows. "Complaining?"

"Nope."

"Good."

"Seems to me a woman walking around without underwear has sex on her mind. Is that true?" He carefully slipped the material past her thigh. The wound had healed so much that she no longer wore a bandage. "That why you're drooling over me like I'm dessert?"

"You conceited—"

"Is it why you washed for me?" He cupped the backs of her legs and slid his hands up, from knee to thigh, then back down.

"You followed me to the shower. I only wanted to get clean."

"Right."

Her smiled widened. "Can't help it if you get off on watching."

"That's not what gets me off." He slid his index finger lengthwise between her legs, finding warm, wet folds.

"You talk too much," she breathed.

"That's not what you used to think."

She angled her head down to meet his gaze. Direct. Challenging. "I've changed."

"Yes," he whispered against the skin of her belly. "I think you have."

Jenna pushed him back against the bunk and stepped out of her pants. Then she attacked his jeans, ripping open the top button, unzipping his fly, and yanking the denim down over his hips. His briefs came next. All the while, she ate him with her eyes, every inch of skin flaming beneath her fierce stare.

With one hand propped on either side, she leaned down along his naked body. Hot as a brand, her tongue flicked out and touched just above his bellybutton. Mason hissed and tensed. She pushed farther up until her face was level with his chest. She inhaled deeply and grinned.

"What was that you said, John? *Mine.*"

She bit down on the flesh of his pectoral. At first he clenched his muscles against the sharp pain, fighting it. But her teeth sank deeper. Mason closed his eyes and submitted to her sharp, testing hold. He let the pain numb him, a drug in his veins. She'd break the skin soon, but he didn't care. And all the while his cock pulsed hard and thick, caught by the mindless friction of her belly against his.

Her teeth sank in, just deep enough. Blood welled from the broken skin, and she tasted him, savage and erotic. He lay quietly beneath her mouth, heart thudding in his ears. The glow around her intensified, as if by taking his blood, she'd done . . . something. Maybe even magic—the most powerful kind of all. He sure as shit felt trapped under her spell.

She raised her head from his chest, green eyes scared and stricken. "Oh *shit*. I'm sorry. You should've stopped me—"

"I can take it," he said, breathing her in. "If it's going to happen, I want it to come from you, not them." He grabbed her wrist and gently sucked the pulse there. Her mouth went slack on a low moan.

She pressed her lips to the still-tender mark. "But you don't need more scars."

"We're talking again."

"Don't want that."

"I want inside you."

The connection between them amped up. He was so turned on he couldn't stand it. Couldn't wait for her. Her need to fuck clamored inside his head too, as sexual frustration urged him out of his own skin.

Sinking into her willing body would erase every horror they still faced. He could forget it all if she opened for him. Jenna was *his*—beyond time, beyond death. *Mine. Mate.* And he didn't know whose thought that was.

He palmed her thigh and positioned his cock, but she protested. "Not that way."

Puzzlement washed through him, and he hesitated. But when she rolled over and spread her thighs, all uncertainty fled. It was a submissive pose, offering him dominance. And he liked it. She took hold of his shaft and rubbed a drop of fluid around his swollen head. Bright spots burst before his eyes.

"Don't," he growled, his teeth clenched. "Inside. Now."

She whispered *yes* on an exhale as she guided him in. Mason kept his body up, away from hers. He liked the distance—needed it, just as his body needed its grinding release. They only touched where her hands kneaded and gripped his upper arms, and where his cock surged between her legs. All teasing fled, leaving only the bone-deep need to possess. If he fucked her hard enough, if he pushed in deep enough, he'd fuse them together. No fear there. Just oblivion.

Mason rocked his hips, thrusting up and in. She arched and hooked her legs around his lower back. Her silky, hot depths tightened. Blunt nails scored his biceps. His mouth watered with the need to suckle the soft skin of her neck, but he stayed up, his arms holding him aloft. His strength kept them separated.

The clenching pressure of orgasm built in his balls and at the base of his cock. He doubled his pace, their bodies coming together in a sharp, determined rhythm. Jenna matched his pace, thrashing tangled, damp hair across the pillow. She bit her lower lip. Fierce little noises in the back of her throat urged him on until, eyes open, she shuddered and cried out his name.

So attuned to her now, Mason growled as her orgasm ripped a wide, white-hot blast of pleasure through his mind. His body followed. With a final pump, he ground his pelvis against hers and rode the last tremors of his release.

He rolled onto his back beside Jenna, quivering and light-headed. Only minutes later, as his breathing returned to normal, did he realize that they hadn't kissed. He'd held back as much of himself as he could.

He touched his lips to her hair in silent apology, but she'd already retreated into sleep.

The walkie-talkie popped to life. Mason bolted upright, and Jenna rolled into the wall. "Damn," she said. "What's that?"

"Tru, I think." The glowing hands on the wind-up clock read one in the morning. They'd been asleep for three hours. He jumped out of the bed and grabbed the handset. "What is it?"

"Mason, get your ass down here now!"

And then the sound of gunshots.

THIRTY-EIGHT

Jenna scrambled into her clothes and followed Mason, who'd headed for the stairs at a dead run. *Jesus.* It no longer seemed strange to sleep with weapons close at hand. She checked her rifle as she ran. Loaded and ready for a fight.

She could have passed him, but that would piss him off. John did his best to ignore the wolf part of her, so she shouldn't press. He could fool himself if he wanted, pretending he had a choice. She wasn't letting him go. No more questioning or wondering.

Mine. The last trace of their harsh pleasure teased through her body. She'd bonded to him in a way she never could have imagined.

But was this how it would be? Living in permanent crisis mode? She didn't know if she could take it, never making plans, just running headlong from one disaster to the next. Something had to give. Jenna just hoped it wouldn't be her. Or John.

"Tru?" He barked into the walkie-talkie.

More gunshots, closer now.

They pounded past the generator to the weak door, where they found Tru surrounded by corpses. The beasts had finally popped the hinges, forcing the file cabinet away. The kid was covered in blood and gore, shell-shocked. Beyond him lay a tunnel curving into darkness. John stepped through to scout. .

"You all right?" Jenna asked.

"I think so. Yeah."

John returned but didn't take his eyes off the breach. "What happened?"

"I fell asleep," Tru said. "They must've hit the door at the same time, using all their weight. The hinges on the cabinet snapped, and they took the door down."

Jenna's scalp tingled. "That's tactical."

"We had to expect this sooner or later," John said. "You did great taking them down by yourself."

"Did they howl before you got them all?" Jenna's instinct drove the question.

Tru nodded. "Before I got the last one, it did. You think that's important?"

She double-checked her gun. "Could've told the others something."

"We should expect more of them," John said, grim in the ruined doorway.

"Is there any way to get the cabinet back up?" Jenna studied where they wrenched the hinges out of shape. "Or maybe not."

"The door's not the solution," John said. "It's in the tunnel."

Footsteps sounded behind them. Ange and Penny trailed Chris. They all looked scared, but Chris seemed to have found some steel in himself. He summed up the situation with a glance and an under-his-breath "Damn it."

Ange passed her daughter to Chris and took a step toward Tru. Funny—her first thought didn't seem to be dead wolves, weapons, ammunition, or the tunnel. Instead she ran exploratory hands over Tru, seeking injury and ignoring him when he tried to shrug her away.

We need her for that. Someone who thinks about people first.

If that had ever been Jenna's role, it had changed in the woods. She would look after John; she had no doubt of that. But he belonged to her on a cellular level. Everyone else—well, however much she liked them, they were expendable. With practical certainty, she knew she'd let them all die to save John. A colder and more savage part of her insisted it had to be that way. Wolves mated for life.

"I'm fine," Tru said, shaking free of Ange. "Damn, lady. They didn't get close enough to take a chunk of me. I scrambled back when I heard the first hit, and I was on the other side of the room by the time the door came down."

John nodded, looking proud. "You emptied your magazine."

"Yeah." The kid inclined his head, acting like the approval didn't matter, but Jenna saw his small smile as he glanced away, his shoulders hunched.

"Welsh, what's the strongest door in the place?" John asked.

Penny held her bear, and the doc still held Penny. At some point he'd gotten pretty good at it. The blond girl laid her head on his shoulder and closed sleepy eyes. She didn't seem worried. After everything, she had faith the grown-ups would figure it out.

Must be nice.

"The maintenance room," Chris said. "That's fire-rated eighteen-gauge reinforced steel. It's meant to prevent the spread of harmful materials during cleanup, which is why the shower's there."

"Then that's where I want you, Ange, and Penny." Mason handed the man his nine-millimeter. "If it comes to it, if we fail out here—"

"No." Chris's face went ashen and rigid. Then with more conviction, he said, "I'm not doing that."

Jenna blinked in surprise as Ange reached for the gun, her hands steady. "If you won't, I will. If we could make sure that what happened with Jenna worked for all of us, that'd be different. But we have no guarantees, and I'm willing to do whatever I must. Neither Penny nor I will end up a half-turned thing . . . or food. I'd rather die."

Chris looked horrified, one hand coming up to frame the girl's head. "You'd *do* that?"

"Being a mother means making a thousand hard decisions before breakfast," Ange said. "Sometimes that means terrible choices, things you'd never otherwise consider—except that's what your child needs. Goddamn it, that's what you do. Over and over again. So if a quick death is the best I can manage for her now, I'll do it."

"You shouldn't have to." Chris reached out for her.

Instead Ange took Penny from him. "No, but there's a lot of *shouldn't* in the world now. Regret hasn't helped me a whole lot. So if you can't, I'll take the gun."

Chris squared his shoulders, looking as if he'd taken a fist to the face. Jenna hurt for him. He didn't belong in this world. Too logical, too thoughtful, and too mired in cause-and-effect. A new god had arisen, one that valued only survival.

"No, it should be me." He tucked the gun into the back of his pants, then pushed his glasses back into place.

Ange nodded, apparently trusting his resolve. "So why'd they attack now?"

"It's the snow," Chris guessed. "This is the worst storm we've had yet. While we were watching earlier, we got at least a foot of new powder. Imagine being out there in that. And their numbers are down. Whatever cannibalism they'd managed before won't be an option much longer."

No hope. Jenna didn't feel sorry for the evil beasts, but she could identify with their instinct for self-preservation. That bothered her, and she feared what it said about her true nature that she had adapted so quickly.

"Nothing to lose," John said. "This is it. All or nothing."

Jenna set her jaw. "We can fight. They'll need time to gather what's left of the pack. They'll be split up, hunting in smaller groups—easier to sustain in harsh conditions. But they'll muster on the orders of their alpha."

Only when she felt the weight of their combined stares did she realize she'd spoken with utter conviction. Not speculation. This was just something she knew.

"You're sure?" Chris asked.

Ange licked her lips, her hands coming up to shield Penny's head, as if she thought Jenna might suddenly go wolf with a taste for little girl. That's me, Jenna thought darkly. *Just call me Big Bad.* The urge to snap and snarl swelled inside her.

Don't, came John's voice in her mind. *For me? We don't need this now.*

With effort, she uncoiled her muscles. Only because he asked.

"Canine is canine," she said. "Pack structure is similar. And you could say I have a new wealth of insight." She flashed her teeth.

John shook his head at her.

What? It's a smile.

"Then let's get down to it." Her mate eyed the tunnel, as if expecting dark, rabid shapes to come flying through, despite what she'd said. But that was John. Always on point. Possessive warmth settled in her belly. "Their leader shows signs of higher thought. He deploys forces with strategy—or he did earlier. We need to be ready for the same here."

"I'm not hiding," Tru said quietly. "I'm not waiting around, listening to the fight until those things take the last door down. Then what? I eat a bullet. No."

John stepped over and laid a hand on his shoulder. "You up for this?"

A shudder worked through the kid. "Sure. So what's the plan?"

"I need you at our back, covering us, while Jenna and I fight to the curve. We'll push them back, collapse the tunnel, then hoof it back